NERVES
OF
STEEL
A Hart & Drake Thriller

CJ LYONS

Also By CJ Lyons:

Lucy Guardino FBI Thrillers:
SNAKE SKIN
BLOOD STAINED
KILL ZONE
AFTER SHOCK
HARD FALL
BAD BREAK

Hart and Drake Medical Suspense:
NERVES OF STEEL
SLEIGHT OF HAND
FACE TO FACE
EYE OF THE STORM

Shadow Ops Covert Thrillers:
CHASING SHADOWS
LOST IN SHADOWS
EDGE OF SHADOWS

Fatal Insomnia Medical Thrillers:
FAREWELL TO DREAMS
A RAGING DAWN

BORROWED TIME
LUCIDITY: A GHOST OF A LOVE STORY
BROKEN
WATCHED
FIGHT DIRTY

Angels of Mercy Medical Suspense:
LIFELINES
WARNING SIGNS
URGENT CARE
CRITICAL CONDITION

Caitlyn Tierney FBI Thrillers:
BLIND FAITH
BLACK SHEEP
HOLLOW BONES

PRAISE FOR NEW YORK TIMES AND USA TODAY BESTSELLER CJ LYONS:

"Everything a great thriller should be—action packed, authentic, and intense." ~#1 *New York Times* bestselling author Lee Child

"A compelling new voice in thriller writing...I love how the characters come alive on every page." ~*New York Times* bestselling author Jeffery Deaver

"Top Pick! A fascinating and intense thriller." ~ 4 1/2 stars, *RT Book Reviews*

"An intense, emotional thriller...(that) climbs to the edge of intensity." ~*National Examiner*

"A perfect blend of romance and suspense. My kind of read." ~#1 *New York Times* Bestselling author Sandra Brown

"Highly engaging characters, heart-stopping scenes...one great rollercoaster ride that will not be stopping anytime soon." ~Bookreporter.com

"Adrenalin pumping." ~*The Mystery Gazette*

"Riveting." ~*Publishers Weekly Beyond Her Book*

Lyons "is a master within the genre." ~*Pittsburgh Magazine*

"Will leave you breathless and begging for more." ~Romance Novel TV

"A great fast-paced read....Not to be missed." ~4 Stars, Book Addict

"Breathtakingly fast-paced." ~*Publishers Weekly*

"Simply superb...riveting drama...a perfect ten." ~Romance Reviews Today

"Characters with beating hearts and three dimensions." ~*Newsday*

"A pulse-pounding adrenalin rush!" ~Lisa Gardner

"Packed with adrenalin." ~David Morrell

"...Harrowing, emotional, action-packed and brilliantly realized." ~Susan Wiggs

"Explodes on the page...I absolutely could not put it down." ~Romance Readers' Connection

NERVES

OF

STEEL

A Hart & Drake Thriller

CJ LYONS

EDGY READS

CHAPTER 1

·—————·⠿≡◆❱❍❰◆≡⠿—·—————

THE SIKORSKY HELICOPTER thundered through the icy February night, its blades chopping against wind gusting off the Ohio River. In the rear-facing passenger seat, Dr. Cassandra Hart swallowed hard to keep down the chilimac she'd eaten earlier. Wishing it was only motion sickness, she tugged at her safety harness. There was no room to breathe, not enough air.

Motion sickness she knew how to fix. Irrational claustrophobia was another story. A curse, a weakness she refused to reveal, forcing her to mask her panic.

The view outside Cassie's window wasn't helping. The helicopter's blades tore into the low-hanging clouds, shredding them into tattered, ghostly remnants. Rain pelted the scarred Lexan windows, ricocheting like shrapnel.

Typical of Pittsburgh, a city constantly teetering on the edge of bankruptcy, few of the buildings they passed were lit. The ones that were, such as the Cathedral of Learning and PPG Place, stood like sentries in the dark, guarding against a pre-dawn invasion.

She bit down against another wave of nausea, her

pulse drumming through her ears in time with the rotor blades. Across from her, Eddie Marcone, her flight paramedic, lounged in his seat, playing a hand-held computer game, oblivious to her distress and their impending doom.

A blast of wind catapulted the Sikorsky skyward. Cassie's restraints tightened against the sudden motion, squeezing against her chest. Gravity yanked them back down with a jolt strong enough to snap her jaws together.

"Weather's moving in fast," Zack Allan, their pilot, said. His voice reverberated through her headset. "Might have to turn back, doc."

Turn back? Cassie rubbed her clammy palms on the legs of her Nomex flight suit. Right now the landing pad at Pittsburgh's Three Rivers Medical Center seemed like a distant Nirvana. A Nirvana that would have to wait. The patient they were flying to retrieve, a girl found in the frigid waters of the Ohio River, couldn't.

"Ten minutes," she told Zack, denying the fight or flight instinct raging through her, every muscle quivering with the desire to escape. "We'll scoop and run, just give me ten minutes."

The Sikorsky bucked again. "They can send her by ground," Eddie said, his glare reminding her that her decision affected all of them, not only her patient.

"It'll take too long. This girl doesn't have that kind of time."

That was the problem with living in a city built around three rivers and several mountains. Tunnels, bridges and roadwork conspired against the rapid transport of trauma victims.

Zack's sigh resonated through her headset and she knew she'd won. Hah. If you could call being locked inside this flying death trap winning.

"You've got five minutes," he said.

They flew lower. The turbulence decreased from head-swimming, stomach-flipping to mere filling-rattling. The Sikorsky shuddered then landed on the last intact slice of macadam remaining at the on-ramp of the West End Bridge. Rotor wash overturned several orange PennDOT barrels, sending them skittering across the broken asphalt. Sleet pounded the helicopter. Cassie didn't need to look; she knew Zack was scowling.

"Hey, Hart," he shouted over the rumble of the engine, "one second late and I swear—"

Cassie ignored him as she wrenched the door open, stepped out into the night and moved away from the rotors, ducking her head until she cleared the blades. Straightening, she turned into the westerly wind and stole a moment to breathe.

Her fear drained away, replaced with the adrenalin of anticipation. A rescue squad sat at the entrance to the bridge, its lights aimed down the embankment that led to the Ohio River. At the water's edge two medics struggled to roll a small, pale form onto a neon orange backboard. Her patient.

Eddie joined her and they scrambled down the gravel slope. "Why do you have to always push the envelope? You know the pilot's got the final call."

"Zack's a worrier." Her gaze focused on the medics, and the girl's unmoving body.

"There's nothing wrong with that. Not when it's my ass on the line." He slipped in the wet scree and fought to catch his balance. "What makes this patient so important you're willing to risk my life?"

Cassie ignored him, rushing forward as one of the medics slipped, almost dumping her patient into the river. She reached out to help stabilize the backboard, splashing icy water over her boot tops while Eddie arranged their gear on a pile of torn-up paving bricks.

"What've we got?" She raised her voice to be heard above the wind whistling through the bridge girders as they sloshed their way onto solid ground. A dark, tangled curl whipped free of its barrette. She twisted it behind her ear where it joined the rest of her rain-frizzled hair dripping down the back of her neck.

"Don't know. Could be a jumper," one of the medics shouted.

The girl was maybe fourteen, fifteen tops. Her lips were blue, her face pale, her blonde hair waterlogged. For a long moment Cassie couldn't find her pulse. There. Slow, thready, but definitely there. *Good girl. Don't give up now.*

"Severe hypothermia." Mud squished beneath her, revealing sharp rocks below it as Cassie knelt at the girl's head. "She's apneic. I need to tube her."

"We don't have time," Eddie said.

"Just give me a second," she muttered, her attention focused on her patient. The girl's skin felt cold, waxen. *Wake up, Sleeping Beauty.* Cassie's fingers parted her patient's blue-tinged lips. It was a difficult position to maneuver in, but she slid the endotracheal tube into place in one smooth movement. She reached for the ventilation bag to force oxygen into the girl's starving lungs.

"Slick," Eddie said in grudging admiration as he secured the tube with a few quick wraps of tape.

"Now or never, Hart," Zack shouted down from the helicopter.

She acknowledged the pilot's words with a nod but did not alter the rhythm of her hands. The February wind burnt her face as she leaned over her patient, trying to shelter the girl. Cassie couldn't spare a hand to wipe the rain away, so she ducked her face into the shoulder of her bomber jacket.

The acrid, smoky smell of wet leather jolted through her, and suddenly she was twelve again, standing in icy water, clutching her father's hand. She shook her head, chasing the errant memory back to its proper place.

"Slow now," she told Eddie and the medics. "Don't jostle her."

Severe hypothermia, trauma from a possible fall, cold-water immersion, shock—the odds against her patient were overwhelming. They slogged their way up the steep, muddy hill, zigzagging around broken pieces of asphalt and other debris left behind by the PennDOT crew.

"Give us a hand already," Cassie called to the policemen huddled beside their cruiser, supposedly directing traffic through the urban wasteland of deserted warehouses and road construction. Not that there was any traffic in the predawn hours of a Monday morning.

With the extra manpower they were able to quickly haul her patient up to the waiting Sikorsky. Cassie jumped in and positioned herself at the head of the stretcher.

"Hang on, it's gonna be a rough ride," Zack announced.

The helicopter's powerful engine revved. Cassie's heart slammed against her rib cage as the craft shook. After an initial upward lurch, winds began to buffet them without mercy.

A coffin, she was riding in a metal coffin.

She squelched the thought, forcing her attention onto her patient. The girl's oxygen level was marginal, heart rate low, blood pressure non-existent. Cassie slid her trauma scissors along the seams of the girl's Pitt sweatshirt, tugging the heat-stealing sodden cotton away. A shower of small green tablets spilled from a plastic bag tucked into the girl's bra.

She scooped up the pills, examining their unique triangular shape. "FX. Looks like it's the real thing, too."

Fentephex, or FX, was the drug industry's latest "miracle" analgesia that had crossed over from hospital use to street abuse. Already this year, the drug had killed six of Cassie's patients. She wasn't about to lose a seventh.

Eddie finished securing the IV line. He ran his fingers over the purplish raised needle tracks lining the girl's thin arms. "She's been shooting it."

"Push the Narcan. I'll set up a drip." There were at least two dozen pills twisted into the baggie. How had the girl gotten her hands on that much FX? Cassie shoved the bag of drugs into her pocket and reached for a syringe.

Without warning, the helicopter dropped. Gravity grabbed Cassie, tearing her away from her patient. Her stomach somersaulted, and she scrambled for a handhold. She looked up. One of the pinnacles of the PPG Tower rushed toward them. Normally, the glass tower with its fairytale spires stretching toward the sky was one of her favorite Pittsburgh landmarks. Tonight it seemed a nightmarish dagger.

The Sikorsky lurched. "Damn it, Zack!" Eddie's voice sounded through her headset.

Cassie couldn't tear her gaze away from the gleaming lights of the tower. They pulled at the helicopter, a siren song beckoning them to their doom. The helicopter pitched to the right. She squeezed her eyes shut.

A blink of an eye. A split second. If anyone knew how fast a life could change, it was Cassie. Who would come to her funeral? She had no family left.

How careless of her to lose everyone like that—how foolish of her to be the last one standing.

The helicopter climbed, then dropped once again, engines screaming in protest. Acid scratched at the back of Cassie's parched throat. She forced her eyes open. The tower filled her window. Thirty years weren't enough, she decided. Not nearly enough. Her mind filled with a vision of twisted steel, smoke and fire. Would there be anything left to bury?

Focus on your patient. You're not dead yet. Neither is she. Cassie reached for her patient's wrist, her fingers automatically feeling for the pulse. It was stronger now that they had fluids going, but there were a few irregular beats. And the girl's skin was still deathly cold. All this jostling around wasn't helping her over-stressed heart.

The glass tower loomed over them. With a shriek and a final howl of its engines, the Sikorsky righted itself, swerving away from disaster.

A few minutes later, the lights of Three Rivers Medical Center came into view. Before they could land, the shrieking of monitor alarms filled the cabin.

"V-fib." Cassie reached for the girl's carotid artery. "No pulse."

"Hell." Eddie began chest compressions.

Cassie charged the defibrillator. She forced air into the girl, squeezing the bag valve mask. The defibrillator buzzed, signaling its readiness.

"Clear!" Cassie planted the paddles on their patient's chest. Electricity shot through the girl's chest. "Nothing." She exchanged the paddles for the epinephrine and injected the heart medication into the IV.

The helicopter thudded down onto the landing pad. The doors slid open, and helping hands reached in to move their patient. Cassie took over chest compressions. She wove her fingers together and pistoned her palms against the girl's breastbone. The wind hurled wasp-stings of sleet against her skin. Cassie ignored it, pausing only to fling her hair out of her face with an impatient shake of her head. The barrette that once restrained it was long lost, probably at the bottom of the river.

Damn it, Cassie thought in rhythm with her chest compressions. *You are not going to die. Not on my watch.*

CHAPTER 2

If Detective Mickey Drake closed his eyes, the rain pounding against the dumpster lid sounded a lot like gunfire from a modified TEC-9. *Splat-patta-pat-pat.* Not as loud as the movies made it out. Less bang, more pop.

Drake didn't close his eyes. Instead, he kept them riveted on the third floor window of the East Liberty apartment building where Lester Young was rocking the night away with his woman.

The wind did little to dissipate the stench of urine, rotting chicken, and sour milk that clung to the alley. Gray mist swirled past Drake in tatters as transparent as promises from old lovers.

He shifted his weight, crammed his bare hands deeper into the pockets of his navy peacoat, and tried to ignore the thud of the rain against garbage bags overflowing with moldering, dirty diapers. The only light on the block came from the apartment's naked window and one overworked street lamp whose yellow glow struggled to make it as far as the pavement below.

Yesterday was Drake's first day off in two weeks. But

when Lisa Dimeo, the straitlaced prosecutor working with the Pittsburgh Police Bureau's FX Taskforce, called to tell him she'd finally convinced her boss that they had enough probable cause to go for a warrant, he had joined in the hunt. No way he was going to let a little thing like sleep stop him from bringing in Lester Young.

Drake had scoured all of the drug dealing, murdering, sonofabitch's hideyholes until, about one in the morning, he tracked Lester to his strawberry's Ruby Avenue apartment. Drake had been a good boy, called for backup, and waited for Kwon to arrive with the warrant. Lester wasn't walking on any technicality. Not this time.

"You need some help out there, DJ?" Janet Kwon's voice drilled through his earpiece. "Thought you went to take a leak. That was twenty minutes ago."

Her voice was good humored, but colored with concern. Not solely concern about his well-being. Kwon's concern was that he'd done something to screw up. Again. Which was why he stood out here, freezing his butt off, instead of trapped inside the Intrepid with Kwon and her discerning glances.

"Found a better vantage point," he said into his radio.

"I think we should go in now. Nothing's moved up there in the last half hour, good time to catch them sleeping."

"Or with their pants down," interjected Summers from his position at the rear of the building. He sounded excited by the prospect, but then Summers was young, his gold shield so fresh it squeaked.

Drake wanted Lester more than anyone. Taking down Lester would be better than sex—at least better than Drake remembered sex. For the last six months, he'd been living like one of those monks up the mountain in Loretto. It was all part of getting his life back together. Seeing Lester get what he deserved was a big piece of that. But still . . .

"There's a kid in there," he told the others. With his binoculars he could see a red jacket, too small for an adult, hanging on the back of the door. Beside it was a backpack emblazoned with the iridescent green figure of the Incredible Hulk.

"What kid?" Summers asked. "I didn't see any kid."

"If there is a kid," Kwon put in, "he'll be in the rear bedroom. We can contain him."

"Too risky. We wait."

"Could be fucking forever," Summers muttered.

"Don't worry, Eric," Kwon assured him. "Lester's got to come out for more Viagra sooner or later." The caffeine and adrenalin jazzed cops chuckled.

Drake was silent. He waited, rain puddling under his wool peacoat, soaking his jeans and canvas high-tops until he couldn't move without squishing. He watched, despite the fact that he'd been averaging less than four hours of sleep a night and his eyelids scratched like fifty-grit sandpaper.

He blinked against the sting of sleet against his face. Lester's window blurred then refocused once more. Lester left the front bedroom and walked naked in front of the curtain-less window.

Yes, come on down, Drake urged. Time to play the *Price is Right.* Or better yet, *Truth or Consequences.* Because he had a little truth for good ole Lester—you didn't shoot at a cop, miss him and hit a van full of kids and walk away on a technicality without sure as hell paying the consequences. Damn, would feel good to nail Lester. It was the drug dealer's third strike and he was O-U-T.

Lester stepped into his pants. Drake raised his radio. "Actor's getting dressed. Looks like show time."

Kwon and the other team members acknowledged.

Drake crept through shadows to the end of the alley until he stood directly across from the tenement. His gaze never left the window. Lester reached for his shirt, his jacket.

Come on, come on.

Lester jerked upright, his mouth open, calling to someone as he fumbled through his jacket pockets.

Lester's strawberry sauntered from the bedroom, wearing only an unbelted chartreuse kimono. Her expression went from seductive to fearful in one quick blink. The words "double cross" and "whore" filtered down to the street. The woman was speaking rapidly, backing away. Lester struck her with an open handed slap, and she went down. He hauled her up, shook her, hit her again; blood flew from her nose. Lester twisted his fingers in her cornrows, drew his gun and pointed it at her face.

A little boy in Superman PJ's came out of the hallway, rubbing his eyes. He saw the woman and ran over, tugged on Lester's arm, his mouth open in a scream.

Drake flew across the street, pounding through the puddles, ran up the stairs leading into the building. He took the slippery concrete steps two at a time, shouldered through the heavy glass door, shouting into his radio for backup.

His chest was tight, his grip on his Glock sweaty as he raced up the steps to the third floor apartment. Drake braced himself, waiting to hear a gunshot, certain that once again he was going to be too late.

CHAPTER 3

"WAIT FOR BACKUP! Damn you, Drake!" Kwon's voice shouted from the radio, loud enough to be heard over the pounding of his heart and his feet. Drake skidded to a stop outside the apartment door, and caught his breath.

There was a kid on the other side. And a woman. And a man with a gun.

SOP in a hostage situation was to call in the boys from Special Response. Unless there were civilians in imminent danger. Drake leaned against the wall, straining to listen. He heard a woman crying—or was it the little boy? Sounded like imminent danger to him.

He'd love to bust in and shoot the bastard, take him out of the game permanently. But Lester was his only lead to the source of the FX flooding the streets. Drake needed him alive.

Kwon reached the top of the steps. She put a hand on Drake's shoulder while she murmured into her radio, checking on the rest of the team's positions.

A woman's scream pierced the flimsy door, cut short by a heavy thud. The sound of breaking glass followed.

"Where is it, bitch?" Lester bellowed.

It was totally against regs, but there was one sure way to draw Lester's attention away from the civilians. Lester had a hard-on for Drake. He knew Drake was behind his impending downfall. If he busted through that door, there was no way the dealer would refuse the bait.

"I'm going in," he told Kwon. He squeegeed the water dripping from his hair out of his eyes, wiped his hands on a dry patch of T-shirt, and adjusted his Kevlar.

"No. We wait." Kwon was meticulous, almost always as by the book as Dimeo.

"When I go in, Lester will turn on me. You get the kid and mom out."

For once, Drake was thankful for the Housing Authority's penny pinching. The door was so cheap, Lester's shouting had it rattling in its frame. Drake raised his Glock, nodded to Kwon, and popped the door open with a well-placed kick. It dangled crooked on its hinges and scraped across the pine floor as he pushed through. Kwon followed him.

"Lester, old buddy, old pal," Drake called out, focusing the drug dealer's attention and gun on him, while Kwon moved behind him. His gaze raked across the room. The boy looked to be okay, huddled in the far corner, crying. The woman was down, but breathing. He stayed near the door, giving Kwon more room to work so she wouldn't be at risk of crossing his line of fire.

"We gotta talk, man," he continued his singsong patter, ignoring the Taurus Raging Bull Lester aimed at him. Not easy, given the revolver's six inch barrel.

The room reeked of marijuana and Southern Comfort. White gleamed all around Lester's pupils, and the overhead light bulb reflected off sweat beading across his forehead. Lester was smiling, a dopey grin, all teeth, that made Drake wonder if he'd broken his rule and sampled some of his own product.

"Neighbors complaining about you making too much noise." Drake's focus narrowed to the few feet separating him and the drug dealer, alert to the slightest shift in Lester's weight, tightening of his muscles, flick of an eye. He forced his smile to mirror the drug dealer's.

Lester stumbled toward Drake, ignoring the bloody woman Kwon dragged out of the line of fire. He was definitely high on something. Lester was crazy enough to take potshots at a cop on a crowded street when he was stone cold sober. How would he act now? Drake's finger curled around the Glock's trigger guard, prepared to send Lester to the morgue if he had to.

"Drake, you lil' fucker. Been a while. Thought they finally fired your drunken ass."

Lester waved his cannon of a gun, aiming it at intimate parts of Drake's anatomy. Drake swallowed back his joke about the size of a man's weapon. In the state Lester was in, he might take it the wrong way, but watching Lester lovingly stroke the chrome barrel of the Taurus, it was damned hard to resist.

"You wear that thing to bed? What happened to the TEC-9 you used to carry?"

The drug dealer's smile widened. Dudes loved talking about their guns. "Jammed on me one time too many. 'Sides, I'm a big man, got big needs, know what I mean?"

Kwon closed the bedroom door. The civilians were safely behind it. Her own weapon now aimed at Lester. Drake could hear the rest of the team running up the steps behind him. He didn't turn to look. Lester and his foot long, bad boy revolver had his complete attention.

"Guess'n maybes you don't," Lester continued, his voice slurring. "Heard how your bitch died on ya."

Enough of this shit. Slowly, Drake holstered his weapon, extended his hand, palm up, toward Lester. "C'mon Lester, you can insult me all you want on the ride over to the House."

"Don't think so." Lester raised his gun, his hand shaking so badly Drake was surprised he didn't drop it. The Taurus weighed a good three and a half pounds. "You're a hard mo'fucker to kill, Drake," he said, his words strangled, difficult to understand. "Guess I'll hafta do it myself."

"What the hell? Drop the gun, Lester. Unless you wanna die. That your game—you too chicken to come talk to me? I thought you were the big guy on the streets. Maybe I was wrong. Maybe you've got a boss, someone who scares the shit out of you."

As he spoke, Drake tried to keep the drug dealer's attention and gun focused on him. He edged forward and to one side. Lester looked confused, his mouth clamping down in a frown as if he was having a hard time understanding Drake. "That how it is, Lester?"

When he was in range, Drake rushed forward, crossing Kwon's line of fire, and grabbed Lester's arm. The Taurus went off, the boom of the .45 Magnum deafening at such close range. Lester pitched forward. Drake elbowed him hard over the kidney, and sidestepped as the man fell to the ground. He yanked the Taurus from Lester's slack grasp.

Drake ignored the fist-sized hole the bullet had punched through the hard wood floor, safed the long-barreled revolver, and turned to Kwon. She glared at him. Her hands trembled as she holstered her own weapon and yanked the Taurus from him.

"What kind of idiotic stunt was that, moving in front of me? I could've shot you," she said as Summers and the rest of the team swarmed into the room.

"Glad you didn't."

"Too much paperwork. You're not worth it."

Lester was still face down. Summers was reading him

his rights when his body began convulsing as if possessed. Summers jumped off the dealer.

"Fucking A! He pissed himself." Summers flicked the fluid from his hand, the grimace on his face making him look younger than the twenty-something he was.

"Turn him over, check his breathing." Drake squatted to help Summers roll Lester's writhing body. He smelled the rank odor of human feces. Lester's eyes were rolled in the back of his head, the whites of his eyeballs blossoming with the scarlet plumes of broken blood vessels. His lips were blue and his mouth was open, but no sound came from it.

"Judas H." Drake tried to hold Lester's head still long enough to open his airway, but the force of the seizures kept bouncing it off the hardwood floor. Then everything stopped.

⁕

SUMMERS WAS STRADDLING the drug dealer, still doing CPR when the paramedics arrived several minutes later.

"Give it up. He's dead, man," they told the detective.

Drake watched as Summers did a backward scuttle, placing as much distance as possible between himself and the dead body. Summers, a lean, six-two black man, looked as if he might throw up. Drake gave him a break and ushered him into the hall before he added to the mess in the crime scene.

"I never seen anything like that. I mean I've seen DB's before, some of 'em really rank, but that . . ." Summers trailed off, wiped his hands on the seat of his jeans.

Drake leaned against the wall, rubbed his eyes with the heels of his palms, caught a good whiff of himself, and grimaced. He felt soggy, bruised, ancient.

He rammed his hands into the sodden fabric of his

jacket pockets. Ice-cold water slid under his collar and down his spine as he stared impassively at the drug dealer's body. Leave it to Lester to die without telling them what he took or where the hell he got it. Selfish bastard.

With Lester dead, Drake was out of leads. And if there was more of this shit out on the streets, they were in big trouble.

CHAPTER 4

CASSIE WRAPPED HER fingers around the cold steel of the bed rail as she walked alongside the gurney transporting her Jane Doe to the ICU. Jane Doe's resuscitation had left her exhausted, and she leaned on the gurney for support as much as she helped to push it.

The glass doors of the ICU swished open. They steered Jane Doe to bed space four, her new home. Nurses and respiratory techs swarmed over her gaunt form, transferring her to the bed, attaching licorice whip monitor leads, switching IV lines, connecting her to the ventilator.

"We've got it, Dr. Hart," one of the nurses said after bumping into Cassie as she reached to turn on the overhead monitor.

Cassie edged to the foot of the bed where she wouldn't interfere with the well-rehearsed choreography. After spending the last two hours fighting for Jane Doe's life, she wasn't about to abandon her now. "Her last core temp was still only ninety-five."

"I know. I ordered a bear-hugger warmer. As soon as I get her situated, I'll hook it up."

"And neuro will want a continuous EEG."

"Already paged them." The nurse pivoted, placing herself between Cassie and Jane Doe. "We'll take good care of her, Dr. Hart."

"Thanks. I know you will. I'll check on her this evening before my shift starts." Satisfied that Jane Doe was in good hands, Cassie squeezed the girl's foot in encouragement and retreated to the nurses' station to finish her charting.

She searched her pocket for a pen and chanced upon the twisted baggie of drugs she had taken from Jane Doe. A stack of zipper-lock bags used to transport lab specimens sat on the corner of the counter near the requisition forms. Cassie grabbed one and sealed the plastic bag with its contraband inside. Ignoring her charting, she stared at her enemy.

Innocent looking pale green pills, each with the power to destroy a life. Of course, the kids on the street never saw FX in its pure form. It was already ground down, adulterated with mannitol, baking soda, and lord only knew what else, then re-pressed into tablets bearing street names like Storm and Funky Shit. One enterprising dealer had combined FX with ephedra and called his creation "Kennywood" after the local amusement park famous for its roller coasters.

Cassie's fist tightened around the bag. She'd lost three kids to that particular variant until word got out on the street about a "bad ride".

After watching Richard, her ex-husband, descend into the black hole of addiction, Cassie had tried to learn everything she could about the why's and how's of drug abuse. She still couldn't understand playing Russian roulette with the product of an illicit chemist's imagination—half the kids she treated had no idea what they actually took.

Her gaze returned to Jane Doe, now dwarfed by the machines keeping her alive. Why would a beautiful girl throw her life away like that? What was she running from? It must be so horrible that dying became a viable option.

Anger seared through her. The waste. Young kids, grown men, professionals like Richard—she clamped down on the anger and the thought. Richard wasn't her worry anymore, she hadn't even seen him in a year, yet somehow he continued to infiltrate her life, leaving her with unanswered questions, doubts about her own part in what happened to him—to them—fear that she was destined to repeat her mistakes.

A queasy feeling not unlike the claustrophobia she'd felt in the helicopter churned through her. She took a deep breath, held it for a count of five, and then released it, hoping to banish her fears with it. It helped. A little. She forced her attention back to the bag of FX.

Protocol called for the charge nurse to lock any drugs in the narcotics cabinet until the police arrived. But she was currently busy with morning report. Using her fingernail, Cassie traced the markings etched into the back of the FX tablets.

"Son of a bitch."

The ward clerk glared at her outburst in the otherwise still and quiet ICU, but she ignored him. She held the bag up, scrutinizing the pills. There were twenty-seven of them, all imprinted with "3RMC." Three Rivers Medical Center.

To hell with protocol. She swiveled in her chair, slamming her elbow against the counter, her anger and surprise drowning out any pain.

The FX that had almost killed Jane Doe came from right here, from Cassie's own hospital.

Abandoning her paperwork, she pocketed the FX, glanced at the clock, and hurried through the doors. Seven-thirty, her shift was over. But Fran Weaver's was just beginning.

Cassie jogged down four flights of stairs to the basement. Here, amid the bang and hiss of ductwork and pipes, was the concrete tunnel that led to the Annex, the oldest part of the medical center.

The inpatient pharmacy was temporarily housed here while their permanent facility in the main tower was renovated and enlarged. Instead of the Bunsen burners and microscopes Cassie once used as a medical student, the black laboratory benches were now stacked with wire baskets brimming with medications.

Fran Weaver sat at her computer, sorting patient orders from the night before. The pharmacy assistant looked up with one of her perennial smiles. Fran had helped Cassie several times with difficult cases, once even rushing additional drugs up to the ER after several kids had been sprayed by bullets during a drive-by shooting in East Liberty last summer. Some drug dealer aiming at a cop, the police had said.

When their schedules overlapped, Fran, Cassie and Adeena Coleman, a social worker at Three Rivers, often got together. They'd gorge themselves on Primanti Brothers' take out, Fran and Adeena bemoaning the Pittsburgh dating scene while Cassie kept silent, uncomfortable with the idea of letting any man back into her life.

"Don't tell me you're flying in this weather," Fran said.

"Not since around five this morning." Cassie perched on the edge of the desk and tossed the FX to Fran. The halogen desk lamp made the pills glisten like candy. "They're some kind of counterfeit, right? Please tell me this shit didn't come from here."

Fran whipped her head around, looking for her boss. "Hush. You know Mr. Krakov hates swearing."

A bonus in Cassie's mind. She didn't like Krakov. Something about the arrogant pharmacist reminded her of Richard, her ex-husband. But this morning she had better things to focus on than pissing off Fran's boss. "Just tell me where these came from. It's important."

"Every lot of fentephex is stamped with a tracking code." Fran scrutinized the pills. She cleared her computer screen. Her fingers flew over the keys. She nodded as the screen flashed with information. "These are ours, from inpatient stock received last week. Where did you get them? Every pill is accounted for, both here and on the floor."

"They almost killed my patient. And could have gotten me and my team killed as well." Cassie explained about her Jane Doe and their harrowing helicopter ride. "How did a girl living on the street get a hold of this much FX? And why doesn't it show up as missing in your inventory?"

Fran twirled a strand of blond hair with her pinky. If she was really agitated, she would gnaw on it like a schoolgirl; if she wanted to flirt with a guy at a bar, she'd tug on it while batting her eyelashes. Cassie wished her own rambunctious hair could be half as useful as Fran's.

"ER, outpatient pharmacy, and same day surgery have a different lot number." Fran's fingers resumed their race across the keys. She was clearly unhappy with what she was finding.

An image of Jane Doe's frozen body lost in the dark waters of the Ohio flashed through Cassie's mind. "You're saying someone on one of the inpatient units stole these?"

"No, I'm not. We don't even know—" The door opened, and a trim, thirty-something man with round wire-rimmed glasses and an engaging smile pushed a cart inside. Fran looked up to greet the newcomer, the warmth returning to her face. "Neil, how are you? Neil Sinderson, this is Cassandra Hart, she's one of our ER docs."

"Nice to meet you," he said, taking Cassie's hand and shaking it with a firm grip, his smile widening as he looked her straight in the eyes.

"Neil runs the MedMark service," Fran told Cassie.

"MedMark?"

"Most of the HMOs subscribe to it," Neil explained. "We provide all their patients' medications while they're in the hospital."

"Neil's a lifesaver," Fran said. "He even found a stock of amphotericin for us when there was a nationwide shortage."

"All part of the service," Neil said with a self-deprecating shrug. He glanced at his watch. "I've got some Level Two narcotics here." He gestured to a locked metal box welded to the cart. "You want to tell Gary?"

"I'll get him for you." Fran left her seat to go to the pharmacy director's office.

"You carry narcotics also?" Cassie asked.

"Sure, whatever the doctor orders."

He rolled his cart down to the counter where the inpatient drugs were sorted by nursing units. Cassie watched as he efficiently began to dispense his merchandise. Maybe it wasn't someone inside the hospital responsible for the FX thefts and Jane Doe's overdose.

"Do you carry FX, then?"

Neil turned around and smiled at her again. He had a skier's tan with pale rims where his goggles would fit and an athletic build. "No, sorry. Fentephex is shipped directly from the manufacturer to the distribution site, no middle man."

So much for that theory, she thought as Fran returned.

Gary Krakov, the pharmacy director, popped out of his office like Alice's White Rabbit, his red bow tie centered precisely, the cuffs of his white shirt pressed and starched. He frowned at Cassie, one finger stabbing his glasses up against the bridge of his nose.

"Dr. Hart, despite these temporary facilities," he intoned, "may I remind you that we are still running a pharmacy here." Krakov glared at her mud-splattered Vasque boots, and her equally stained navy blue Nomex flight suit and leather jacket. Then he turned his gaze on Fran. "I'm certain you have more important things to do than hosting a coffee klatch, Ms. Weaver."

Cassie slid from the desk to confront the prickly pharmacist. "Fran is helping me find—"

Fran pinched her arm, and Cassie broke off. "Find a dosing protocol for patients with antibiotic resistant organisms," Fran finished, pulling a stack of order sheets overtop the bag of FX.

"She can find that in the pharmacology database just like every other physician in the hospital," Krakov said. "There's no need to waste your time."

"You're absolutely right, Mr. Krakov." Fran took the director's arm and walked him over to where Neil Sinderson waited. "Neil just needs you for a moment to sign in these narcotics."

Fran returned to her desk, clearing the screen with the FX information before Krakov could see it. "Are you trying to get me fired? Fentephex is a controlled substance. If he saw that much laying out in the open instead of under lock and key, he'd go nuts."

She slid the bag containing Jane Doe's drugs back across the desk with the tip of her pen as if it was contaminated.

"I need to find out who stole these, and how Jane Doe got them," Cassie protested, shoving the bag into her coat pocket.

"I told you, all of our stock is accounted for. If there is

any fentephex missing, it's police business," Fran said in a low voice. "You should let them deal with it."

"Easy for you to say. You're not the one who has to face the families of the patients I've lost." Cassie's voice rose enough to draw Neil Sinderson's gaze her way as he and Krakov stood at the narcotics safe in the far corner.

"I can't violate patient confidentiality and you know it."

"I'm not asking you to. Just see if there's any way to track down exactly where this FX was stolen from."

"You don't even know if it was stolen. Besides, Mr. Krakov will fire me if he finds out."

Cassie waved her hand, dismissing Krakov and setting Fran's Mario Lemieux bobble-head nodding. "Inventory control is part of your job. That's all I'm asking, that you track some missing inventory. You'll just be doing your job. No worries."

Fran's eyebrows lowered into a frown. "Right. Unless Mr. Krakov catches me doing it on his time."

"You want to come up to the ICU and tell that to my Jane Doe?" Cassie flattened her palm against the desk, leaning forward to meet her friend's eyes with an imploring gaze. It was hitting below the belt, but she didn't care. Not if there was more FX out on the street, coming from her own hospital.

Fran blew her breath out, glanced over her shoulder at Krakov, and nodded. "Anyone ever tell you that you don't play by the rules?"

"All the time—drives the charge nurses crazy." For the first time since that morning, the tension in her shoulders eased. "Thanks, Fran, I appreciate it. You could be saving lives here."

"And losing my job."

Fran was over-reacting. Even Krakov would admit that stopping the FX thefts was more important than following hospital protocol. She squeezed Fran's shoulder and gave her an encouraging smile. "If you get in trouble, just blame me."

"Don't worry. I will."

CHAPTER 5

CASSIE LEFT FRAN working on the FX mystery. After returning to the ER's locker room, she changed into the jeans and Shaker knit sweater she'd worn to work the night before. She touched the bag of drugs in her coat pocket and scowled. It was a macabre equation. Twenty-seven pills of pure FX. Equaled how many dead kids? She had no idea.

She yawned and tucked her hair behind her ears. She thought about simply turning the drugs into a charge nurse and going home to bed.

No. It didn't matter how tired she was, didn't matter what the rules were, all that mattered was stopping more FX from making it onto the streets and killing more kids. The best way to make certain the police gave the FX thefts at Three Rivers top priority was to speak to them in person.

The police substation was less than a mile from the medical center, housed in a squat brick cube of a building that brought back memories of her grade school. It was sandwiched by St. Andrew's Episcopal Church on one side and a Methodist one on the other. Perched higher up the hill stood Our Lady of Sorrows, its stained glass a flickering light of hope in the gray morning mist.

Who was protecting whom? Cassie wondered, skirting oil slicked puddles as she crossed the parking lot. Across the street sat a McDonald's, that other bastion of American worship.

Inside, the desk sergeant escorted her to a glass-walled waiting area on the third floor. He closed the door behind her, muffling the noises coming from the squad room beyond.

A tall man in jeans and a grimy Rolling Stones' T-shirt sprawled across a vinyl couch peppered with cigarette burns. His feet hung off the couch cushions. The water dripping from his red canvas high-tops had formed a sooty puddle on the floor. One arm was flung up to cover his eyes, and a sheaf of unruly black hair cascaded over the arm of the couch. A gold hoop hung from his left ear, winking in the flickering fluorescent light, giving him the appearance of a Barbary Coast pirate.

The tiny room was sweltering, a tropical fish bowl for humans. As she slid out of her jacket, Cassie wrinkled her nose against the smell of urine, sweat, stale cigarettes, and day old Chinese food. Her slumbering roommate appeared oblivious to both the heat and the stench. She watched him for a moment, noting the regular rise and fall of his chest. At least he wasn't dead.

Maybe he was a witness or informant. Her hand went to the plastic visitor's badge the desk sergeant had given her. The man wore no identification. A drunk left to sleep it off?

There was no place to sit except for the couch, but there was a vending machine. Coffee, that's just what she needed. She fumbled in her jeans pocket for change.

"Make mine black, extra sugar." A sleep-choked voice came from the sofa.

Cassie glanced over her shoulder in surprise. The man's arm was now behind his head, his eyes still closed.

"Excuse me?"

At the sound of her voice, one of his eyes popped open, drifted for a moment, then lit on her like a beacon in a storm. He blinked twice, his lips curling into a smile that might have been charming if they weren't shut up in a glass sauna and if he didn't look and smell like a refugee from a third-world insurrection.

"I said extra sugar, sweetheart." He sat up, looking at her expectantly as he yawned without bothering to cover his mouth. "Please."

Several detectives worked in the squad room beyond the window. She eyed her companion once more, not liking the way he looked at her. His gaze was that of a cat searching for a weakness in the canary's defenses.

"Mister, I've had a really lousy night," she said, pushing up her sleeves and shifting her weight to the balls of her feet. "I don't need any grief from you. I'm not your waitress or your sweetheart, all right?"

"Sure, honey, whatever you say."

She stepped to the machine, dropped her coins into the slot, and jabbed the button for her coffee. Sweat gathered between her breasts, but she took her time, refusing to let him see how nervous he made her.

She turned back, glad to have even a lukewarm cup of coffee in her hand as a potential weapon. He watched her with surprisingly blue eyes, inclining his head slightly as if he knew exactly what she was thinking.

He yawned again and raked his fingers through his hair. "I don't suppose it would make a difference if I said pretty please? I'll bet my night was worse than yours."

She doubted it. But his voice was raspy with fatigue and haggard circles shadowed his eyes. She sighed. "Here, take it. You look like you need it more than I do."

She handed him the paper cup. His knuckles were scraped and grease stained. Maybe a car thief?

"You're a life saver." He took a sip of the hot coffee and closed his eyes in rapture. Then he patted the seat beside him on the couch. "Sit."

She might have been tempted if he hadn't flashed her a lecherous grin. Con artist was probably more like it. "No thanks, I'm fine."

"Suit yourself." He finished the coffee in one large gulp and crumpled the cup, aiming it at the trashcan beside the door. He missed, and it joined the pile of take-out cartons on the floor.

Stifling her own yawn, she ran her fingers over the coins left in her pocket, shifting her jacket to her other arm as she pulled them out to count. The bag of FX fell from her coat pocket, tumbling to the floor before she could catch it.

Her derelict companion had faster reflexes than she would have guessed. He snatched the bag from the mud-colored linoleum and scrutinized the small pills inside.

"Give me that." She reached for the bag but he closed his fist around it. Damn, how would she explain this to the police? *Gee, I brought you all this evidence, but some homeless wino took it?* She planted herself in front of him and held out a hand, backing up her confrontational stance with a glare guaranteed to make med students jump. Too bad the pirate before her was no med student. "Give it to me, now."

His eyes narrowed in an expression resembling a scheming Wiley Coyote. "Looks like you brought enough to share."

"It's not mine."

"Whose is it? Where'd you get your hands on this much FX? It looks to be the real deal—worth a couple thou on the street."

"How would you know? Have you seen this much FX before?"

He gave a low chuckle. "Only in my dreams. Darlin',

you've hit the mother lode. If you know where to get your hands on more, you and me, we could really shake things up. Know what I mean? So where'd you get it?"

"I told you, it's not mine. Now, give it back." She reached her hand out to him once more. He gazed upon the FX with covetous eyes, then sighed and dropped it into her palm. Cassie crammed the bag into her jeans pocket.

"Sweetheart, if you only knew what you just passed up," he said, stretching his arms above his head. His t-shirt shifted to give Cassie a glimpse of well-defined abdominal muscles and a thin v of dark hair that vanished beneath the snap of his jeans.

She turned away. His image was a shadowy reflection in the filthy glass wall, but she could see enough to keep an eye on him.

He rubbed the stubble on his face. "Guess I'd better go," he said to her back, rising to his feet. "Thanks for the coffee. I'll be seeing you." He sent another smile her way, this one more predatory than grateful, and left.

Watching him saunter through the squad room. No one paid him any attention at all. She wondered who he was. Mr. Invisible Man. Should she tell someone he was leaving? Let one of the detectives know?

Cassie took the seat he had vacated, the vinyl still warm. She had more important problems than a vagrant wandering loose among armed cops.

⋅⟨⊙⟩⋅

DRAKE EDGED INTO the shadows of the narrow hallway that led to the washrooms and janitor's closet. He pulled his cell phone from his back pocket, his gaze never leaving the dark-haired woman in the waiting area. His Fair Lady of Caffeine.

"Kwon."

"It's me," he said, watching as the woman sat down then bounced back up again a moment later. Jeezit, could the woman look more guilty?

"What would you say if I told you I found someone with more FX in their pocket than we've seized in two weeks?"

"What? Hold on. Miller's here, I'm putting you on speaker." He fidgeted, his body rocking as the caffeine surged into his veins. There was a click of static, followed by Commander Sarah Miller's voice.

"Is this a joke, Drake?"

"No, ma'am. Not unless someone's playing it on me. I was crashing in the third floor waiting room when Whitman brought this woman in. She dropped a small bag and I swear it has at least two dozen FX pills in it. Looks like the real deal, too."

"What did you do?"

"I played along, in case she'd spill anything useful. Didn't want to force her hand and lose a chance to see what's going on." Drake squirmed to get a better view of his Lady as she began to pace, her thick hair whipping against her shoulders with every staccato step. For the first time in months, images cascaded through his mind in rich, vibrant hues of color and light. "She didn't give me anything. But she has bruises on her arms, some look pretty fresh. I'll bet she's here to drop the dime on someone."

"Whitman just told Kwon that her name is Hart and she asked to see someone on the FX taskforce. You stay out of sight. I'm on my way."

He dropped the phone into his pocket and waited. One by one, each of the detectives in the bullpen received a call. Within a few minutes the area was clear of civilians and the other cops had positioned themselves at strategic sites. The clipped sound of Miller's footsteps reverberated down the stairs across from Drake, announcing her arrival.

Hart seemed oblivious. Whoever she was, she sure was an amateur. She took two steps to the door, hand reaching out as if she were about to leave, then spun and resumed pacing, a ferocious scowl tightening her features. He hadn't seen any track marks, but you could snort FX that pure. Although, she didn't seem like a user. Most junkies wouldn't be so generous, even if it was only coffee. Instead, her agitation reminded him of his own restlessness last night. Anticipation of action, more like a caged tigress than a scared rabbit.

Kwon appeared behind Miller, her Glock drawn. She'd even put her Kevlar back on. As Miller approached the door to the waiting room, every cop in the place had a hand on their weapon. Every cop except Drake.

His service piece was upstairs, locked in his desk at Major Crimes. He still had his backup Baby Glock in an ankle holster, but he made no move toward it. Instead he was fascinated by the way his palms were tingling, his fingers itching. As if they'd been numb, dead to touch for months, and were finally coming to life.

Drake shoved the thought aside, forcing himself to focus on what was happening in the glass walled room. He blew his breath out, surprised that he'd been holding it. Afraid that this feeling might vanish.

The fluorescent lights glared off Miller's shiny blonde hair, styled into a sleek bob. Her posture would have drawn compliments from any drill sergeant. Even the pinstripes in her slate gray suit stood at attention. She marched into the waiting room. The direct approach. Typical. The Commander was intent on climbing the Pittsburgh Police Bureau's career ladder in record time and breaking the FX case would be a major step on her path.

"I'm Commander Sarah Miller, in charge of the FX Task Force. I understand you have some information for us."

CHAPTER 6

DRAKE STAYED IN the shadows, out of sight, as Miller and Kwon escorted Hart through the bullpen and into Miller's office. Hart emerged twenty minutes later, her face and neck flushed with scarlet plumes of anger, head erect as she looked straight ahead and bolted down the stairs. He waited until he was sure she was gone and joined Kwon and Miller in the Commander's office.

"So, what's her story?" he asked, ignoring Miller's look of distaste at his disheveled appearance.

"Her name is Cassandra Hart." Miller drummed her Mont Blanc against the pristine surface of her bleached oak desk. Drake found himself only half-listening, his attention focused on stray motes of dust caught in the air, sparkling ever so slightly as a narrow beam of sun forced its way through the clouds. Winking at a private joke. "She's a physician at Three Rivers' ER."

"A doctor? What's she doing with all that FX?" The sunbeam lost its battle as sullen gray clouds scudded through the small patch of sky visible in the window behind Miller.

"Says she found it on a patient she was life-flighting last night," Kwon put in.

"Who's the patient? Maybe we can trace the source from them."

Miller's drumming stilled. She scrutinized the Mont Blanc as if it were the Holy Grail. "The patient is a juvenile Jane Doe, in a coma."

"I'll get someone over to Three Rivers to get her prints and photo," Kwon said.

Drake thought about the scenario as the clouds continued their dance in the stiffening breeze. Things just weren't making sense. "How does a kid get her hands on that much FX? And why would a doctor bring it here herself?"

"More to the point," Miller said, "how does that much FX disappear from a hospital without anyone realizing it is gone?"

He straightened at that, shot an inquiring look at Kwon. She arched an eyebrow and nodded. "That's what Hart says. See for yourself."

She skidded the bag of drugs across Miller's desk to him. He snagged it and examined the pills. The doctor, Hart, had sealed the original baggie in some sort of lab bag and Kwon had deposited the entire thing in an evidence bag. He held it under the light of Miller's banker's lamp, and saw the markings on the back of the pills.

"According to Hart," Miller continued, "she had Three Rivers' pharmacy track the lot numbers. They're from their own inpatient stock."

"According to Hart." Kwon's voice was colored with disbelief. "She could still be covering something—maybe she never came here to tell us about the FX at all. Maybe Drake was right, she came to rat out whoever gave her those bruises. Then when she dropped the pills, she knew that people had seen her with the FX, and she made the story up."

"There's too many what ifs," Miller conceded. "I don't like the idea of Hart ignoring hospital protocol to come here herself. Everyone over there knows to call us to secure evidence. What I really don't like is that the police bureau has already publicly cleared the area hospitals as being sources of FX. Last thing we need is to look like fools."

"That was the narcotics guys who checked the hospital inventories," Kwon protested. "Before the task force was even formed."

"Then I guess you all have your work cut out for you. Check them again. But at least we finally have a lead on the FX source. I want you and Drake in Three Rivers by tonight, monitoring the wards. See how the drug distribution works, who could have opportunity. And someone needs to keep an eye out for this Hart woman. Who does she associate with? Can anyone back up her story about what happened last night? By tomorrow morning I want to know everything there is to know about Dr. Cassandra Hart."

.⊚.

DRAKE LEFT CHEN doing Hart's background check. He retrieved his coat and service piece and jogged down the steps leading away from the Major Crimes Squad, eager to get going. Because of Hart, they had their first good lead, now that Lester was dead.

He turned the corner onto the landing at the second floor, and a stocky man wearing a gray fedora blocked his way.

"Hey, Jimmy," Drake greeted his partner from Major Crimes. "Thought you were in court this week."

Jimmy Dolan stopped, and brushed the rain from his wool overcoat. "In recess for motions. Where you going in such a hurry?"

"Nowhere, just over to Oscar's for a hair cut." Drake buttoned his worn navy pea coat, but not before noting Jimmy's disapproving glance at his T-shirt and grease stained jeans.

"Heard about Lester Young. Tough break. So how much longer's Miller gonna keep you with the task force?"

"Aw, you miss me. Didn't know you cared."

Jimmy snorted and moved up onto the landing to slouch against the wall opposite from Drake.

"Miller's sending me over to Three Rivers to work undercover on the night shift. Kwon, too."

Jimmy arched an eyebrow at that. "Three Rivers? I thought you guys already cleared the hospitals."

"So did I. But some doctor from the ER convinced Miller someone there's stealing FX. And Miller, being Miller, suspects everyone, including her." Drake ran his fingers over the three-day beard that was beginning to itch. At least he thought it was about three days old. He couldn't remember the last time he'd bothered to shave. "So now I've got to go get cleaned up so's I don't scare the patients."

He started down the steps, and then turned back to his sartorially superior partner. "You ever get a shave over at Oscar's?"

"You mean like with hot towels, fancy lotions, all that jazz?" Jimmy removed his fedora, exposing the flat top Oscar kept close shorn for him. "This doctor, do you think she's behind the FX thefts?"

Drake thought a moment, remembering the way he'd been able to con a cup of coffee from Hart. He hadn't had to work very hard, and he didn't think that was because Hart was a soft touch, either. "I'm not sure. She doesn't seem the type, that's for certain."

"Is she *your* type?" Jimmy gave him a stern, remember-what-happened-last-time, look.

If it had been anyone but Jimmy asking, Drake would have just shot him the bird. But Jimmy had taken a chance, still partnering with him after last summer. "Don't worry. She's about the exact opposite of my type. Besides, nothing's going to happen. She's a suspect."

CHAPTER 7

AT SIX-FORTY THAT night the ICU bustled with activity. Flocks of white-coated students and residents wearily followed their attendings from bed to bed, trying to put out any fires before leaving their patients in the care of the on-call doctors. Two shifts of nurses crowded into the small dictation area behind the nurses' station, the day shift giving report to their night colleagues. In the middle of it all, there was one island of solitude.

No one approached Jane Doe's bed. She lay there, pale and unmoving, the IV tubing and monitor leads her sole connection to the outside world. The only sound from her was the faint whoosh of the ventilator filling her lungs.

No friends or family—so she was probably still Jane Doe. Cassie pulled the chart from the rack at the ICU nurses' station and sat down beside Adeena Coleman, the social worker assigned to the case. Cassie pushed her sweater sleeves up and flipped through the already thick binder, finding the neurology consultation. As usual, they were hemming and hawing, taking a wait-and-see attitude. She turned to Adeena.

"Anything?" she asked the social worker.

Adeena shook her head, rattling the copper beads woven into her braids. "Not yet. The police are working on her fingerprints. I'm sending her information to the National Center for Missing and Exploited Children."

"The milk carton people."

Adeena nodded then pointed her ballpoint at Cassie's forearm. "Nice bruise. Should we talk?"

Cassie smiled and twisted her arm over to admire the latest patch of purple forming there. It *was* a nice bruise, almost as nice as the move that had followed when she twisted beneath Mr. Christean's guard and cut his legs out from under him with a sweep kick. First time she'd been able to best her instructor. "Kempo. I'm testing for my brown belt next month."

Adeena's eyes narrowed in concern. "Maybe you should give yourself a break," she suggested. "No karate belt is worth getting hurt over."

Hurt? This was nothing. Cassie knew *real* pain— Richard had taught her that. She yanked her sleeves back down and focused on Jane Doe's chart.

They sat in silence for a moment before Adeena surrendered. "Right. I keep forgetting you're superwoman. Able to kick butt, then patch them up afterwards. Tessa was asking why you haven't been by to take her to Mass."

Cassie sighed. Between her boss, Fran, and Adeena's Aunt Tessa, she had enough people anxious to meddle in her life than any one person deserved. She glanced at Jane Doe's bed and choked down her sarcastic reply. At least she had people in her life who cared for her. At least she would never be alone and anonymous like her patient.

"Tell her I'll be there Sunday."

"Great. You know she makes her fried chicken whenever you come over."

"Why's everyone always trying to fatten me up?"

"Because." Adeena reached out and laid her own plump hand over Cassie's. "Tessa promised your Gram that—"

"She'd take care of me." Cassie rolled her eyes. Even from beyond the grave, Gram Rosa somehow still managed to interfere with her life. *Love is stronger than death,* Rosa would say. Right before telling Cassie everything she had done wrong with her life and exactly how to fix it. "One of these days you guys will figure out that I can take care of myself."

Adeena didn't take the bait and instead turned back to the data sheet from the Center for Missing and Exploited Children. Cassie looked over the social worker's shoulder, reading the scant information collected on Jane Doe.

Adeena jangled her braids in impatience, shifting so Cassie no longer blocked her light. "Am I in your way?"

"Yeah, thanks." Cassie took the paperwork and scanned through it. "There's so little here. How can we know next to nothing about her?"

"One good thing. As far as the police can tell so far, she hasn't ever been arrested."

"Is that the only thing they care about?" Cassie scoffed. "Idiots. They practically accused me of stealing the FX I took to them this morning."

Adeena looked up at that. "What were you doing with FX? You're lucky they didn't arrest you or something."

"Tell me about it. I think they would have liked to. Seems they had no idea where all the FX flooding the streets is coming from or how to stop it."

"They're doing the best they can."

"Right." Cassie focused on her patient again. "It really burns me that people get more upset over a beached whale than they do about homeless kids on their own streets. Look at her, she was somebody's beautiful baby, but they all abandoned her."

"More likely she abandoned them," Adeena reminded her. "She's probably been out on the street for a while now. Long enough to get hooked on FX at least. Who knows what kind of life she ran away from."

The monitor above Jane Doe's bed traced a regular, green wave across the screen. Family members sat beside loved ones at all the other beds, except bed space four, where the stark glare of the overhead lights made Jane Doe's pale skin appear transparent. As if there wasn't a real girl there, but only the too-thin ghost of one.

"Still, it's wrong. She shouldn't have to lie there without even a name to call her own."

"I'm doing the best I can."

"I know." But that wasn't enough.

Leaving Adeena to deal with the paperwork, Cassie crossed over to Jane Doe's side. What could have caused this girl such pain that she was willing to throw her life away before it really even began? She thought about her own life. By the time she was fourteen, she had already seen both her parents die.

If not for people like Gram Rosa, she might have run away from her own future, just as Jane Doe had. She remembered her morbid thoughts when the helicopter almost crashed last night, her fears that no one would mourn her. Hiding her face from Adeena, she blinked hard, suddenly ashamed of her own weakness. She'd been so very wrong to feel that way.

Cassie ran her fingers through the girl's pale hair. Some kind soul had taken the time to comb it out and wash it, she noted with a small smile.

"I'm not going to let anything happen to you," she promised the comatose girl. Maybe Jane Doe couldn't hear her, had no idea who this strange woman standing over her was. But it didn't matter. Cassie was not going to allow

Jane Doe to lie here unmourned and unloved. "You're not alone anymore."

CHAPTER 8

CASSIE LEFT ADEENA and jogged down the steps to the ER. Ten 'til, she had just enough time to change. In the ER locker room, she grabbed a pair of cotton scrubs and inventoried her equipment: radio at her waistband, hemostat holding trauma scissors and tape cinched beside it, stethoscope around her neck, and penlight and name tag clipped to her shirt pocket. Ready for battle.

She knew she was no general waging a war against disease, certainly no genius like her boss, Ed Castro, the best physician she knew. She was just another grunt in the trenches, trying to get the job done. Since leaving Richard, it seemed like the job was all she had. It was safe to focus on work and avoid the rest of the world—until she'd met Jane Doe. Now she felt like she was being pulled in, against her will, that she was risking herself by becoming emotionally involved.

It scared the hell out of her. Richard had overcome her defenses, swallowed her whole, and she'd barely survived.

She plodded through the first half of her shift determined to remain objective and professional and refused to think about the nameless girl lying alone in the ICU. Well, not much, anyway.

"Med Five coming in code three." Her trauma radio sounded the alert. "Overdose victim."

"Room Two," Cassie instructed the dispatcher. "What's their ETA?"

"Three minutes."

Typical Med Five, the hotshots liked to cut it close. They were the best in the city, so they got away with it. As she wrapped her yellow Tyvek gown around her, Cassie felt her heart rev into high gear, savoring the familiar jolt of adrenalin. Just enough to keep her focused as she readied her team.

The two critical care nurses prepared IV lines on both sides of the gurney, the respiratory tech had her vent set up and ready to go, and the lab tech jogged into the room as the paramedics arrived with her patient. One of the medics glanced at his watch and flashed the recording nurse a smile.

"Must be the A-Team on tonight, Tony," he said to his partner.

"What's the story?" Cassie asked.

"Name's Brian Winston. Nineteen years old. Found at a rave over by the West End Bridge," he told Cassie amidst the tangle of arms involved in transferring the patient, monitor and lines to the ER personnel. "We tried high dose Narcan, but no change."

Cassie bent over her patient. His eyes were open, but he was unresponsive, his pupils pinpoint. "Any idea what he took?"

"Nope. The cops are right behind us with his friends."

"Get me a tox screen, blood gas, and set of lytes." The heart rate and blood pressure alarms shrieked. She glanced up, absorbing the overall picture in one quick look. It wasn't good. None of the FX overdoses had presented like this. She needed to figure out what Brian took and come up with a plan to counteract it.

A third alarm added its strident voice to the chorus. She didn't have much time—neither did her patient.

She stepped into the hallway and spotted a uniformed police officer towering over two teenaged girls sitting on plastic chairs arranged along the wall.

"I'm Dr. Hart. I'm taking care of your friend." Both girls had streaks of fluorescent color in their hair and body makeup to match. One of them had been crying.

"Is Brian gonna be all right?"

Cassie squatted and met the girl's eyes. "I don't know. I'm trying to help him, but I really need to know what he took." The girls exchanged glances.

"Don't tell them anything," the second one said.

Cassie glanced up at the police officer. "I think there's fresh coffee, Officer Rankin." He hesitated, then nodded and moved down the hall. "What's your name?" she asked the first one.

"Linda."

"I need to know what Brian took," she insisted, locking her gaze on the girl. "Don't you want to help save his life?"

The girl sniffed, and then reached into her designer jeans and pulled out a single square shaped pill. She handed it to Cassie.

"Hey, where'd you get that?" her friend asked. "Brian said he didn't have enough dough to buy more than one. Not at fifty a pop."

"Well, he bought me one. Said it was an early birthday present."

"What is it?" Cassie examined the pill. The only markings on it were two large X's.

"It's Double Cross."

"What's in it? Is it a new form of Ecstasy?" But

Ecstasy alone didn't explain her patient's symptoms.

"It's FX times X, double crossed. Don't you get it?"

Cassie did, all too well. She returned to the trauma room just in time for all hell to break loose.

CHAPTER 9

DRAKE LEANED AGAINST his mop handle, eavesdropping. He beckoned to Rankin, the uniformed officer, who joined him in an empty suture room.

"What's up?" Drake indicated the trio across the hall with a terse nod of his head.

"Kid overdosed at a rave. Those two were with him. Wouldn't tell me nothin'."

"They gave it up to the doc. Said he was doing a new combo of FX and Ecstasy."

Hart finished talking with the two girls and shook their hands before returning to the resuscitation room.

"Get their particulars for me," he asked Rankin. "Miller will send someone from the task force to interview them."

"Sure thing."

With the help of the ER's director, Dr. Castro, it had been easy to infiltrate the department and hide amidst the shadows and chaos—the guy cleaning the trash was always a non-entity. It was a bit harder to stay out of Hart's sight all night. But thankfully the ER provided plenty of hiding places and Hart was too focused on her patients to pay attention to anyone else.

Drake pushed his mop over the linoleum until he stood at the door of the trauma room. Hart's patient had taken a turn for the worse. She barked out commands, somehow managing to be everywhere at once. She shoved a plastic tube down the kid's throat, and then started a special IV up near his collarbone. Every few seconds she would whip her hair back and glance up at the monitor, her eyes blazing with fury at the bad news she found there.

It wasn't compassion that drove this physician, Drake realized, but passion—pure and simple. Her expression forced a smile from him, despite the grim circumstances. She didn't look like someone who would accept failure gracefully.

He stood, riveted by the battle raging in the small room. At least six people crowded around the boy's still form, moving in a choreography of controlled chaos. He gripped the mop handle, his fingers growing sweaty, frustrated by his inability to do anything but watch.

⚜

"SOME IDIOT GOT out his chemistry set and combined FX with Ecstasy," Cassie told her team. "As if one alone wasn't lethal enough."

A new alarm on the monitor clamored for attention. "Temp's 105 and climbing, oxygen level dropping."

"He's getting the worst from both drugs. The FX made his chest muscles too rigid for him to breathe, and the Ecstasy is giving him heat stroke. We need to cool him down and intubate." Cassie prepared her equipment, thinking rapidly. Use the wrong medication, and she could make things worse. "Valium. It should sedate him and help any seizures."

She wiped the sweat from her forehead and bent over

her patient. She had to get this right the first time. She tried to pry open her patient's mouth, but his jaw muscles were still in spasm. Cassie forced herself to take a deep breath and wait for the Valium to work.

"Damn, that's not doing it. Give me pentobarbital," she ordered. The oxygen alarm sounded, adding to the cacophony bouncing off the tile walls. It was now or never. She forced her patient's mouth open and slid the lighted blade past his tongue until she could see the vocal cords. Like his chest and jaw muscles, they were clenched tight.

God, damn it, cut this kid a break. She gingerly threaded the endotracheal tube to the level of the cords and waited for the opportunity to pass it all the way through them.

"Pulse ox is down to sixty-eight."

Cassie nodded, her eyes never leaving the stubborn, slender cords of muscle. She saw them part. <u>Now</u>. She pushed the tube past them. Hanging onto the tube as if it were made of gold, she whipped the stylet out and straightened up. "Bag him."

"Pulse ox coming up, eighty, ninety, ninety-eight."

Cassie let her breath out and wiped her sweaty palms on the back of her scrubs. Brian Winston was not out of the woods yet, not by a long shot. But he was alive.

CHAPTER 10

IT WAS AFTER three in the morning before Drake had a chance to check in with Janet Kwon, who was assigned to the surgical floor upstairs. He stepped into the medication room, which was the closest thing the ER had to privacy, unless you counted the padded lock-down room reserved for psych patients.

"How's bedpan duty going?" he asked after Kwon answered her cell phone. "Get any chance to do some real police work?"

"Nothing on our actor, but there's an orderly up here who's creeping me out. Keeps wandering into the female patients' rooms while they're asleep."

"Don't blow your cover, he's not going anywhere."

"Tell that to those women."

Drake leaned against the window in the door. He could see Hart over at the X-ray view box, the bright lights gleaming in her hair. He'd been watching her all night, staying out of sight, following Miller's orders. He couldn't complain about the duty. Hart was explaining something to a resident, her face animated.

He closed his eyes. Suddenly she was looking at him

like that, her lips brushing his, warm, promising more. His head knocked against the window, and he jerked awake.

"Sorry, what was that?" he said. Kwon clicked her tongue in exasperation. Drake stifled a yawn. "Haven't gotten much sleep in the past few days."

"Thought Miller gave you the afternoon off so you could catch some zzz's," she said.

Drake smiled as he remembered how he had spent the afternoon. After Oscar's, he'd gone home and relaxed in his studio, playing around with some charcoal studies, the first real work he'd done in months.

"I don't think that Dr. Hart has anything to do with the FX," he told Kwon. "You should've seen her with the Winston kid. I don't think he would've made it she hadn't fought so hard to save him."

"Careful, big boy—starting to sound like you're getting personally involved." Kwon, always the voice of caution and logic. "And we both know that can't happen. Right?"

He sighed. Six months was a hell of a long time. "Yeah, I guess."

"Besides, turns out Hart's ex is a doc here, too. Some surgeon. And he was mixed up in drugs awhile back. I'm figuring you were right this morning, they're in it together." She paused, and Drake could almost hear the pieces of the puzzle dropping into place for her. "Think about it. Winston is in a coma, so is Jane Doe, our one possible lead. Both treated by Hart. Ever think that a smart doctor could put a patient in a coma while making it look like she was trying to save them? I'm going to get Miller to run Hart's financials and a full background check on her. And the ex."

Before he could reply, Drake heard footsteps behind him and saw Hart watching him. Shit. How much had she heard? "Gotta go."

"Hey," Cassie called to the strange man in scrubs who came out of the med room.

He looked over his shoulder. It *was* the vagrant she'd met at the police station. Her stomach did a quick flip-flop. Had he been following her?

"Wait!" She glanced around. No security guards or burly paramedics nearby. Cassie rushed after him, skidding around the corner to see where he went. He was gone, probably out the ambulance bay doors.

She slowed to a walk and started toward the security office. Maybe the security cameras had gotten a picture of him or where he was headed.

As she passed Trauma One, a hand reached out and pulled her inside the dark room. After a panicked breath, Cassie's Kempo training took over. She grabbed her attacker's forearm, twisted inside his embrace, then rammed a knee up. She missed his groin when he sidestepped. A roaring filled her head—it was her pounding pulse.

Cassie didn't let her fear slow her as she twisted under his arm and wrenched his wrist up against his back. His free hand flailed behind him, grasping at her scrub top. She bent his wrist into an almost impossible angle, leveraging all her weight against the fragile collection of bones.

"I'm a cop!" His words penetrated her adrenalin haze just before she pushed his wrist past the breaking point.

"Prove it." Her voice emerged higher pitched than usual, tight with fear.

She tightened her grip, propelling him forward until he lay face down on the floor with her knee on the small of his back. The sound of their breathing rushed through the dark room.

"My badge," he gasped. "In my back pocket."

She kept her weight pinned on his wrist. He exhaled and his body relaxed, signaling his lack of threat. She skimmed her free hand up the back of his leg, felt his muscles twitch through the thin cotton scrub pants he wore.

"Find what you want yet? I don't usually get this physical on a first date." His voice was too loud, too bright. She wondered if he was as scared as she was.

Her fingers found his waistband and slid down to the pocket, retrieving a slim wallet. She rolled onto her feet, scrambling to the shelter of the gurney in the center of the dark room.

Keeping the gurney between them, she re-oriented herself in blackness broken only by a small amber light glowing on top of the blanket warmer across from her.

"I really am a cop," the man said.

Where was he? Still on the floor, or had he followed her? She kept silent, trying to conceal her position.

"Why do you think I was at the station this morning? Why do you think I'm here? Commander Miller sent me." His earnest words were delivered in a calm, friendly voice that almost convinced her. But Cassie remembered the eager gleam in his eyes when he'd held the FX. Besides, he could have seen her and Miller together.

She edged along the wall, searching for the door or the light switch, hoping he wasn't waiting there to ambush her. She realized she was holding her breath—not good, especially if she needed to fight—and inhaled through her nose, slowly, quietly. Her fingers found the light switch and she flipped it on.

She blinked in surprise as the stark overhead lights gleamed from the metal and glass cabinets. The man was still in the center of the room, although he had gotten to his feet.

"See for yourself," he said, leaning forward and pressing his hands against his knees as if recuperating from a marathon. Sweat stained his rumpled scrub top. He heaved in several deep breaths, his eyes never leaving hers.

Cassie tried hard to slow her own adrenalin-jazzed breathing, but failed. She opened the thin wallet and scrutinized his identification. Detective R. Michael Drake, she read. The photo was him. She stared at him, unable to speak, her nerves still buzzing.

Since yesterday, Drake had shaved and cut his thick, black hair so that it now merely grazed his collar. But the flashing blue eyes were the same, still filled with mischief. "Nice technique. Where'd you learn it?"

Remnants of fear, adrenalin, and anger choked Cassie's throat. Of course he'd let her take him down—as a cop, he wouldn't want to hurt her by drawing his gun or fighting back. Disappointment surged through her as she watched Drake edge across the room, keeping a wary gaze locked onto her. As if she were a threat.

"Why didn't you tell me you were a cop yesterday?" she asked, still comparing the photo in her hand with the man before her, ignoring the trembling in her fingers.

"You never asked."

"R. Michael Drake. What does the R stand for?" She returned his ID.

"Ready, willing and able," he replied with a wink.

Obviously their little scuffle hadn't upset him like it had her. She had honestly, for a few brief moments, thought that all the hard work with her Kempo training had paid off, and that she didn't need to fear being a victim again.

"Or if you prefer, remarkable, resourceful, and really, really good." He braced his foot against the gurney and re-tied one red high-top that had come undone in their struggle. She couldn't help but notice the gun strapped to his ankle—he could have drawn it at any time.

"Just my luck. I ask the police for help, and they send the class clown. So, R. Michael Drake—"

"That's Detective R. Michael Drake." He leaned against the gurney, seemingly relaxed.

"Detective," she amended. "You're Commander Miller's idea of thoroughly investigating the FX case? And you do that how, exactly? By romping through the halls of the hospital?"

"That wasn't my fault, Dr. Hart. I was just trying to keep you from making a scene and blowing my cover." He frowned and stepped toward her so that only a single square of linoleum separated them. "Just what were you thinking, chasing after me like that?"

Cassie's cheeks burned with embarrassment. Looking away from him, she smoothed out her wrinkled scrub top, tucked it back into her pants, and tightened the drawstring. "I wasn't planning on catching you."

"What was your plan?" His voice deepened with anger. "You had no idea I was a cop. What if I was the real deal? Anything could have happened."

He was wrong. Nothing would have happened. Not right here in her own ER.

She started to tell him that, to point out the video camera that had begun recording as soon as the lights were turned on in the trauma room, but his expression was so damned smug, superior, that her own anger rose to the surface.

"If you people did your job, I wouldn't have to worry about the possibility that some lowlife was stealing drugs from my ER!" She met his gaze head on.

"You can stop worrying now, I'm here."

"Right, and you're doing a hell of a job so far."

He leaned closer, and she thought for an instant that he was going to touch her. His eyes darkened to a deep indigo. She held his stare, ignoring the sudden kick in her pulse rate, and the moment passed.

"You could have gotten hurt."

"No, I wouldn't have." She needed to believe that, to hang on to some semblance of control. This was her turf. "I didn't."

His lips clamped tight, and he took a deep breath before speaking again. "Look, Dr. Hart. You do your job and leave me to do mine. No more amateur detective work. You hear or see or find anything, you come to me," he said over his shoulder as he stormed out.

It wasn't a request, it was an order.

CHAPTER 11

BACK AT THE nurses' station, Cassie scribbled a note on a resident's chart. This tedious paperwork was meant to distract her from what had happened in the trauma room with Drake. She sighed, shoving the papers aside. It was annoying to admit, but Drake was right. The FX was a police problem. She should stay out of it. Before someone got hurt.

"I've got Ortho for you," the desk clerk called out.

"It's about time. That hip fracture has been waiting for hours. What line are they on?" She reached for the phone.

"They're, ah, right behind you."

She turned around in her chair. Leaning against the cubicle wall, his arms crossed and a smirk on his face, was a tall man with short blond hair and large gray eyes. His white coat gleamed in the bright lights, pristine and wrinkle-free, making him look like a soap opera actor who had just stepped on stage.

"Ella," he drawled. "Long time no see."

Cold flooded Cassie's veins as tendrils of fear worked their way through her body. She winced at his use of the nickname she hated. She tried to grab onto anger, to force out the panic. "Richard."

He pushed himself from the wall and came over, grabbing the back of her chair, trapping her against the desk. She shoved her chair back hard, banging into his legs, and rolling over one Ferragamo clad foot. Childish, but it felt good. Like maybe she was in control, and could remain in control. She spun out of the chair to face him on solid ground.

"Same ole Ella, I see." He slid the chair out of the way., leaving no barricade between them. He was dressed in blue scrubs and a surgical cap spilled over the rim of one of his pockets.

"I thought you lost your privileges." A nurse glanced up at her raised voice, and Cassie fought to regain a façade of professionalism. Her jaws ground together. Leave it to Richard to get her flustered here in her own territory.

"Finished rehab and got reinstated." He held out a hand. "What, no hug, not even a handshake for your husband?"

"Ex-husband. You're lucky I don't have a restraining order." The words emerged clipped, filled with venom. Good. Hang on to the anger; it kept the fear at bay.

Richard's smile hardened. "C'mon now, Ella. You never got anything you didn't ask for. Besides, I know it was you that called the Medical Board and turned me in."

She wished. But someone else had done her that favor. "I'm not having this conversation." She handed him a chart, forcing her hand to remain steady. Her mouth was dry, parched by fear. "Your patient is in room six."

She turned and marched down the hall. Footsteps echoed on the linoleum behind her. She ducked into an empty suture room.

The door banged open, and she jumped.

"You still have feelings for me," Richard said, easing

the door shut behind him.

Cassie backed away until the tile wall halted her. Again. Memories flooded over her. Her heart began to pound as if trying to escape the cramped confines of her chest. She struggled against the knot of panic constricting her chest. "Go take care of your patient, Richard. You wouldn't want to lose your privileges again."

"Don't worry, that won't happen." He straightened to his full height, towering over her. "I'm a changed man."

"Fine. I'm glad. How about if you go do your job, and I'll do mine." Wasn't that what Drake had told her earlier? She wished the detective would make an appearance now. Why was there never a cop around when you wanted one?

Richard reached out a hand. Cassie flinched, old habits hard to break.

"Ah, Ella, you're always so serious," he said, caressing her cheek. "Don't you remember all the fun we had?"

"How would you know?" She batted his hand away. "You were drunk most of the time."

He took a deep breath, looked away for a moment, and then returned his gaze to her. "I never said I was sorry, did I?" His hand rested on her shoulder, and this time she did not flinch at his touch. "That's one of my greatest regrets. Losing you."

His voice was sincere, but Cassie knew Richard was an accomplished actor when it came to getting something he wanted. She met his eyes. A warm gray, they had promised her the world when they first met. They promised now to grant her that dream once more. Could he have changed that much in a year?

She edged away. "I've patients to see."

His fingers closed on her shoulder, and his other arm came up, boxing her in, her back against the tile wall. She swallowed, gulped in air as if she was drowning.

"Ella, this is important." A note of pleading entered his voice. He leaned his body toward her.

The scent of his cologne overwhelmed her. Drakkor Noir. Once upon a time she had painstakingly chosen it for him, hoped that he would like it, yearning to please. Now she inhaled its aroma and terror filled her, burning and choking.

The room seemed suddenly empty of oxygen, the walls moving in on her. She felt dwarfed, a scared rabbit caught fast in the hand of a giant. Cassie fought against the panic even more than she struggled against Richard's physical advances.

"Get off me, Richard. I swear I'll—" She clamped her lips shut, immediately realized her mistake. Don't agitate him. Don't fight back. It will only make things worse. Damn, when would she learn?

"You'll what?" he demanded. "Call the Medical Board? Afraid it'll be hard to play that card twice, Ella. Especially when I've had squeaky-clean drug tests. Why can't you give me a chance?"

His leaned forward, his body pressing against hers, his erection obvious beneath the thin cotton scrubs. She knew what would come next. He would force her to her knees to finish arousing him, then he would take her on whatever surface was handy: the floor, the scrub sink, the gurney. It wouldn't matter to Richard. Not as long as he was in control.

Cassie wasn't about to let that happen. She'd wasted almost three years of her life on him. He wouldn't get another second.

She placed both hands against his chest and shoved him back. Finally, air to breathe that wasn't polluted by the smell of his cologne. She turned away, but he grabbed her wrist.

"Dammit, Ella. What we had meant something. You

can't ignore it, pretend it never happened." He spun her back to face him. "One chance, is that too much to ask for?"

"Yes," she said. His eyes narrowed, and she knew her small act of defiance would cost her dearly. Richard was used to getting what he wanted out of life. Rehab hadn't changed that. His grip on her wrist tightened, and he raised her arm over her head, pinning her against the wall.

"You folks need anything?" came a voice from the doorway.

Richard jerked away. Cassie slumped against the wall, shaking the blood back into her numb hand. Drake, playing his role as an orderly, carried a stack of suture trays into the room. How much had he seen?

"Private conversation," Richard snapped.

"I'll just be a sec," Drake replied with an amiable grin. "They asked me to stock in here."

The two men stood staring at each other, neither fooled by the other's veneer of civilization.

While Richard was distracted, she sidled away from him, out of reach. She fought to slow her breathing, to regain any sense of the woman she'd thought she'd become since she'd left Richard. Who did she think she was fooling? No amount of Kempo lessons, no amount of time could repair the damage she'd done to herself when she allowed Richard into her life, her heart.

Richard glared at Drake, whose grin never wavered, then turned to Cassie. "We'll finish this later, Ella."

CHAPTER 12

As HE WATCHED the door close behind Hart's ex, Drake clenched the suture trays hard enough to leave indentations in the plastic. Hart and her personal problems were none of his business. Unless the ex had been hassling her about FX? Didn't sound like that from what he'd heard, but he might have missed something.

He set the trays down on the counter and opened the small refrigerator below. Stacks of bright blue chemical ice packs were arranged in the freezer door. He grabbed one and approached her. She stood against the far wall, her gaze darting from him to the exit, searching for an escape.

He cradled her wrist in his hand and saw the dusky imprint of finger marks marring her pale skin. She shuddered at his touch. Reflex. From what he'd seen, one born of long habit.

"Hold still," he told her. "Trust me, this helps." He raised his own arm, still reddened by her wrist-lock-from-hell and was surprised to see a faint blush of scarlet color her cheeks.

"Your timing always so good?" she asked.

"It's what they pay me for." He wished it had been better. Wished he'd heard the entire conversation and could be certain it had nothing to do with stolen drugs. "Did that have anything to do with my case?"

She shook her head, still looking down, hiding her features behind a veil of dark curls.

She was so different from the woman he'd seen fighting desperately for her patient. He curbed the urge to reach out to her, to stroke her hair, to pull it back so he could see her face. "So, who was that creep?"

Hart slid the ice pack from his hand as she stepped away from him. Her posture was stiff, brittle. The fading bruises on her arms were a yellow-ochre color made garish by the bright lights. "That creep was my ex-husband, Dr. Richard King."

"Domestic dispute." Drake pretended he'd never heard of King or his recent problems with drugs. He opened and closed his fist, keeping his face impassive. "You want to press charges?"

"No, it won't happen again. He caught me by surprise, is all."

"I see. Just like I did earlier?" Her dark eyes flared at his sarcastic tone, but then her gaze sidled away from his to stare resolutely at the Ethicon poster on the wall. He opened the door. He could take a hint. Hart was none of his business other than proving if she had anything to do with the FX thefts. "Guess I'll get back to work."

And why not? She'd given him a cup of coffee. He'd given her an ice pack. Because of her, he'd done his first real art in months. Because of him, she'd been saved from an unpleasant encounter with her ex. It all evened out, just the way Drake liked it. So, why couldn't he force his feet past the threshold?

He turned back to her. The case could wait another minute or two. "Why was he calling you Ella?"

Her head jerked up at that. "What's the R in your name stand for?" she flung back at him.

"Rembrandt."

She scowled in surprise, and then laughed, a rich, bubbly sound that echoed through the tile-walled room and was choked off too soon. Drake wasn't certain if she was more surprised by his answer or that he'd answered at all. He leaned against the open door. "My mom wanted an artist in the family."

"So you became a cop to spite her?"

"No, just following in my father's footsteps. And—" He returned to her side, let the door swing shut. "I'm good at it."

"Modest, too. Rembrandt Michael Drake."

"Mickey to my friends," he added, and immediately chided himself for it. This woman couldn't be a friend. She could not be anything but another suspect until this case was over.

"Think I'll just stick with Drake."

"What are you going to do about King?"

"Nothing." Her grip threatened to strangle the ice pack. It bulged, ready to explode from the pressure. She stalked to the door. "Just forget about it."

"Anything you say, Ella." He delivered the name with a grin, wondering how she'd gotten the nickname.

She whipped the ice pack at him. He snatched it from the air with ease.

"Don't call me that."

⚜

DRAKE TRACKED RICHARD KING into one of the cast rooms. He was surprised to see the surgeon treat his patient, an elderly woman, with kindness. King could be charming when he wanted, Drake noted as the woman laughed at the surgeon's jokes. He watched King closely. The way he moved, the way his eyes shifted, the catch as he turned with a jerk, and regained his balance.

The man was on something. It was just a hunch. Drake had no reasonable—or even unreasonable, as Miller would tell him—grounds for suspicion.

King patted his patient's hand and looked up. His confident grin didn't falter when he saw Drake staring at him. "Mrs. Kertesz will be needing a bed pan," he told Drake, brushing past him.

"I'll send someone right in," Drake assured the woman. He followed King out to the empty corridor.

"Didn't catch your name earlier," King said, his speech slow, unhurried. He slouched against the wall as if they were waiting to tee off on the back nine.

"It's Drake, Mickey Drake." He mimicked the surgeon's posture, giving the man one of his best eat-shit-and-die smiles.

"You're new here, Mickey. So let me fill you in on the situation. Dr. Hart is my wife, my business. Understand?" The surgeon's gray eyes tried to issue a challenge, but it was lost on Drake. King turned on his Italian leather clad heel and stalked away without waiting for a reply.

He left Drake more curious than ever about the conversation he'd interrupted. And Dr. Cassandra Hart.

CHAPTER 13

———— ✦ ⊰⊙⊱ ⊰⊙⊱ ✦ ————

IT WAS FIVE 'til seven and the ER was empty. Knowing Ed Castro would be there any minute to relieve her, Cassie erased the last patient's name from the board at the nurses' station with satisfaction. Nothing like a clean board at the end of a shift.

"Med Five rolling up with a MVA," the dispatcher's voice sounded from her radio. "Fifty year old male, unrestrained driver, T-bone collision. They just lost vitals."

"Level One Trauma, room one," Cassie told her. The trauma alert began to sound throughout the ER. Cassie grabbed her Tyvek gown, mask, and goggles, and raced out to the ambulance bay to meet the medics. Med Five backed in with a squeal. She opened the door as soon as it braked to a stop.

"Fifty-year-old male, closed head injury, left pneumo needled in the field, dislocated right hip, compound fracture right radius and ulna with arterial bleeding. No BP in the field, lost his pulse about two minutes ago," the paramedic told her as he performed chest compressions.

Cassie and his partner wrestled the gurney out of the ambulance, and together they rushed down the hall to the trauma bay.

"Get him on the monitor. Someone take over CPR, push epi," she called out her orders as she assessed her patient. "Get me a chest tube tray. And four units of Oneg." She nodded to the senior resident who quickly placed a chest tube. Blood poured out of the man's chest and into the waiting pleurovac. Cassie finished inserting an IV into the man's subclavian vein, and the nurse hooked up the blood.

"Pulse is back. We've got a pressure."

"Score one for the home team. Let's get another gas and crit and start our secondary survey." Cassie began addressing her patient's less life-threatening injuries. She looked up to find Richard smiling at her from across the man's body.

"I forgot how good you are at this," he told her as he examined their patient's open fracture.

He reached a hemostat into a pool of blood and deftly snagged a gushing artery. Cassie wasn't the only one good at her job.

Once she had the man stabilized, Richard moved to tackle the dislocated hip. He nodded at her. "You mind?"

She hated dislocations. That clunk the bone made when she popped it back into the joint echoed through her body. But it was a two-person job. And in such a critical patient, she didn't want to delegate it to someone else—like Richard's linebacker-sized resident who might cause more harm than good.

Cassie climbed onto the gurney beside the man's hips and wrapped her hands around his pelvis to stabilize it. She leaned her weight into the maneuver, bearing down while Richard pulled against her. Then he flexed the leg, easing the head of the femur back into place. She gritted her teeth against the clunk and tried to suppress her shudder. Richard offered her his hand as she scrambled back down.

"Nice job," he said, his hand squeezing hers. "I'll meet you up in the OR," he told the trauma surgeons as they wheeled the patient out. His eyes went wide, and he smiled. "God, I forgot what a rush this is!"

It had been a long, long time since she'd seen Richard genuinely excited about anything—her or his work. Sometimes, she could almost understand why he had turned to drugs and alcohol for stimulation, to escape the life he felt was smothering him. Almost.

He grabbed her other hand and pulled her close, waltzing her through the debris scattered on the floor. "You were amazing." He beamed down at her. "You saved that man's life, Ella."

Sickened by his touch, she pushed him away, escaping from his embrace. "Just because we work well together doesn't mean you should get any ideas."

Richard stood in the center of the room, the overhead surgical lights glinting from his perfect white teeth. "I made a promise to myself when I left that clinic. I vowed I'd get my life back. All of it. And this—" He gestured to the trauma room with its resuscitation equipment. "Is the first part." He stepped to her, took her hand once more, his finger caressing the space where her wedding ring used to rest. "The first part, but not the most important part."

She yanked her hand free. "Richard, you can't—"

His cell phone rang, and he released her before she could finish.

"Got to go, they're ready up in the OR." He sped from the room, his trauma gown flying behind him like a superhero's cape, and Cassie lost her chance to set him straight.

She frowned. Words would never dissuade Richard. When they first met, he'd coaxed and cajoled, charmed her with surprise gifts, beguiled her with thoughtful acts, until she finally relented and agreed to go out with him.

And what a first date. A cruise past the Point on a chartered yacht, caviar and champagne, he'd even bought her a ball gown. And they danced on the deck for hours. Cinderella had finally met her Prince Charming.

She squeezed her eyes shut against the memory of that night. Waltzing under the stars, how could she not fall in love with the man who had offered her that?

The familiar smells of Betadine and cautery smoke — sharp, acrid odors that belonged in no fairy tale — jarred her back into reality. Cassie opened her eyes and surveyed her kingdom. Here, surrounded by blood and pain, there was no playacting, no fairytale dreams. Here she made a difference. Here she was the one in control.

Right, she was in control. She just had to figure out how to convince Richard of that. She stripped off her trauma gown, wadded it up and threw it into the trash.

CHAPTER 14

CASSIE STEPPED INTO the hallway, her nerves still jangling with adrenalin from the trauma. Not to mention Richard showing up with no warning.

Ed Castro had some explaining to do about that. As department head, he sat on the Executive Committee, the group who would have granted Richard permission to return to Three Rivers. Cassie gritted her teeth, pacing through the nurses' station to the chart rack where her bantamweight boss waited.

"You could've told me Richard got his privileges back."

"Good morning," he said, keeping his voice bright, ignoring her accusatory tone. "How was your night?"

"How do you think my night was?" she demanded. "Richard ambushed me, and we had another kid overdose. We almost lost him."

Ed stroked his perpetual five o'clock shadow. "FX?"

"Combined with MDMA. Together they have some kind of synergistic effect. Kid had a temp of 106, chest wall rigidity, laryngospasm. The worst of both drugs, multiplied."

"How'd you stabilize him?"

"Tried Valium, got nowhere. So I put him in a pentobarbital coma and paralyzed him. That worked, but I almost lost him. Might still, I don't think there's much left upstairs." She tapped the side of her head.

"Do the police know about this new combo?"

Her face grew warm, and she turned to the board. "I'm sure their hotshot detective passed the word by now. I don't like him skulking around down here."

"So you met Detective Drake. He comes highly recommended. He was a part of the task force that broke up the drug dealers and gangs that were turning Ruby Avenue into a war zone."

"The FX was stolen upstairs. Why is he wasting his time down here?"

"I just do what I'm told."

"When I went to the police yesterday, they acted like I was a suspect. Was he down here to spy on me?" If he was, he'd gotten an eyeful, walking in on her and Richard. She rapped her pen against the chart rack in irritation. "I didn't do anything wrong. I was just trying to help."

"By breaking hospital protocol?"

"If I have to." She leveled a stare on him. Ed returned it full force—no surprise, it was hard to intimidate the man who'd helped change your diapers when you were a baby.

But, as usual, he gave in. "I'll see what I can do to keep the police off your back. And the Executive Committee."

She sniffed at the mention of the governing board of the hospital. "They're too busy recruiting drug addicts to the medical staff to worry about doctors actually trying to make a difference."

"I'm sorry about Richard. I argued with the Committee, but he threatened a lawsuit if they didn't let him back. And you know how powerful his family is."

"Not to mention his father being on the Committee, himself." Richard's father was head of orthopedic surgery, while his uncle was the senior partner and his brother the managing partner of the largest law firm in Pittsburgh.

"If he becomes disruptive in any way," Ed continued, "tell me so I can bring him before the disciplinary board."

"Why? So they can feed him coffee and doughnuts while they lecture him?"

"My hands are tied."

She realized he was sorry about more than just Richard. She regretted shutting Ed out of her life, but all she could think of when she saw him was Ed proudly leading her down the aisle on the happiest day of her life. The day when she'd made the biggest mistake of her life.

"Have a good shift." She left to change and get breakfast.

⚬❦⚬

CASSIE WALKED INTO the "dirty" room of the temporary pharmacy and found Drake already there, head to head with Fran, the glow of the computer screen bathing their faces in blue. Fran laughed charmingly over some shared joke, and then looked up to greet her. "Food. You're an angel."

Cassie deposited two cheese Danish and a blueberry muffin on the desk. Drake snagged the muffin for himself before Cassie could make a grab for it. Another strike against him. He was making it damn hard to pretend he didn't exist. She saw the gleam in his eye as he bit into the muffin and wondered if that was the point. To annoy her into acknowledging his presence.

She glanced around. Drake perched on the corner of the desk, looking over Fran's shoulder. There were no other chairs available. She settled for the safety of the lab bench

79

behind Fran's computer station. It was as far away from Drake as she could get and still see the monitor.

"I rechecked our stock of fentephex." Fran typed one-handed as she nibbled on a Danish. "Every pill is accounted for. But what if someone were replacing it with look-a-likes? It wouldn't take a lot. One legitimate pill to duplicate, anyone could do it."

"FX is kept locked up, right?" Drake asked. "How would they make the switch?"

Cassie fielded that one. "Think of how many are dispensed in a day. Almost every post-op patient, a lot of the cancer patients, even ob-gyn uses FX. That's hundreds of patients every day, which translates into hundreds of times someone familiar with the hospital and how the wards are run could have opportunity to sneak a few here or there."

"So you think that's what they did? Stole FX and replaced it with sugar pills?"

"I'm sure of it," Fran said. "Instead of trying to track the fentephex and where they all went, I did a search of medication failures, times when nurses had to give more sooner than expected or gave a different drug because the fentephex didn't work."

"Because it was a placebo." Cassie filled in the blanks.

"How many?" Drake asked.

"I only went back a month, but I found over two hundred. Way above average. And that was just inpatient. I didn't have time to check the outpatient stock."

"Two hundred?" Drake pursed his lips in a silent whistle. "That's about ten thousand dollars on the street. Can you get me dates and times? Anything we can use to narrow down who'd have opportunity?"

"Sure." Fran saved her data to a disk and handed it to him.

"Thanks, Fran. It was wonderful meeting you." He gave the pharmacist a quick salute and was gone.

Fran was blushing from Drake's attentions. Cassie rolled her eyes. The detective appeared to be in his mid thirties, but acted like a hormone-driven schoolboy.

"We need to find those placebos and get them off the floors," she told Fran. "Is there a way you can tell the difference? Maybe we could have them analyzed—" She stopped as Neil Sinderson appeared in the doorway, carrying a small box of medication.

"Here's the extra pentobarbital you wanted, Fran." His smile was directed at Cassie. "It's nice to see you again, Cassie. What time do you want me to pick you up on Saturday?"

She stared at Fran, who grinned in delight, mouthing the words, "Pay back," behind her hand, out of sight of Neil. Cassie groaned.

"Eight works for me and Mike," Fran answered.

"Sounds good." Neil cleared his throat and stood in embarrassed silence, looking at Cassie with an expectant expression.

Fran elbowed Cassie in the ribs, nodding at the pharmacist. "Eight's fine," Cassie said, grudgingly, plastering a saccharine smile on her face.

"Good. See you then. I'll go restock the chemo." Neil walked past them to the rear of the pharmacy and the "clean" room with its laminar flow hoods.

"What's going on?" Cassie asked.

"Yesterday after you left, he asked about you—"

"No, you didn't!"

"Oh yes, I did. C'mon, where's the problem? He's cute, the nicest guy ever, and you'll be doubling with me and Mike. It's bowling, what could go wrong?"

"Fran I can't—" The excuse stalled. She couldn't say no—who could when Fran truly had her best interests at heart? But Fran's constant attempts to help her "get over" her divorce were misguided at best. She'd never told anyone the real reason she and Richard split up. Or the real reason Cassie couldn't let anyone into her life again—she couldn't trust herself not to make the same mistake.

"Give him a chance. Besides, you owe me." Fran leaned over her desk to make eye contact with her Mario Lemieux bobble head. "What do you think, Mario?" she asked, flicking the hockey player's oversized head into a nod. "Mario agrees." She slanted her gaze up at Cassie. "And nobody argues with Mario."

Before Cassie could reply, Gary Krakov bounded from his office. "Ms. Weaver, I want—" He stopped to frown at Cassie and the food she'd brought. "Dr. Hart, I've asked you repeatedly not to bring food into the pharmacy."

"Sorry." Cassie edged toward the door at an angle that wouldn't intersect with Neil Sinderson's path. He flashed an amiable smile in her direction that only confused her more. He was nice looking, friendly—but Cassie just wasn't ready to get involved. With anyone.

"See you Saturday," Fran called out. Cassie glared back at her friend, not at all amused. Fran's laughter rang after her.

Krakov followed her out the door, slamming it shut behind him. "You can't continue to disrupt my workers or their routines," he said, looking over his glasses at Cassie.

His thick, unnatural hair was the same color as brown shoe polish. Combined with his pasty complexion and beady stare, Krakov resembled a zombie extra from a fifties horror flick. And he was just as hard to take seriously.

"All I did—" she started.

"All you did was to distract Ms. Weaver from her duties. Not to mention imply that there's a discrepancy in my accounting procedures. If I wasn't already short-handed, your friend would be out of a job."

"You can't fire her. She didn't do anything wrong."

"I can and I will if you and she persist in this ridiculous crusade. There is no fentephex missing from this hospital."

"Then how do you account for my patient, or the fact that she overdosed on FX that came from this hospital, from your pharmacy?"

Krakov shot his cuffs and shrugged. "She must have obtained them from a legitimate source. There are no drugs missing from my pharmacy. If you don't cease in your accusations, I'll have no choice but to ask the Executive Committee for disciplinary action. The medical staff bylaws delineate strict penalties for disruptive physicians. As, I'm sure, you are well aware."

"How is trying to save kids' lives considered disruptive?" Cassie's molars ground together as she fought to keep her voice civil.

"Anything that interferes with the smooth functioning of my department is disruptive, Dr. Hart." He emphasized her title with a sneer. "After all, we are all in the business of saving lives."

Before Cassie could respond, he spun on his heel and returned to the pharmacy, closing the door in her face.

CHAPTER 15

———— ◆ ⌒❉◆❖◐❖❉⌒ ◆ ————

"WE'RE GOING TO need more than that for an arrest,"
Dimeo, the ADA reminded Drake once he told her about
Weaver's theory.

As if, after ten years on the force, Drake had no idea
what the District Attorney needed to make a case stick. He
pulled the cell phone away from his ear and glared at it.
Dimeo's voice continued its tinny lecture on the merits of
probable cause. It was one thing for his friends in Major
Crimes to be watching him, he knew their intentions were
good. But it was another for this Perry Mason wannabe. Six
months ago, she would have never said something like that
to him.

Finally, she finished. He hung up the phone, more
determined than ever to nail the actor stealing drugs from
Three Rivers.

Hart stomped around the corner, her face flushed
with anger, heading toward the stairwell, obviously
surprised to see him still there.

She skidded to a stop, hands on her hips, head raised
high, as if issuing a challenge. "I suppose you heard about
my kid with the Double Cross overdose?"

Drake punched the elevator button.

"What are you going to do about it?"

The elevator chimed its arrival. Drake took her by the arm and ushered her inside with him.

"I thought I'd start with a real breakfast," he told her, immediately embracing the idea. Hart could join him, tell him more about hospital routines, and help him on the case. It had nothing to do with Hart as a woman, it was all about the case. Yeah right, that was why his hand was still on her arm.

He dropped the offending hand. He just needed sleep then he would be back on his game. Breakfast, then sleep. That was the ticket.

"Breakfast? That's not going to help my kids in the ICU."

The elevator doors slammed shut, and it started up with a jerk. He was surprised to see her face blanch as they moved, a thin sheen of sweat form above her lips. She was afraid. Of what? Was she claustrophobic? He'd heard how she insisted on flying for Jane Doe despite the weather, how they almost crashed on the way back. But a slow, smelly elevator scared her?

Nice to know she was human after all. He tried his best to distract her, take her mind off the small cage they were temporarily trapped inside. "A good breakfast might put you in a better mood. When was the last time you ate? I didn't see you take any breaks during your shift—unless you count your *tete a tete* with your ex."

At the mention of Richard King, her cheeks flared once more with streaks of fury. At least she wasn't scared anymore. Just good and pissed.

The elevator ground to a halt, and the doors slid open, releasing them.

"Why don't you find someone else to annoy?" She strode across the lobby toward the main doors.

Drake hustled and got there in time to hold the door open for her. "I'm sorry. I promise not to mention King again. Join me, it's only breakfast." She looked up at him, suspicion in her eyes. "C'mon, everyone has to eat."

She hesitated, and he heard her stomach growl. He swallowed his smile, afraid he might frighten her off.

She nodded her agreement. They began to walk toward the street. Dark clouds scudded in the west wind. "Snow soon."

Beside him, Hart jammed her hands into her jacket pockets and hunched into the wind. The leather bomber jacket was much too big for her, it practically swallowed her whole.

"Where are we going?" she asked as he led her past the employee parking lot.

The wail of an ambulance sounded in the distance. Hart's gaze jumped to follow it. Her body tensed, at full alert, battle ready.

"The Blarney Stone." It was difficult to resist the urge to touch her, to draw her focus back to him. "You know it? Just a few blocks down, corner of Aiken."

Her shoulders relaxed, and they resumed walking. "Brick place, pictures of JFK and the Pope?" He nodded. "We used to go there when I was a resident. Didn't know they served breakfast."

"My first partner, Andy Greally, bought it when he retired. Does the best breakfast in town. And it's close to the station house."

"Tell me again how eating breakfast is going to help you stop the FX thefts."

Relentless. And stubborn. "I called for a court order to release the hospital's work records. It should be ready by the time we finish. Then, with the help of your friend's information, we can start looking for our actor."

"That might take days—I've got kids out there taking

shit that could kill them!"

Drake stopped and turned toward her, enjoying the play of color crossing her face. Alizarin crimson with just the faintest hint of Rose Madder. "That's the best I can do for right now."

He reached for the brass handle of the Stone's front door. She bit her lip, and he could see she wasn't satisfied, but she said nothing. He followed her inside.

The Blarney Stone was quiet. Two uniformed policemen coming off duty perched at the bar, one foot apiece resting against the brass foot rail as they drank their Guinness. Drake remembered when he used to be one of their number, the warm stout and whiskey chaser filling the void the night's dramas had carved out, giving him a blissful reprieve from responsibility and memory.

"Hey DJ," Andy Greally called out a greeting from his position behind the bar. "Where've ya been? Heard you finally nailed Lester Young. Straight into his coffin."

Drake strode to the long walnut bar, its surface polished to a mirror finish. With his cherubic face and ruddy complexion, Andy Greally would have been at home anywhere the Irish infiltrated the gene pool. But a glance at his constantly roaming sharp eyes that missed nothing, confirmed that this man hadn't spent his life hoisting pints.

Cop eyes, Drake had called that look when he was young. The same all-absorbing gaze his father had had. Andy had been Drake Sr.'s partner in those days; both men young and trim versions of modern day knights in shining badges.

"Too bad we didn't get anything useful from him before he died." Drake frowned at the memory of Lester's body convulsing.

"Way of the world, my lad." Andy shrugged philosophically. "Still one less actor on the streets." He raised an eyebrow at Hart.

"Andy, this is Dr. Cassandra Hart. She works over at Three River's ER."

"Pleased to meet you, Dr. Hart." Andy leaned his impressive girth against the bar to reach over and take her hand.

"It's Cassie," she told him, shaking his hand firmly.

"Done. Now what can I get yunz?" Andy moved his bulk out from behind the bar and led them to a booth. "I've got corned beef and home fries ready to go, pierogies with onions, sausage and broiled tomatoes, or I can rustle up some steaks if you want and about any kind of eggs you're in the mood for. What'll it be?"

"Pierogies sound good to me. And lots of coffee, please."

"Coffee and dippy eggs here," Drake said, watching Hart hang her coat on the brass hooks at the end of the booth. She moved with a fluid grace she seemed utterly oblivious to.

Andy nodded. "I'll have it right out."

Hart was silent, her gaze moving away from Drake to glance around the bar with its collection of police memorabilia. He allowed the silence to settle into a comfortable length of time, waiting for her attention to return to him. Finally she gave a nod of approval and looked back. Her eyes were rimmed with red and dark circles smudged the pale skin below them.

Andy set their coffee in front of them then returned to the bar. Drake watched him go and saw another uniformed officer join the two already at the bar. Tony Spanos. Last person he needed right now.

He tightened his grip on his paper napkin, wringing it into a choked, twisted coil. It had been a stupid idea to bring Hart here. He should have stuck with his original plan to ignore her, to stay far away from her. Drake tried to think of an excuse to leave before Spanos noticed him. Or worse, noticed Hart.

CHAPTER 16

CASSIE WIPED HER palms on her jeans before raising her cup of coffee and hoped Drake didn't notice. Although so far, he'd shown himself to be the kind of man who noticed everything.

"Why does Andy call you DJ?" she asked, searching for a conversational opening. Fran was right. She did need to get out more. Aside from work, this was her first prolonged conversation with a man since she'd left Richard.

"Andy used to partner with my father. Dad's father was Robert Michael Drake, so Dad was technically a Junior."

"But he went by Mickey," she guessed. This was nice. Sitting here, talking like a normal person. Drake had surprised her with his invitation, she was certain he'd bring up the incident with Richard. Instead, he'd been, well . . . human.

"Right. And my mother dreaded making me a third, so to speak, hence my—" Drake rolled his eyes, "colorful first name. But since Dad was already Mickey Drake, I became Drake Junior."

"DJ."

"My dad's been gone seven years now, but no one on the job will call me Mickey. I'll always be Junior to them." He finished with a tinge of regret.

He tensed when the door opened and a man in uniform entered. Drake stared past her toward the bar and the other policemen.

"If the FX is being stolen from the floors, why were you in the ER all night?" she asked.

Drake shook off his reverie and turned his attention to her. The muscles at the corners of his eyes had tightened, she wasn't sure if it was with amusement or skepticism. "You want the truth?"

"I wouldn't have asked if I didn't."

His expression grew serious, as if he'd just now realized she wasn't making idle conversation. Were all cops so intense? Or was it just that Drake needed to control everything, including how much information he shared with a civilian?

"The surgical floor and the ER are the two places where FX is used in a high volume. Even though the supply you found didn't come from the ER, we weren't certain it wasn't a source."

"I'm a suspect? You were there to spy on me?"

The toothy grin he shot her did little to relieve her outrage. "A civilian waltzes in off the street with a few thousand dollars worth of FX and you think we're not going to think twice about her? Come on, Hart. It's our nature. We're suspicious of everyone. Especially someone who involves themselves in a case like you did."

She looked away, tried to choke down her anger. The uniformed officers seemed to be staring at her, sharing some secret joke. Was it at her expense or Drake's?

"I was only trying to help," she said. It sounded even weaker said out loud.

The corner of his mouth twitched as he raised a skeptical eyebrow at her. "No. You didn't trust us to do our job. You felt you had to get involved, to make sure it was done right."

She hid her dismay by searching the depths of her coffee mug for a reply. "Trust no one, assume nothing," she muttered. "That's the first lesson of ER medicine I teach my residents."

He set his coffee cup down, his hand resting alongside hers, almost touching. "Same with us cops. But it feels different when you're the one nobody trusts, doesn't it?"

"Yeah. You're right. I was naive, thinking I could actually make a difference. But if you'd seen my Jane Doe—she's just a kid. I had to do something."

"Don't worry, Hart. You're clear in my book. But you need to let me do my job. I can't if I'm worried about civilians getting caught in the middle."

Their food arrived, and Cassie couldn't resist the aromatic, hearty fare. She dug in.

"Sorry," she said when she came up for air. "Occupational hazard, eating fast." The silence imposed by eating also gave her a chance to subdue her anger, to try to see things his way. She glanced at Drake's barely touched plate.

His phone went off with a raucous chirp. "I have to take this." He began to slide from the booth.

"You stay," she said. "I'm going to the restroom."

Cassie left Drake and headed toward the rear of the bar where a heavy oak door was labeled "conveniences". Through the door she found a narrow hallway with the men's and women's rooms along one side and a door marked Private at the end. When she finished, she emerged from the restroom to find a large man in police uniform waiting for her in the corridor.

"Hi there, Dr. Hart." His smile bordered on a leer. "I'm Tony Spanos." He held his hand for her to shake. Cassie took it, wondering if Drake had been called away and sent Spanos to relay the message. The patrolman had shaggy, dark blond hair, thick eyebrows, and brown eyes that drilled into hers.

"Nice to meet you," she said. He kept hold of her hand with a gentle but firm grip. Nothing overtly threatening, but alarm bells went off in her mind.

Alarms that were confirmed when he broke his stare to flick his gaze down her body.

"I'm sorry, Officer Spanos. Detective Drake is waiting for me," she said, trying to keep her voice neutral.

"I'm sure he is." Instead of releasing her hand, Spanos shifted his weight so that one foot was between hers. "Which is why I needed to talk to you, to warn you, Dr. Hart. It's Cassie, right?"

His free hand reached out to rest against the wall at her shoulder, one more wall of the cage he was constructing around her. She pointedly turned her gaze to stare at the hand, but he didn't move it.

"What do you want, Officer Spanos?" She jerked her hand free of his grip and saw his Adam's apple jump in anticipation.

The odors of Murphy's Oil, fried onions, and coffee swirled around her as the walls of the corridor receded, vanishing from her sight. She channeled her anger, used it to sharpen her focus, to search out his vulnerable spots, just as Mr. Christean had trained her to do. She wasn't wanting violence, but merely listening to her instincts and preparing. Just in case.

"You don't want to get involved with a drunken piece of shit like Drake," he said, his tone conversational as if they were discussing Andy's pierogie recipe. "He's unstable. People around him get hurt—innocent bystanders. I

93

wouldn't want anything to happen to you, Cassie."

"Is that supposed to be some kind of threat?"

"A warning. Just a friendly warning. You know us cops, serve and protect."

"Leave her alone, Spanos." Drake's voice came from the doorway. Spanos pivoted, straightened to his full height, his broad shoulders threatening to brush the walls of the narrow corridor.

Leaving Cassie trapped between the two men.

She took Drake's arm. "It's all right. Let's just go," she urged him, surprised by the rigid tension in the muscles beneath his flannel shirt. She turned to see Andy holding the door open, surrounded by the other breakfast patrons, all of them police officers. Several held coffee mugs aloft, toasting Cassie in a mock salute.

Both Spanos and Drake had their hands bunched into fists. Her face burning with anger and embarrassment, Cassie abandoned them to their testosterone-laden standoff, and walked through the door, brushing past the other men in blue.

She kept going until she got to the coat rack. As she reached for her jacket, Drake's hand was there an instant before hers. He lowered the coat and held it out for her. Conscious of the stares of his fellow officers, she resisted the urge to yank it from his hand.

"Now, you see boys, that's how a real gentleman treats a lady," Spanos observed loudly from the bar, trying to regain the upper hand. "Hey, Cassie. Ask him about what happened last summer. Ask him where his last girlfriend ended up."

CHAPTER 17

DRAKE IGNORED SPANOS' jibes and joined Hart outside. Thick snowflakes swirled through the air, melting as soon as they hit the street. It would turn to sleet or rain soon enough.

He had to jog to catch up with her. Damn, she moved fast for someone so short. Suddenly, she pivoted and stared at him. He was tempted to reach out and brush the melting snowflakes from her hair, but the look on her face stopped him.

"What was that all about?" she asked.

"Sorry 'bout that." No sense dragging her into this mess.

"You're just like him, aren't you?"

He winced at the tone of disappointment before realizing he'd similarly judged her after witnessing her encounter with her ex. Lumping her in with all the domestic violence calls he'd taken over the years. Not the same thing, he told himself. Not the same at all.

"Hell, no," he said. "I'm much better looking, don't you think?" They stopped at the light on Aiken. Hart's glare could have drilled through diamonds. How could he tell her that he was worse than Spanos; that because of him a woman died last summer?

"Is anything going to happen because of what he did?"

Drake took a step closer to her. The light had changed, but neither of them moved from the curb. "Why? What did he do?"

She frowned, looked away. "Nothing. He—nothing."

He took her arm, but she shook him off. "What happened?"

"Nothing. That's the point isn't it? Someone like Spanos, a cop for chrissake, doesn't need to do anything to intimidate someone, to make them feel . . ." Her face colored once more. "Damn, I hate bullies. He just made me so angry." She darted across the street and he followed, ignoring the honking from a gray Olds.

"Don't worry, Hart. After the way you walked out on him," Drake smiled at the thought of her exit from the Stone, head high, stride firm—regal, that was the word, "it's going to get around that Spanos let a little woman get the best of him."

"Damn it, don't you see? He shouldn't be allowed to treat anyone, man or woman, that way. How'd a Neanderthal like him get on the force anyway?"

"Spanos is a good cop. You just caught him at a bad time."

"Why's that?"

"You were with me," he admitted.

"I take it you two tangled over a woman."

"You could say that." Now Drake was the uncomfortable one.

They reached her car, a blue Subaru Impreza coupe. Drake liked the color for her—bright yet rich at the same time. Five speed, he noted as she opened the door and slid inside. It suited her need to control, to take responsibility for everything.

"I'm going to nail whoever's stealing the FX," he told her, breaking one of his cardinal rules. Never make a promise you can't keep—it was written in stone, along with: always watch your partner's back, first call for backup.

Her gaze was bleak as she looked past him at the towering medical center. "I only hope it's before I have to send more kids to the ICU. Or the morgue."

"Nice to know I inspire such confidence."

In response, she merely shrugged and closed the door. He watched her drive away. Every time he and Hart got together, he forgot about the case or being professional. Somehow he seemed destined to always piss her off.

Drake hunched his shoulders against the wind, lowered his head as he trudged toward his Mustang. Probably safer that way. Otherwise things might end up like they had last summer with Pamela. With him suspended. And a woman dead.

CHAPTER 18

―――・⋇≡✦◆◗◎◖◆✦≡⋇・―――

"CASSANDRA ROSE HART." Kwon addressed the task force members, sounding like a schoolteacher in front of a group of unruly students. Which was pretty much what they resembled. Drake, Kwon, and Summers from Major Crimes, two guys from Narcotics, and one of the DA's investigators, the only one wearing a suit and tie, of course. And Dimeo, watching from the rear of the room, the school principal waiting to send someone to detention.

"Age thirty, native of Pittsburgh, parents deceased, no other family that we've found. Residency at Three Rivers, been there as attending ER physician almost two years now."

He stretched his legs, resting them on the back of Summers' chair. They had appropriated roll call to meet and brainstorm new approaches to the investigation now that it was focused on Three Rivers Medical Center.

Kwon continued, "No wants, no warrants, record's squeaky clean."

The others raised their heads at that. Squeaky clean usually meant something dirty hidden somewhere. And money or influence to hide it with. Drake remembered

Richard King's shoes that cost more than a month's salary and wondered about that.

"Finances?" Lisa Dimeo asked from the back, echoing his thoughts. She was a thin, bony blonde who favored conservative suits and an even more conservative attitude to the concept of probable cause. Dimeo was not there to make a case, she was there to make a career. At every meeting, she would stand against the back wall as if afraid to contaminate herself by getting too close to the grunts who gathered her evidence.

"Worked as a waitress and hotel maid to put herself through Duquesne, then Pitt Medical School," Kwon said.

Drake could tell by the gleam in Kwon's eye that she was holding something back. Dimeo nodded in dismissal, her face resuming its bored expression. Hunters and gatherers, that was what they were to Dimeo.

"Married and divorced Richard King," Kwon continued, her voice bland. "Divorce settlement sealed by King's attorney, his brother Alan."

Summers sat up, jostling his chair and knocking Drake's feet from the back rung. "King? As in Asshole, Asswipe and Pee-U?"

A snicker came from one of the Narcotic guys. Every cop knew the law firm of Arthur King, Alan King and Paul Ulrich. Knew and dreaded. The Kings were known for shredding cops on the witness stand, and took pride in making Pittsburgh's finest look like idiots.

Kwon smiled and nodded. "Richard is Alan's brother and Arthur's nephew."

"Shit, we'll never nail this fucker."

Dimeo strode forward, her heels clicking on the linoleum. The six detectives swiveled to look at her. Her face held the gleam of a predator scenting blood. "One of our principles is connected to the King family?"

Drake groaned. He could see where this was going. A

chance for a prosecutor to derail the powerful King family was worth more than a pair of Steeler season tickets. A solid gold chit to bigger and better things: State's Attorney office, judgeships, political office.

"Hart divorced Richard King last year. The paperwork's sealed, but King recently returned to Pittsburgh after attending a drug and alcohol rehabilitation clinic. The State Board of Medicine restored his license. Now he's back at Three Rivers." Kwon paused, her eyes gleaming as if she were ready to hit a home run. "King's brother, Alan, is Lester Young's attorney of record. And," the men all hunched forward in their seats, listening, "I found Richard King's name in two separate incident reports involving Young."

"What kind of incidents?" Summers asked.

"Routine witness statements surrounding two drug busts. One at the downtown Hilton, the other at Gateway Plaza. Both times King claimed he was just at the wrong place, wrong time, didn't see anything, didn't know anything. Fine upstanding citizen that he is, no one pursued it. Alan King was able to get the charges on Young thrown out on both occasions, so the investigations stopped before they went farther."

"Until now," the DA investigator put in.

"Either one, King or Hart, could be our source." Dimeo mulled this over, liking it. "Or both. Supplying Young with drugs they picked up at Three Rivers."

"What about the new rave over at the West End Bridge?" Drake interjected, trying to deflect their attention from Hart. It was too early to be focusing on only one suspect. Especially when he was certain Hart had nothing to do with the FX thefts.

"That might be where the teeny-boppers are buying, but we need to get the actor behind all this. And now we know it has to be someone with a connection to Three

Rivers Medical Center," Dimeo said. Kwon nodded her agreement. "We can't afford to let another high level source slip through our fingers." They all looked at Drake, as if he was responsible for Lester's death.

"So we focus on Three Rivers," Kwon said. "Especially Richard King."

"If they're divorced, spousal privilege no longer applies," Dimeo said. "Nail Hart. Then we can use her to get King."

CHAPTER 19

ONE OF THE advantages of working nights was being always able to find a parking space when you drove home in the morning. Cassie pulled into an open spot halfway up Gettysburg Street's hill. Point Breeze was one of those Pittsburgh neighborhoods whose residents still sat out on their stoops in nice weather, and if you put a kitchen chair out to save a parking place, no one would dream of moving it. People who lived in the upscale condos Downtown or in chic Shadyside thought of Point Breeze as "quaint," but to Cassie it was just home, the only home she had ever known.

She waved across the street to Mrs. Ferrara who, despite the flurries and the rain forecast for later that day, was washing the outside of her front parlor windows. Cassie noticed the streaky grime that coated her own windows and grimaced. Gram Rosa would have been mortified.

She climbed the concrete steps to her front door, closed the solid oak door behind her, leaned against it, and the turbulence of the night's events faded from her mind. A few breaths later, and she felt the calmness of the house begin to envelope her. She looked around her living room with its comfortable familiarity. Her father's favorite chair still waited for him, his pipe and tobacco resting nearby. Rosa's silk shawl sprawled over the back of the sofa, its bright colors repeated in the pillows at either end.

Cassie hung up her coat, kicked off her boots, and traced one finger over the fringe of the shawl. Hennessy, her fat tortoiseshell cat, head-butted her shin, pushing her into the kitchen. Cassie translated the accompanying meows as: feeding fat cats should come before everything else. Conceding the point, she measured a cup of the special diet cat food the vet charged outrageously for. Hennessy sat back on her haunches looking from the bowl with its meager offerings to Cassie.

"Sorry, girl, that's all you're allowed." She scratched behind the cat's ears. Hennessy stiffened her tail in indignation and stalked from the room.

Cassie sighed. Some days you just couldn't please anyone.

After an hour in the basement with her weights and heavy bag, she finally exhausted herself enough to entertain sleep as an option. She fell asleep in her sweat soaked T-shirt and shorts, face down on her bed, Gram Rosa's heavy velvet patchwork quilt blanketing her.

Sleep for Cassie was often elusive and never restful. How could it be with so many people clamoring for her attention? Patients she could have saved. Her mother, who she'd never known and who had died because of her. Gram Rosa with her scent of lilac and lavender. Her father's face, gaunt and twisted by pain, silhouetted by broken glass glistening in winter sunlight.

All the people who loved her—all gone now, except in her dreams.

Today she dreamed of dancing on the deck of a ship, a man's arms holding her close. She closed her eyes, her body humming with anticipation, but then opened them as his grip on her waist tightened. Richard grinned down at her.

"You'll always be mine, Ella," he said, holding her fast when she tried to run.

She thrashed beneath the heavy quilt, fighting to escape Richard. The thick collection of satin and velvet had once saved Rosa's life, but it was powerless to protect Cassie from her nightmares.

Finally, she left her dreams behind. As always, she woke alone in a silent house. The same dark gloom that had greeted her this morning shadowed the room even though her bedside clock said four-fifty pm. Cassie lay in bed a few minutes, fantasizing about sunlit beaches and ocean surf.

Her grandparents had taken her to Wildwood every summer when she was a child. A month before he died, her grandfather, Padraic, had won the ceramic ballerina sitting on her dresser there, at a Boardwalk arcade. As the ancient furnace fired up, making the lace curtains ruffle, she tried to pretend the movement came from an ocean breeze.

The February wind rattled the windows, its icy tendrils shattering her fantasy, and she gave up. She gathered enough energy to shower and feed herself while the cat watched, forever hopeful.

Several messages had come in while she slept. The first was from Richard. "I'm sorry about what happened last night." His voice sounded sincere and earnest. "I'll see you tonight. I promise things will be different this time."

Fran's voice came through the machine next, eager with excitement. "I've been playing around with this treatment failure idea and I think there's more going on. The fentephex is just the tip of the iceberg. I'm staying late at work, come talk to me before you start your shift. Bye."

More to the FX thefts? Did Fran mean more than one

person involved? Or had other drugs gone missing as well? Cassie tapped the edge of the buffet. Maybe she should call Drake. No, Fran would have already called him. Best just to get over to Three Rivers and see what Fran had found.

Drake would probably already be there, huddled with Fran, both sharing a joke, the mystery solved by the time Cassie arrived.

⁘

THE ROADS WERE slick as she drove from Point Breeze to Three Rivers. Sleet flung itself at her windshield with the ferocity of a kamikaze. Cassie pulled her Impreza into the employee parking lot and raced across the blacktop, dodging raindrops.

Fran would be waiting for her. It would be nice if she had solved the riddle of the FX source. Anything to put a stop to this epidemic of dead and dying children.

Cassie hesitated at the stairwell, wanting to go up to the fourth floor and check on Brian Winston and Jane Doe, but there was no time. As she opened the door leading down to the Annex tunnel, her cell phone trilled. Probably Fran.

"I'm on my way," she said into the receiver.

"You'd better hurry," came a muffled voice.

Cassie frowned, definitely not Fran. "I'm sorry, who is this?"

"How fast can you run?" the voice continued. "Your friend is counting on you. Hurry or it will be too late."

"Who is this? I think you have the wrong number." A clenching in her chest told her the caller had not misdialed.

"Ask your friend."

"Cassie." Fran's voice now, high pitched and strangled with fear. "Please hurry. He says he'll hurt me."

"Fran?" Her voice reverberated from the concrete

walls of the stairwell, echoing with the pounding of her heart. "Where are you? Are you all right?"

"Head back to your car, Dr. Hart," the first voice returned. "Run. Run fast."

Clutching the phone so tightly she feared it might slip from her sweaty grasp, she did as she was told and raced back the way she'd come. "Please, don't hurt her."

She rushed past a security guard at the hospital entrance and beckoned for him to accompany her. The guard looked at her as if she was crazy, but heaved his bulk from his stool and plodded after her. She pushed through the doors, scanning the parking lot.

"Where are you?" Fear slashed at her, as icy as the sleet. She turned towards her Subaru.

"Who you talking to?" the guard asked her as he stumbled out into the rain, fumbling with a golf umbrella.

"Too late, Doctor." The voice returned. "Maybe if you move fast you can still save your friend."

The sound of a gunshot echoed in Cassie's ears. "Fran!" she screamed, but the wind devoured her voice. A dark form ran from the parking lot, quickly lost in the night.

"Get a trauma team out here," she shouted at the guard as she sprinted toward her car.

Fran lay beside the Impreza, blood bubbling from a jagged wound in her neck. Cassie knelt in the freezing rain, frantically applying pressure to the massive wound, ignoring the lurching in her stomach as she focused on Fran. Bright red blood sprayed between Cassie's fingers, showering her with crimson warmth. Fran's eyes were open, life still in them, but she was unable to speak.

"Sshh, it's all right," Cassie crooned. Fran's wrists were bound with strapping tape, but she somehow found the strength to reach up and clutch Cassie's arm. Blood gurgled around Cassie's fingers. Fran's lips formed words

Cassie was powerless to translate.

"Fran, I'm sorry. It's all my fault. I should have never gotten you mixed up in all this." She bent over Fran, trying to keep the rain out of her friend's face. There was little other comfort she could give and nothing more she could do until the trauma team arrived.

She heard the sound of voices, glanced up to see the trauma team rushing a gurney stacked with equipment toward them. Thank God. "Help is on the way," she told Fran. "Hold on."

Fran's eyes closed. Her body fell limp. Cassie reached for a pulse. It was gone. No! She straddled her friend's body and began chest compressions, but each one forced more blood from the awful wound.

The surgeon examined the damage and shook his head. "You can stop CPR."

"No—we can get her up to the OR, repair the damage. Damn it, why isn't someone getting me a line, we need to push Oneg!"

The team stared at her. The surgeon took her arm. "Look around you. She bled out, it's too late."

Cassie blinked hard, finally looked down. Blood streamed off her clothes. Fran lay in a large puddle of dark red fluid so thick the pounding rain couldn't begin to wash it away.

A silent scream tore through her, lodging in her throat before she could give it voice. She rocked back on her heels, raising her bloody hands from Fran's still chest.

"She never had a chance," someone murmured.

CHAPTER 20

WHAT EVERYONE FAILED to understand, Cassie thought as wind and sleet and people swirled around her, was that Fran did have a chance. She would be alive if she hadn't been Cassie's friend, if she hadn't agreed to help her.

If she hadn't trusted Cassie. The thought reverberated through her, a church bell tolling a call to worship. She was jostled by yet another uniformed policeman attempting to cordon off the crime scene.

"Lady, you're gonna have to move," he told her in a brusque voice.

"I'm not leaving her." Her eyes never left Fran's face, now chalky white against the blacktop.

"If you don't leave on your own, I'll move you myself," he said, placing his hands on his hips.

Cassie wrapped her arms tighter around her body. She couldn't feel her feet, they were as numb as blocks of concrete. She shuddered as the corner of the sheet covering Fran's body danced in the wind, giving the illusion that Fran was still moving, still alive.

"Please, lady," the cop's voice dropped now, almost

pleading. "Just move back a little. We got to take care of her now. Won't you let us do that for your friend?"

Blue and red flashing lights surrounded her, bathing her in their surreal colors. Cassie nodded and shuffled back a few steps, still in eyeshot of Fran, but out of the way.

She choked back tears of frustration. Why didn't the killer come after her instead of Fran? It wasn't fair, wasn't right.

No one ever promised the world would be fair, she heard Gram Rosa's voice whisper through her mind.

Cassie raised her hand to her lips, sealing in her cries of anguish. Her vision blurred as she stared at Fran's body.

It should have been Cassie.

Chills cascaded over her flesh as she stood in the sleet, her friend's blood soaking her skin and clothes.

"Harley, would you move this lady," a uniformed officer called out, this one with Crime Scene Unit emblazoned on his jacket and carrying a tackle box. "Jeez, this place is a circus."

"Yeah, we're gonna do a lot of good here," his partner said, banging Cassie's hip with his camera bag. "Fucking rain just won't give us a break."

"Harley," the first one shouted. "Who taught you to secure a scene? Would you get this woman out of our way?" He glared at Cassie as if his eyes held enough force to move her. She merely stared back, willing her trembling to stop.

The uniformed cop returned to plead his case. "Miss, I asked you before—"

"I'm staying with her." Cassie was surprised by how level her voice was.

"C'mon lady, give me a break. It's freezing out here, don't you want to go inside where it's warm?"

She turned her gaze back to Fran and ignored him. She liked the cold, it numbed her to her pain. Right now the cold was her only friend.

"I've got it, Harley," a familiar voice came from behind her.

She didn't turn. Drake was the last person she needed right now. He might try to reason with her, talk her out of this rage building within her.

"Hart, go inside," he told her, his voice commanding. When she didn't respond, he moved in front of her, blocking her view of Fran. Cassie shot him a quick glare and took a step to one side. He paralleled her movement.

"I mean it. Your teeth are chattering, you'll make yourself ill. Then what good would you do Fran?"

Logic. Just what she'd expect from him.

"I'm staying." She took another step.

Instead of moving with her, Drake stepped toward her. He wrapped his arm around her shoulder, hugging her close. But he didn't try to force her to move. Together they stood, his body pressed against hers, sharing his warmth, as they stared down at Fran.

"I'm sorry." His whisper barely carried over the rain bouncing off the pavement.

A wave of exhaustion crashed down on Cassie, crumpling her strength. She leaned against his shoulder. He wore an old wool peacoat that smelled of lanolin and musk. The rain had curled his hair, and there were goose bumps on the back of his neck. His arm tightened, pulling her closer.

"You ready to go inside and tell me what happened?"

Too numb to speak, she nodded. Fran was gone.

Drake led her through the maze of cars and cops and gawkers, then into the shelter of the ER. They moved down the rear hallway, and he turned slightly to bump through a swinging door.

"You can't come in here," Cassie said when she saw where he had brought her. The women's locker room was empty. Drake didn't seem to notice, steering her past the gray metal lockers and wooden benches to the shower stalls. He reached out an arm and turned on the water as hot as it would go.

"You're freezing." He slid her leather jacket from her shoulders and pushed her under the hot water.

"Let me out!" The tiny jets stung her frozen skin. She raised her face to the stream of water. God, it did feel good.

"Not until your lips stop turning blue."

Newly awakened by the warmth of the water, Cassie looked down at her body. Her fingertips were blue, and shivers rippled across her flesh. She tried to pull her sweater off, but her hands fumbled uselessly at the sodden cotton.

Drake reached into the stall. With a firm grip, he turned her around and tugged the clinging sweater over her head. His hand, hot against her chilled skin, rested for a moment against the small of her back, steadying her. Cassie watched, mesmerized by the vivid, technicolor swirls of blood circling the drain. She wished she could drown out the memories as easily, muffle the gurgling noise of Fran's last breath echoing through her mind, bury the sight of crimson splashing through her fingers, smother the smells of blood and sweat and terror . . .

"This has got to stop," she said through chattering teeth. She wasn't talking to Drake in particular, more to herself, but she heard him sigh. He removed his hand from her flesh. She missed his warm presence with a yearning that surprised her.

"I know," he said. "Can you manage the rest on your own?"

Cassie turned to him, clothed now only in her sports bra and jeans. His eyes were fixed on her face, searching for her answer.

"I'll be all right."

He stared at her for a long moment, the muscles at the corners of his eyes tightening into small crow's feet of concern. And then he nodded, and left.

CHAPTER 21

DRAKE ALREADY HAD an account of Weaver's death from the security guard. He would've liked to hear more from Hart, but that could wait. She would've told him if she had any urgent knowledge.

His footsteps echoed through the dimly lit tunnel to the pharmacy. Janet Kwon was supervising the scene. Kwon knew better than wasting effort outside in the rain.

"What've you got for me?" Drake asked, resting against the door jam, hands in his pockets until she cleared him to enter.

"Come on in. It's not much." Kwon handed him a pair of vinyl gloves. "Tons of prints—will take us a long time to go through them all. Looks like she was grabbed here." She gestured to an overturned cup of coffee at a debris-covered desk.

"Didn't put up a lot of a struggle. Here's the tape he used to restrain her." She indicated a roll of reinforced strapping tape. "Our actor was too smart to take it with him. It's that damned Discovery Channel, it's like Criminal U."

Drake nodded, he'd heard it before. At least it wasn't

duct tape. That would have Kwon, who worked sex crimes before she came to Major Crimes, ranting about how the omnipresent silver tape should be bought by licensed non-rapists only. He was more interested in what was missing from the desk. "Where's the computer?"

Kwon crooked a finger at him. "No disks or hard copy anywhere, but the CPU is over here." They rounded a corner and Drake groaned. The computer unit had been torn open, the individual components immersed in a sink full of, he sniffed, isopropyl alcohol. "Looks like he tried to torch it. It didn't catch. Maybe we can recover something useful."

"How long?" he asked. She shrugged her answer.

"Not much else to see, except that the narcotics vault, if you can call it that, is empty."

He looked past the sink to the corner of the room where a metal lock box sat on the counter, its door twisted off its hinges. "That can't be standard hospital issue. It wouldn't stop any serious thief for more than a few seconds."

"Apparently these digs are only temporary while they're remodeling the real thing. You'll have to ask the boss man, Krakov's his name, for more details. He's not too happy about finding his pharmacy a crime scene, either."

Drake turned around, surveying the scene for anything Kwon might have missed. As usual there was nothing. "Guess I'd better go talk to Krakov."

"Did you know the vic?" Kwon asked.

"I met her this morning," he told her. "Why?"

"No reason, you just seem a bit off your pace, that's all."

Drake stripped off his gloves, wadded them into a ball and aimed for the trash bag Kwon had hung at the entrance to the crime scene. He missed. "No sleep for a few days will do that to an old man like me."

"If you say so. Just you haven't looked like this since what happened last summer."

He frowned, retrieved the gloves and deposited them in the bag. "Where's Krakov?"

"The office." She nodded her head toward the open door on the opposite side of the room. "It's clean, I already checked."

He left her to do her job.

⋅⊙⋅

CASSIE BOWED HER head against the stream of hot water. Finally, she took in a shuddering breath and collapsed onto the tile floor beneath the stream of water. She hugged her knees to her chest and leaned her forehead against the wall.

It should have been her. Why wasn't it? Why hadn't he killed Cassie? Maybe he would have if she hadn't grabbed the guard at the entrance. The thought should have left her cold with terror, but it didn't.

She felt nothing.

Cassie sat there long enough for her skin to prune. Trembling, she climbed to her feet and turned the water off. She stripped free of the wet jeans and underwear and threw her bloodstained clothes in the garbage. Wrapping one towel around her hair and another around her body, she went to her locker. Not much to chose from: her Nomex flight suit, bright with its reflective stripes and brass pins, a white lab coat, or a sweaty black cotton *gi* in a forgotten gym bag.

Her hand brushed against the white lab coat and flinched away. No, she would not dress like a doctor, not tonight. The *gi*, with its flowing pants and loose fitting top, would be more comfortable against naked skin than the itchy Nomex. A spare pair of running shoes, *sans* socks, completed her ensemble.

She sat on the wooden bench and dried her hair, exhausted by making the simple decision. How could that be? She made decisions all day long—life and death decisions. Like asking her friend to help her, introducing Fran to Drake.

What was she going to do next?

At first she fought against the need to make another choice—who would she hurt with this one? She flung her head upside down, rubbing at her hair with the energy of a maniac. She remembered Rosa combing it with infinite patience every morning before school.

Gram Rosa, the one ghost whose presence she welcomed.

What would Rosa say now?

Suddenly Cassie heard Rosa's voice echo through the locker room with absolute clarity. *You must live forever or die trying.*

Cassie straightened. The scent of lavender and lilacs filled the room. Despite the weight of sorrow and unshed tears, she found her lips easing into a reluctant smile. Rosa had outwitted the Nazis, fought with the Resistance, once even escaping from the Gestapo. But more important, Rosa was a Rom, a gypsy of the Kalderasha tribe. If anyone could speak from beyond the grave it would be her.

Live forever or die trying. Typical Rosa advice. Not to be taken at face value. Rosa did not mean to cloister herself away from her problems and thus stay safe and sound until old age took her. Cassie knew her gram's wisdom better than that. Rosa's message was to go out fighting, to risk everything on what she did today because there may not be a tomorrow.

Die trying.

Maybe. As Cassie stood up and shut her locker door, she realized that she no longer felt empty. Where there had been a frozen void, she now felt anger, an anger as sharp and brilliant as a scalpel blade.

The man who killed Fran made a mistake when he didn't take Cassie as well, she decided as she reached for her father's jacket on the bench. There was nowhere to hide. She would make certain that he was brought to justice.

Whatever it took.

CHAPTER 22

CASSIE STEPPED INTO the hall and headed toward the ER. She blinked in the bright lights. Wherever she looked, rainbow halos glimmered around her. Before facing her co-workers, she leaned against the wall and wiped her eyes on the sleeve of her top. When she opened them again the halos had vanished. But the knot twisting her gut, pushing against her lungs so that it was hard to breathe, remained.

She turned the corner and saw a familiar figure ahead, near the med room. Richard spotted her immediately, his long strides quickly cutting the distance between them.

"Are you all right?" he asked, taking her elbows in his hands and holding her at arms length as if inspecting her for damage. "What happened?"

Cassie was silent, wishing she had an adequate answer. He wore a tan trench coat draped over a silk suit ruined with rain and mud splatters. His shoes were also soaked through, leaving gray smears of footprints in his wake. Her glance traveled past him down the hall the way he'd come. What was he doing here?

"Ella," he gave her a small shake, returning her focus

to him. "What happened? What did you see?"

"Fran's dead." It was an effort to choke out the words. Her voice sounded small, tinny—as if it came from a great distance.

"I know. What were you doing, getting involved in this? What were you thinking!"

She tilted her head, her gaze sliding from his shoulder to his eyes. Their dull, sheet metal gray had been almost swallowed whole by his dilated pupils. His rapid blinking couldn't disguise the slight twitch at the corner of his left eye. She jerked away from his touch, shifting her weight to balance on the balls of her feet. "Are you using again?"

His upper lip pulled back in a sneer. She met his gaze without flinching. He couldn't scare her. Not tonight, not after what she'd just seen.

"None of your business, Ella. None of this is any of your damned business. You'd better remember that."

He took a half step toward her, trying to intimidate her with his height advantage. Cassie stood her ground. He stared at her for a long, hard moment, then lowered his hand.

"Did you have anything—Richard, were you involved—" She broke off, unable to finish. The man she'd seen running away from Fran had seemed shorter than Richard, but it was dark and with all the mist and rain . . .

"No! Of course, not. I'd never let anyone hurt you, Ella." His tone changed to one of possessive concern again. He gave a quick glance over his shoulder, frowning as if he expected someone to be there. "I have to go," he said abruptly. "I need to call Alan. The cops want to talk to me." He spun back to her in a move that caught her by surprise. He raised a finger to trace her jaw. His flesh felt icy against hers, as if he'd been the one caught outside in the rain. "I guess I have you to thank for that."

CASSIE CLIMBED THE stairs to the ICU, still puzzling over her conversation with Richard. If he knew who killed Fran, if Richard was somehow involved in the FX thefts . . . her nails bit into her palms as she thought about the possibility. He was obviously using again, which made him a danger to patients as well.

The glass doors of the ICU swished open, admitting her. She stopped at the nurses' station and called the Medical Board's 800 number.

"I'd like to report an impaired physician," she said, leaving Richard's information on the anonymous recorded hot line. Richard was the one abusing drugs, not her, so why did she feel so guilty? But rational thought couldn't erase feelings reinforced during the three years she'd spent with Richard.

Or the fact that she was betraying the man she once loved.

Tapping her finger against her lips, she listened to the automated voice thanking her for her interest in aiding impaired physicians. She held onto the phone long after the dial tone began to buzz. Finally she lowered it back into its cradle. There, it was done.

She found Brian, the young man who overdosed on the new combination of FX and MDMA, in a bed two spaces down from Jane Doe's. He was now on dialysis. A portable EEG machine sat at the foot of the bed, needles scratching against paper in a monotonous hum. His nurse glanced at Cassie's unusual garb, and then looked away again. So, the news had traveled up here already. Hospital grapevine, the original instant messenger.

"How's he doing?" Cassie asked, glancing at the EEG tracing. The ink lines were flat and unvarying. Not a good sign.

"They're still trying to find his parents, hoping they might consent to organ transplantation before . . ."

Before his body deteriorated to the point where the vital organs became too damaged to donate. Which meant the boy in front of her was, for all intents and purposes, just as dead as Fran. Cassie reached a hand out, stroked her fingers along his well-muscled arm. She blinked hard, felt a pressure building behind her eyes as if something was trying to escape.

"Kind of makes you think of that old commercial, doesn't it?" the nurse went on. "You know, the one with the frying pan and the egg. This is your brain on drugs."

Cassie sighed and gave Brian's lifeless hand one last pat. "And my Jane Doe?"

"Bed Four?" The nurse pursed her lips. "A little better, they're starting to wean her vent."

At last, some good news. Cassie left Brian and walked past two sleeping patients to bed space four. She took the seat beside Jane Doe, holding her hand as she leafed through the chart, now the size of a bible.

"It all started with you," Cassie told the sleeping teenager in a low voice. "If you would just wake up and tell us where those pills came from, we could end this before more people get hurt." She returned the chart to the bedside table and leaned over to straighten the girl's sheets, tucking them around her thin body.

"I lost a friend tonight, to the same man who gave you those drugs. Fran was doing me a favor, she didn't want to get involved in this. She just wanted to get me to go out on a date, she thinks I spend too much time alone." She squeezed Jane Doe's limp hand in hers. "Fran's like that, always looking out for everyone else. She shouldn't even have been there tonight—"

Cassie looked away, blinking hard against the glare

of the overhead light. Once the tears had been subdued, she turned back to stroke the straight, blonde hair away from Jane Doe's face. "You know, when I was a little girl, I would have killed to have hair like yours. I begged and begged my father to let me bleach mine. I even tried washing mine in Clorox. I was only six, I didn't know you needed hydrogen peroxide."

"I'll bet that was a pretty sight," came an amused but tired voice behind her. Cassie looked up to see Drake standing at the foot of the bed. "Thought I'd find you here." He scrutinized her outfit. "Not going ninja on me, are you?"

"It was the only thing in my locker."

"How's she doing?" He nodded to Jane Doe.

"Better. Stable. Progressing nicely. Take your pick."

"When's she going to be able to talk to me?"

Cassie's sigh rattled through her, leaving her empty. "Maybe tomorrow. Maybe never."

"You're a big help. How 'bout if I give you a lift home?"

"Thought you needed my statement."

"I do, but you've been through a lot."

"I'd rather get it over with."

"You make it sound like getting a root canal," he joked. Cassie said nothing to that. "All right, I'm set up in the break room down in the ER."

After giving Jane Doe's hand one final squeeze, she followed Drake downstairs to the ER.

⋅◉⋅

"YOU KNOW THE pharmacy's narcotic safe was emptied?" Drake asked as he slid a small recorder from his pocket.

"Does that mean there's more FX out on the street?"

"More of a lot of drugs: Percocet, Dilaudid, Oxy-Contin, you name it. This actor also trashed your friend's computer. They didn't want us to find something she was working on. Any idea what it was?"

"Fran called me. She said the FX thefts were only a part of the problem, that there was more going on." She hesitated, gnawing on her lower lip for a moment. He waited, allowing her to set the pace, wondering if she was going to finally tell him about her ex. "Gary Krakov, her boss, knew she was looking into the FX thefts. He was pretty upset."

"I know. Practically reamed me a new one for suggesting there could be anything wrong in the way he ran his pharmacy."

"Sounds like Krakov. Could he have had anything to do with . . ." she faltered, "this?"

"I wish I knew." His voice was throaty, raw. He cleared his throat. "Anyone else you can think of who might be involved?"

A faint sheen appeared on her upper lip and she raised a single finger to her mouth as if telling herself to hush. Her head bobbed in a nod, but she said, "No. I don't think so."

"How about your husband?"

Her head jerked up at that. "Ex-husband," she corrected him firmly. "The man I saw, it wasn't Richard."

She didn't exactly answer his question, but he allowed it to pass. Maybe later. After he had a chance to see what Kwon found out from her interview with King. There were too many coincidences piling up, all pointing to someone with intimate knowledge of Three Rivers Medical Center. "What did Weaver mean by only a part of the problem? Did she mean other drugs were taken?"

Kwon had said it would be tomorrow before they could get the work schedules and compare them to Weaver's data. Maybe they should be looking at other narcotics, testing to see if they were substitutes as well.

"Or did she mean that more than one person was involved?" He tilted his chair back, steepling his fingers, and continued, "This morning Weaver said she found at least two hundred pills that had been stolen." He looked to Hart for confirmation.

"Right."

"But this hospital goes through five hundred pills a day, give or take. And our guy only got two hundred in a month? Makes me suspect someone with sporadic opportunity, like a resident or orderly or nurse."

"Or physician assistant or maintenance man or ward clerk. Do you have any idea how many people that would be?"

"I'm beginning to get the picture. Thing is, it's hit and miss. Our guy seems much more organized and systematic."

"Our guy?"

"My guy. I've been tracking down leads on a major source of the FX. This guy, my guy, has a network extending over into Ohio and as far south as Morgantown, West Virginia."

"Is that who the task force is tracking?"

Drake brought his chair down and shook his head. "Miller thinks I'm cracked. Thinks I've fabricated one super-dealer out of a lot of little fish. Not a single person I've spoken to has seen him up close. He's very methodic, cagey." More he learned about Richard King, the more it looked like the surgeon could be a good fit for the part.

"That's why you're so interested in Jane Doe."

"I figure if she was close enough to wrangle some real FX from him, she probably knows who he is or at least can give me a good description. But if it's some kid just sneaking a pill here or there—" He shrugged. "Maybe Miller's right, I'm getting too involved in this case."

What was he doing, telling her all that? Hart was a

suspect. Drake fixed his gaze on her, she was still far too pale. The image of her kneeling over her friend's body haunted him. The silence lengthened as he tried to convince himself that she was still a suspect. He rubbed the heels of his hands over his eyes and blew his breath out before acknowledging the truth.

Hart wasn't a suspect. Not anymore. Not for him.

"When was the last time you got any sleep?" she asked, jarring him back to reality.

"You mean like a full night?" He suppressed the urge to yawn at the mere mention of sleep and kept his face impassive. He was still a cop on the job. Nothing could change that. "Can't remember. You ready to get started?" He turned on the recorder.

He led Hart through the events of the evening. Not that she needed much leading. She was clear, concise, and didn't seem prone to either self-doubt or hyperbole, two traits that perennially plagued witnesses. She'd be great on the stand. Her voice was clear as crystal, her face revealed honest emotion, and those large brown eyes . . . a prosecutor's dream.

If he ever got this actor to trial, that was.

Remembering Hart in the shower, covered in blood, his hand below the table drew into a tight fist and pounded against his thigh. Suddenly getting the job done right had never seemed so important.

He rubbed his chin and frowned at the stubble of growth there. What would Hart say if he told her that lately she was the main reason for his lack of sleep? After the task force briefing, he'd gone home to toss and turn until memories of her face finally drove him from his bed. He had done several quick-fire sketches in charcoal, then a more leisurely study in pastels. That one almost captured her elusive luminescence that compelled him, drew him like Icarus to the sun.

Finally he'd fallen asleep in the battered recliner in his studio. For the first time in months he had not been chased from slumber by visions of Pamela. Instead he dreamt of Hart, tactile dreams where her body came alive beneath his touch, vibrant colors swirling around them as they embraced.

Exactly what you'd want to tell a witness who just watched her friend die. That she's the new star of the investigating officer's erotic fantasies.

Wouldn't Miller love that? The Commander wasn't very sympathetic after Drake returned from his suspension last summer. She'd made it clear that if he didn't start getting results from his work on the task force that she would reassign him. To motor pool duty if she had her way. To Siberia if she could figure out how to extend her jurisdiction that far.

Hart's eyes closed as she described Weaver's death. She reverted to medical jargon, distancing herself from the victim, but still he saw her pain. Nuances of emotion played off the planes of her face. She had excellent bone structure. What kind of ethnic blend had combined to form those high cheekbones, deep-set almond shaped eyes, rich, full lips and that hair—he could bury himself and get lost for days in those rich, dark curls.

She opened her eyes and he startled. When had he moved so close to her? Drake carefully rolled his chair away from hers. He wanted to touch her, comfort her, but he couldn't. He shouldn't.

"So you never saw his face?" he asked, not because he thought she was holding out on him, but to break the uneasy silence that had settled over the room.

"No. I can't even be certain if it was a man." Her eyes flashed for a moment, and he watched the muscles of her jaw clench. "I think it was. The voice sounded masculine." She turned the full weight of her gaze on him. "What are you going to do next?"

Drake cleared his throat, surprised by the intensity behind the question. He shut the recorder off, stood and held her jacket out for her. "I'm going to take you home."

She slid out of her chair and turned toward him, ignoring the waiting coat. Her cheeks flushed with color that spread down her neck and chest. He couldn't help but notice she wore nothing under her karate uniform.

"When is Fran's autopsy?"

Uh oh. He could see where this was headed. "You're not going."

She glared at him, stood toe to toe, head tilted back to meet his eyes. Why was it he was the one who felt intimidated into looking away first? He could pick her up with one hand. Then he remembered how she'd used his own bulk against him last night and decided maybe he wouldn't try. She didn't wear a belt on her karate top, but she definitely was no novice.

"I signed her death certificate. As physician of record, I have a right to be there." Her words emerged in a flat, clinical tone as if she was telling him to take two aspirin and call her in the morning.

Ah, there was a picture he didn't need right now. Hart in the morning, hair tousled, face relaxed in sleep. Drake's fingers curled, itching with an urge to sketch the image that flashed in his mind.

He looked down at Hart and realized that somehow his hand had risen to rest on her shoulder. It was a nice shoulder, well rounded with firm muscles, but it belonged to a witness and definitely was off limits.

"You don't have to go," he heard himself telling her, forcing himself to remain professional when every instinct in him wanted to gather her into his arms, to tell her everything would be all right, to comfort and protect her. "I'll see to it that you get a copy of the protocol."

She shook her head, curls bouncing against her shoulder. If he opened his fingers the slightest bit, he could have slid the silky strands between them.

"No, I have to be there."

"Why would you want to see your friend carved up like that?" Her eyes widened at his words, but he saw resolution there. And fear. Now he knew what she needed from the autopsy. "There was nothing you could have done. She would have died even if you had been right there when he shot her."

Hart shrugged his hand away, grabbed her jacket and slid into it herself. "You can't be sure. I was there and I'm not sure. But one way or the other, I need to know."

CHAPTER 23

CASSIE WAS SILENT as Drake led her to his car. A '68 Mustang convertible, candy apple red with a black top and interior. She slid into the low-slung passenger seat and wrapped her arms around herself, shivering while he turned the heat up as high as it would go. The car fit him. So masculine, so independent. *Don't need nobody*, it seemed to sing as it glided out of the parking lot. She almost smiled when it fishtailed on a patch of black ice while taking the turn onto Penn. The Mustang might be a classic muscle car, but not the most sensible for the streets of Pittsburgh. Especially in winter.

"We should have taken my car."

"I'll take you back for it if you'll change your mind about going." He turned away from the road to look at her. Cassie saw the movement but kept her face forward and said nothing. "All right, it was worth a try."

They drove in silence through the Strip District. Drake pulled into the small lot behind the newly relocated coroner's offices on Penn Avenue. A small, wooden sign along the curb revealed the address but no hint as to what the anonymous, bunker-like building contained: the morgue and a level three bio-lab. The squat, narrow concrete building was punctuated with deeply recessed windows that seemed designed to block more sunlight than they would admit. Not that there was much of a view. Across the street was a four-story windowless warehouse and a vacant lot.

Cassie missed the old medical examiner's building with its soaring sandstone facade, as intricately carved as a gothic cathedral. Its solemn atmosphere seemed suitable, granting its unwilling denizens the respect they deserved.

Drake let the engine idle. He turned to face her. "You don't have to do this."

"Yes. I do." She pushed open her door and slid from the car before he could say anything else. Icy rain blew into her face, dripped inside her coat and down her chest. The pressure behind her eyes grew, keeping time with the rain beating against the Mustang's soft-top. She steeled her shoulders and stepped through the puddles leading to the side entrance, the only one open after official business hours.

Whenever she lost a patient and there was an autopsy, Cassie would try to attend. They were her patients, she was responsible for their care to the end. Tonight, she was just hoping to make it through the procedure without falling apart.

The night watchman looked up at them. Drake waved his credentials, and they both signed in. The guard frowned at Cassie's appearance, then shrugged and went back to his *Sports Illustrated*.

Their footsteps echoed through the empty tiled corridor. They passed the subdued, beige on beige family waiting area, then turned down the rear hallway that was restricted to authorized personnel. Here the smell of Ozmium—the vanilla scented disinfectant that smelled of anything but vanilla—clouded the air, burning Cassie's throat and nose.

The door to the staff lounge stood open, a metal sign over the microwave instructing visitors to please not feed the animals. As they passed dark administration offices and approached the exam rooms, the decor changed to white tile everywhere: floor and walls, gleaming in the overhead fluorescent lights. The only relief from the absolute stark whiteness was the occasional black scuffmark left by gurneys skidding on the tile. Everything seemed brighter, harsher, and brittle—as if it might break at any moment. As if she might break.

Drake took her elbow and steered her toward the autopsy viewing area across the hallway. There, from behind a glass wall, they could see and hear everything. Cassie allowed herself to be led. She would not be scrubbing in to observe more intimately, not tonight.

Fran's body had already been processed for trace evidence and now lay on a steel table with a sink at one end. The diener was preparing the equipment: electronic scales, camera, Stryker saw, scalpels, and other dissection tools.

Cassie flattened a palm against the window. She held her breath, waiting in vain for Fran's chest to expand. Cassie exhaled, a long shushing sound, a pressure valve releasing the constriction in her chest.

Drake took her by the shoulders and turned her away from the viewing window. She barely registered his touch, she was so numb. He held her like that, his eyes boring into hers as if searching for life. His hands were warm, threatened to thaw the protective barrier that encased her. She shrugged free of his touch, surprised when he hesitated, his fingers tightening instead of relinquishing her.

"I'm fine," she told him, her voice creating a jarring echo in the tiny space, making her wince. His hands hovered for a moment before he jammed them into his jacket pockets.

The outer door opened and a figure dressed in scrubs entered. Cassie was relieved to see Isaiah Steward, her favorite deputy medical examiner. Isaiah, a slightly built black man in his thirties, moved to greet them.

"Cassie," he said in his deep baritone, "I'm so sorry about your loss." And she knew he meant it. "We'll take good care of your friend."

He took her hand and she allowed him to grasp it for a long moment. "Isaiah," she started. The syllables emerged in a choked croak. She tried again. "I need to know—" her voice faltered once more. Isaiah nodded his understanding.

"After the external, I'll start with the wound and determine cause as best I can," he assured her. He turned to Drake. "Good to see you again, Detective. I trust that would also be amenable to you?"

Drake nodded, but his gaze was fixed on her, not the medical examiner. Did he think she would crumple? That she couldn't handle it? Her fingers dug into the thin metal ledge along the bottom of the window. He didn't know her at all. Or what she could handle.

They watched in silence as Isaiah changed into his protective suit, double gloved and carefully adjusted his face shield so it wouldn't bang against his thick, wire-rimmed glasses. He and his assistant entered the autopsy suite to begin their work of witnessing for the dead.

Cassie's breath fogged the glass, her entire reality telescoped into the well-lit circle around Fran's body. When she thought of Fran she was already beginning to use the past tense. Was that good or bad?

Isaiah's voice carried clearly through the speaker as he dissected her friend into her essential elements. She heard the scratch of a pen and saw Drake scribbling notes in a small pad.

Was she the last one to hear Fran laugh? Cassie knew she was the last to hear her speak. And scream.

"Body of a Frances Jennifer Weaver," Isaiah intoned, moving around the table, not yet touching the corpse in front of him. "External exam reveals a three centimeter by two centimeter irregularly shaped wound in the anterior neck at the level of the thyroid cartilage and slightly laterally displaced to the body's left side. There is extensive stippling and abrading around the wound edges." He paused and fixed a ruler in place while the diener took close up photos.

"Our guy held the gun directly against her skin," Drake translated unnecessarily. If there was one thing Cassie had seen too many of, it was gunshot wounds.

Isaiah placed a probe into the wound, reproducing the track of the bullet. "The entrance wound was at approximately a thirty degree angle, aimed downward," he continued his litany, "placing the victim below the perpetrator and directly in front of him." They rolled the body and he examined the back briefly. "No obvious exit wound. Lividity has set in and is consistent with the victim's position as supine immediately after death. There are also abrasions circumferentially around the victim's wrists and across her mouth."

More photographs. Cassie closed her eyes against the bright stab of the macroflash, but her vision still flared red, pulsing in time with her headache. She felt herself begin to sway and snapped her eyes back open, holding herself upright with her grip on the ledge. She darted a glance in Drake's direction just in time to catch his narrowed gaze watching her intently. He was hovering again as well, his hand stretched out behind her, ready to steady her if need be.

"I'm fine," she repeated, stepping to her left, out of his reach.

He shrugged and returned his focus to the proceedings beyond the window. "You're the doctor."

Isaiah began the Y-shaped incision and carefully removed the chest plate, preserving the tissue around the neck.

"The heart is virtually empty, consistent with ex-sanguination," Isaiah continued, removing each vital organ and weighing it before handing it to the diener for photos. In his large, green-gloved hands, Fran's heart looked like a dark amorphous blob of meat. There was no sign of the living, caring woman the compact mass of muscle had once kept alive.

After the chest cavity was empty, Isaiah ran his fingers over the tissue along the rear of the rib cage, working his way up until he found the bullet. The diener photographed the site of the bullet, then Isaiah dug it out with painstaking care. Pinched between Isaiah's forceps, the bullet with its flattened tip looked small. Too insignificant to be lethal.

"Thirty-eight caliber bullet with little deformity, removed from the cervical spine at approximately the level of C-7." Finally he turned to the neck itself, carefully reflecting away layers of tissue. "Trachea is completely disrupted, the larynx has sustained a comminuted fracture, and there is obvious penetration of the left jugular vein and common carotid artery."

Cassie's sigh rattled through her body like wind through a haunted house. She took a step back, able to breathe again. Isaiah turned the recorder off and gestured for the diener to take some close-ups. He stepped out to join her and Drake, wrapping his bloody hands around his chest and tucking them under his arms.

"You heard?" he asked Cassie.

"Thanks, Isaiah." She raised her hands, flexed and stretched them, relieved that they didn't have blood on them after all. She caught Drake staring at her and dropped them to her sides once more.

"You want to translate for us poor slobs?" Drake asked, pen poised over his notebook.

"Death was inevitable," Isaiah emphasized the last word, his gaze on Cassie. "It's a toss up which came first: ex-sanguination or hypoxia. My bet is the rapid blood loss did her in, but I can give you an exact answer after I review the micro. Either way, manner of death is homicide."

Drake nodded, satisfied, and closed his book. "That's all I need. You'll send over your final report as soon as possible, right?"

Cassie saw he said this with a smile and knew the two must have worked together before. Because if there was one thing Isaiah Steward was noted for, it was his painstaking search for all the answers before he made a final commitment. Which was why she appreciated him disrupting his routine to give comfort to a friend.

Right now, she'd take comfort wherever she could find it.

Isaiah started back through the door. "You'll get it when it's ready." The door to the autopsy suite swung shut behind him, and she was alone with Drake once more.

Cassie zipped her jacket, avoiding the detective's gaze. He laid a hand on her shoulder.

"Was it worth it?" he asked in a low voice. Not his cop voice, but the same tone he'd used in the suture room when he'd asked her to call him Mickey.

She nodded, looking away so he wouldn't see her blink back the tears fighting to spill from her eyes. He handed her a clean handkerchief. Where the hell had that come from? She ignored it, and sniffed. She looked down at the floor, at anywhere but him. His hand on her shoulder radiated heat, even through the thick leather of her jacket.

"It's all right if you want to cry," he told her, folding

the handkerchief into a neat square and returning it to his pocket. "You've just lost a friend."

"She would still be alive if it weren't for me."

The words burned, but it was good to have them out in the open where she could deal with them. Left inside, they threatened to eat away at her. Now they joined the ranks of the other enemy, the man who had actually pulled the trigger.

"Who died and made you God?" Drake asked, his voice back to normal, mocking and without a trace of compassion. "You think you're responsible for everything bad that happens around you. Is that why you let that creep, King, run roughshod all over you? Do you somehow feel you have it coming? That you deserve to be treated that way?" He shook his head, blue eyes blazing at her. "I don't understand you."

Cassie gathered herself up to her full five foot four and wished she were taller. "I hope this isn't how you handle all your witnesses, Detective," she flared back. "I'll call a cab, if it's all the same to you."

She reached for the phone on the wall. He intercepted her, snatching it from her hand. "No. I said I'd take you home and I will."

"This isn't the prom. I don't have to leave with the same adolescent I came in with."

They shared a glare for a moment, then he chuckled. "Adolescent, huh? Guess you're right. I'm sorry, Hart. I owe you an apology. I had no right to bring up your ex-husband."

"Damned right. And it's Dr. Hart."

He gave her a gracious bow, mitigated only by the fleeting grin that played over his face. "Dr. Hart. Your carriage awaits."

Cassie looked past him and saw Fran, now completely eviscerated, a shallow husk of flesh all that remained of her friend. Her gut twisted as if she'd been sucker-punched and her vision filled with black spots. It took effort to stumble through the door Drake held open for her.

He was wrong. It didn't have anything to do with playing God. It was all about right and wrong and taking responsibility for her choices in life. Both the good ones and the bad. It just seemed that, with the people she loved, her bad choices far outweighed the good.

She turned to tell him this, but he was walking closer to her than she realized. She lurched against him and fell off balance. His hand was immediately there, supporting her, righting her. She stood, bemused by his proximity, her back against the wall.

Cassie flashed to when Richard had cornered her in a similar position. This time she felt no fear, none of the deep-seated emotions that unraveled her whenever she was around Richard. Instead she felt a strange calm. Her vision cleared, the world stopped its gyroscopic spinning.

Drake looked down at her, blue eyes flashing in the fluorescent lights. His hand fell away, hovering an inch or so from her body, as if he were afraid to break the spell that had embraced them both.

The sound of Fran's screams, the heat of her blood pumping into Cassie's hands, the dull film that clouded her eyes—all these vanished. Leaving only the man before her. Cassie raised her hand, her palm gently caressing his cheek, the stubble of his beard. His chest caught with a sharp intake of breath and he looked away.

Damn it, when would she learn? She'd crossed some line, done something offensive to him. She began to lower her hand, disappointed.

Drake surprised her and took her hand in his, burying his mouth in her palm, tasting her with delicate strokes of his tongue. She arched her neck, reached up to pull his mouth down to meet hers.

Her fingers tangled in his hair, her mouth opened beneath his, eager. She moved his hand to rest inside her jacket, over her breast, where he could feel the desperate pounding of her heart. He made a small noise as he shifted his weight, the better to align his body perfectly against hers.

She took a deep breath, mingling her exhalation with his, and for the first time that night, the sight of Fran's bloody body did not haunt her.

CHAPTER 24

—— •⸗✦ↀ◉ↂ✦⸗ↈ•—— ◆——

A SHRILL BUZZ echoed down the hallway. Drake jumped back and shoved his hands in his coat pockets. The security guard moved past them down to the service entrance where the buzzer sounded once more.

He dared a glance over at Hart and saw that her face was flushed with color. She stood with her arms crossed over her chest.

"Necking in the morgue," he muttered, certain the spell was irrevocably shattered. "What would the guys say about that?" He reached for her arm, but stopped short of actual physical contact. No sense courting danger.

She seemed fascinated by the tiled floor, and didn't say a word as she walked out the door. After scrawling their initials on the guard's clipboard, he followed her out to his car. He climbed into the driver's seat. She remained silent in her seat, her eyes focused straight ahead into the darkness.

"I'm sorry." He cleared his throat twice before his voice normalized. "That was totally unprofessional of me. I know fear can sometimes trigger certain," he stumbled over his words in his effort to sound impersonal, "emotional reactions. I hope you don't think I would take advantage of that vulnerable state. I haven't ever, I shouldn't—" He decided to stick to basics. "You're a witness. Now," he turned the ignition on, "let me take you to your home."

She perched on the edge of her seat, her back straight, shoulders hunched high, neck rigid. She said nothing, swiped at her face with her hand although she still hadn't cried, and stared straight ahead.

He fiddled with the heater, watching her from the corner of his eye. Wan light from the building's security spots filtered in through the rain-streaked window, etching her face in blue-gray shadows as if she were carved from granite. Just when he feared she was having some kind of catatonic breakdown, she spoke.

"I know she's just another case to you," she started. Her voice was a hair above a whisper, but not gentle by any means. Each word emerged clipped, as if she were biting off pieces of glass. "Not even a case. Part of your big drug conspiracy. I know you can't let yourself get personally involved. It's just—" She cleared her throat and her voice returned, stronger now.

"Damn it, Drake, you met her. You saw how vivacious, how full of life she was. She's not just another DB!" He looked up at her use of the cop talk. "Yeah, everyone has their own name for it. Dead body for you guys, crispy critters for the firemen—you know what we call 'em? MM's: morgue meat. I know it's the only way to keep your sanity in a job like ours, but forgive me if I'm feeling more than a little insane right now. You got a fancy speech to cover that?"

"I'm sorry." He shifted in the seat, the butt of his Glock digging into his side, reminding him of his responsibilities. To Hart. To her friend. "It's nothing personal."

"Don't you dare say that to me! Not here, not after

what we just watched."

He reached for her hand, trying to offer the dispassionate comfort of a professional. Part of him was afraid of what might happen if she accepted it—he still felt the heat of her lips on his.

She jerked away before he could make contact and shoved her door open. Wind rushed in, biting rain slashed at them both. He leaned over her, past her, reaching for the door handle. She jumped out into the freezing rain, avoiding him.

"Know what, Drake? You can just go to hell! I'll walk home."

Drake scrambled after her. Judas H! Couldn't she see he was trying to help her? Icy water sloshed over the tops of his sneakers.

Help her or handle her? It wasn't her fault he had responded to her touch in the hallway. She was distraught, it was his job to take control of the situation.

Except that ever since he met Hart, he'd felt totally out of control. Until he held her in his arms. Then, for the first time since last summer, everything felt right, his world had tilted back into balance at last. Only for a few seconds, but he already missed that feeling. He missed her touch with an intensity that was frightening.

"Wait!" Drake called out to her.

He splashed through puddles, followed her onto the rain-slicked grass. She skidded to a stop, hunched over the waist-high wooden sign in front of the building. He slipped, almost fell, then caught himself and quickened his pace, not certain if she stopped because of him or because she was getting sick.

He raced over to her, caught her in his arms. "Are you all right?"

She hadn't gotten ill, but she was gasping for breath, hyperventilating. Wrapping his arms around her for support, he pulled her back against his chest, bent his head over hers.

"Breathe, slow, slow," he coached her. Her heart skittered like a hummingbird beneath his hand. Finally her breathing slowed to normal. He spun her around to face him.

"Can we please start over?" He wiped rain and strands of her hair out of her face. God, how long had he imagined the feel of her skin beneath his fingers? She tilted her face up to his, and he could see she was just as terrified as he was by all this. He framed her face in his hands and lowered his lips to hers.

Her mouth opened beneath his, inviting him to deepen the embrace. He leaned her back against the sign. A small sound, half sigh, half urging, caught in her throat.

Oh yeah, there was nothing wrong with this, he thought as the cold and the rain and the house of death behind them all vanished from his awareness. There couldn't be, not when everything felt so right.

Even if it probably was the biggest mistake of his career.

CHAPTER 25

DRAKE COULDN'T REMEMBER getting Hart back into the Mustang, but somehow he did. Before he released the brake and started the car, her hand slipped onto his right leg. Drake tensed. Her palm slid down to the inside of his thigh and began a slow, firm stroke up. He sucked in his breath, the heat of her touch as jolting as a shot of good whiskey. It burned through his jeans, moving relentlessly toward his groin.

"Take me to your place," she whispered in the darkness.

He almost stalled the car in his urgency to comply.

It wasn't a long drive to his building on Ravenna Way. Hart remained silent, her only response when he tried to speak was to squeeze her fingers against his groin, inflicting a wave of pain and pleasure that choked any words before he could utter them. His mind churned with conflicting emotions. This was not a good idea. He couldn't get involved with a witness—Miller would break him for certain. The clammy touch of fear pierced him as he remembered Pamela and how that had turned out.

He had purposely avoided any romantic

entanglements since last summer. It wasn't safe, it wasn't fair to them—let's face it, he told himself, you just weren't ready to handle it. And, he realized as he pulled into the garage beneath his building, he wasn't certain he could handle it now. For the first time in his life, Drake felt nervous around a woman.

He reached out a hand to help her from the seat. She looked up and met his gaze with a calm radiance, a certainty that made him tingle all over. Hart's smile promised that this night was not a terrible mistake. Her hand tightened over his, so small and delicate, yet so strong. He led her through the door and up the polished oak steps to the third floor.

"I need to tell you something." Somehow he managed to put together a coherent string of words by the time they reached the landing in front of his door.

She laid a finger over his lips, took the keys from his trembling hand, and opened the door to his apartment. "It can wait," she told him, pulling him inside, her hands already working the wool jacket from his shoulders.

Drake barely had the presence of mind to remove his Glock and deposit it on the foyer table. Hart tugged his shirt open, sliding her lips over his chest. She pushed the flannel shirt back to his elbows, and he was caught, helpless as an inmate in a straight jacket. Which worked out just great, because if Miller ever found out about this, temporary insanity would be his only defense.

She feathered one hand down his back with a delicious, tickling movement that jolted through his nerve endings. Her fingers came to rest at the sensitive spot at the base of his spine, moving in small circles, sending shockwaves of pleasure through his body. *Judas H! Where'd she learn to do that?*

"I really need—" his voice was hoarse and throaty.

"Shh. Do you have condoms?"

"Yes." The single syllable was all he could manage as her hand slid under his waistband.

"Trust me, everything will be fine. No more talking."

As she released him from his jeans, he knew she spoke the truth. Drake wrenched his arms free from their cotton bindings and buried his hands in her hair, tilting her face up so he could look into those fathomless brown eyes as he kissed her.

·❧·

CASSIE OPENED HER mouth to him and was jolted by his hunger; it matched hers in intensity. Their bodies tangled together, hands and mouths exploring, pleasuring, tantalizing. She had the impression of a large open space where the city lights illuminated them from tall windows. As she and Drake moved in their dance of passion, the dim light embraced them in an ethereal glow.

As if this wasn't real. *It couldn't be real,* was her last formed thought before she surrendered herself to her urgent need to forget herself, forget this awful, dreadful night.

Drake propelled her backward against a leather couch. His hands left her for an aching moment, just long enough for him to shed his clothes. Then they returned to her, their light touch skimming over her as he pulled her clothing from her. Now both naked, on equal ground, they regarded each other.

Cassie felt her breath quicken as she saw that he was already hard. She looked up and met his eyes, two stars caught in the dim light, eyes that seemed to see right into her soul. Feeling wicked, she allowed her fingers to lightly trace the length of him.

She was rewarded when he grabbed her shoulders and shuddered beneath her touch, exhaling a low, animal moan.

"Condoms," she whispered, her lips close to his ear, her breath ruffling his hair.

Drake turned his head and kissed her roughly, his tongue scraping over her teeth, his fingers tightening their grip on her shoulders. Their eyes met, small sparks reflecting the light from outside. Suddenly he stopped, pulled away for the barest of moments, before kissing her once more.

This time his touch was tender. His lips trailed down to the sensitive area at the base of her throat. He paused, tasting her, her pulse throbbing against his mouth. She inhaled, had to fight back tears once more, the sudden intimacy overwhelming.

Intimacy wasn't what she'd come here for. Intimacy wasn't what she needed. Not tonight, not after what she'd just seen. She wove her fingers in his hair, yanked his face back to her, capturing his mouth in hers. His eyes narrowed as she usurped control, then he gave her a small, quick nod. Not surrender, more like a challenge.

He lifted her into his arms, carried her into another room and lay her on the bed. Cassie turned her head, listened as he rustled in the bedside table, smelled the musk and sweat of his sheets. There were only two walls with windows in this room. The city lights spilled in, unimpeded by shades or curtains.

His form appeared over top of her, and she smiled in anticipation. He reached above her head and pulled a pillow out, sliding it under her hips as she spread her legs around his waist.

"Now," she told him, rewarded by the flash of his grin. When he waited, she leaned forward, reaching for him, guiding him. Still, he held back. She felt him throbbing inside her. Her muscles clenched, pelvis rocked, drawing him in further. He allowed her to work, entwined his fingers in hers, gripping them with an intensity that told her what his restraint cost him.

Finally when neither could bear it another second, his hips arched up to meet hers, and he began to thrust, long slow strokes that increased in speed and intensity. Her mouth was open, but no sounds able to escape as her throat tightened with pleasure. His lips found hers. He climaxed with a last, long shuddering thrust, his mouth on hers, sharing her breath.

She felt the vibrations tremble through his body, into hers, and she joined him. Then he collapsed on top of her, their heartbeats racing in synchrony.

Drake reached a finger up, wiped the tears from her face. "I didn't hurt you, did I?" he asked in a quiet, concerned whisper.

Cassie's mind was still reeling. For one precious moment she'd abandoned her barriers, and Drake touched her soul, set it chiming like fine crystal, a vibration echoed in every cell of her body. She wanted to savor that feeling, that pure tone of unity, the promise that she was not alone, that for one brief moment in time the universe stood in perfect balance.

Had he hurt her? "No."

CHAPTER 26

DRAKE PUSHED HIMSELF up onto his elbows, surprised he had enough energy to do that. He felt both drained and energized at the same time. How was that possible? He smiled down at Hart. Who the hell cared?

"I've been wanting to do that ever since I first laid eyes on you."

She flushed at his words, her cheeks glowing in the faint light.

"I feel like we exorcized some demons," he continued in the same low voice. The words sounded strange, unable to encompass the feelings swirling through him, but they were the best he had to offer.

"Demons?" Her eyes popped open, startled.

"I mean, I haven't let anyone, any woman . . ." He trailed off when she frowned. Guess this wasn't the right time to tell her about last summer. But he needed to. He owed her that.

Hart raised a finger to his lips. "No talking."

She pulled his face down to meet hers. He slipped his lips down her neck until he rested his cheek against her chest, the rhythm of her heartbeat mesmerizing him, banishing all thoughts of Pamela and last summer.

All he could think about was the woman in his arms tonight.

She had to have some Irish the way she colored so easily, he thought, rolling onto his side to watch her. Italian, too. And those high cheekbones—Indian? Eastern European? Maybe Greek or Armenian. Didn't matter, the whole was greater than the sum.

And all that hair. He lifted a fistful and held it to his cheek. Soft as lambswool. He inhaled deeply. "I love the way you smell."

She gave him a mock frown. "Excuse me?"

This was so unlike him—why couldn't he just shut up? He never talked this much in bed—and spouting off nonsense at that. Jeezit, what the hell was wrong with him? Drake grinned; he couldn't help himself. "Like a fresh apple when you slice it, and there's this faint blush of color on the inside." His eyes closed as he sniffed deeply of the handful of hair. "Lace curtains dancing in a summer breeze, that's what you smell like."

She let out a short laugh. "Really? I think you're mistaking me for a shampoo commercial."

He shook his head. Leaning forward to nuzzle her neck, he buried his face in her hair. "No, it's you," he whispered. "All you."

⚘

WAVES OF FREEZING rain splashed over Cassie as she ran. She was late, so late, she'd never make it in time. Dread and panic seized her lungs so that each breath was a struggle. She looked around wildly, searching for a familiar face. There was no one there to help her.

She gasped for breath, forced her legs to keep moving, keep running. The night closed in on her,

149

smothering her, confounding her as she raced through the darkness. Her head pounded in time with her heart, a driving beat so intense it drowned out the sound of her footsteps.

Faster. Faster. Late, she was too late.

Icy fingers of fear squeezed her heart tight, and she collapsed onto the wet pavement, gasping for breath. She looked down at her hands. They were covered with blood.

Fran's pale face stared back at her. Blood gurgled from her mouth and throat, a fountain of death. Her lips moved. "Cassie."

Fran's eyes opened wide, staring into Cassie's even as life faded from them.

Cassie reached out to her friend, her hands dripping blood. But she was too late.

She jerked upright, fleeing the realms of nightmares and memory. Her vision was choked with tears. Cassie covered her face with her hands, muffled her sobs until her breathing quieted. Sweat soaked sheets tangled around her legs. She looked over at Drake. He slept peacefully, his face unlined with worry or fear.

She slipped silently from the bed, grabbed one of Drake's shirts and walked barefoot into the living room.

What was she doing? Fran was dead, and here she was, making love to a man she barely knew. Had she gone crazy?

But being with Drake felt good. It felt so right. And she wanted more. Much more.

She moved to the dark windows. Vulnerable. Because of Drake, the way he made her feel, she was vulnerable, weak. Out of control.

Cassie saw her reflection floating in the glass. Pale as a wraith. She reached a hand out, placed her palm against the cold glass, and absorbed the chill into her body. The glass was black, a scrying pool. She gazed into it, allowed herself to fall into the darkness of the winter night.

Fran's bloody image floated in the glass, and Cassie was overwhelmed. She was so sorry. Sorry for everything, everybody. Her father's image appeared beside Fran. *I need you to be strong, Cassie.*

Then her mother's dark shadow joined them. The worst of all because Cassie could conjure no image, no memory, just a stab of emptiness that threatened to devour her soul. The woman had given everything for Cassie, how could she ever live up to that? Ever repay it?

Grief shuddered through her body and she collapsed, her hand sliding down the length of the window as her body sagged to the floor.

⚬

DRAKE TRIED TO wake up, tried to stop the dream, at least he prayed it was only a dream. He opened his mouth to shout a warning, but no sound came. He watched helplessly while Hart screamed. Then her screams were silenced to a croaking gasp, and her mouth filled with blood. He tried to move, to see who had done this to her, but he was powerless to control anything. Helpless to save her, her blood gushing out, covering her face, Drake shuddered and turned away.

To see Pamela. God, why did it always have to come back to her? The one face he never wanted to see again, but the one he saw every night. He sat up in bed. Pamela turned to him, his off duty Beretta in her hand. She raised the gun to her head and, this was the most horrible thing, the thing he had never told anyone about that night, she smiled at him. Just before she pulled the trigger, she smiled.

The scene played out in slow motion. He leapt toward her. The sound of the shot reverberated through the room, deafening him. He fell down beside her, grabbed her arm, tried to find a pulse. He held her head in his lap, her blood covering him, saturating him with the smell of copper and salt, a rank smell that turned his stomach.

He looked down on her face. It no longer was Pamela, it was Hart.

That was when he woke.

Drake sat up, tried to control his breathing. He looked around, disoriented for a moment. He reached for his gun, and then remembered he had left it on the foyer table. Where was Hart? He was afraid to look beyond the foot of the bed, his nightmare still clouding his thoughts.

He shook his head, freeing himself from Pamela's image, and ran his fingers through his hair. He hadn't imagined tonight—could he have? Then he heard a small sound coming from the living room. A woman sobbing.

Drake unraveled himself from the sheets and grabbed a pair of sweat pants. He moved into the other room. Hart was crumbled against the window, her body shaking with grief. Drake watched the pain overwhelm her—but still she did not cry. Something wrenched inside him. He knew she needed to grieve, expel all those churning emotions before they consumed her from within, but it was impossible for him to see her in such pain.

He joined her on the floor, cradled her in his arms, and held her frozen hand safe inside his own. He rocked her like a baby, he crooned a melody from a distant memory, and made up nonsense syllables when he could not remember the words.

Never before had he had such an overpowering need to care for someone. He hoped she wouldn't realize that he was the one weeping as he buried his face deep in her hair. Seeing her like this had undone him completely. He wanted to be her champion, to slay her dragons, to heal her body and soul.

If she would only let him.

CASSIE TOOK A deep breath and swallowed her grief. Unshed tears threatened to choke her, but she gulped them back. She didn't want Drake to see her like this. She slid from his lap and stood once more. He rubbed the heels of his palms against his eyes then looked up at her.

"Are you okay?" he asked.

She couldn't talk, not without risking an explosion of pain. She turned away, faced the window and bowed her head, resting it against the dark glass. He joined her, standing behind her, his arms encircling her waist, fitting just right.

Cassie leaned back, enjoying the warmth of his bare chest against her body. The city lights spread out before them like luminous jewels cast on a black velvet blanket. Jewels she had been blinded to until he joined her.

She placed a hand on the window, connecting with her reflection there. Drake reached his own hand forward and covered hers. He eased her hand from the glass and raised it to his mouth, his lips sending a wave of heat through her body.

Cassie turned within his embrace, slid her hand away from his mouth and behind his neck. She reached up to kiss him. He lifted her, pressing her back against the glass. She tugged the shirt over her head. His mouth eagerly searched for hers after the momentary break in contact.

Her body was flushed with heat on one side and growing numb with cold on other. The window rattled with the winter wind, its vibration echoing through her. Cassie left the cold world behind as Drake carried her back into the bedroom.

CHAPTER 27

CASSIE LURCHED FROM sleep, fleeing another nightmare. She opened her eyes, disoriented, startled by the sound of a man's breathing beside her. Richard? She steadied her own breathing, fearful of waking him.

No. Memory slowly returned. Not Richard.

Drake. She rolled over and watched him. Pale dawn light picked out glistening strands of silver woven through the thick, black hair spread over his pillow. Cassie liked the idea that, although he seemed to live life like one long beer commercial, Drake already had a few gray hairs. She smiled, traced a finger over the v-shaped scar on his chin, wondered where he'd gotten it.

She might never know.

Cassie slipped from beneath his arm and walked naked through the open door into the bathroom. After using the toilet and washing her face, she grimaced in the mirror. Puffy circles cradled her eyes. It would be a long time before she would sleep soundly again. She couldn't count on Drake always being there when the nightmares hit. Maybe never again.

She dabbed some toothpaste on her finger, scrubbed

her teeth, and then gargled with mouthwash. Looking with yearning at the old fashioned, oversized claw foot tub, she decided against taking the chance on waking him before she left. Best just to slip away. They both knew this was impossible. Better to end it now, before it became painful for either of them.

But she would miss the man, and the feeling of wholeness, of contentment he had given her last night.

She crept out to the living room and slipped into her clothes. All those crazy things Drake told her—no other man had ever treated her like that. But finding Fran's killer took priority. She couldn't become involved with Drake, not if it might jeopardize the investigation.

It wasn't only the investigation. Part of the queasiness that stirred in the pit of Cassie's gut was good old-fashioned fear. Why should she trust Drake, especially now that she knew how easily he could stir her emotions and make her lose control? What proof did she have that Drake would not reveal a secret side akin to Richard's?

Richard had been handsome, talented, and treated her like a princess. Look how that had turned out. Banishing the ghost of Richard and the pain he'd caused would take more than one night of passionate escape.

She took a few minutes to appreciate Drake's place in the rose tinted early morning light. He had the entire top floor, which explained the many windows that climbed from just above knee level to elaborate cornices in the ceiling twelve feet overhead. The windows themselves were large, composed of leaded panels joined by intricate carved mullions. The extensive woodwork continued past the cornice, crisscrossing over the plaster ceiling above.

How did he afford this on a cop's salary? The building was old, probably dating from the twenties or thirties judging from the elaborate ornamentation and solid construction. The leather sofa, love seat, and overstuffed chair that circled a thick oriental rug all must have cost a good bit. The dining room table, a spare Shaker style crafted from a light cherry sat on a similar rug. The little wall space free of windows was covered with artwork.

Maybe there was more to Drake than the shallow he-man her imagination had conjured. Too bad she wouldn't have the chance to know him better. At least not until after Fran's killer was caught.

Once outside, Cassie jammed her hands in her pockets. She wasn't dressed for the blustery weather, she didn't even have any socks on. Shuffling toward the front of the building, she refused to look up. In case Drake was watching.

She glanced down the street, trying to get her bearings. There was no traffic, and the street dead-ended at his building. Damn it, where was she? She knew she was somewhere in East Liberty, they had driven around Penn Circle last night, hadn't they? Her mind wasn't exactly on the landscape at the time.

Fool. How could she let this happen? Surrender control to a man who was a virtual stranger. Let him get so close.

Cassie shook her head. Last thing she wanted to think about was Drake.

She looked back at his building. It was brick with large, wide windows ringing each floor. Signs in the windows advertised commercial space available on the first and second floors. He must be the only residential tenant, she realized. She was tempted to go back in and borrow a phone, but there was no way she could face him again.

As the sky gradually lightened, she jogged down to the corner. Ravenna Way—never heard of it. The cross street was wider, lined with brick row houses, several that appeared abandoned. Pierce Street. That rang a bell. And there was the busway. At least she knew where she was, about two miles from home.

She turned the corner and began to run.

•◖◗•

DRAKE GOT TO the living room window in time to watch Hart run down the outside steps, her hair streaming behind her. He wanted to race after her. He told himself it was pride that held him back, but knew that to be a lie. What would he say when he caught up with her? His palm pressed against the chilly glass. He watched her run away.

He'd never felt like this before. An unsettling mixture of fear, excitement, and anticipation twisted in his gut. Along with the knowledge that whatever this feeling was, he wanted more.

Why had she run from him? Did he scare her?

She hadn't seemed frightened last night. But she'd been in shock then. He raked his fingers through his hair, tugging at it in frustration. Was there something more going on?

The phone rang. "Drake here," he answered, glad of any diversion from his thoughts.

"Remy." His mother used her pet name for him. "I know you're probably headed out to work, but I wanted to see how everything was going."

Drake smiled. Typical Muriel, her ESP working overtime. "Fine, Mom. Sorry I haven't called, my hours have been pretty crazy."

"Still that drug thing?" she asked, disapproval in her voice. Muriel Drake couldn't wait for her son to return to Major Crimes and the more structured and less dangerous world of murder and mayhem.

"Yes, Mom."

"Well, be careful. It's seventy degrees and sunny

down here, why don't you come for a visit?" Muriel had retired to Ft. Myers, Florida.

"I can't leave this case." Drake listened to the silence on the line and imagined the frown on her face. "Maybe once it's wrapped up."

"The Weather Channel says you'll have snow today or tomorrow. Make certain you dress warmly. Do me a favor and leave the Mustang. That car is a deathtrap on icy roads."

"Sorry, it's part of my cover." He could have heard her sigh of resignation even without the help of Verizon.

"Just be careful."

"I will," he assured her, ready to hang up.

"Remy, is something going on? You sound different. Did something happen?"

He almost choked on his laughter. Yes, Mrs. Drake, your son had his world rocked by a beautiful woman last night. Aloud he just made a noncommittal noise. "Everything's fine, I'll talk to you later."

"I love you," she said and hung up.

Drake replaced the phone in its cradle and started the coffee. He returned to the bedroom, and began to get ready for work. He had just enough time to make it to the morning task force briefing.

In the shower he found himself humming as he imagined Hart's exquisite hands, soap sliding from her fingers, moving over his body.

He jabbed a hand out to the temperature control and was immediately jarred by freezing water. He forced himself to endure it. He needed to be especially sharp, make certain Miller never found out about him and Hart. He had to close down the FX ring and find Weaver's killer.

Then he could figure out what to do about Hart.

❦

THE PHONE RANG just as Cassie was climbing into bed. She grabbed the receiver, her pulse jumping as she wondered if it might be Drake, then immediately chided herself for her adolescent thoughts. Drake wasn't going to call. He knew as well as she did that they had no future together. She wasn't even certain if she wanted him to call.

"Cassie? It's Adeena. How're you doing?"

She sank back against the headboard. "All right, I guess."

"You don't sound so good. Listen, you can say no if you want, but Fran's parents are coming over to Three Rivers this morning. The police said they could collect her stuff from her desk. Some of the people who worked with her are going to meet them, and I didn't know if you wanted to join us."

Cassie was silent. Her knuckles whitened as she gripped the phone. Damn, she should have called Fran's parents. But facing them was the last thing in the world she wanted to do. She looked longingly at her bed.

"We thought maybe we could pack everything for the Weavers," Adeena continued. "Then they could go through it when they felt ready."

Cassie ran her hand over the quilt, savoring the rich velvets and silks. "What time?"

"Around ten."

"I'll be there." She hung up and stood, ignoring the warm comfort beckoning to her from the bed.

CHAPTER 28

CASSIE STEPPED OUT of the fourth floor stairwell and headed toward the ICU. It was only nine-thirty, she had time to check on Brian Winston and Jane Doe before meeting Adeena. A familiar face popped out of the waiting room — Linda, one of the girls who had accompanied Brian into the ER.

"They won't let me see him 'cause I'm not family," she told Cassie. "Please help me, I need to see him, be with him."

"Did you ask his parents?"

"They're flying back today. They were skiing in Switzerland." She looked up at Cassie with hope in her eyes. "He's gonna be okay, isn't he? He just has to be."

She led the girl back into the family waiting area and sat her down on the couch. "Brian's not doing so well. The Double Cross caused some brain damage."

Linda gasped and covered her mouth. "Oh my God. And I almost took it too! What would have happened if I did?"

Cassie looked at the thin wraith of a girl with her plaid Catholic High skirt, leather shirt and pierced eyebrow and nose. "You might have died." She waited a beat and went on. "We have another girl in the ICU who almost died from FX. We found her under the West End Bridge."

Suspicion hardened Linda's eyes. "So?"

"We haven't been able to let her parents know she's here because we don't know her name. If I take you in to see Brian, would you look at her, see if you can tell me anything about her?"

"Are you gonna tell the cops?"

"No. I just want to find out who this girl is. I'm only trying to help her."

"You'll let me see Brian?"

"For a few minutes, yes."

Linda considered it, drumming her ring-studded fingers on the arm of the couch. "Okay."

Cassie waved off the nurses' protests as she brought Linda into the ICU to see Jane Doe. They stood together at the foot of the bed, Linda's eyes fixed on the pale form of the girl. Cassie watched for any hint of recognition from her.

Finally the older girl nodded. "Yeah, I've seen her. She was hanging around T-man, trying for a piece of the action. But I don't know her name."

"T-man? Who's he? Where can I find him?"

Linda cut her a hard look. "He's the creep who sold the Double Cross to Brian. Hangs out near the bridge, got some sort of crib there. I don't know exactly where. I wouldn't mess with him if I were you."

"I won't." Cassie walked her over to Brian's bed.

"Remember, you promised you wouldn't tell the cops. If T-man found out I was even talking to you, he'd kill me for sure."

Cassie looked down at the girl. She had grown pale, obviously frightened both by T-man and her friend's condition.

"I won't tell the police," she assured Linda, and she left her with Brian.

"Be careful down there," Linda called as Cassie walked away.

Cassie waved goodbye and kept going. She made it to the stairwell, her favorite thinking place, and perched on the concrete steps.

She had no proof that this T-man was connected to Three Rivers. He could be some low level dealer who knew nothing. Or he could be the key to everything: Jane Doe's identity, stopping the FX epidemic, getting the deadly Double Cross off the streets. And Fran's murder.

Logic told her to call Drake, let him handle it, even if it meant breaking her promise to Linda. But Jane Doe was her patient, her responsibility.

Cassie got to her feet and brushed off her jeans, trying to convince herself that her reluctance to call Drake had nothing to do with the churning emotions he stirred inside her last night.

⚬

DRAKE SLOUCHED IN his customary place behind Summers, avoiding eye contact with Kwon or any of the others. They were in Miller's conference room this morning, all bleached oak polished to a high gloss. One good thing about a front-page killing, it had gotten them nicer digs.

A stack of coasters beside the coffee pot reminded them to mind their manners. Kwon had plastered the cork board with stills from the crime scene, the pharmacy, blow ups of Weaver's, King's, and Hart's DMV photos, a floor plan of the Annex, and a time line of the events leading up to Weaver's death.

"Security guard didn't see shit, and can't confirm Hart's description of the shooter, vague as it is," Kwon was saying.

Everyone nodded except Drake, who wanted to groan and crawl under the table. While the rest of his team wanted to pin a murder on Hart, all he wanted to know was why she ran away this morning. Like he was a goddamn plague carrier.

Maybe that just proved how smart she was, the devil's advocate in his brain whispered. Good survival instincts.

But not good enough to keep Kwon and Dimeo off her case. Drake could see they were focused on Hart's involvement, as if she were responsible for her best friend's murder. Dimeo he could understand, lawyers would twist facts to suit their purpose without a qualm, but Kwon knew better than to allow her imagination lead the case.

"Where was King last night?" Dimeo asked.

"At home. Says he was watching TV," Summers answered. "No witnesses. And his brother, the lawyer, made him shut up after he gave us that spectacular tidbit of information."

"King doesn't match the description Hart gave us," Drake said. "He's too tall. Surely his ex would know him by the way he moved—" he broke off when he saw Dimeo's smile. Idiot. He'd just made her point for her.

"King could easily be the shooter while Hart set herself up with an alibi from the security guard," Kwon said. "Then Hart made certain Weaver died before talking. Just like Jane Doe and the Winston kid."

Drake's fist bounced against his thigh. "Why?" he interjected, drawing everyone's attention to him. "Why would Hart do that?" he pushed on, braving Kwon and Dimeo's frowns of disapproval. "Weaver already talked, gave us her info."

He gestured to the list of the ten possible suspects Kwon had listed on the dry erase board. Suspects gleaned from Weaver's data and Dimeo's court order of the work records. Suspects besides Hart and King. "We got anything on these others?"

"No convictions other than moving violations and two with sealed juvenile records. Trautman and Conroy," Dimeo said, placing red checks by the two men's names. "I'm working on getting them unsealed, but it's highly unlikely without more—"

"Probable cause," the two narcotic detectives chorused. It was a refrain they were all sick of hearing.

"Drake and I have the parents this morning, then he can take Trautman and I'll take Conroy," Kwon said. "You guys divide up the rest and start working them."

Great, Drake thought as he scraped his chair back. All morning with two grieving parents and Kwon. Could this day get any worse?

CHAPTER 29

"WHERE WERE YOU last night?" Adeena Coleman asked as Cassie entered the social worker's office. "Your car was here, but I couldn't find you anywhere. I was worried sick."

Cassie sank into the metal chair beside Adeena's desk and rubbed her eyes. The pressure was back, building like a river in flood stage. "One of the detectives took me to Fran's autopsy."

She kept her eyes shut, but that didn't block the sound of Adeena's disapproving whoosh of breath. "You went to Fran's—did you watch?"

Cassie nodded. Adeena laid a hand over her arm, squeezed it.

"I'm sorry, I should have been there with you."

Cassie's eyes popped open at the memory of what happened afterward at Drake's. "Trust me, it was better this way."

"But you shouldn't have to go through that alone."

Typical Adeena, the professional mother hen. "I wasn't alone," Cassie admitted. "After, I kind of lost it, and," she felt her cheeks burn with embarrassment, "the detective and I, we went home to his place."

"You slept with him?" Adeena reached behind her and shut the door to her cubbyhole of an office. "Good God Almighty. What were you thinking?"

"I wasn't." Cassie's voice shuddered to a stop. "All I could see, think of was Fran. I couldn't get the sight of her face out of my mind. And then he was there, and suddenly I could breathe again. How could I do that—act like that—when Fran was dead?"

"And you're still alive," Adeena said. "Isn't that the point? Isn't that what sex is really all about?"

"But I was enjoying myself—Fran's body wasn't even cold yet!"

Adeena caught Cassie's eye and grinned. "Enjoying yourself, huh? That good, was he?"

"How can you think about that at a time like this?"

"Because I'm only human, and so are you." Her braids bounced as she nudged Cassie, eager for all the details. "So tell me, how was it?"

"It was better than anything I ever imagined," she blurted out. "God, what's wrong with me? This can't be normal, and don't give me some cliché about how everyone grieves in their own way."

"What's abnormal is a fine young thing like you throwing away your life on scum like Richard King," Adeena retorted. "And then waiting eighteen months before you let another man touch you. Which Detective was it? That cute Summers guy?"

"No. Drake. Mickey Drake."

To Cassie's surprise, Adeena pulled away, her back rigid, eyes narrowed. "Drake? You slept with Drake? What the hell were you thinking? That man—"

"What? What's wrong with Drake?" She thought about her misgivings this morning. Had she made a terrible mistake?

"Remember those kids that got shot by that drug

dealer last summer?"

"Yeah. The dealer was aiming at a cop."

Adeena nodded, her braids jangling. "That cop was Drake. While I was working with the families he came in to interview one of the mothers and he reeked of beer. Wasn't very happy when she couldn't give him a description of the shooter. Didn't seem to care that her son was in the OR getting his spleen removed."

"He was upset," Cassie protested. She sucked in a breath. She used to make excuses for Richard as well. A cold sweat broke out, raising goose bumps on her skin.

"Yeah, but now two nights ago that same drug dealer died. One of the medics told me he was in police custody. Said they'd busted in the door and there was a gunshot near the body. Guess who the arresting officer was?"

"Drake," Cassie said through clenched teeth. She remembered him and Andy Greally talking about Lester Young's death. Making jokes. "Wouldn't they have taken him off the case if there was anything suspicious?"

Adeena gave her an elaborate shrug. "It's the police, who knows? But take my advice, you steer clear of that man. He took advantage of you last night and you don't need any more trouble in your life."

Cassie blew her breath out, reluctant to admit that Adeena might be right about Drake. It had been a long time since she'd felt as safe and secure as she had last night in his arms—not to mention the fabulous sex. She'd been hoping that after Fran's case was solved she could return to that feeling, but maybe Adeena was right, she should think twice about getting involved with Drake.

She changed the subject. "How's the search for Jane Doe's family coming?"

Adeena gave her a long, hard stare before answering and Cassie was thankful when she didn't bring up Drake again. "I've sent her information to all the major databases.

Her face is up on every website, but no one's come forward with anything helpful."

"I can't believe anyone would let a child lie in a coma, alone, without even a name. And—"

"And," Adeena finished for her, "you thought Jane Doe might give you a clue to Fran's killer. Don't you think you should leave it to the police?" Cassie nodded, avoiding Adeena's eyes. "But you're not, are you?"

"Someone here at Three Rivers knew Fran and I had stumbled onto the FX thefts. Jane Doe had drugs that were stolen from here, so she must have had some contact with the thief."

"Do you think Jane Doe is in danger?"

"No, not while she's in the ICU."

"Then what?"

Cassie shrugged, tried to act nonchalant. Adeena pursed her lips, watching Cassie's face closely. "My other consult in the ICU, Brian Winston, he isn't doing so good, is he?"

"No. They're talking about a perfusion scan. If there's no blood flow to his brain and his EEG stays flat. They may suggest that the parents withdraw life support."

"Didn't he get the drugs at a rave near the West End Bridge? That's where you found Jane Doe, right?" Cassie said nothing. "There are several abandoned buildings nearby that homeless kids crash in. You know, the cops won't get anywhere with those kids, but the right person might be able to parlay an introduction for you."

"Who?" she asked.

Adeena smiled. "Me," she said with satisfaction. "I go there with the outreach van a few times a month."

Cassie looked away, the corners of her mouth turning down in reluctance.

"Don't worry about me," Adeena said. "I can take care of myself."

"That's what Fran said."

CHAPTER 30

GARY KRAKOV AND Neil Sinderson sat head to head, huddled over inventory sheets when Cassie and Adeena entered the ransacked pharmacy. The two pharmacists were warped mirror images of each other, Cassie noticed. Same height and build, Krakov with horn rimmed glasses, Neil with wire rims; Krakov had thick, brown hair that Cassie swore was a toupee, Neil a full head of natural blond, sun-bleached hair.

"Thank goodness they didn't get any of our more expensive stock," Krakov said. "As it is, I have no idea how my budget is going to recover."

Typical Krakov. The cost in human life paled in comparison to the prospect that his precious budget would not balance. She narrowed her eyes at him, seeing the pharmacist in a new light. Could he have been involved in Fran's murder? Even if he wasn't, he should have seen how important Fran's research was, allowed her to do it during regular hours instead of forcing her to stay late, working down here alone.

Neil looked up from his Palm Pilot. "Hi," he said, his gaze fixing on Cassie with embarrassing attention.

"Neil," Krakov interrupted, "did you get that? Four dozen more of Percocet."

"I got it. Hold on a moment." Neil left the pharmacy director to join her and Adeena. "Are you all right?" he asked Cassie, taking one of her hands in both of his. "I heard you were there."

The pharmacist's solicitude made Cassie squirm. She looked to Adeena for help, but the social worker had moved over to Fran's workstation.

"I'm fine," she said.

"What a shock. I know you did your best for Fran . . ." He trailed off. "We'll all miss her," he finished in a low voice.

Cassie sighed. Was this how her life was going to be now? A constant reliving of the one moment she wanted to erase forever from her mind. She took a shuffling half step toward the door.

"You actually saw him, the killer?" Behind the thick lenses of his glasses, his eyes grew wide.

"No, I didn't get a good look. I couldn't even tell the police if it was a man or a woman." She edged further away, but he still held her hand fast in his.

"Well at least you're safe," Neil continued, squeezing her hand.

She eased her hand free. "About Saturday—"

"Of course, I understand. We'll reschedule."

She was spared the need to reply by the arrival of the Weavers. Fran's parents appeared frail beyond their years, dwarfed by the weight of tragedy. Mr. Weaver was tall and slender, wearing a dark suit rumpled with wrinkles. He bent over his wife, guiding her into the room, his eyes scouring it, in search of anything that might cause her further distress. Fran's mother wore a navy blue polyester dress, her blonde hair pinned back in a tight bun that only accentuated the lines of grief already etched into her face.

Cassie began to approach them, and then froze. Drake, accompanied by a slim Oriental woman who was obviously another detective, entered behind the Weavers. He wore a gray tweed sports coat over a pale blue shirt and jeans along with his trademark red high tops.

Damn, she should have realized he was going to be here. What would she say to him? She should never have run away this morning, she should've found the courage to stay and talk things over face to face.

But when face to face with Drake, talking was the last thing on Cassie's mind.

Drake stared at her as if she were a total stranger, his expression blank with indifference. Cassie felt her face color. Fool. Just because he had a pretty line of pillow talk didn't mean last night meant anything to him. Maybe Adeena was right about him.

Neil approached with the Weavers. "This is Dr. Cassandra Hart," he told the bereaved parents. "She was a good friend of Fran's."

Mr. Weaver grabbed Cassie's hand and pumped it, while his wife dabbed a tear-stained tissue to her eyes. "Thank you. We heard you risked your life to help Fran."

"Detective Drake told us how you tried to save her," Mrs. Weaver said, the words smothered by tears. "I can't tell you how much that means to us."

"We just don't understand," Mr. Weaver said. "Fran would never hurt anyone. Why would anyone—" He couldn't finish, his face twisting in grief.

"I'm sorry I couldn't do more," she said. Damn Drake, he had no right to make her out to be any kind of a hero in this. These people deserved to know the truth. "I'm afraid I'm the one who asked Fran—you see, someone was stealing drugs," she faltered. How could she explain to them that she'd gotten their daughter killed?

"Yes, the police told us how Fran was helping them,"

Mrs. Weaver said. "She was such a good girl, so conscientious."

The Weavers seemed oblivious to Cassie's attempt to claim responsibility. She opened her mouth to try again, but Gary Krakov joined them, awkwardly inserting himself into their circle.

"Do the police have any idea who's behind this?" he asked instead of offering condolences. Cassie wanted to shake the self-centered prick, but restrained herself.

Mr. Weaver hung his head and shook it. "No. They said Fran had some information, but never had a chance to tell anyone."

"We're certain Detective Kwon and Detective Drake will find out," his wife added, looking over to where Drake and his partner were helping Adeena clear Fran's personal items into a carton. "It's just so hard to believe she's actually gone," she finished, tears overwhelming her once more.

Fran's father wrapped his arms around his wife, guiding her to a seat Krakov hastily cleared for them. Cassie wondered if he even noticed that it was Fran's chair he offered to her mother. Mr. Weaver knelt beside his wife, his fingers intertwined with hers, ignoring the tears sliding down his own face.

Cassie's breath escaped her, left her feeling hollow inside. She closed her eyes against the sight of the grieving parents but that only invited Fran's image. Her throat burned, it was hard to swallow.

A man's hand touched her elbow. She opened her eyes again, grateful for Drake's support. But it wasn't Drake. It was Neil Sinderson. The pharmacist patted her hand again. His skin felt dry, cool.

"Are you all right?" he asked in a solicitous tone. "Do you need something?"

Yes. But it wasn't anything Neil could provide. Her

gaze speared across the room, caught Drake as he bent over, rescuing Fran's Mario Lemieux bobble-head from where it had fallen behind the desk. The sight of the small, cartoonish hockey figure stabbed through her. Whenever Fran was trying to talk Cassie into something, she'd ask Mario's opinion, then flick his head to nod in agreement. No one argued with Mario.

Drake balanced the statue in the palm of his hand, his gaze cutting over to Cassie. She sniffed. Was it only yesterday the three of them had been gathered around Fran's desk? She met Drake's eyes and for a fleeting instance thought she saw them tighten in concern. But it was over too quick for her to be certain she hadn't imagined it, and replaced by a blank look that slid past her to the Weavers, then back to Adeena. He turned and placed the bobble-head in the box.

Something Krakov said renewed Mrs. Weaver's crying. Her sobbing grew in intensity, the high-pitched keening drilling into Cassie's bones.

She slipped away from Neil's grasp and broke for the door, the weight of her grief making her stumble.

· ✦ ·

DRAKE HADN'T COUNTED on Hart being at the pharmacy. He wanted to find a way to talk to her in private, but between Kwon's eagle eye and Adeena Coleman's icy stare, it wasn't happening. Kwon he could understand, she had heard about his taking Hart to the post mortem last night, but every time he looked up Coleman was glaring at him like he was the one responsible for Weaver's death.

He ducked under the desk, escaping both women's scrutiny, and retrieved Weaver's Mario Lemieux mascot. When he straightened back up, he caught Hart's gaze. She stood rigid, hands balled into tight fists, her lips pressed so tightly that all color had been blanched from them. One look at him, and she turned and fled.

Nice to know he hadn't lost his touch with the women, he thought as he tucked the box lids under each other.

He grabbed the box and took a step to follow Hart, but Kwon intercepted him. "I'll take it," she said, lifting the box from his arms and walking it over to Weaver's grieving parents.

It left him empty-handed and with no good excuse to leave and track down Hart. Adeena Coleman tapped his arm, and motioned him into the pharmacy director's empty office. "Could I have a word, Detective?"

He shrugged and followed her. He'd never gotten along with the social worker. She was often overly protective of the victims she tried to help, hampering his efforts to interview them. Once she'd even complained that he was insensitive, and had harassed a witness. Jeezit. Like a victim was going to feel better knowing the perp was still running loose instead of talking to Drake?

Coleman closed the door behind them, crossing her arms over her ample chest. "Do you get some kind of kick out of using your authority to seduce vulnerable women?"

Drake straightened at that. "What the hell are you talking about?"

"I know what happened last night," she continued in a low voice. "How could you? You knew how vulnerable Cassie was. She'd just watched her best friend die, for Godsake. You took advantage—"

"I don't know what Hart told you," he began, "but she knew exactly what she was doing."

Coleman glared at him. "Right. I'm certain you did everything according to regulations."

Not even close. "Is she—is Dr. Hart—making a complaint?"

"Maybe. Maybe you'd better be certain not to do anything more to hurt her. Or anything stupid, Detective."

Drake balled his fists and turned away, stalking back into the pharmacy without another word.

CHAPTER 31

CASSIE RACED THROUGH the Annex tunnel, up the stairs back to the ER, and back to where she could take a moment to regain control. She fled inside an empty trauma room, left the lights off, and leaned against the welcome warmth of the steel cabinet that heated blankets.

Choking on her tears, she lay her cheek against the warm metal, its rhythmic thrumming a heartbeat echoing through her. Pull it together. She couldn't do this, not now, not here. Her fingers clawed at the unyielding metal, desperate to regain her control.

Footsteps sounded, and the door opened. The room lights snapped on. She jerked up, fearing it was one of her colleagues, and saw Drake standing before her.

He was the last person she needed right now. "Go away."

He didn't move.

"This isn't a game," he said, his face unreadable except for the slight narrowing of his eyes. "You're an adult. Why blame me when you can't make up your mind about what you want?"

"That's not true," she protested. "I know exactly what

I want. I'm just mature enough to get my priorities straight. Solving Fran's murder takes precedence over anything I want. I'm not going to do anything to jeopardize the investigation, Detective."

"Really?" He arched an eyebrow at her, his face more stony than ever. "You think getting me kicked off the case is in the best interest of the investigation?"

He unclenched his hands and ran them through his hair. "Look," he lowered his voice, "I'm good at what I do, Hart. Damned good. Getting me suspended won't help find your friend's killer."

She frowned. "What are you talking about?"

"Your complaint about last night. Adeena Coleman, she told me—"

"That I was going to file a complaint?"

"Practically implied that I raped you." He dropped his gaze to the floor before looking back up at her, his eyes now filled with concern. "That's not really how you feel about what happened, is it? That's not why you ran away this morning?"

No, of course not. How could he think—how could he think anything when she hadn't stopped to discuss it with him? "I was worried how it might affect Fran's case. And," she sighed, "I was ashamed about jumping into bed with you when Fran—ashamed about feeling so good, about wanting more."

She leaned back, angled her head to meet his eyes. He blinked and his face relaxed, lost its stony resolve. One corner of his mouth rose in a hesitant smile. She felt her own lips respond in kind. Adeena was wrong about Drake. She had to be.

He crossed the distance between them, placed his hands on her shoulders and leaned forward until their foreheads touched.

"I wanted more, too." He lowered his mouth to hers.

The kiss was long and deep. Cassie kept her eyes open, watched his darken with emotion, changing from indigo to a deep violet. She slipped her hands inside his jacket, her fingers sliding over the smooth broadcloth of his shirt. His grip on her tightened when she found the sensitive area at the small of his back. She felt his hips rock against hers, and his hands moved down to her waist. Heat flushed her entire body and it had little to do with the blanket warmer she leaned against.

"DJ, we've got to—" A woman's voice cut through their passion.

Drake straightened, snatching his hands away. Behind him, Cassie saw the oriental woman who had accompanied him earlier standing in the doorway. She spotted several white-coated figures just beyond. The woman's hands were on her hips, her face pinched in irritation. Drake stepped back from Cassie.

"We're late." She shot a disapproving glare at Cassie, turned on her heel, and closed the door behind her.

"I've got to go," Drake murmured, stroking Cassie's cheekbone with his finger. His touch left a tingle in its wake that made Cassie shiver.

"But I'll be back," he promised.

The door closed behind him. Her hand rose to touch her face, shadowing his caress. Then she yanked it down, and shoved it into the pocket of her jeans. She and Drake didn't exist, couldn't exist, she told herself firmly. Not until Fran's killer was caught. The fact that last night had meant as much to him as it did to her didn't change that.

Nothing could.

She turned the lights back off as she left the room. Unable to face the Weavers again, she turned toward the nurses' station and the hall leading out to the employee entrance. Then she froze.

Lounging against the wall, a smirk creasing his face, was Richard.

CHAPTER 32

WHAT HAD HE SEEN? Or heard? Enough—more than enough from the look on his face. Richard waited for her to come to him, his gaze never leaving her face.

"That's a nice way to mourn your friend," he said. "Want to try it with me next?" He reached out to snag her waist, but she easily sidestepped and batted his hand away.

"Out of my way, Richard."

He looked down at his hand—his left one. A familiar gold band encircled his ring finger. "Ella. Please. I know you're in pain. Won't you let me help?"

He sounded genuinely concerned—but the only person Richard cared about helping was himself. It had taken her years to figure that out. She might be a slow learner, but she wasn't about to make the same mistake twice. "You can help by leaving me alone."

She stepped forward but he blocked her path, his eyebrows lowered into a glower.

"Richard, what do you want?"

"Already told you. I want my wife back."

"Not gonna happen."

There was a breath of silence, like the moment between lightning and thunder. His face changed from concerned and caring to murderous.

"You'd rather screw the guy who mops the floor than me?" His eyes glittered with an unnatural light, and the twitching had returned. "I don't think so. You're playing games with me, Ella. And I'm tired of it."

He yanked her toward him. Cassie resisted, enough to pull him off balance, then she twisted free of his grasp. She backed away from him. "Stay away from me, Richard. Next time you touch me, I'm calling the police."

His laughter chased her down the hall.

•◉•

"WHAT THE HELL was that all about?" Kwon slid into the driver's seat of the Intrepid and turned the ignition on. "Tell me you aren't screwing the main suspect in my case, DJ."

"Our case," Drake reminded her. "And she's a witness, not a suspect."

"Everyone's a suspect, and you know it. Hart's off limits."

"It was just a kiss."

"A kiss? You two were dry humping like a pair of horny teenagers."

"Look, it was nothing. Forget it."

Kwon backed out of the parking space. "Didn't you learn anything last summer?"

Drake sat in silence.

"I know that if Jimmy Dolan was here, he'd slap you on the back, turn this into some kind of testosterone-ridden male bonding moment. But I'm not Dolan and I'm not going to cover your ass while you do something stupid and fuck up my case. Is that clear?" She pulled into traffic, cutting off a Fed-Ex van.

"Crystal clear."

Later, Drake left Kwon and Dimeo clucking over an out of state arrest record on another subject from their short list. He snagged one of the few Intrepids that had a working heater and drove back to Three Rivers.

His subject, Victor Trautman was working the seven to three shift on the Orthopedics ward. Drake located Trautman's truck in the parking lot. A two-year-old Ford Ranger, hardly the vehicle of choice among urban drug dealers, but smart if Trautman wanted to keep a low profile. It was the only vehicle registered to him, but Drake made a mental note to check with the DMV to see if any sisters or mothers were suddenly new registered owners of BMWs or Mercs.

Drake walked in through the ER. Trautman still had a hour or so left on his shift, might as well change into scrubs and push a broom behind him, and see what his routine at work was. Drake was good at blending into the background so that people treated him like part of the scenery and forgot he was there.

But he *was* there. Watching and waiting with a mind that absorbed all the details. He could remember verbatim conversations that took place years ago. A useful talent for a cop. Not so helpful for forgetting the things he would rather forget.

Like the sounds of Hart's sobs when he walked in on her earlier. Tiny, swallowed sounds that barely made it past her lips, but spoke of greater pain kept reined tight inside. Pain so immense he feared it would strangle her if she didn't find a way to release it.

"Hey, Drake!" He spun around. Ed Castro, the head of the Emergency Department, steamed out of his office. "Get in here," Castro gestured behind him, "we have to talk."

Drake obeyed before Castro could make a scene. Did

no one here understand "undercover?" Castro slammed the door behind him, marched over to his desk, but instead of retreating behind it, turned and squared off. Drake saw his weight was balanced evenly on the balls of his feet, noted the shift of the smaller man's shoulders, and knew the Cuban had done some boxing in his past.

"What the hell were you thinking, taking Cassie to Fran's autopsy?" Castro's voice wasn't raised, but the force behind the words made them feel like a shout. Drake hid his smile; this guy was good. Jimmy Dolan was the only other person he knew who could do that with his voice.

"I was thinking it was better she went with me than driving herself and going alone," he replied. Castro stared at him as if debating Drake's veracity, but his posture relaxed.

"She would do that." Castro collapsed back against his desk. "What am I going to do with her?"

Drake was still trying to figure that one out himself.

"I caught her filling out Fran's death certificate, told her to take a few days off, and she jumped all over me." Castro blew his breath out. "She did all right, then? At the post mortem."

Drake leaned against one of the chairs piled high with journals. "Better than most." Castro nodded as if he expected no less. "She's worked here two years?"

Castro seemed to have a deeper relationship with Hart than employee-boss. Drake's eyes went to the framed pictures that filled the wall behind Castro's desk. No vanity photos or glitzy diplomas. Castro had framed finger-painted portraits, photos of earnest high school and college graduates and an assortment of family gatherings. Including several with a young Cassandra Hart.

Castro followed Drake's gaze, took a five by seven photo from his desktop, and handed it to Drake. "Cassie and my daughter, Maria." Two girls waved from a vintage

Cadillac convertible. Hart was driving, Maria was in the passenger seat. "They're only three months apart. Cassie's my goddaughter."

Drake looked again at the family photos. No sign of parental figures except for Castro, a short, buxom woman he assumed was Mrs. Castro, and a fierce looking older woman.

"That's Rosa, Cassie's grandmother." Castro shuddered. "Crazy old witch." He caught Drake's expression of skepticism and chuckled. "I mean that literally. Rosa was a gypsy, from the old country. She moved here, and raised Cassie after Patrick died."

"Cassie's father?"

Castro nodded. "Patrick and I were roommates in college and best men at each other's weddings. I was there when Cassie was born. It was a C-section, I scrubbed in with the pediatrician." He raised his hands, looked at them briefly, and then tightened them into fists. "These were the first hands to touch her. Her mom died three days later." He sucked in his breath. "And I walked her down the aisle on her wedding day, gave her hand away. Biggest mistake of my life, letting her do that. She had no one then, Rosa died a few weeks before. Just me and Tessa Coleman."

Drake looked up at the name. "Any relationship to Adeena Coleman?"

"Her great aunt." Castro raised an eyebrow. "You've met Adeena, then?"

"Yeah, we know each other. She read me the riot act too." He didn't tell Castro why. "Seems like Hart has a lot of people looking after her."

"Don't you forget it. Is Richard King involved in this, in Fran's death? Because so help me, if that bastard ever does anything to hurt Cassie again . . ." He trailed off, having the good sense not to vow violence in front of a cop. Drake didn't have the heart to tell him King had already laid a hand on Hart, or that she hadn't done a damned thing about it.

"I don't know," he answered Castro's question. "If he is, how do you think Hart will feel about it?" What Drake really wanted to ask was: how would she feel about the man who sent her ex to jail?

Castro thought for a moment. "Betrayed. Cassie takes her oath as a physician very seriously, probably why she's such a good doctor, always going above and beyond. For a man she once loved to be involved in drugs that are killing kids—"

"Would she protect King?"

"God, no. She'd be the first to want to see justice done. And to protect patients from King if he is using again." Castro looked up at Drake. "So you do think he's involved."

"What makes you think he might be?"

"Nothing more concrete than wistful thinking, I guess." Castro sighed. "She doesn't talk to me much now, not after what happened with King. I think maybe there was some abuse there, physical or otherwise. She sure as heck didn't tell me," he said with a hint of bitterness. "Before she died, Rosa gave me a heads up about King, said he had gold around his neck and the devil in his heart."

"What the hell is that supposed to mean?"

"That's what I said. I was so happy Cassie had found someone that I ignored Rosa—big mistake. Anyway, after, I had my suspicions, but Cassie never said a word to me. I just had to suck it up, and watch her ride that roller coaster—try to help her where I could."

Drake heard regret in the older man's voice. Castro wanted to protect Hart, to be a surrogate father to her, but she wouldn't allow him into her life. Stubborn woman—and proud.

They both fell silent for a moment. "Well, whatever happened with King," Drake said, certain Castro's suspicions of abuse were correct, "she got herself out of it. She can take care of herself."

"That's what she keeps telling me. But she could have been killed last night. She's no superwoman, can't outrun a speeding bullet."

"She's not stupid enough to put herself in danger again," Drake said, but he had the same thought as Castro.

Castro rolled his eyes. "Intelligence has nothing to do with it. Some of it has to do with being raised by a crazy old woman spouting gypsy curses and nonsense. Mostly, I think she's always trying to repay her parents. She feels responsible that she's alive and they're both dead. The rest—well, you've seen her. Cassie's not one to let go.

"Believe me, I've raised six kids. And let me tell you, Cassie Hart has caused me more pain, sleepless nights, and heartache than the rest of them put together."

Drake had the sudden feeling Castro knew all about him and Hart. Maybe raising six kids invested a father with a special ESP, because Castro wasn't looking at him like a cop who was disrupting his ER's routines. Castro's stare felt heavy, as if he expected Drake to volunteer for dangerous duty.

He cleared his throat, and tried not to squirm under the intensity of the older man's gaze.

"Get the bastard before he hurts anyone else, all right?" Castro finally broke the silence. "And watch out for Cassie, keep her safe."

"Yes sir," Drake said, nodding slowly as if he had just taken a solemn vow. Castro relaxed, moved behind his desk, dismissing him. Drake left the office feeling like a schoolboy released from detention.

CHAPTER 33

ARMED WITH POLAROIDS of Jane Doe, some cash, her Maglite, and most importantly, several bags of burgers and fries, Cassie pulled off Route 51 and into the abandoned industrial complex at the foot of the West End Bridge. Up ahead, orange PennDOT barrels marked where the road and bridge were closed for repairs. The construction crews were gone for the day, their demolition equipment casting shadows like those of prehistoric beasts across the jagged field of broken asphalt.

No sign of Adeena's car. Cassie couldn't believe Adeena came here alone on her outreach visits. The place spooked the hell out of her—and she had yet to meet the kids who called it home.

They were only kids. Still, she'd feel better waiting until Adeena arrived. Not that the slightly over-weight and very out of shape social worker would be much of a help if anything happened. Cassie grabbed her cell and called Adeena. "Hey, where are you?"

"Didn't you get my message?" Adeena said. "I texted you. We need to re-schedule, I'm having dinner with Fran's parents. You're invited too."

Cassie stared out the window at the strange shapes of the construction equipment. That was one message she was glad to have missed—there was no way she could handle an entire evening with Fran's parents. Give her a bunch of homeless kids to deal with any day.

"That's okay," she told Adeena. "But I think I'll skip dinner—I haven't gotten much sleep lately."

There was a pause, and she could almost hear the social worker dissecting her words. "So you're not thinking of going over there alone, right?" Adeena asked.

Not thinking of it, already doing it. "No big deal, you do it all the time."

"Promise you'll wait for me. We'll go tomorrow." A voice in the background distracted Adeena. "Fran's parents are here. I have to go. Sure you won't change your mind?"

"Absolutely sure. Bye." She hung up before Adeena could question her further. The smells of hamburgers and French fries filled the car, leaving the air slick with grease. No harm dropping off the food—it would be a gesture of good will, even if the kids didn't trust her or talk to her without Adeena there with her.

The closest building was a squat tin-roofed affair, a faded sign above the door proclaiming its former incarnation as a Westinghouse distribution facility. Cassie rocked open the wide door, allowing the fading sunlight to silhouette her, revealing her lack of threat to those within.

"Anyone hungry?" she called out. The odor of sweat, urine and rotting food swarmed over her. She remained in the doorway, not just as a safety precaution, but also to give her fresh air to breathe. How did these kids stand it?

She hefted the large Burger King bag into the light of the doorway. At least it had stopped raining, she thought, thankful for the wan February sun.

As her eyes grew accustomed to the darkness inside the warehouse, she began to discriminate a few body-sized masses huddled amidst the debris. Several stirred, a few even dared to make eye contact, but no one came close to her. Then one emaciated young man appeared from out of the darkness, his flat, dark eyes appraising her.

What caught her attention was the wicked looking butterfly knife he held, ready to attack at the slightest provocation.

"Who're you?" he asked, the sunlight glancing off pale skin wracked with acne. Both ears were pierced and the spirals of a tattooed serpent traced its way up his arm.

"I'm a doctor from Three Rivers," Cassie told him.

"Here to give us some checkups, doc? Don't think our HMO will cover it, y'know?" He grinned at her, his teeth blackened by decay.

She gestured with the bag of food. He looked over his shoulder and nodded to his comrades. One of them scurried forward, grabbed the food and returned with it to the others.

"I'm taking care of a young girl, maybe fourteen years old," she went on, holding Jane Doe's photo out to the boy. "She's in a coma. We don't know who she is, or how to find her family."

"Why should I care?" he asked reasonably, using his left hand to eat a burger one of the others brought to him. The right hand, the hand with the knife, never wavered.

"We found her down here, under the bridge. I thought you might be able to help. She may have been hanging out with someone named T-man."

The boy looked up at that. "Then she's lucky she's not dead, or worse." He spat a piece of gristle at her feet. "What's in it for us? A reward?"

Cassie wasn't stupid enough to waltz in here with a wallet full of money. She'd brought just enough to bargain with, not enough to tempt violence. She hoped.

"No reward. But," she added when his attention

drifted away in disinterest. "I can give you twenty dollars for helping."

"A hundred," he countered readily. "Now, in cash. How's I know you won't get what yunz lookin' for and forget about us?"

"Forty." Cassie pulled two bills from her jeans pocket. The boy narrowed his eyes. "If someone can help me." She closed her fist on the two twenties when he reached for them.

He shrugged and took the photos from her, handing them off to another boy without looking at them. He and Cassie remained where they were for several minutes until the boy returned and whispered something in his ear.

"Her name's Sarah," he told her as she pocketed the photos. "From either Ohio or Indiana. Been hanging 'round here a few weeks, mainly over at the Barn." He gestured at the next building toward the bridge. "She's a strawberry, will whore for anything—crack, FX, heroin, Contin, whatever's around."

"Is there anyone at the Barn I should talk to?" Cassie held the money out of his reach.

He looked her up and down. "Depends how much a fool you are. That's T-man's territory, he holds his parties out of there."

"Is there a party tonight? Will he be there?" She looked at her watch; it was almost six o'clock.

Her new friend shrugged. "I look like a fucking social calendar or what? Yunz got your money's worth." He held out a palm scarred with the crisscross marks of a street fighter, and she gave him the money.

"Thanks," she told him, backing away from the building.

"Anytime, doc," he yelled after her. "Just bring more cash next time."

Yeah, right. Cassie picked her way through the refuse

littered lot to the large Quonset type building he'd called the Barn. Bone jarring music thundered through the air from fifty yards away. Christmas lights were festooned over the entrance, illuminating a straggling line of colorfully clad people waiting to get inside.

As she drew closer, she saw it wasn't just kids who were attracted by the rave. There were several older couples and a few single men all wearing frayed jeans, metal chains for belts and leather biker jackets. An assortment of giggling girls, their hair sprayed to match the colors of the rainbow, passed a joint back and forth. More kids shuffled through the line, interspersed with sports-jacket clad men with fake tans and sunglasses dangling from their open shirt collars as if it were August in Miami instead of February in Pittsburgh.

She considered calling Drake then imagined the condescending lecture he'd most likely deliver. Not to mention the dirty looks his partner would give her.

The hope of avoiding another humiliating encounter made up her mind. Cassie straightened, rolled her shoulders, and joined the line into the Barn.

·₪·

DRAKE WOULD BE the first to admit that he was no super-cop. But after successfully running a one man tail on Trautman and following him to an address in Homestead that didn't match the one listed in DMV records, he was starting to feel like he had a little of that old black magic coming back. *Timing*, Jimmy would say, *it's all in the timing.*

He circled around the block, and found a good vantage point in the alley behind the brick row house Trautman had parked in front of, just in time to see Trautman appear in an upstairs window. Changing his clothes, Drake guessed. Settling in for the night? Or getting dressed to go out, do some business?

Drake began to trace the property's ownership through the car's computer, one eye on the house, following the lights as they went on in the kitchen and living room, the other on the computer screen.

And none out the rearview mirror. Which was how the old man snuck up on him. The old man with the shotgun, that was.

CHAPTER 34

"HEY THERE."

Drake jerked his head up. A white-haired man stood on the other side of the car who looked disturbingly like his grandfather—same stooped posture, same crows feet, same loose upper dentures that clicked when he talked. He whacked a shotgun barrel against the passenger side window. "Hands where I can see them. Out of the car, now."

Another rap with the gun. "I said out of the car!"

Judas H! Anyone could see this was a cop car, who else would be caught dead in a piece-of-shit Dodge with a radio and computer on the front console? Drake rolled down the passenger window.

"I'm a police officer, sir," he said, hoping the old guy wasn't deaf as well as blind. "Please move away from the car."

The old man shook his head, the barrel of the shotgun moving with it. Drake was definitely within target range no matter how bad the guy's aim might be. The back of his neck began to itch. In a way this was more frightening than staring down Lester's Bulldog. At least he knew Lester wanted to kill him. This idiot might kill him totally by accident.

God, what a stupid way to go. Cop's worst nightmare: becoming fodder for training lessons for years to come. *Don't pull a Drake and get your head blown off by some old fool who thinks you're there to steal his TV and Viagra.*

"Ya deaf?" the geezer yelled.

"Just wake up the neighborhood, why don't you?" Drake risked a sideways glance at Trautman's house. All the lights were off except the one in the living room, the TV's flickering glow visible through the open drapes. Guy was acting like he didn't have anything to hide.

He held his hands up in plain sight, edged across the seat, and then stepped out of the car. "If you reach into my inside coat pocket, you'll find my identification," he told the old man as he walked around the front of the car. The guy was so excited, his hands were shaking.

"Please don't aim that gun at me, sir." This old coot was really starting to try his patience.

"Don't you tell me what to do. Angie Myerson got attacked by two guys who said they're cops just last month. Pushed past her inside her house, shoved her down, and ransacked the place. Who you working with? Where's the other'un?" The man spun around as if expecting an ambush at any second. As he did, he swung the shotgun with him, and Drake saw his chance.

He grabbed the gun, twisting it from the old man's hands. The man fell to the ground, landing in a mud puddle.

"Don't shoot, it's not loaded," the man cried out, holding his hands in front of his face.

Drake didn't try to follow the logic there, instead he broke the shotgun open and verified that it was empty. As he flipped it closed again, he heard the growl of a motorcycle's engine. He looked around just in time to see

Trautman speeding off down the street. *Damn it!*

He bolted toward the car, but the old man was a stubborn coot. He latched onto Drake's leg, and tried to drag him down. Trautman was out of sight before Drake could break free.

"I ought to run you in for obstruction of justice, you old bastard!" he shouted at the mud-covered man still clutching at his jeans.

The man released him, scooted back. "You really a cop?" he asked in a doubtful voice.

"Yes, goddamn it! What the hell you think you're doing, running around with a shotgun and pointing it at people?"

"It wasn't loaded," the man protested. "I was just trying to help."

"Next time dial 911." Drake threw the empty shotgun in the car and opened the driver side door.

"Hey, you can't leave me like this! I think I broke my hip." The old man grabbed his leg and winced. "Yeah, you broke my hip. I outta sue!"

"I'll break something for you," Drake muttered as he helped the man to his feet. Both legs seemed to work fine as the man alternated limping dramatically on first one, then the other. His name was Maurice Coffman—not related to those Kaufmann's, the rich ones, Coffman with a C—and he gave Drake the history and life story of every house and homeowner on the block while they waited for the ambulance Coffman insisted upon. At last he came to Victor Trautman.

"That's his aunt's house. She passed two, almost three, months back. Right afore Christmas. Probably gave herself a heart attack—that was one mean old lady. She'd have shot yunz first, then asked what ya were doing on her property after."

Tough block, Drake thought, glad he hadn't come

while Trautman's aunt was still alive. "Does her nephew bring anyone home with him? Lots of strange cars come by here?"

Coffman shook his head. "Nah, he pretty much keeps to hisself. Goes out a lot on that noisy bike, comes home late. Mostly there to eat and change clothes it seems. Must be pulling double shifts, 'cause he's doing all right money-wise. That bike's brand new and he's got a nice looking sports car in the garage. One of them foreign jobs."

The medics came, assured Coffman and Drake that everything was fine and gave Drake a copy of their report. He couldn't wait to hear what Miller said when she saw that. The old man fetched beer and stale kalatke's for them all, tried to convince them to stay longer, watch the Pitt basketball game with him.

When Drake was finally able to break away, he found Trautman's house and garage were both locked up tight. Nothing that could remotely resemble probable cause was in the sight of his flashlight when he looked through the window. He kept half an eye out behind him, hoping there weren't any more senior citizens on the prowl.

He called a report to Kwon and got back into the Intrepid. Out of leads. Should just call it a night.

His cell rang, a number he didn't recognize. "Drake here."

"It's Adeena Coleman. From Three Rivers?"

"I remember." Why the hell would the social worker be calling him? To accuse him of rape again? "Do you need more information about that complaint you were going to file?"

There was a lengthy silence. "No. I'm worried about Cassie and I didn't have your partner's number."

"Hart? What's wrong?" He sat up, on full alert.

"She had this idea that Fran's death was connected to the Jane Doe she found—you know about her?"

"Yeah, the girl from the Kills Deer Bridge."

"Cassie went out there to talk to some homeless kids—she was supposed to wait for me, but I know she didn't. And now she's not answering her cell. I'm worried."

"I'm on my way."

CHAPTER 35

CASSIE TOOK A moment to orient herself once she crossed the threshold into the Barn. The atmosphere inside the rave club was a tsunami of color and noise. Strobe lights spiraled over the gyrating crowd, reflecting off fluorescent body paint, jewelry, and glowsticks. A gray haired couple in Birkenstocks and tie-dyed shirts danced as if it were the Jerry Garcia Band playing instead of nerve wrecking technofunk.

She shook her head at a vendor selling bottles of water for five dollars each and another with a display of pacifiers, glowsticks, and assorted miniature feather dusters. She saw no one openly selling any drugs.

Since it was fruitless to try to talk above the roar of the music, she navigated through the crowd to a rear room. The door was open, the floor coated in a fog of dry ice, and several people lay on thick futons and old mattresses. None of them appeared to be in distress. Maybe the Double Cross wasn't being sold tonight. She thought of Brian Winston lying in a coma at Three Rivers and hoped word about the deadly drug combo had gotten out.

It was quieter here. She moved over to the first group

of kids and knelt down beside them. Two boys and a girl, none looked old enough to drive. Their clothes showed them to be affluent, at least enough to buy Tommy Hilfiger and Doc Martens.

"Aren't you hot," the girl asked in a dreamy voice, her fingers stroking Cassie's leather jacket. She spoke around a pacifier that she sucked at greedily.

"A little." She held out the photo of Jane Doe. "I'm trying to find this girl."

"That's so sweet," she crooned. "Sarah, horse and buggy Sarah." She frowned, shook her head. "But can't go home when you're a bad girl like me."

To Cassie's surprise the girl began crying, then wrapped her arms around Cassie's neck in an embrace.

She gently disengaged her. The girl was blubbering now, incoherent. The two boys looked on, their smiles wolfish. They weren't as high as the girl. They weren't as young, either. She saw as one of them lifted the girl onto his lap and began to stroke his hand over her belly in a possessive manner.

"Sarah's gone," the other boy said, clearly wishing the same fate on Cassie. He slipped the girl's legs onto his lap, moving her bare feet over his crotch. The girl giggled, her head drooping forward as the two men smiled at each other.

"I know. She's in a coma at Three Rivers." Cassie shifted her weight, calculated the distance to the door. How could she get this girl out of here before something happened? "I'm trying to find out who she is so we can notify her parents."

"You a cop? Social worker?" the first boy snapped, his disdain for either profession clear.

She considered lying, thinking it might intimidate them into releasing the inebriated girl. The second boy raised the girl's foot to his mouth and began sucking on her toes, making her squirm in delight.

"What if I was?" Cassie hedged, uncomfortable with these budding sociopaths. Was their behavior the result of drugs or something more pernicious, like a complete lack of conscience?

The first boy shrugged, his hand opening the girl's blouse, exposing her breasts. "We'd still let you join in on the fun if you wanted." His eyes gleamed with anticipation. "Or," his tongue flicked over his lips, "we could just watch you and Sherry here."

Cassie got to her feet, hauling the girl up with her. The girl was still giggling, her body a dead weight as she struggled to find her balance.

"How about if Sherry and I just go now."

"Then you'd have to discuss the matter with me," a sober voice came from the doorway.

She whirled, dragging Sherry with her. A large, stocky man filled the doorway. He gestured at the two younger men, and they got to their feet and sidled past him, back out into the crowd. Cassie stared at him. She recognized this man. From Three Rivers.

"I know you," he said slowly, ignoring Sherry and focusing his attention on Cassie. "You're Richard King's wife."

Orthopedics, that was where she'd seen him. He was an orderly on Orthopedics, worked with Richard. He sometimes came down to the ER to help with fracture patients. What was his name? Victor Trautman, that was it. T-man.

"You checking up on the Mister?" he asked, his head cocked to one side. "He ain't gonna be too happy about that." He nodded to Sherry. "Why don't you let her sleep it off? I think we need to talk, Dr. Hart."

She looked around the room. Everyone else studiously ignored them. No help there.

"Is Richard here?" she asked, assuming a worried tone. "This is his niece. I came to get her before something happened. If you just help me get her outside, I have my car waiting." She poured every ounce of sincerity into her performance. Trautman wavered for a moment, but then his eyes hardened.

"Don't ever play poker, Dr. Hart," he said. "You can't lie for shit." He pulled a large chrome plated gun from his waistband. "Drop the girl. Let's go for a walk."

Cassie stared at the gun. Despite the room's chilly temperature, sweat began to pool under her sweater. Sherry squirmed in her grasp, severely limiting their defensive options. But Trautman didn't seem interested in the girl, only Cassie.

Confident of his superior position, Trautman stepped forward, and Cassie saw her opening. She pushed Sherry at him and darted through the door back into the maelstrom of music and gyrating bodies.

She pulled out her cell phone. There was no signal under the metal roof. She plunged through the crowd, ignoring the curses that followed in her wake.

No phone meant no cavalry. Looking around at the glazed stares of the partygoers, she couldn't expect much help from the crowd.

She shuddered, searching past the shoulders of gyrating dancers to survey her options. No other exit visible except the front door. Was there a rest room with a convenient window? Bad idea. If she went in and there was no way out, she'd be trapped.

The crowd spun her around, and she saw T-man's head above the others. He was gesturing to men at the door, talking into a small radio.

Cassie ducked, taking advantage of her short stature as T-man began to scan the throng of dancers. She allowed the tide of gyrating bodies to move her closer to the disc jockey's platform. The noise became deafening, but it was the only corner of the building she hadn't explored for a possible exit.

The DJ had his equipment set up on a chest high platform draped in black muslin. The walls behind him were draped as well, and a silver disco ball spun overhead, dazzling in the strobe lights. Cassie saw T-man turn her way and she crouched down, slipping under the drapes beneath the platform.

The pounding, driving beat of the music rattled her fillings as she crawled to the rear of the DJ's station. Dust swirled around her, and she sneezed, but had no fear anyone would hear her. She thought briefly about staying here in her dark but noisy shelter, but knew it would be one of the first places T-man would look when he didn't find her in the crowd.

Cassie tried her phone again. Still no signal. She edged from the back of the platform. The DJ, ears protected by bulky headphones, swayed to the beat as he rapped with the crowd. He didn't notice her behind him. She looked around. Amen—a door!

She crept over to it. The drapes partially hid it, and the shadows would hopefully do the rest. She hugged the black fabric around her, trying to blend in with the darkness as she edged the door open and darted through it.

Cassie took a deep breath of fresh air and oriented herself. She was facing the bridge. Wind whipped across the river and cut through her clothes. She didn't stop to zip her jacket, but turned and ran.

She pulled out her cell phone once more as she rounded the corner of the building. She collided with a young man fumbling with the zipper of his jeans, and the phone went flying.

"Sorry, man," he mumbled without looking at her,

"just looking for a place to take a leak."

Before she could chase after the phone, Trautman stepped from the shadows and aimed the gun at her. "Hold it, doc."

Staring into the maw of the large gun, Cassie did as she was told.

"Not here," Trautman growled at the drunken reveler who blinked and staggered away. "C'mon doc, let's find someplace private to talk."

He wrapped his arm around her waist, the hand with the gun tucked inside her jacket, aimed at her heart. Together they walked through the dark, away from the Barn and toward the bridge.

"Wanna tell me who sent you down here?" he asked.

Cassie's jaw clenched with fear as he propelled her toward the river. She remembered Jane Doe's frozen form when they pulled her from the water. Did the same fate await her? Only she might be weighted down with the lead of several bullets.

"The girl in these photos," she told Trautman as he hauled her over the guide rail and onto the chopped up pavement.

He stopped under the lone functioning streetlight and looked at the photos of Jane Doe. A frown creased his brow. "Where is she?" he demanded, his free hand reaching over to squeeze her face. "That bitch stole my stash."

Cassie searched the deserted bridge and the road that ran past it. Just one car, she prayed. That was all she needed, one person to pass this way.

"When was that?" she asked.

He shook her hard and began dragging her up onto the bridge. "Don't play games with me," his voice raised over the roar of the wind as they climbed the slope. "You know damned well it was Sunday. Damned strawberry said she'd do me for a hit of FX. I threw her down on a slag heap and told her she'd fucking well do her best, then I'd decide what it was worth. We was in the middle of it when the bitch hit me on the head with a brick."

He pulled back a sheaf of dingy yellow hair, revealing an ugly bruise above his right temple. A little harder or lower and it might have been fatal.

Too bad for her it wasn't. She searched in vain for any sign of traffic. Trautman saw what she was doing and laughed.

"Relax, doc. Ain't no one coming up here, not with the construction."

They reached the apex of the bridge, the deep hungry waters of the Ohio swirling below. Trautman bent her over the railing, pushing her head forward to look down on the water.

"Where's Sarah?" he asked. "That bitch and I have some unfinished business."

Cassie grabbed the railing with both hands, straining against his greater weight to no avail. She'd have better luck moving Mount Washington with a butter knife.

"I'll take you to her," she lied, trying to gain time.

He spun her back to face him and brandished the gun once more. "Tell me where she is or you're going for a swim. Tell me now!"

CHAPTER 36

DRAKE PARKED THE Intrepid alongside the old Westinghouse warehouse, beside Hart's Subaru. The engine was cold to touch. He looked over to the rave club, its lights blazing, several groups performing impromptu dances outside the front door. Movement on the bridge behind it caught his eye.

A large figure moved into the light of a street lamp. From here it looked like Trautman. A woman was with him. Christ, it was Hart.

Then he saw the gun.

A CAR TURNED off Route 51, raising Cassie's hopes. Would they come near enough to see her?

"You don't need the gun," she told Trautman. "I'll take you to her."

Trautman's laugh was high-pitched for such a large man. The glare of the street lamp revealed violaceus craters of inflamed acne pockmarking his face. Steroid abuser? That was almost as frightening as the gun he held so casually.

Her gut twisted with fear. She forced herself to focus and watch for any opportunity to escape. He slid the gun into his pocket, and she momentarily relaxed. Then he grabbed her hair, pulling her head back so that she that she had no choice but to look into the empty, dark void of his eyes. An ugly smile stretched his mouth.

"No, you'll tell me, now," he said, slapping her so hard her ears rang. "Where is she?"

As his palm connected with her face a second time, he released her hair. The force of the blow sent her flying into the railing. Trautman laughed again. She pushed herself upright, leaning her weight against the railing, as if she were too stunned to stand on her own. Before his laughter died, Cassie rammed a knee into his groin.

Trautman staggered back, his hands dropping to his crotch. She raced past him, setting her sights on the road. T-man was faster. He grabbed her around the waist and dragged her back to the railing.

Effortlessly, he raised her up high, her legs dangling uselessly. Cassie gulped in a lungful of the frigid night air. She stared down at the water far below.

"Bitch!" Trautman shrieked. He leaned back, ready to heave her over the side.

Cassie shot her hand down, aiming at his eyes with her outstretched fingers. Her index finger popped through tissue into viscous, jelly-like liquid. She gagged at the sensation that shuddered through her but forced herself to not pull her strike.

Trautman screamed in pain and dropped her, his hands clawing at his face.

She bounced off the top railing. The impact jarred through her, snatching her breath. She flailed, tried to gain a handhold, foothold, anything to stop her free fall. Her hands scraped over the twisted steel, searching, grasping.

But she kept falling, slipping, her legs kicking against air.

She clawed against the side of the bridge, refusing to give an inch. A small rim of metal, no more than a few inches wide, stopped her. Cassie locked her fingers around the ledge. She dangled, her entire weight supported by the muscles of ten digits.

Her fingers strained with agony. She forced herself to stop kicking. When she opened her eyes, all she could see was the metal spider web that formed the underbelly of the bridge. She looked down and immediately regretted it as a wave of nausea ripped through her. The river was a black vortex, hungry for her arrival.

Wind whipped mercilessly beneath the bridge, drowning out the chattering of her teeth. She tried tilting her head up but that sent a searing pain through her back and shoulder muscles. Instead, she kept her gaze forward, focusing all her energy on her fingers above her. Trautman's screams died down to a primeval wail. She didn't want to think about what she'd done to him—she'd think about it later, after she got off this bridge.

Which wasn't going to happen unless she moved one of her hands and began to climb. She heaved in several deep breaths, trying to convince her fingers to loosen their precious hold. Her hands burned with the cold, her arms were trembling.

Die trying. The wind carried Gram Rosa's whisper to her ears. Why did the old woman have to always be right? Cassie gulped down one last breath and transferred her weight to her right arm. She stretched her left hand, ignoring the screaming that tore through her right shoulder, and tried to find a more secure handhold. Her fingers hit a solid wall of steel. Her breath came in jagged gasps as she tried to stretch further. Nothing.

Just as her right hand was about to give away, she grabbed the ledge again with both hands. She clenched her fingers tight around the ice-cold steel.

"Hold on!" a man's voice shouted, muffled by the wind.

She didn't waste energy on an answer. She wasn't even certain she hadn't imagined it. Her fingers were numb now. Cramps spasmed her arms and back. Sooner or later her grip would break. Her breath caught as she choked on tears of rage and frustration. What would kill her, the fall or the freezing water?

There was movement at the railing, and she dared to swing her glance up. Drake straddled the railing, extending an arm to her. She hadn't imagined it—he was there.

"Take my hand," he shouted.

She could not move, much less make the Herculean effort necessary to reach an arm up to meet his.

"C'mon, you can do it," he coaxed. "Don't be afraid."

"Not. Afraid." The words stuttered past her chattering teeth. "Frozen."

"Hold on. I'm coming."

Cassie hung there, unable to control the shaking in her arms, powerless to stop her fingers from slipping.

A red high top landed between her hands. She felt Drake's strong hands grasp her wrist. Still she could not let go, her fingers were locked into rigor.

"All right," he said as if discussing directions to Ikea. "This is how we're gonna do this." She raised her gaze and saw his blue eyes staring down from the darkness. His face alternately glowed red then silver as colored lights played off his features. Despite his grip on her, she felt as if she was falling.

And she was. Pain jolted through her arm as her fingers tore away from their precarious grasp on the steel. Suddenly she was dangling in the air, the river below roaring its welcome.

CHAPTER 37

CASSIE DROPPED LOWER for a heart wrenching moment. Drake gave a grunt of pain.

"Okay, we'll do it the hard way." He began to hoist her up. With one final heave, he propelled her to a level where she could roll her leg and hip on top of the steel beam.

"Almost there," Drake whispered, his voice hoarse with straining. Cassie barely heard him; she was too busy appreciating the solid surface supporting her. He never let go, even though she was in a less precarious position, his fingers warm against her frozen skin. It was the only part of her that did feel warm.

He climbed back over the railing. Once his feet were safely on the other side, he lifted Cassie over the railing. They both collapsed onto the metal grating on the other side.

"What took you so long?" Her words emerged in a low rasp, as if not even her vocal cords had escaped the punishment the rest of her muscles had suffered. She swallowed, trying to force down the wave of hysteria that threatened to consume her.

Drake cut her a look, his eyes wide, his brow furrowed, and a snorted a short laugh. He circled an arm around her.

She leaned against his warmth, her entire body quaking, out of control. There was blood on her, but she felt nothing. Yet. There would be hell to pay in the morning. But at least there would be a morning.

A few feet away, in the middle of the road, Trautman writhed in pain, his ragged moaning piercing the night. Blood streaked his face. Cassie's stomach roiled in nausea. She had done that—she had brought a man to his knees in pain, most likely destroyed his vision. She held her hands up, inspected them as if they belonged to a stranger. Trautman's blood mingled with her own.

"Trautman didn't kill Fran," she told Drake, her voice almost back to normal.

He sighed as if reluctant to return to reality. "You sure?"

"He's much taller, bigger than the man I saw."

Rolling off Drake, Cassie knelt on the pavement, trying to control the nausea that wracked through her, wrenching muscles that already seared with pain. Her ears roared with her gasps as she fought to breathe. Below the metal grating, the river churned, echoing her vertigo, mocking her. She'd been so stupid.

"Are you all right?" Drake's voice broke through her haze. "An ambulance is on the way. Are you hurt?"

She ignored him, focusing on squelching the revolution in her stomach. She took a deep breath, cleared her vision and began to rise to her feet. She needed to check on Trautman. Drake's hands helped her up. Her vision darkened for a second, then she was steady once more.

"I'm fine," she lied.

"What the hell were you thinking?" She knew Drake

must be shouting because his voice cut clearly through the ringing in her ears. "You could have been killed! Didn't I tell you to leave the detective work to me?"

Cassie blinked up at him, unable to find the words to answer him. Especially since she knew he was right.

She was saved by the blare of more sirens. A patrol car and ambulance arrived, bouncing past the construction debris at the foot of the bridge, and then screeching to a halt beside them. Drake's mouth opened, clamped shut again. He spun on his heel to intercept the other police officers.

The first paramedic recognized Cassie and approached her, but she waved him off and sent him over to Trautman. "Bilateral eye trauma," she told him, surprised by how normal her voice sounded. "The globe may be ruptured."

It took both of the medics to move the drug dealer's hands away from his eyes in order to assess the damage. "Yeah, looks like one is gone," one of them told her as he grabbed supplies from the squad. "Might be able to save the other." He looked at her, appraisal in his eyes. "He's saying you did it, doc."

Cassie nodded. "Yeah, I did."

He pursed his lips and slid the gurney out from the ambulance. "Guess he had it coming, then. You going with us to Three Rivers? You ought to have those hands looked at."

She stared down at her grime and blood streaked palms. Wincing, she flexed them; no tendon damage, just abrasions.

"No thanks. I'll be fine."

"All right, but at least let me clean 'em up a little. Won't take a second." She shrugged and allowed the paramedic to clean her hands, and then salve them with antibiotic ointment. Two fingernails were torn to the quick, but other than a few scrapes, there was no serious damage. Cassie didn't even need the bandages he applied, but it was warm in the ambulance and she didn't feel up to facing Drake again.

Finally she was forced from her temporary refuge. She watched the ambulance pull away, her hands bundled under her armpits to keep them warm and out of sight, the glaring white bandages marking her as a victim. Her body was covered in streaks of grime from her sojourn on the bridge.

Drake was busy talking with several more detectives. One of them, a tall, willowy blonde wearing a tailored pantsuit turned, Cassie recognized as Commander Miller.

Miller looked angry. Cassie braced herself for another lecture. She saw Drake glance her way and flinched at his glare of disappointment. She'd acted recklessly, stupidly. She could have gotten herself or someone else hurt—like Drake, what if she'd gotten Drake killed? Trautman could have shot him.

She walked along the bridge, heading over to where her car was parked. She flexed her hands encased in their cocoon of gauze.

She started shaking again. Her shoulders hunched, and her throat tightened with anger. The fact that she almost died was frightening enough, but she'd let Trautman make a victim of her. It was a feeling she despised, but a familiar one just the same. Three years with Richard had made her an expert on the self-loathing that came with accepting the role of victim.

Cassie ripped the gauze from her palms. The wind swept the wisps of cotton over the railing and down into the dark abyss of the Ohio. Shoving her hands deep into her jacket pockets, she bowed to the wind and continued over the bridge.

The sound of running footsteps stopped her. "Wait,"

Drake's voice came as he joined her.

She didn't move. He took two steps around her until he faced her. He was silent, looking down at her in the glare of the single streetlight. Then he surprised her by taking her chin in his hand, tilting her face toward the light. He slid a clean handkerchief from his pocket, licked one corner and used it to wipe her face.

Cassie's vision blurred. The act was so intimate, so familiar. Suddenly it was her father standing over her, cleaning her face before they went in to Mass. Those same gentle strokes, that same concentrated look of concerned appraisal. She blinked, and Drake's image returned, but he still wore her father's soft smile. He bunched the now filthy cloth into his pocket.

"There. At least you look halfway human again."

They continued walking beside the guide rail. Cassie finally broke the silence. "Thank you."

"For saving your life? You're quite welcome. It's not often that I get to come to the aid of a beautiful damsel in distress."

He was mocking her now. She should've known better than to try to have a serious conversation with him.

"It's not funny. I almost—" she couldn't finish.

"Died?" He supplied the word with a light tone, but she saw the frown tighten his face. In the glow of the headlights, he looked haunted.

"I needed to do something."

"You needed to trust me to do my job!"

Indigo blue eyes blazed down at her as she searched for a reply. And failed.

Drake shook his head. "You can't trust anyone, can you? After last night I thought—" Before he could finish, Janet Kwon pulled up beside them in a gray sedan.

"DJ," Kwon called through the driver's window. "Miller wants you to stay here and find Trautman's stash."

"Give me a minute, Janet," Drake told her, his eyes never leaving Cassie's face.

"And she wants me to escort your witness," Kwon flavored the last word with sarcasm, "home. Now."

Drake cut his eyes at Kwon, glanced at Cassie once more, then shrugged and spun on his heel. Cassie watched as his long legs easily took him over the guide rail and into the vacant lot beyond. She wanted to run after him, to explain—but her feet refused to move.

"I don't exactly have all night," Kwon said.

Cassie pulled her eyes away from Drake's receding form and crossed around to the passenger side of the car. Kwon pulled away before she finished closing the door.

CHAPTER 38

———— ＊ :=≡◆➤◑◖◗≡¦ ＊ ————

THE POLICE CAR lurched over the uneven pavement as Kwon deftly steered through the construction debris. They narrowly missed an orange barrel before bouncing over the curb onto Route 51.

"My car's parked beside the old Westinghouse warehouse," Cassie told the detective. "I can drive myself home."

Kwon twisted the wheel furiously, spinning the car into a controlled skid as she made the turn into the lot where Cassie's Impreza sat in the shadow of the abandoned warehouse. Several patrol cars had moved from the Barn over to the Westinghouse building, their headlights illuminating the open doors.

"I'm trying to figure out why you're messing with my case," Kwon finally said as she brought the car to an idle. The police radio crackled in the background. "You don't seem stupid to me. Surely you realize that fucking DJ will only destroy any chance of seeing your friend's killer convicted. And, getting him suspended from the job is no way to get Drake into bed. So," the other woman turned, her dark eyes boring into Cassie's, "exactly what are you trying to accomplish here?"

She flushed at the detective's crude description of her relationship with Drake. Kwon had no business speaking to her that way.

Except for the fact that she was right.

"Thanks for the ride." Cassie opened the car door.

"Think about what I said, Hart. And stay out of my case."

The sound of two shots ripped through the night. "Shots fired, shots fired, officer down!" a frantic voice shouted over the police radio. "Westinghouse warehouse, front entrance. All units, officer down!"

Cassie jumped back into her seat. Kwon gunned the sedan, speeding them around to the main entrance of the building. Sirens screamed as the other police units responded to the urgent call for help.

"Stay here," Kwon said. She pulled her gun and joined several uniformed officers crouched behind a patrol car.

Cassie slid over to the driver's seat, rolled down the window and craned her head out. A uniformed figure stumbled from the warehouse, clutching his right arm. It was Tony Spanos, the policeman she'd encountered yesterday morning. He ran past the cordon of police cars and collapsed against the rear of one. His fellow officers quickly surrounded him.

Even if Spanos was a jerk, it looked like he needed medical attention. Cassie left the car and pushed through the crowd.

"What happened in there?" Kwon asked. "Where's Rankin?"

"Son of a bitch stabbed me," Spanos said, his eyes focused on the blood dripping from his arm, oozing between his fingers.

"Does he have a gun? Who fired the shots?"

Several officers were pulling shotguns and riot gear from their units while more cars squealed up behind them, their flashing lights cloaking the scene in a surreal glow.

"Kid's high on something. I dunno, PCP maybe," the wounded officer continued. "Rankin got off two rounds and hit him at least once, but he just kept coming."

Cassie reached Spanos' side, pulled his fingers aside to examine his wound. One of the other officers handed her a first aid kit.

"Where's your piece?" Kwon asked.

Spanos looked down at his empty holster, and his face grew pale. "Must have dropped it."

"Shit." Kwon spat the word. Then she glared at Cassie. "He gonna be all right?"

It was a nice, clean laceration through the outer forearm. No exposed muscle. She moved Spanos' fingers. No tendon damage that she could see.

"Just a few stitches," she told the detective as she wrapped the wound in gauze.

"Fine. Get him back to my car and out of here until the ambulance arrives." She took a Kevlar vest from a patrolman and slid it over her head.

"What did the kid look like?" Cassie asked Spanos as she helped him to his feet. They headed back toward the gray sedan.

"Skinny, pale, bad acne. Pro with the knife." She opened the passenger door for him. He slid into the seat, wincing as he jarred his arm. "Am I going to be okay?"

"You'll be fine," she assured him. "Just keep pressure on it."

"Guess I screwed up royally." He stared down at her, eyes narrowed, lips pursed in disapproval. "Almost as bad as Drake did last summer. Heard you were here with him, doc. You should've listened to me."

She ignored him, watching as Miller moved toward

the knot of police officers. Where was Drake? she wondered, hoping he hadn't done something dangerous like run inside the building. "Stay here, I'll be right back."

"Dr. Hart, what are you doing here?" Miller asked.

"She was helping Spanos," Kwon answered.

"I think I know the boy inside," Cassie said. "I spoke to him earlier today—he's the one who told me about Trautman and Jane Doe."

"Thank you, but that's not very helpful right now." Miller's voice was cold, her eyes never leaving the entrance of the warehouse. "Please, go take care of Officer Spanos. Let us do our jobs."

"I gave him money for the information," Cassie persisted. "I think he used it to buy some Double Cross. If he did, the combination of FX and MDMA could have effects similar to PCP. It might make him difficult to deal with."

"Nothing we can't handle." The uniformed officer beside her punctuated his words by chambering a shell into his shotgun.

The noise of an ambulance siren cut through the night air. It pulled alongside Kwon's car, and paramedics jumped out to attend to Spanos.

Drake slipped behind the patrol car, seemingly appearing from nowhere. He spread a piece of paper open on his knee as he crouched beside Kwon.

"I've got the layout of the place," he told Miller. He glanced over at Cassie, his brow creasing momentarily before he composed himself once more. "Doors here and here. They're secure—we'll have to ram them." He pointed with his pen at the sketch. "Windows low to the ground along this side. I could see the suspect and Rankin about here." He indicated their position, just inside the main entrance. "The suspect had a knife held to Rankin's throat."

Tires squealed close behind them as the news vans

returned. "Great. Here come the vultures," Kwon said. "Everyone smile for the cameras."

"I'll deal with them." Miller nodded to several officers to accompany her. "Get them back and get a perimeter established," she instructed the patrolmen. Then she turned to Kwon and Drake. "Once we have all the civilians at a safe distance, you can proceed," she told Kwon. "Detective Drake, will you please ensure that Dr. Hart leaves the scene and returns to her home?" Miller barely spared Drake or Cassie a glance as she moved to intercept the media.

A frown crossed Drake's face as he surrendered his sketch of the building layout to Kwon. He took Cassie's arm and began to escort her away from the scene.

"Go away!" The shout came from the entrance to the warehouse. "This is my place. I want you all to just go away!"

Cassie turned and saw the leader of the homeless kids push Officer Rankin through the doorway. Rankin's hands were handcuffed behind his back, and he stumbled to his knees. The boy held his knife at Rankin's throat. A dozen police officers focused their attention on the teenager, most of them through the sights of their guns.

The boy's gaze jumped around, his eyes squinting in the headlights. Then his eyes fell on Cassie. His face broke into a broad grin. "Hey, it's Dr. Feelgood," he shouted a greeting to her. "Thanks for giving me my fix, doc! This stuff rocks!"

Cassie felt the weight of the police's attention fall on her. She took a step forward, hoping to distract the boy from his hostage, but his blade never wavered.

"You all get out of here," the boy shouted again. "All except her, she can stay. I saw you and T-man all cozy. Think you can score me some more?" Then he frowned. "Why'd you let T-man call Five-O out on us? They took everyone—they're all gone 'cept me." The last was delivered in a plaintive wail. Rankin jerked as the boy twisted his free hand in the officer's short cropped hair and yanked his head back. "You took everyone away, Five-O!" he screamed at the captive man. "Don't think I'm gonna forget that!"

"It wasn't his fault," Cassie called out. "It was T-man's."

"Be quiet," Drake told her, pulling her back. "You could get Rankin killed."

"Hey, you leave her alone!" Drake froze. "Let her go, now—or I'll slit this pig's throat!"

Drake's hand tightened on her elbow. "Don't," he whispered.

She bit her lip and stepped forward, leaving Drake behind. "He didn't hurt your friends," she called to the boy. "It was T-man." She kept her voice level, the same voice she used with drunks and psychotic patients. Her gaze remained focused on the lower half of his face, not challenging him with direct eye contact.

Kind of like dealing with a rabid dog. A rabid dog with a man's fate in his hands.

"But T-man's gone," the boy said, releasing Rankin's hair, his hand rubbing over his neck and chest as if he were having difficulty breathing. Cassie noted that his voice had tightened. His flushed skin gleamed in the headlights.

"I can take you to him. I know where he is. But you have to leave the cop here."

"You know where T-man is? Can we raid his stash? He's got some good shit there. You'll share with me, right?" The last came out a strained whisper, barely audible.

"Sure, no problem. Just drop the knife and come with me."

The boy's hands began to tremble. A drop of bright red blood appeared on Rankin's neck, but the officer didn't flinch.

A look of surprise came over the boy's face. One hand flew to his throat, and his breath came in a strangled gasp.

There was a blur of motion as Drake rushed past her and tackled the boy, forcing his knife hand away from Rankin. Rankin rolled away, scrambling to his feet as the other officers joined Drake. They swarmed over the boy's prone form.

Kwon had Rankin uncuffed by the time Cassie reached him.

"It's only a scratch," he told her as she examined his wound. She had to agree. "Hey doc," Rankin continued, rubbing the feeling back into his hands, "that was really something. Thanks a lot."

"Yes, we're all so lucky the good doctor was here tonight," Kwon added in her dry tone. "Lucky she didn't get someone killed."

Movement from the cluster of police officers surrounding the boy caught Cassie's attention. "Get an ambulance," she told Kwon. "Don't handcuff his arms behind him," she shouted to the other cops. "Turn him over, he's not breathing."

The uniformed officer straddling the boy's prone body looked up at Drake. "Do what she says," Drake told him, kneeling in the mud to help roll the boy over.

Cassie ran to the boy's head, his face now a dusky blue. She placed her lips over his and tilted his head back, trying to force air into his lungs. Nothing.

"His vocal cords have clamped shut." She felt for a pulse. It was there, but weak. His skin was fiery hot and dry to the touch. Blood was starting to congeal around a bullet wound in his right shoulder. "Where's the ambulance?"

"On the way," Kwon answered. "Should be here in five, ten minutes at most."

"He'll be dead by then." She looked around. "Someone give me a knife. And I need a tube of some sort—something skinny, about quarter inch in diameter."

"Here." Drake handed her a short-bladed folding knife. He grabbed a flashlight from one of the uniformed officers and shone it over the boy's neck. "Evans," he ordered, "grab the first aid gear from the back of a squad."

The uniformed officer nodded and took off at a run. Cassie ignored the activity around her, focusing on the small area of skin below the boy's cricoid cartilage. She had to be careful not to damage the tissue of the trachea. She took a deep breath and with a swift, sure movement cut the skin. After using her sweater to blot the blood away, a second cut parted the membrane of tissue that lay below. A small gush of air rewarded her.

"I'm in. Where's the tube?" She didn't dare take her hand away from the tenuous opening she'd created. Drake's hand entered her field of vision, his fingers wrapped around the hollow bore of his pen. Cassie spread the tissue with the blunt handle of the knife and slid the pointed end of the pen into the opening. She clamped her fingers around it, bent forward and tried to force air into it.

The air went in, but slowly. The boy's chest barely moved. Cassie tried again, but the boy's chest wall muscles were rigid, restricting the flow of air.

"Let me," Drake said. She kept hold of the improvised airway as he leaned forward from his position on the opposite side of the boy's body. She felt for a pulse once more.

"No pulse. Get that defibrillator over here," she shouted. A uniformed officer complied, opening the shoe box sized automatic defibrillator and attaching the pads to the boy's chest. The lights on the command unit lit up. "Everyone clear," she ordered as the unit charged. At the last possible second she released the pen. The boy's body jerked as three electric charges in rapid succession surged through him.

CHAPTER 39

"STILL NO PULSE," the paramedic announced.

Cassie sighed. They'd been working on the boy for over twenty minutes and even with the advanced equipment the ambulance brought, it was futile. "All right," she said. "Call it. Time of death eight twenty-nine."

"It was a good try, doc," one of the medics told her as they disconnected their equipment from the boy's body.

She rocked back on her heels, spasms of pain shooting through her cramped legs. A strong hand reached down and lifted her to her feet. Drake. The rest of the police had scattered, searching the warehouse for drugs and evidence, but he had remained behind.

She glanced around. Her sight had been so focused on such a narrow area for so long that it took her a few moments to reorient. "Rankin all right?"

"He's at Three Rivers. I think he wants to thank you again."

Cassie grimaced and shook her head. "I should have warned them about the Double Cross," she muttered. "I was too excited about getting a lead on Jane Doe's identity to bother to stop and warn them."

"Kids like this—warning them about the Double Cross might have made them want to try it more."

She looked down at the body at her feet. The boy—she didn't know his name either. John Doe, just another disposable child like Sarah, her own Jane Doe. Her jaw clenched in frustration, she pulled her gaze away from the boy's body to study the silhouette of the bridge, a dark, ominous form lurking in the night sky.

"I can't believe you did that," Drake continued.

"I didn't do anything but talk to the kid," she answered. "You're the one who rushed him."

"Only when I saw he was ready to collapse anyway. I remembered the Winston kid from the other night. I was worried that this actor," he nodded to the body on the ground, "might jerk the wrong way and cut Rankin."

"Don't you have work to do?" She was more than ready to end this conversation about dead and soon to-be-dead boys. "I thought Miller wanted you to lead the search for Trautman's drug cache."

He shrugged. "It can wait."

Cassie remembered Kwon's words about her interference with the investigation and Drake's career. "I don't need you to babysit me."

She spun away and started toward her car. The bridge filled the sky behind the warehouse, towering over the landscape like some malevolent beast of the night.

"Bricks." She stopped, her eyes fixed on the West End Bridge.

"What?" Drake asked, and Cassie startled. She hadn't heard him following her, she'd been so preoccupied by her thoughts.

She nodded at the bridge. "Trautman said Jane Doe—Sarah—hit him over the head with a brick when she stole the drugs from him."

"So?"

"Old paving bricks, PennDOT must have torn them up." She began to jog over the jumbled pavement, heading toward the foot of the bridge. Drake caught up to her and pulled her to a stop.

"What do paving bricks have to do with anything?"

"There was a pile of broken paving bricks near where we found Jane Doe," she explained, her words tumbling over each other in her excitement. "I remember Eddie putting the jump bag on them. That must have been where Trautman raped her, and she hit him."

Drake frowned, then nodded with comprehension. "Why would she go back to where she knew Trautman might be, unless—"

"Unless she knew his stash was near there, and she wanted to steal more drugs. That's why she was there at four in the morning on a night when there wasn't a rave. She went to look for Trautman's stash." They scrambled across the broken pavement to the other side of the road and down the embankment where Jane Doe had been found.

Drake paced the bank of the river, his eyes moving over possible hiding places. Then he stopped, head tilted back, looking up at the concrete blocks that formed the foot of the bridge. He aimed the flashlight up, illuminating a narrow shelf between the last row of concrete blocks and the steel foundation of the bridge. Handing the light to Cassie, he began to climb the graffiti-covered slabs.

"Hold the light up higher." At the top, Drake stretched his arm out, reached behind some tumbled fragments of cement. "Got ya!"

The wind ripped through the underpass like a Chicago bound freight train. Cassie tried to hold the light steady, but her shivering made the beam skip. Drake skidded down the interlocked concrete slabs, and landed at her feet.

"Trautman made himself a nice cache up there." He pulled his cell phone from his jacket. "Cemented a big old lock box right onto the bridge supports."

Cassie stomped her chilled feet. While Drake called for back up, she watched the black water of the Ohio lap against the edge of the gravel. Every time she looked away the water came near as if trying to sneak up and ambush her. She took a step toward Drake, not liking the banshee howl of the wind wailing through the bridge struts or the icy fingers of water stretching out to her. A rumble above them came as one of the police cars pulled off the bridge.

Gravel flew down from the road surface. She gazed out over the stretch of river heading west. Suddenly a bright red flame came shooting over the railing of the bridge above them, twirling end over end as it spiraled through the darkness. It splashed into the black water with a ribbon of sparks quickly devoured by the greedy river.

She froze, unable to move her eyes from the spot where the roadside flare drowned. That could have been her.

Wrenching her eyes away, she stared up through the darkness to the railing high above. If Drake had been slower, a second longer . . . she would have dropped, spun through the air as the flare had. Plummeted into the water.

Cassie crouched down, plunged her bare hand into the icy water. No mercy there, a few minutes perhaps before hypothermia overwhelmed the body.

She closed her eyes, remembering Jane Doe's limp, blue body. She'd be there but the grace of God — and Drake.

Her body shuddered as she realized just how lucky she was that he had been there.

"What the hell—" Strong arms yanked her back before she could slump forward into the water. Drake pulled her to her feet. She opened her eyes and looked up into his. Dark as midnight now in the dim light, they narrowed in concern. "You're like ice. C'mon, we've got to get you out of here."

"What about the lockbox?" she stammered through trembling lips. He wrapped his jacket around her, propelling her up the slope.

"Kwon's coming to get it processed."

Her numb feet slipped on the rocks, and she fell back against his body. Drake's body was so solid, so warm against hers. Definitely not the quivering mass of overwrought and exhausted nerves she had deteriorated into. She pulled away. She could take care of herself, she was no one's damsel in distress.

Cassie plowed up the scree slope on her own, wincing as the gravel bit into her abraded palms. At least she could feel her hands again, she thought, cursing herself for not bringing gloves. She tucked her hands under her armpits once she reached the pavement and headed toward her car.

"Wait. My car's right here." Drake steered her across the pavement to his Intrepid.

She hesitated, steeling herself to refuse his offer. But then he was holding the door open for her, and she found herself sliding into the warm embrace of the front seat.

Drake hurried around to the driver's side, got in, started the car and turned the heat on high. He turned to her. "Thanks to you, I think we just made major progress on the FX epidemic."

"Tell that to that homeless kid. Or my patient. I still don't know who Jane Doe is, and Fran's killer is still out there." Everything she'd gone through had been all for nothing more than a first name and the hazy possibility of an origin for Jane Doe. Not much to work with, but she'd call Adeena with the information as soon as she got home.

She slumped against the seat, wishing that the heater could go higher. Her body was numb with exhaustion.

Maybe she'd call Adeena after she got some sleep.

"Didn't it occur to you that once Trautman knew you linked him with Jane Doe, he'd have to kill you? That he couldn't allow you to connect him back to Three Rivers or the FX?" He shook his head. "Just how far would you go to help a patient?"

The edge in his voice forced a flare of indignation from her. "My patient, my job, my responsibility—a lot like yours, Detective."

"It's my job to risk my life, not yours. My job to find Fran's murderer, not yours. You could have been killed." Now his eyes flashed with anger.

Cassie sighed. Didn't they go through this already? "You wouldn't understand."

"Try me. What makes an intelligent woman fool enough to take risks to help a girl she doesn't even know? What makes you think that Jane Doe wants to have her family back in her life? Maybe she made herself anonymous in a strange city for a good reason."

She massaged the scar on her thumb and stared out the windshield. *Because she was Cassie's,* was the answer that she could never articulate. How to explain that someone had to stand for the helpless, the hopeless, that she cared for day in and day out? What words would make that feeling of responsibility sound real and not like some grand delusion?

"I do what needs to be done." It was the best explanation she could come up with.

He nodded slowly at that, and Cassie thought she saw some glimmer of understanding cross his face.

"Why were you there tonight?" she asked, trying to keep her voice level.

"Doing *my* job," he replied. She was silent, and he continued, "I remembered you found Jane Doe here and that other overdose was brought in from down here, so I headed over, hoping to find Trautman, his stash, or both."

She gave a taut laugh. "And you got lucky."

He exhaled loudly, and his hands tightened on the steering wheel.

"I got lucky," he agreed, but his voice had lowered. "I saw Trautman toss you over the railing. If I'd been a minute later . . ." his voice trailed off, and he looked away.

"Thank you," she said in a quiet voice. The trembling returned. It was as if the river had frozen her from the inside out. No matter how high the heat blew at her, it would be a long time before she felt warm again.

Or completely safe.

CHAPTER 40

DRAKE TURNED BACK to her, his face carefully neutral. "You're welcome," he said. "Do you want me to drive you home? I can have uniforms bring your car by later."

"I'm okay. Can I just sit here a moment?" Hart leaned against the door, pulling her knees up and wrapping her arms around them, his jacket hanging loosely from her shoulders.

"You can stay as long as you like," he said, his voice dropping into a near-whisper. He couldn't help himself, the way his throat tightened when he thought of how close she'd come to dying, the way his pulse raced at the prospect of her sitting so close, yet still so very far away from him. She looked like an angel: the mist of their breath surrounding her, hair tumbling over her shoulders, that porcelain skin.

He took a deep breath. *She's off limits,* he reminded himself, trying not to remember their passion the night before. Suddenly the Dodge seemed drenched in the smell of apples and vanilla.

She was an angel with her wings folded around her. The image formed clearly in his mind. He knew he would have to get it onto paper or canvas before his mind would allow him a moment's rest.

Then the angel opened her eyes, and he was drowning in their depths. *Hell of a way to go*, a voice whispered even as he raised a hand to stroke an errant strand of hair from her face. He snatched his hand away, stunned by the flame that surged through him with the touch of her flesh.

Steady boy. He returned his hand and gaze to the neutral steering wheel. It had been a long time since he'd felt this way—too long.

Was this angel worth taking the risk?

•❦•

"YOU'RE SHAKING." Drake's voice penetrated the icy chill that had enveloped Cassie.

Her teeth chattered as she answered. "It's just adrenalin."

He raised her hands, unclenching them to inspect the damage. "Maybe I should take you over to Three Rivers."

"No." The single syllable took all her strength. He looked away and dropped her hands. She wanted to ask him to hold her, to share his warmth, but knew it was impossible. There was too much at stake—and not only his job and Fran's case. Cassie couldn't risk re-opening wounds that had taken eighteen months to heal, wounds that last night had come perilously close to exposing.

Her stomach lurched as if she were still falling, dropping into an abyss. It was terrifying to feel like this, as out of control as when T-man hurled her from the bridge. Right before Drake pulled her back from the chasm.

Drake turned back. He surprised her by taking her wrist once more and raising it to his lips. With gentle precision he kissed the moon-shaped scar at the base of her thumb. Her pulse vibrated beneath his touch.

She froze. What should she do next? Damn it, she'd never been any good at this. Was he trying to tell her goodbye? Or something else entirely?

He reached his other arm to gather her close to him, and she had her answer.

The kiss was sweet, filled more with compassion than the passion that drove them last night. Cassie felt her trembling slowly ebb away. She slid closer to him, craving contact with him.

After savoring the long, sweet exchange, she pulled back. Focused on reality. "I'd better go now. I don't want to keep you from your duties."

"Seeing you home safe is pretty much my last job for the night." Drake's hand closed over hers. "We can get your car in the morning."

Her resistance crumbled with his touch. She squeezed his hand in reply. But not her house, it was too crowded with memories and old ghosts. "No, your place. We need to talk."

A tiny frown tightened his mouth and his gaze flicked away from her as he put the car into gear. He drove with one hand on the wheel, keeping the other entwined with hers. They rode in a comfortable silence over to his building in East Liberty. He parked the departmental car in the side lot. She waited for him as he moved around the car to open her door and give her his hand once more.

Together they climbed the wide oak steps. Cassie admired the carved banisters and intricate twisting of wrought iron on the railings, details that she had overlooked last night. "This is a great building."

"Thanks. I worked hard on it."

"You own the entire building?"

"My uncle advised me to invest in real estate. I fell in love with this place. It was built in 1922 to house the

Liberty Times newspaper. Now, I'm just trying to find the right tenants for the other floors."

"I can't believe nobody's interested."

"A dot-com start up wanted the second floor, but they fell through. Monsignor Newman from Our Lady of Sorrows is going to take the ground floor for a new food bank and daycare center once we get the funding approved."

She paused on the landing outside his door. "I have a friend who wants to start a community clinic," she told him. "Ed Castro—my boss in the ER, you met him, right? He's had this dream for as long as I've known him."

"A free medical clinic?"

"Not just medical. A place to help serve all of the needs of the community. Social services, job training, literacy counseling, financial planning—every time he talks about it, he comes up with more ideas."

"That would tie into Newman's ideas. I should get the two of them together."

"You'd do that? Let them use the building?"

Drake nodded. "Sure, why not? Maybe your friend the social worker would be interested as well."

"I'm sorry about what happened this morning with Adeena. She was just—"

"It's all right. You have good friends."

"Sometimes I wish they'd let me live my own life."

Drake opened the door to his apartment and flicked the lights on. After depositing his gun and badge on the foyer table, he took her coat and hung it on the coat rack with his jacket. The door behind clicked shut behind them, and Cassie felt a shiver run through her.

Drake moved with slow, precise movements—as if his mind were elsewhere. He led her into the living room.

"Can I get you anything?" he asked once she was settled on the sofa. His voice sounded hollow, his face was expressionless.

"No thanks." What was going on? She stole a look back over her shoulder at the closed door, trying to ignore her clammy palms. Had she said something wrong? Everything was fine when they were talking outside—wasn't it?

But things had changed. All they did was cross the threshold. It had only taken a split second. Something was going to happen, something bad. She looked up at Drake, wanting to convince herself that her anxiety had no basis in reality. But he wouldn't meet her gaze.

"We have to talk," he started.

Here it comes, get ready. Where was her escape route? Cassie clenched her hands and forced herself to remain where she was. She remembered the look of concern on his face out at the bridge. *He's not Richard.* Drake would never hurt her. Oh, but he could, without even trying, he could cut her to the bone.

Then it dawned on her what he was trying to say. She let her breath out in relief. "I know," she replied before he could go on. "Finding Fran's killer has to come first. And we can't see each other as long as you're on the case. We have plenty of time. I'll wait as long as you need."

Drake stepped away from her to the window. He stood frozen, his gaze fixed far beyond the streets of East Liberty.

"I should have told you last night," he said. He cleared his throat and turned around. "I'm sorry I didn't. But things moved so fast."

She grimaced. That was her fault, not his. She started to tell him that, but he spoke again. His voice was distant, remote.

"I used to drink a lot—" he started.

Her head swam. It *was* Richard, all over again.

She wiped her clammy palms on her jeans, strained

to concentrate, listen to his words. *Drake wasn't Richard,* she repeated, hanging onto the thought even as her stomach tightened with fear.

"It comes with the job," Drake was saying. "Your friends are cops, and you drink with them. Your dates meet you at bars or parties so you drink with them. You're a detective working all hours, and sometimes a drink helps you sleep. At least that's how it used to work for me.

"I never had a black out, and I was never drunk on the job. In fact I never thought I had a problem. Until last summer, that was." He stopped.

"What happened last summer?" Cassie remembered what Spanos had said. She'd ignored the patrolman's warning. She thought his angry words were the product of jealousy.

"Someone died because of me."

Cassie couldn't meet his eyes. Her mouth was dry. She fought to swallow as she waited for the rest.

"This job wears you down, you know that," he continued. "There's only so much you can see before it gets to you. But you can't let it affect you because then it affects the job. You can't share it with anyone else because either they wouldn't understand or they'd think you were weak.

"So you build a persona, an alter ego. Joe Cop—you watch enough bad TV shows and you can get it down real fast. Life imitates fiction. And boy, do the women go for Joe Cop." He shook his head. "It's unbelievable how sexy they find him," he said, speaking of himself in the third person.

"Last summer I'm seeing this woman, Pamela. She'd been a witness in a case, and afterward she started hanging around, calling me, stopping by bars where we hang out. We hooked up, but then things got too serious, and I decide to call a halt to it. No big deal, I had the routine down pat. I did it all the time after I got bored or scared or whatever. Even prided myself on letting them down easy.

"Anyway, a few weeks later I get a call from Pamela. Can we meet for drinks, just as friends, no strings attached? There's something she wants to tell me." He paused. "I'm afraid she's pregnant or something, so I'm scared shitless. But I decide to face the music like a man and agree to meet her. I go to pick her up at her place, we have a few drinks there, then a few more, and to make a long story short, we end up in bed."

Cassie stiffened but kept her eyes focused on her clenched hands. She knew she wasn't the first woman in his bed, but it still hurt. Did he have any idea how much last night meant to her? What she had risked, allowing anyone to get that close?

"Afterwards I'm sleeping, and I hear a voice whispering my name." His voice was low and raspy as if what he had to tell her should not be said out loud. "I roll over, thinking I'm dreaming, but I'm kind of half awake, and I see Pamela standing at the foot of the bed. She turns around, and there's my nine millimeter at her head." He cleared his throat and raised his hands to rub at his eyes.

"Before I could shout or move or blink, she pulls the trigger and there's this godawful explosion that echoes through the room, and blood is raining down on me, the bed, the walls, everywhere.

"I call 9-1-1," he continued, his voice now reduced to a hoarse whisper, "and I hold her until they come. I have her head in my lap, trying to stop the bleeding. I can't even tell where her mouth is anymore but there's this awful bubbling and gurgling noise."

Cassie drew her breath in. What he described was so close to Fran's death that for a moment she was back in the parking lot, cradling Fran's face, blood covering her own hands. A shudder raced over her. She wrapped her arms around herself, trying to ward off the cold, chill vision of death.

"And then it stopped. Everything stopped." Drake kept his hands over his eyes, pressing them shut. "She was only twenty-six, just a kid, her whole life in front of her. I was suspended while the department investigated, but they couldn't determine any wrong doing on my part, and they re-instated me. Of course, that didn't stop everyone for blaming me for her death."

There was silence. He lowered his hands and opened his eyes. "You know, I really think she was going to tell me. I don't think she'd planned to kill herself, not until after she realized that she just didn't have the courage."

"Tell you what?"

"I found out after the autopsy. Pamela was HIV positive."

She stared at him. She remembered last night, how fast everything had happened, how nervous he'd been at first. Then all that time talking afterward—why hadn't he said anything? Did he think all those pretty words would make up for his silence?

He hung his head and turned back to her. "Anyway, I took the cocktail, and I've tested negative twice since then."

She considered that. The odds were in Drake's favor as far as the HIV exposure. Hers, too. Still, he should have told her. What did he think, that she just jumped into bed with any man who came along? Did he assume that she was like Pamela? Another witness, another woman to fall for his charms?

Anger roared through her mind. Anger and humiliation. She'd been such a fool. In the back of her mind, Cassie heard Richard's laughter mocking her.

"I'm sorry," Drake continued. "I just never expected—"

"You never expected what? To care about what happens to me?" The hot flash of fury propelled her to her feet. She shifted into a fighting stance, her hands fisted at her sides.

She thought Drake would never hurt her—and she had sat there and allowed him to flay her open! She should've known that just because a man didn't raise his hand to you, it didn't mean you could trust him.

"Did you think I was just another one night stand?" She flung the last at him even as she strode across the room, reaching for her jacket. This time she didn't hide her tears from him. To hell with him, anyway.

CHAPTER 41

"WAIT!" HE SHOUTED. "That's not what—damn it, would you stop!"

How could she have been so stupid? Thinking that he had felt anything at all for her? When would she learn to trust no one, assume nothing, especially not handsome men with clever hands and smart mouths? She grabbed the door and flung it open.

"Don't go." His voice—softer now, pleading almost, caught her on the landing. "Please."

The word was so quiet Cassie could almost convince herself she'd imagined it. She slowed her breathing and tried to still the fight or flight nausea that filled her stomach. She turned, eyes narrowed, and to her surprise he stood there, motionless, hands at his side, palms out. He looked so harmless. So sincere.

Drake had the potential to hurt her more than anyone else alive. Still, she took a reluctant step toward him. Could she trust him? Lord knew why, but she wanted to. The idea seemed so foreign that she almost laughed. It was as frightening as this dreadful need he stirred within her. And as compelling.

She edged back inside, handing him her coat, her eyes never leaving his for an instant.

"Thank you," was all he said, as if she had given him a rare and precious gift. If he only knew.

He met her gaze and took her hand once more, his touch gentle as his thumb caressed the scar at the base of hers. Maybe he did know.

⁕

DRAKE OPENED THE third door in the foyer. Cassie had assumed it led to another bedroom. He opened it and flipped a light switch. Beyond him a cavernous space that occupied the rear of the building brightened with the gleam of overhead track lights. He led her inside, looking over his shoulder at her.

Large windows took up all three outside walls. There was an elegant wrought iron spiral staircase in the corner, leading to the roof, she guessed. Beside it was an old-fashioned freight elevator enclosed within an intricately worked metal cage. A battered leather recliner along with a large table were the room's only furnishings. But what stole her breath were the colors.

Swirling colors covered canvasses of all sizes. There were easels, angled to capture the light at certain times of the day, each holding works in progress. She began a slow walk around the room. His work was evocative, breathtaking. The way he turned light into a vibrant force converted the simplest of landscapes into living moments of time temporarily imprisoned by the pigment. His portraits, they moved beyond two dimensions as if he were capturing the subject's soul rather than their mere physical appearance.

She stopped in front of a large canvas depicting a man of indeterminate age sitting on the steps of the

Carnegie library, his earthly possessions packed tightly in paper shopping bags surrounding him.

"I know him. That's Morris," she said, her fingers reaching out and almost touching the figure. Morris was a frequent visitor to Three Rivers on nights when it was too cold to sleep on his grate. In the portrait he looked up at the viewer. The rage and impotence in his eyes was so palpable she wanted to step away. Instead, she was actually drawn forward because, beneath all that anger, she saw the strength of the man revealed.

"It's wonderful," she whispered as if she were in church.

"I'm rather proud of that one myself." Drake joined her. "It's almost done, just needs a touch of something—I'm not quite sure what. I haven't really done any work since last summer."

"There are always so many people there, walking right past him like he doesn't exist." Cassie remembered the last time she'd seen Morris during a visit to the library. The homeless man had spat and cursed at her.

Drake cocked his head and looked at the painting. The white marble steps spread out from the seated figure, dwarfing him while also shedding a reflective light that created a halo, bathing the homeless man, illuminating him in sharp contrast to his surroundings. Drake grabbed a length of charcoal and leaned forward. With a few quick strokes he added a distant figure emerging from the library, his shadow descending over the steps, almost reaching Morris.

She watched in awe as the few, almost careless, sweeps of charcoal suddenly redefined the painting. Now Morris was not just a man who had left society behind, but who existed in a life on the other side of an invisible border.

"You've a good eye," Drake told her. "Thanks."

"Your mother got her wish," she said, remembering his story about his first name.

"It's something I've done all my life, scribbling on any scrap of paper I could find. It's my escape."

She moved on to look at a view of jumbled rooftops. "Why do police work at all? When you have so much talent—"

"I love being a cop. That's when I feel most alive. Most of what I do in here comes directly from what I do out there on the streets."

"I know what you mean. The rush, the adrenalin—they are addictive." She turned and spotted a scattering of paper sketches on a battered table behind her.

He moved to intercept her. "When I said I didn't expect anything to happen last night, what I meant was that I didn't expect you to want—I mean, you're so—hell, I don't know what I mean." He ran his fingers through his hair in frustration.

She glanced down at the figure in the drawings. Her hand shot out to grasp the paper, she stopped herself and looked to him for permission, but his gaze was turned away from her, fixed on the floor at his feet. She scrutinized the sketch, gnawing at her lower lip for a long moment. "Is that supposed to be me?"

"They're only from memory." He took the sheet of paper from her, and she was surprised to see that his hand was trembling.

Cassie stepped away from him. He couldn't see her that way, it was impossible. The woman in those sketches was beautiful, full of passion and sensuality. She was none of those—couldn't he see that? Then she saw the date scrawled in the corner. Two days ago. Before last night. She turned to him in confusion.

DRAKE CLENCHED HIS hands, waiting for her verdict. She knew all his secrets now, she could hurt him without even trying. But when she looked up at him with surprise and wonder in her eyes, he didn't think that would happen.

"You didn't know me at all when you drew this," she said. "Not even my name."

He risked stepping closer to her. "I knew everything I needed to. I knew everything in here." He placed a hand over her heart. To his amazement and delight, she blushed.

"So, you like them?" he asked.

She nodded, her teeth still worrying her lower lip, gazing at the sketches with wide-eyed fascination that was enchanting to watch.

"Like them? I love them, but this isn't me." Her finger softly stroked the air above the charcoal lines.

A surge of pleasure warmed him and he straightened as if released from a burden. "I draw what I see," he assured her, encircling her with his arms. He turned her toward him and lifted her hands in his. "How do you do your job with such tiny hands?" Her palms were angry red where the skin had been stripped away. He gently kissed the small areas of intact skin.

Drake raised his gaze when she took a sharp breath in. Her eyes were sunken, her face pale beneath the remnants of grime and soot. He thought of all she had been through in the past two days. Enough to decimate a strong man, but she refused to bow to exhaustion.

"You need sleep," he whispered. In answer, she slid her hand from his and feathered it up his arm, sending a delightful shiver through his body. She gave him a tiny smile and encircled both hands around his neck, standing on tiptoe to kiss him.

The kiss resonated through Drake. At last he felt free to totally respond to her. There were no secrets, no fears left, only his desire for her.

"You're all I need right now," she murmured when their lips parted. If she only knew how true those words were for him as well.

Drake encircled her waist with one arm and swept the table clean with his other. She wrapped her legs around him, and he placed her on the table. His hands slid under her sweater, playing over her skin as his lips slipped down her neck.

She reached down, drew her sweater up. Before it was over her head, Drake's mouth and hands returned to savor her flesh. She tasted of sweet apple blossoms rustling in a springtime breeze. She bent her head over his, her hair cascading forward, and he was drowning in the rich, dark tresses.

Her mouth was at his neck, his cheek, his ear, filling him with tiny thrills as her tongue caressed him. His hands continued to roam over her, evoking small noises of delight from her whenever he found a particularly sensitive area. He pulled her jeans off and continued his exploration of her body, enjoying the pleasure he was able to give her.

Her hips rocked in time with his hand as he caressed her. He moved his mouth down her chest, slow and relentless, wanting to taste every inch of her, to know her in entirety. Finally he knelt between her legs. Her fingers tangled in his hair, pulling his head forward, and she cried out.

She grabbed the edge of the table, relaxing her merciless grip on his hair. Another cry of release escaped her lips, this one a soft mewing. She fell back, limp. He straightened and looked down on his handiwork.

Hart said nothing, her breath coming in rapid gasps as if she'd just finished a marathon. When she opened her eyes, her pupils were wide with pleasure. Her body glistened with sweat and a healthy glow, her eyes were bright, her hair hanging tousled like a child's as she leaned back on her elbows, totally relaxed.

"My god," she said when her breathing normalized.

"Something wrong?" he asked with a smile, his fingers teasing a small circle below her belly button. She weakly swatted his hand away.

"You need to give me a moment here."

Drake kept his hand still, and felt the trembling in her body begin to subside.

"I hate that you can do that to me." She sat up again, swinging her legs on either side of him.

"Do what?" he asked innocently as his fingers slid up to cup her breast.

"Stop it. That. Turning me into jelly. I hate needing you, wanting you, letting you make me feel so—"

"Vulnerable?" He supplied the word that had echoed inside him ever since they had shared that first cup of coffee, when she had brushed her fingers against his, restoring them to life.

They were both still now, staring at each other. "Yes," she whispered, and he was surprised to see a single tear slide from her eye. "Vulnerable."

CHAPTER 42

"WAIT HERE," HE said. Cassie watched Drake go into the guest bathroom next door. He returned with a thick terrycloth robe that he wrapped her in. Before she could tie the belt, he scooped her into his arms and carried her out of the studio. Laughter at his exuberance escaped from her. The constant knot of grief constricting her chest since last night loosened its grip.

"You're exhausted." He deposited her onto one of the cherry, Shaker-style dining room chairs. "First something to eat, then bed." He moved into the kitchen beyond, opening the folding doors over the bar.

"Bed?" she asked with a smile that crinkled her eyes.

"Sleep," he amended in a stern tone. He turned on the heat under a cast iron skillet and gathered eggs, roasted red peppers, green onions, sausage and mushrooms. The kitchen filled with a tantalizing odor.

"Should I be jealous?" She asked as he chopped the vegetables. His knife flew in quick precision with only the slightest movement of his hand. "A woman's robe?"

"I keep it for my mother's visits."

"Where's she live?"

"Florida. She got a job down there a few years ago. Got tired of the cold."

Cassie stood, tying the robe around her and looked out the windows at the bleak Pittsburgh night. "I don't blame her."

She walked around, admiring his artwork, examining his belongings for clues to their owner. One corner of the living room was filled with a large TV, stereo and DVD player. His eclectic collection of music was neatly arranged, but in no particular order. John Coltrane sandwiched between Led Zeppelin and Tantric. She smiled when she saw a copy of her father's favorite, John Lee Hooker. She finished her wandering and returned to the kitchen, perching on the counter beside the refrigerator.

Drake flashed her a smile, then turned to add the vegetables to the browning sausage. She watched him grind some pepper over the mix and sprinkle in some rosemary, basil and a small amount of fennel.

"Have you sold any of your work?"

"I'm lucky, my uncle set me up with an agent who takes care of that end of it." Drake beat the eggs and adjusted the heat before adding them to the pan. "I try not to think of my art as a business. It's more like therapy that happens to sometimes pay."

"Could I see your paintings in a museum or gallery?" she persisted despite his obvious embarrassment.

He looked up at her, as if uncertain if she was mocking him. "No museums, but galleries in New York, Cleveland, Baltimore and DC."

"None here? I really want to see more."

"None here. You're one of the few outside the family who even know about my painting. I'd like to keep it that way."

She nodded her agreement. "That smells great. Did your mom teach you to cook?"

He chuckled and shook his head. "Mom's idea of cooking is ordering take out. My dad was the chef in the family." He shut the gas off, allowing the eggs to finish cooking in their own heat while he poured them each a glass of milk. Cassie carried the glasses to the table, and he followed with the food.

⁕

HART DUG IN, and he was gratified by the smile of delight that crossed her face as she chewed. "Wow. This is great."

She shoveled more of the eggs into her mouth, eating with the same passion she seemed to bring to everything in life. Drake took a small bite, marveling at these new feelings. He chewed slowly, as if he could somehow stretch out this peaceful interlude, and freeze time. He'd never had someone to take care of before.

It felt good, he decided as he washed down the eggs with a sip of milk. The food settled in his stomach with a warm feeling that eased into his veins. For the first time in days, the rigid set of his muscles begin to relax.

"I thought your dad was a police officer," Hart continued once she satisfied her appetite.

"He was. After he died I was going through some of his papers and I found a certificate from the Culinary Institute. Mom told me he wanted to be a chef, to open up his own place, but she was laid off from the steel mill, and then I came along, so he quit. The Police Bureau was looking for people. The pay was decent, the hours not bad, and the benefits good, so he became a cop."

"Do you think he regretted it?" she asked as if she spoke of someone important to her rather than a man she'd never laid eyes on.

Drake thought about that. "No, I don't think he did. He turned out to be a great cop and he loved the work. Of course that was before the damned Consent Decree and spectrum of force and all. He died on the job."

"He was shot?"

"Heart attack. He was a sergeant, usually rode alone, but that day a supervisor, a woman, was riding with him. He spotted a mugging, jumped out of the car and went after the guy on foot."

"Isn't that what police do?"

"Only in Hollywood. Any cop will tell you that four wheels and 300 horsepower are better than two legs for most pursuits. I think Dad did it to impress the skirt, excuse me, female supervisor. He wanted to show her that after thirty years on the force he still had what it took." The memory always brought a curious mix of anger and pride. Drake took another bite but the eggs had grown cold, their texture rubbery. "He got his man, though. Ran him down, cuffed him, then sat back and dropped dead. Right there on the street in front of the old Woolworths."

"I'm sorry. When did it happen?"

"Seven years ago. I was still in uniform."

She cupped her chin in her palm and smiled. "I'll bet your father was very proud of you. What do you like most about your job?"

"To me being a cop is a lot like painting. It's having a vision of how the world should be, then creating order out of chaos so that vision has a chance to become clear."

"And is that what you do?"

"On a good day. Yes." He took a drink of milk, why was it everything tasted better, cooking for someone else? Sharing with someone else? "My turn. I heard how you went after Jane Doe the other night. How did you manage that? Being claustrophobic, I mean."

She flushed and ducked her head in embarrassment. Then she shrugged and faced him again. "Not much to it. Just sit yourself down and strap yourself in."

"Have you always been claustrophobic?" It was hard to imagine Hart afraid of anything—not after seeing her on that bridge tonight.

"It's not really claustrophobia. More a bit of panic about loss of control—"

"Like riding in a helicopter?"

"Like riding in a helicopter. I used to love flying. Ed still gives me extra transport shifts—he thinks he's being nice to me."

"When did it start?"

"Around a year ago." Silence as she pushed the remnants of her eggs around on her plate. "Please don't tell Ed or anyone in the ER. They don't know."

A year ago. When she left Richard King. Drake scowled at his own plate, his appetite vanished.

Hart pushed back from the table and took her empty plate and glass over to the sink, taking longer than necessary. Drake regretted breaking the mood that had been building between them.

Instead of returning to her seat, Hart came up behind Drake, draping her arms over his shoulders. Her tongue tickled his ear as her fingers caressed their way down his chest. "I've had enough talking. How about you?"

Drake pushed his plate away, and she climbed into his lap, straddling him with her legs. The robe hung open, exposing her naked body.

"I thought you were going to bed."

"We will," she assured him as her fingers took ownership of his body once more.

She squirmed on his lap, lifting his shirt over his shoulders. Drake suddenly understood the attraction of lap dances. It was tantalizing to have her naked flesh so near while he was still restrained by layers of clothing. An exquisite pressure began to build within him. He slid his hands over her thighs, keeping rhythm with the movement of her hips.

Her fingers pressed hard on the sensitive spot at the base of his spine. He squeezed his eyes shut as heat jolted through him. Must be something they taught at medical school, some trick of the male anatomy.

Drake could restrain himself no longer. His fingers dug into the firm flesh of her buttocks as he lifted her onto the table. He stood before her. She kept her legs entwined around him, squeezing his hips tight against hers, refusing to release him. He felt his erection grow, constrained within his jeans, painful.

He forced a hand between her thigh and his body, reaching for the zipper of his jeans. The pressure on his spine eased. Her hand tugged on his, pulled it away. Her head moved forward to rest on his shoulder.

"Not yet," she whispered.

Drake felt as if he might burst with the pressure. His vision danced with red swirls, and his pulse pounded in his ears. He nipped at her breast.

"Now," he insisted, breaking her strangle hold on his neck.

He pulled her into his arms and moved into the bedroom, dumped her onto the bed, the robe flying free. He yanked at the snap of his jeans.

Hart sat up, her hand darting into the bedside table's drawer and emerging with a condom. He reached for it, but she moved it away. She tore it open with her teeth.

"Allow me," she told him with a wicked grin, and then slid to the floor to kneel before him.

"I can't—" His mouth clamped shut as a wave of burning pleasure shot through him. She took him inside her mouth, easing the condom over his erection with teasing motions of her lips and tongue.

"Now," he urged her, his hands gripping her shoulders, trying to lift her back onto the bed. His pelvis began to rock harder, and he knew he would come soon, wouldn't be able to wait for her.

"No." She drew her head back and clamped her fingers tight, held him in a vise grip of pain and pleasure. She lay back on the bed, pulled him down on top of her. Drake's mind drifted in a crimson haze. How much longer could he stand this? Part of him hoped it never ended. He wanted to ride this knife-edge of ecstasy forever.

Her legs wrapped around him, and he was inside of her, free to allow his body to release its pent up fury. Hart's fingers gnawed at the muscles of his back, digging, searching for a handhold. Drake opened his eyes as the final wave pushed him over the edge, just in time to see her mouth widen in a cry of pleasure.

He slumped on top of her. Her lips parted in a mischievous smile, and her finger traced the path of a tear that slid down his face. Drake lifted his head and watched as she licked the salty essence from her finger.

"Did I hurt you?" Her eyes twinkled in delight at the prospect.

He bowed his head once more. "My god," he gasped. "Yes."

"Good," was her reply.

CHAPTER 43

LATER THEY LAY together on his bed. Drake traced his finger along the muscles of her back. An anatomy lesson in intimacy. He loved the gentle curve that dipped between her shoulder blades. His hand continued downward to that succulent basin of flesh at the base of her spine. Like a flat bowled champagne glass. Something to drink from, to savor, a celebration. He leaned down, tasting the sweat pooled there. Sweet and tangy, spicy musk tinged with honey. She squirmed, and he smiled, raking his teeth against her skin.

"That tickles." She arched her back further to look over her shoulder at him.

Drake stretched out, facing her, his fingers still skimming, feasting. Touching her, however lightly, sent a tingling through his body, a tantalizing promise.

"You're not going to run away again, are you?" he asked, working to keep his voice light.

"Are you going to watch me go? Again."

Ouch. "You saw that, did you?"

"Uh huh."

"I'm sorry. I was—"

CJ LYONS

"Scared?" Her eyes met his with an open honesty. "Me, too."

"Guess we both have reasons not to be jumping into relationships right now." Drake stroked the curve of her spine. Her muscles rippled beneath his touch. He could do this all night—watching her, touching her, inhaling her—and never tire of it.

"The heart has reasons," she murmured.

"What's that mean?"

She shrugged, cascades of curls brushing against his waiting fingers with the movement. "Something my grandmother used to say."

"The witch? Ed Castro told me about her."

Hart flounced over, and sat up. "Ed and Rosa never did get along. He thinks she put a curse on him because he didn't stop me from marrying Richard."

"A curse? Like the evil eye? You're kidding, right?" He tried and failed to keep the amusement from his voice. Her face colored. Reading Hart's face was like learning a new language. This faint tinge of crimson suffusing her cheeks and nose was anger.

"What would Rosa say about us, then? Is some gnarled old witch going to give me a poison apple to eat?" His chuckle blossomed into a deep belly laugh. "Or spit between her fingers, *cha, cha,* and make all my hair fall out?"

"I'm glad you think it's funny."

"Of course it's funny." He controlled his laughter and looked up at her. "Isn't it?" He sat up beside her. "You can't be serious. You're a doctor for chrissakes—you don't believe in a witch's curses."

Her eyes flashed. "There's nothing to joke about. Curses too often return with a vengeance. And she wasn't a witch. She was Rosa Costello of the Kalderasha *kumpania.* She was Rom, a gypsy to you *gaje,*" she said the last with disdain.

"What did you call me? I didn't like the sound of that."

He was torn between the desire to calm her indignation and the temptation to further stir her anger. God, she was beautiful right now, eyes blazing through the dim light of the bedroom, head held high, regal cheekbones lit by a fire within. He very well believed she was part gypsy. What had she called it—Rom, part Rom.

"*Gaje,* outsider," she practically spat it.

"But your grandmother must have married a *gaje,*" he stumbled. The word had an unpleasant feel to it. "Right?"

She sighed, and her look softened. He missed the blaze of color, but was happy to see her relax once more.

"Padraic Hart. He was Irish."

Drake had the sudden image of whiskey thrown onto a flame—that was Hart. Fire, passion, all smoldering, barely contained beneath the surface.

"Rosa gave up everything for him, even became *marhime,* unclean. No Rom would talk to her, look upon her, touch her, she was dead in their eyes. That's why she and Paddy moved here after the War, to start a new life."

"She was shunned, like the Amish do."

She nodded, her gaze falling away from his. He reached for her hand, turned it over, and stroked the crescent-shaped scar at the base of her thumb. "Do you think something like that might happen to us? That I might be shunned by my people, by other cops, because of my involvement with you?"

⚬◈⚬

CASSIE CLOSED HER eyes for a long moment, savoring his touch, hoping this wouldn't be the last time. They both knew what was at risk if anyone found out about them. It would be her fault. After all, she was the one who had practically jumped him last night, desperate for comfort and damning the consequences.

Reap what you sow. Rosa was right, as always.

"Hart, look at me." The way Drake said her name gave the single syllable a thrill that was sensual, stirring. He took her by the shoulders, and she met his eyes. "What we have, this is very special, precious. I wouldn't jeopardize it for the world—"

"I think we already have," she said in a low voice. "It's not just Commander Miller finding out. Think of the press, how they would twist this, turn it into something ugly. You could lose your job and I—I couldn't live with a spotlight trained on me, everyone watching, waiting to ambush us—I couldn't do that."

"I don't think we're going to be on the next Jerry Springer special." He gave a short, wry chuckle. "But you're right. Things could get uncomfortable." He sighed and encircled her shoulders with his arm, bringing her closer. "We could go back to Plan A."

"Plan A?"

"Yes. Take it slow and easy, like you were talking about before. The patience is a virtue plan."

"After tonight Plan A's going to be a challenge. Maybe I don't want to take it easy," she said, turning her head so that her mouth nuzzled his ear. What she wanted was to take everything he had to offer, to devour him in an endless feast of delight. "There's something you should know about me," she whispered. "I'm not noted for my patience."

"Neither am I."

"So what do we do?" She straightened, raised her hand to cover his where it rested on her shoulder. "I'm certain that Miller suspects and Kwon—"

"Don't worry about Janet. She won't say anything."

"She has a thing for you."

"Who? Kwon? No way. She'd never get involved with anyone she worked with. You don't know Janet, she's a stickler for rules."

"Which doesn't solve our problem."

"It's no problem. I'll go to Miller tomorrow and ask to be reassigned. No big deal."

His face held the same impassive expression it had this morning when he saw her in the pharmacy. His poker face, she was learning. She glanced down and saw that his free hand had crushed the sheet into a twisted knot.

"Who would take over Fran's case? You said yourself that you were good at what you do—"

"I was only trying to impress a pretty girl," he joked. "Besides, I can still stay involved, just not officially."

"When this guy's caught, won't his lawyer ask why the lead investigator was reassigned? Won't people wonder?"

"Let them wonder. Who cares about people?"

"No. I don't want to do anything that might jeopardize Fran's case."

"But if I stay on the case—"

"Then we're back to Plan A."

"That's what I was afraid of." His hand relaxed its death grip on the sheets and moved to pull her onto his lap. He surrounded her with both arms and began to stroke his fingers along the sensitive skin of her inner thigh.

Cassie's body responded instantly to his touch. She tilted her head back, and he lowered his mouth to the side of her neck.

"What about Plan A?" she asked.

"Doesn't start until morning."

His fingers continued their work, and her pelvis arched in synchrony with their movements. "Don't start something you can't finish," she warned him.

"There's something you should know about me," he whispered as he nuzzled her ear. "I always finish what I begin. Always."

CHAPTER 44

"HEY, WAKE UP. It's late." Drake shook Hart's shoulder. She flopped over onto her stomach, ignoring him. "Come on. We still have to get your car, and I've a seven o'clock task force meeting."

"What time is it?" she mumbled without lifting her head.

"Six fifteen."

"Five more minutes."

"That's what you said twenty minutes ago. Twenty minutes that we could have spent together in the shower."

"Go 'way."

"Maybe this will help." He opened the lid of his travel mug, and held the steaming cup of coffee near her face. She unearthed her face and turned it toward the coffee, eyes still closed. "Have a drink, then get some clothes on."

One brown eye popped open and took in his clean shirt and jeans. "You're dressed."

"Seemed like a good idea." She reached for the coffee. Drake pulled it out of reach so that she was forced to sit up. Then he gave it to her, and she took two deep swallows.

"Good coffee," she mumbled, her eyes still at half-mast. She shivered as the covers fell away from her naked body. "Cold. Need clothes."

"Your wish is my command. Just get a move on, will you?" Drake easily dodged the pillow she hurled at him. "You always this cranky when you wake up?"

"I am when I've only gotten an hour of sleep," she called after him.

"Who's fault was that?" He returned with her clothes as she emerged from the bathroom smelling of mouthwash. She lifted the coffee mug to her lips one more time, then dressed with rapid, efficient movements, never once looking at the mirror.

"All right, let's go." She stepped into her boots and grabbed the mug. "You're going to be late."

They shared the coffee as Drake drove them back to the Westinghouse warehouse and Hart's Impreza.

"If Trautman didn't kill Fran, who did?" she asked.

"I don't know. Trautman certainly fits for the FX. We reconstructed his work schedule and correlated it with the treatment failures Weaver found. But using the cell phone to set you up to witness Weaver's killing, why? You're no threat to him. You said yourself you only knew him by sight. And why would Weaver know him at all? She wouldn't have access to the work schedules—how did she discover him? The whole thing doesn't make sense."

Drake frowned. "So far we have no idea who was working with him. It would have to be someone familiar with the pharmacy routine at Three Rivers."

"Guess this blows your one big dealer theory."

"That's all right. Getting that much FX off the street is worth a blown theory." He pulled alongside her car.

Drake turned to her, wanting to memorize everything—from the tousled, unbrushed hair, to the smell of coffee, Listerine, and stale sweat. It didn't matter how unromantic the details were, they were what made Hart who she was. The thought of not seeing her, not touching her, made him seriously consider asking Miller for reassignment. "This is goodbye. For a while, anyhow."

"Not so long. Just until you find Fran's killer."

"Optimist."

"No, just the opposite. But I have faith in you."

He looked up at that, surprised by the quiet, earnest tone of her words. He wished he was as confident in his abilities as she was. After what happened last summer, he had his own doubts.

Hart seemed to read his mind. She took his face between her hands, pulled him closer to her.

"You'll find him. I know it," she whispered. She kissed him deeply and, before he could draw in a breath, she was gone.

⊷⊚⊷

CASSIE CAUGHT HERSELF humming Eric Clapton as she went through her front door, kicking her shoes onto the rug so that she wouldn't dirty the hard wood floors. It was a habit bred by years of Rosa's lectures. When she crossed the living room she saw the message light blinking furiously on her answering machine.

"I can't believe you!" came Adeena's voice on the first message. "You promised you wouldn't go there. Tessa heard it on the eleven o'clock news and told me! She's really upset, Cassie. I don't care if you lie to me, but you'd better not do anything to hurt that old lady. She wants you to call her tomorrow, or better yet . . . come over."

There was a click as she hung up. Cassie frowned. She couldn't face Tessa until she had some sleep, the old woman was as bad as Rosa with her lectures and interfering.

The second message was Ed Castro. "I saw Trautman

263

in the ER, the optho guys think they can save one of his eyes. Thought you'd like to know." He cleared his throat noisily. "I hope you're all right. Please. Be careful. Come talk to me anytime if you need to." The last came in a heartfelt rush.

"Cassie, are you okay?" Neil Sinderson's voice sounded concerned. "You were on the news. They said some drug dealer was trying to kill you. Do the police think he had anything to do with what happened to Fran? Gosh, I hope everything is all right. Give me a call or page me, I'm available 24/7. Whatever you need, I'm here."

The last message was Adeena again. "Hey, sorry I yelled. You know how I get when Tessa's upset. Anyway, I hope you're all right and I'll see you tomorrow. Take care now—and no more crazy stunts, okay? Love ya. Call me."

Cassie climbed the stairs in her stocking feet, thinking of a few more hours of sleep followed by a hot shower. She stripped in the bathroom, tossing her sweat and blood stained clothes into the hamper, changed into the T-shirt and sweatpants she used as pajamas, and crossed the hall into her room. She took two steps toward her bed.

The door slammed shut behind her.

"Morning, Ella."

CHAPTER 45

CASSIE SPUN AROUND. Richard leaned against the door, arms crossed, seemingly relaxed. Until she looked into his face. His pupils were dilated with either excitement or drugs, his mouth set with fury.

"Get out," she snapped, her own anger rising to match his. Even before he left for rehab, Richard never dared violate the sanctuary of her home. Shoulders hunched, jaw clenched tight, she squared off with him, refusing to be intimidated.

"You've kept me waiting." He ignored her command. "After I heard about Victor Trautman almost killing you, I was worried." He opened his hands to demonstrate his sincerity, as if he expected her to rush into them for comfort.

"I'm fine, Richard. Now, go." She fought to keep the anger from her voice. Richard never responded well to ultimatums, but this was her house and she was damned if she was going to beg him to leave.

"You're sure you're all right?" He stepped toward her. She stood her ground, kept her eyes focused on his, not liking what she saw. Fine. If he wanted a fight, they could have it right here and now—all the easier to document so the police could lock him up for a good long time.

"Yes. I just need some rest. Good-bye, Richard."

"You've hurt your hands. Let me see."

His tone was one of concern and his hand reached for hers. Cassie's glance dropped for an instant. He grabbed both her wrists, stepping so close she almost toppled onto the bed. She fought for balance, but couldn't kick at him without falling back. His grip tugging her arms forward, keeping her upright and pinned against him.

He pressed his body into hers, nuzzling her neck. "I can smell him. Taste him on you. You should have waited, Ella. A good wife would have."

"I'm not your wife anymore." She squirmed against him, trying to find space to kick, hit, escape.

"You're still mine, Ella. Forever."

Cassie fought to breathe. The scent of his cologne filled the room, polluting the air she gulped. "Richard, you need help." She tried to find some compassion for the man she once loved. There was none. "Let me go before I call the police."

His larger hands held her wrists in a stranglehold, tightened them until she gasped in pain.

"You won't do that, Ella. See, I finally figured it out. My problem had nothing to do with drinking or drugs. It was you. You never learned how to listen, how to give me what I needed, how to be a good wife. But this time you're going to."

He ground her delicate wrist bones together and she could no longer hide her wince. His eyes widened even farther and he abruptly released her, shoving her back onto the bed. He straddled her, sitting on her legs before she could kick at him, recapturing both her wrists in one hand, pinning them over her head.

"There, now we can talk in peace." He raised his free

hand, his leer widening when she flinched. He brushed her hair away from her face. His palm lingered, his flesh hot and slicked with sweat as he demonstrated his total control over her. The one thing she'd fought against during every second of their relationship.

She blinked against the burning behind her eyes. Her mouth was dry and her lips began to tingle, grow numb. Her chest was heaving, her panicked breathing fast, too fast.

"Let me go, Richard. Now." She tried to put all her pain and frustration into her voice, to find the voice of command she used in the ER. He responded by squeezing her neck, so tightly that she could barely breathe, much less speak. She tried to swallow, it hurt so bad tears came to her eyes. She focused instead on slowing her breathing before panic could cement its hold on her body.

"So here's my plan," he went on, oblivious to her pain. His voice took on a maniacal singsong, and she knew he must have been fantasizing about this moment. For how long?

"You're going to come home with me. Don't worry about clothes or anything." His lips curled into a sneer. He released her face, his palm bracing his weight as he leaned forward, his face inches from hers. "I doubt you'll be leaving the bedroom for awhile. You'll call Ed Castro, ask for an indefinite leave of absence. We're going to start over again."

"You're crazy." She managed to scrape the words together and force them past her bruised vocal cords. She didn't see his slap coming, had no time to prepare or recoil from it. Warm blood flowed from her nose.

"Did I say you could talk?" he bellowed. "You never learn, do you? A good wife listens and does what her husband tells her."

She wondered how he was faking his urine tests. It

was obvious he was on something. Probably a form of amphetamine. Then he would bring himself back down with a barbiturate or opiate like FX. Never before had Richard been so delusional, so out of control.

Which was least likely to get her killed? Playing along or fighting back? She stopped struggling against him, lay there placidly, and watched for her opportunity.

"Want do you want?"

"What every husband wants—his wife, at home, by his side, where she belongs. And that's what you're going to give me. You see, Ella, you forgot one small detail when you took up with that cop—yeah, I know who he really is, it's all over the news. You forgot about the cameras in the trauma rooms."

She froze. Swallowed back a groan. There was nothing Richard could threaten her with, she'd taken the worse he had to offer and had survived, but now he held Drake's career in his hand. For the first time she felt afraid, truly afraid.

"That's right. And I have the only copy from the other day." He shook his head. "Necking in the ER, your best friend barely cold. Imagine what the tabloids could make of it—detective fucking murder witness. I suppose any potential defense attorney would find it interesting. As will Drake's superiors. I checked into this guy, he's been in trouble before. Really Ella, you should use better judgment about who you get involved with."

He cupped her chin in his hand once more, his fingers caressing the bruises he'd caused. "We'll go home. It'll be just like old times, won't it?"

"Give me the tape. I won't tell anyone about you using drugs again," she bargained, hoping she wouldn't be forced to choose between Drake's future and her freedom.

"Wrong answer. You do as I say, and your boyfriend keeps his job. The only right answer is 'Yes Richard'." His face filled her vision, the rancid odor of his breath corrupting the air she breathed. Triumph etched his features into sharp relief. "Say it." He raised his hand for another strike.

He wanted her to resist, to give him a reason to hit her. She squeezed her eyes shut, unable to look at his face, her mind made up. Sorrow and guilt loosed the dam of tears that had built over the past few days. They burned as they slipped past her defenses.

"Yes, Richard," she said in a dull tone, opening her eyes, ignoring the sting of tears. Richard seemed fascinated by her crying—probably because it was the first time she'd ever wept in front of him. Her tears convinced him of her sincerity.

"Good girl. Let's celebrate our new understanding." His lips parted in anticipation, and he released her wrists as he reached down to fumble at his belt.

Cassie watched as he lowered his head. "Richard," she called sweetly.

He glanced up. She smashed her fist into his face.

"Not if you were the last man on earth."

He floundered off the bed, holding his nose. She leapt to her feet and gave him a solid kick in the groin. He doubled over, yelping like a wounded dog. Her muscles surged with adrenalin and unleashed fury. She brought her elbows down on the back of his head. His face ricocheted off the wood floor with a satisfying crack.

Before she could strike again, he scuttled away to the other side of the bed and climbed to his feet. Blood from his nose and split lip smeared his designer suit and silk shirt. Richard always was a clotheshorse.

"Get out of my house, now!"

"This isn't over." He pressed a silk handkerchief to his face. "You'll pay for this, Ella." He swept a hand across her dresser, scattering the few pieces of jewelry, ceramic ballerina, crystal vase and lamp to the floor with a shatter of breaking glass.

He started to advance on her, his face flushed with outrage. Cassie held her ground, her feet in a fighting stance.

"What's going on here?" Drake burst into the room at a run, his gun drawn. He surveyed the damage-strewn room and kept his gun on Richard. "Hart, are you all right?"

"I'm fine," she told him, catching Richard's eye.

"What happened?"

"Nothing, Detective." Richard smiled at her as he shook the creases back into his slacks. He ignored Drake's gun and moved past Drake to Cassie, nodding at her as if they had a bargain. "Just a little morning rendezvous. For old times sakes, you know."

Drake holstered his gun and grabbed Richard by the arm. "Get your hands off her!"

Richard looked down in amusement, then met Drake's eyes. "Surely, you're not arresting me, Detective?"

"Like hell, I'm not. Assault and battery—" Drake began.

Richard's laugh rang through the small room. "I think not."

"Let him go," Cassie said, the words tasting of ash in her mouth. Drake kept his hold on Richard.

"You can't be serious. Hart, think about—"

"She is thinking, Detective," Richard said. "Thinking of what's best for everyone involved." He tugged his arm from Drake's grip. Drake stared at his empty hand, then at Cassie.

"If I ever see you touch her again—"

"It's all right, Detective, I understand," Richard said. "My wife has that effect on men. Remember what I said," Richard told Cassie as he stalked from the room, smoothing the wrinkles in his Italian silk. "I'll see you tonight, Ella."

Drake spun to face Cassie. She knew he wanted to go after Richard. But she'd bought them a little time. She couldn't let him ruin that by arresting Richard now.

"Let him go," she repeated. Confusion swept across his face. She collapsed on the bed, shaking with adrenalin and anger.

The bed sighed as Drake sat down beside her. He placed his arm around her shoulders. She shrugged it off.

She considered telling him about Richard and the tape. What would she say? *My ex-husband comes from a rich and powerful family and wants to destroy you? Now, thanks to me, he has the means to do that.*

"Want to tell me what the hell is going on?" he finally said.

She had until tonight. She could find a way to make things right by then. She had to.

"Go away," she said. "Please, just go away."

After several long moments, Drake stood. She fell back against Rosa's quilt, the thick velvet embracing her, as she listened to his footsteps echoing down the stairs.

CHAPTER 46

CASSIE WIPED HER face on a corner of her shirt. Blood from her nose stained the white cotton. The least of her worries. She sat up, rolled her shoulders. What to do next? How to fix this mess?

A creak echoed through the stairway, and she tensed. Richard returning to finish things? Her pulse hammered in her head, and her palms grew clammy. She searched for a weapon, grabbed the lamp from the nightstand, and crouched near the door.

"Hart?"

Drake. Cassie almost dropped the lamp in her confusion. "I—I thought you'd left. What are you doing here?"

He said nothing, but took the lamp from her hand and replaced it on the nightstand. "He's gone. I've locked all the doors."

She looked at him in amazement. What was this man doing in her bedroom, talking as if nothing had happened?

DRAKE LOOKED OUT into the fenced in square of Hart's backyard. Wind gusted through fallen leaves, creating tiny whirlwinds that swirled across the garden. His mind reeled in time with the small dervishes.

"You left your cell phone," he said, his face still toward the window.

"I'm glad you came when you did." Her voice was tentative.

Drake spun around, both hands fisted at his sides. "What are you hiding from? What really happened here this morning?"

She kept her back to him, slumped down, hands dangling lifelessly between her knees. "It's none of your business," she said after a long silence.

That hurt, especially after last night. He moved around the bed and stood in front of her. "None of my business, or none of the police's business?"

She hung her head, veiling her face in a curtain of dark hair and was silent.

"Damn it! Just tell me."

"Who asked you for help? Have I ever asked you for anything?" She bounced to her feet and went to the door, holding it open. "Thank you for coming, Detective Drake. Please tell Commander Miller that I'll be in sometime later to give her my statement about last night."

"Want me to tell her you're too busy wallowing in self pity?" he asked, knowing it was cruel, a twist of the knife, but willing to do it if it returned her to her senses.

She glared at him, refused to rise to the bait. "Tell her the truth," she said in a calm voice. "I'm exhausted. I haven't gotten much sleep in the past few days."

"Why don't you call and tell her yourself? I'm not your messenger boy. I've a task force meeting I'm late for."

"Then I suggest you go now."

She wouldn't meet his eyes as he passed her, close

enough to touch. Drake reached out a hand, willing to stop this nonsense if she would, but he saw her recoil when he drew near. He walked down the steps without a backward glance.

To hell with her. To hell with everything except closing his case. He let himself out. He should have known better than to allow a woman to distract him from his work.

The words rang hollow. Especially as Drake realized they were the exact words he used after he had learned about Pamela's secret.

⋅⟨⊙⟩⋅

MILLER STOOD BESIDE Dimeo at the back of the conference room when Drake entered. Kwon shot him a look that said he was so busted. He took his customary seat behind Summers and slouched over the table, doodling on a notepad, making eye contact with no one.

"We found Trautman's lab in the basement of his aunt's house," one of the narcotics guys was saying. "Hazmat will have it cleared for processing later this morning. No signs of any of the drugs stolen from the pharmacy the night Weaver was killed."

"Phone records show several to his cell from Richard King," Summers said. "None to or from Hart."

Drake's teeth ground together at the mention of King and Hart.

"What else did Trautman say last night, Summers?" Kwon asked.

Summers darted a glance at Drake before answering. "Said he caught Hart stealing FX from the ER. He was blackmailing her, and she asked to meet him on the bridge to, uh, negotiate."

Drake's pen tore through the top pages of his

notepad, leaving an ugly gouge behind. No way. Trautman was a lying piece of shit, just trying to cover his own ass. Hart wouldn't, couldn't—

"So, do we believe him or Hart's story that she was just in the wrong place at the wrong time?" Miller asked the group.

Silence. Drake felt the weight of his team's eyes upon him. He remained silent, not looking up, his gaze boring a hole through the table.

"Seems like an awfully big coincidence to me," Dimeo said.

"Did anyone talk to this social worker, Adeena Coleman, yet? The one who was supposed to be there with Hart?"

Drake jerked his head up. Talking to Coleman wasn't such a bad idea. "I'll do it," he volunteered, ignoring the stares of surprise the others sent his way.

"Fine," Miller said. "You take Coleman, and Kwon can interview Hart when she comes in later."

Drake glanced over. Kwon's smile was that of a predator circling in on its prey. Who cared? Hart could take care of herself—wasn't that what she kept telling him? She didn't need him to defend her with Kwon. She only needed him to find Weaver's killer.

In other words, to do his job.

⋅✦⋅

CASSIE WATCHED DRAKE'S car pull away from the curb and sighed in relief. God, the man was stubborn. And she didn't like the way he could see right through her—almost to her soul, it seemed. No one else had ever done that, except for Rosa, but she'd never felt confused by Rosa's uncanny abilities.

Drake scared her, and the fact that she was allowing

him into her life, her world. The way her body responded, compelled by the merest glimpse of him. Worse, the way she seemed to be coming to depend on him.

She wished he could help her now, but she refused to risk his career. Or justice for Fran.

She shook her head, chewing on her lower lip. She could fix this, make this right. Somehow. She owed it to Drake.

The phone rang. "Cassie, it's Adeena. The neurologists said Jane Doe's EEG is looking better. It might take awhile, but she's going to make it."

At least something was going right today. "That's great. How about my other patient, Brian Winston?"

Adeena's silence told Cassie all she needed to know. Hell. "They're considering withdrawing life support," she finally said. "I'm sorry. When Jane Doe—"

"Sarah," she interrupted. "Her real name is Sarah."

"How—you found out who she is?"

"Just her first name and a few other hints." Cassie looked at her rumpled bed. She wasn't going to get any sleep or any peace, not after what happened this morning. "I'll be in shortly and explain everything."

A shower did little to revive her. She jogged up the steps to the ICU at half her usual pace, muscles complaining every step of the way. Adeena was waiting at the nurses' station.

"I need to apologize about those angry messages I left," the social worker told her when Cassie took the seat beside her. "I was worried."

"You were right. I shouldn't have gone on my own." Cassie shuddered. "The way those kids are living out there."

"The news said a drug dealer tried to kill you."

"Guy named Trautman, he's an orderly on Orthopedics."

"Did he kill Fran?"

"No. But I think he's getting Richard drugs that aren't showing up on his urine tests."

"Richard? You'd think he learned his lesson already."

"If Sarah wakes up, maybe she knows who Trautman is working with and can help the police find Fran's killer." Cassie flipped to the neurologist's note, pleased with the optimistic tone. She leaned back. "One of the kids said she was from Indiana or Ohio. And another," she frowned, trying to remember Sherry's incoherent ramblings, "said something about a horse and buggy when I showed her Sarah's picture. She was high on something, so who knows what that means."

"I'll add the information to the database."

She walked over to bed space four. Sarah looked like any skinny teenager sleeping, as if you could rouse her with a simple prod and a reminder that school was waiting. But her slumber went much deeper. Her brain had been oxygen deprived. It would be a miracle if she woke completely intact. The neurologists, although now hopeful that someday she would wake, weren't making any bets on that.

Cassie stroked Sarah's hair, and then tucked it behind the girl's ears. Adeena joined her. "Guess there's nothing more we can do but wait."

"There has to be something," Cassie said. "She's so alone."

She wished Rosa was here. She'd find someway to help the girl, even if it was just to spoon homemade soup into her, and fatten her up. Thinking of Rosa led to Drake and their conversation the night before, when he laughed at the idea of gypsy curses, and she told him about Rosa and Padraic. Rosa had sacrificed for Padraic, and she'd been shunned by her own people.

Cassie froze, her gaze riveted on the irregular earring

holes in Sarah's earlobes. "These were all home made, weren't they?"

Adeena leaned forward to look. "Probably. So, she didn't have money to go to Station Square and get them done professionally."

"Most girls her age have their ears pierced—"

"Maybe her parents were cheap. What are you doing?" Cassie had opened the girl's mouth and was looking at her teeth.

"They didn't believe in orthodontists, either." She closed Sarah's mouth, hiding the crooked teeth and overbite once more. "There are a lot of Amish in Ohio and Indiana, aren't there?"

Adeena looked at her and smiled in comprehension. "Horse and buggy. I'll get a list of county sheriffs and start calling." She left for her office.

Cassie held the girl's hand, wishing Sarah would squeeze hers back. The street-worn drug addict might be a runaway farm girl. Who would have guessed? So many things were not what they seemed. Sometimes you had to keep probing to discover what was hidden beneath the surface.

Fran's last message ran through her mind. The FX was just the tip of the iceberg, she'd said. Cassie released Sarah's hand and straightened. She looked at the clock. Five minutes before noon. Perfect timing. If Fran meant what she thought she meant, she might just have found a clue to her killer.

Cassie planted a quick kiss on Sarah's forehead and rushed from the ICU.

CHAPTER 47

THE TASK FORCE meeting finally broke up, and Kwon walked upstairs to the Major Crimes Squad with Drake.

"My money's on the doctor. Your friend, Hart. I'll bet she set up that meet on the bridge."

"No, it wasn't that way," he said, not making eye contact. "She went to the Barn trying to help her patient find her family." It sounded feeble even to him.

Kwon made a small clicking noise with her tongue. Usually that sound indicated that some bad guy was about to have his story shredded to pieces and fed to him with an accompaniment of sarcasm.

Only this time they weren't talking about some skel from the streets. They were talking about Hart.

"Look at it, DJ," she said, walking him through the evidence as if he were a rookie. "You said yourself you had doubts that Trautman was the only actor involved in the FX thefts. What if the good doctor is in it with him? The brains behind the brawn, so to speak. We know her ex is a user, why not her as well?"

"She's the one who came to us," Drake reminded her. "Without her, we'd never have tripped to Trautman."

Kwon nodded, her eyes gleaming as she pieced everything together. "Of course. She reads about the task force. She knows it's just a matter of time, and figures she'll cut her losses. She gives you Trautman, but she's afraid he'll spill the beans, so she decides to kill him. Something goes wrong. He fights back, and throws her off the bridge in time for you to play hero and rescue her."

Drake clenched his fists and shook his head. He knew he should tell Kwon about the scene this morning between King and Hart, but it'd only give her more ammunition.

"What about Weaver? You can't hang that one on Hart."

"You've only her word it wasn't Trautman who offed Weaver," Kwon said. "The guard didn't see squat. Maybe Weaver found out about Hart and Trautman. What better way to deflect suspicion and know everything the police are thinking than to sleep with the lead detective?" Kwon didn't pull any punches. "I'm telling you DJ, she's a slick piece of work."

Drake hung his head. Her words were a gale force wind, battering him.

"You know I have to check it out."

Drake nodded. He knew. Just as the cop in him knew Kwon could be right about Hart. But the man in him prayed she was wrong.

He grimaced and shook his head, moving to take a seat at his regular desk. A pile of case files and memos had stacked up in his in-box during the weeks he'd been assigned to the task force. He busied himself by sorting them as Kwon continued.

"Think she'd be dumb enough to keep any evidence where we could find it? The drugs stolen from the pharmacy, or a gun with her prints on it would be a nice start."

He turned his face away, scrutinizing the latest directive on firearms re-qualification. Great, just what he didn't need. He dreaded the annual re-certification. The results were always the same: Kwon and Jimmy Dolan vying for top honors while Drake would be near the bottom. Who cared anyway? His father had lived through thirty years on the job without shooting anyone. Drake wadded the memo and spun it through the air. It hit the miniature backboard hanging over the wastebasket and ricocheted off onto the floor.

Could Hart have fooled him so completely? The annual memo delineating the Bureau's sexual harassment policy flew through the air and joined the first. He didn't think so, it was too easy to read her every emotion on her face, she didn't seem capable of such subterfuge. He was certain that she had feelings for him—or was that just pride talking? Then what was she hiding from him? Why couldn't she tell him the truth?

"What do you think? Try for a warrant for her house, or locker at work?" Kwon scooped up Drake's two erstwhile basketballs and crossed the room with them. Nothing but net, times two. "Think we have probable cause?"

Drake looked up as Jimmy Dolan, his regular partner, entered the squad room. The burly ex-marine was fresh from court, dressed in a navy wool suit, dark purple tie.

Jimmy nodded to him. "You done clearing the streets of vermin and scum, rescuing damsels in distress, and ready to come back to the real job?" He joined them, unbuttoning his overcoat and removing his fedora. "What's the matter? The *Post-Gazette* get your name spelled wrong or something?" Jimmy looked over at Kwon, a question in his eyes.

Kwon shrugged and rolled her eyes. "I'll leave you

two love birds alone," she told them. "I want to get my ducks in order before I tackle Hart's interview."

CHAPTER 48

JIMMY DOLAN WATCHED Drake's face close down and gave an inward groan. "Bloody hell, not again," he muttered, his meaty hand grabbing Drake's coat from the chair and shoving it at his partner. "C'mon, DJ, it's time for lunch."

To his surprise, Drake didn't argue. Oh boy, this was bad. He led his younger partner down the steps and out into the brisk February air. Jimmy looked up at the thickening clouds. Snow or rain soon depending on how cold it got. He glanced back at DJ, considered driving, but decided the walk would do them both good.

"So what's the story, kid?" he asked as they walked down Penn toward the Blarney Stone.

Drake shoved his hands deep into the pockets of his peacoat in response. Jimmy ignored the silence. DJ was a good partner. One of the best damned investigators he'd worked with. That included Mickey Drake Sr., which was saying a lot.

"Damn. You sure are high maintenance. Like a goddamn thoroughbred or something. Haven't see you this low since last summer." Denise, his wife, still blamed that on him. As if somehow Jimmy was responsible for who his partner took to his bed. That was women for you. One look at DJ, and they all wanted nothing more than to either mother him or screw him. Or both.

Jimmy shot a glance over at his silent partner. What the hell had the kid gotten mixed up in this time?

They turned the corner onto Aiken and came to the Blarney Stone. Jimmy opened the brass-handled door, gestured for Drake to precede him. His partner went inside, eyes downcast, like a teenager headed toward a strapping.

Which was how he acted sometimes. Jimmy nodded to Andy Greally behind the bar and slid into an empty booth.

Andy began to pull a Guinness. He added two coffees and joined them, forcing Drake into the corner seat by the window. Andy set the Guinness in front of Jimmy and placed the coffees before himself and Drake.

"How was court?" he asked Jimmy, while appraising Drake. The younger man seemed fascinated by the view of the alley beyond.

"I think we nailed the bastard." Jimmy took a large drink of stout and sighed in contentment. "Of course, you never know with juries."

"Ain't that the truth." Andy jerked his head toward Drake. "What's with the kid?"

Jimmy shrugged. "He's not saying. Found him like this when I got back to the House."

Andy pursed his lips. Drake Sr. had been his partner before Mickey won his sergeant's stripes. Andy had taken on his son as a rookie, training him. After Mickey died, it seemed like Jimmy and Andy became surrogate fathers to DJ—but the kid didn't make it easy.

"I think," Jimmy went on when Drake remained silent, "it has something to do with that girl he pulled off the bridge last night."

"She's not a girl, and it's none of your business,"

Drake snapped.

Andy and Jimmy exchanged glances. Bingo. Then Jimmy frowned. "Is she the same Hart Kwon was talking about?" he asked, putting the pieces together. Drake's look of misery was answer enough.

"You mean the pretty doctor you brought in the other day? The one that showed Spanos his place?" Andy asked. Drake nodded. "I thought she was a witness—"

"Murder," Drake said. "Janet thinks Hart is involved in Weaver's murder."

Jimmy raised an eyebrow at that. This was getting interesting. "How'd she do it?"

Drake set his cup down with a bang. "She didn't!"

"Whoa, looked who joined the ACLU all the sudden. All right then, how did our innocent until proven guilty suspect allegedly kill Weaver?"

"Kwon and Dimeo want to nail Hart's ex, Richard King, so they're building this big conspiracy theory that Hart set up Weaver, and that Hart is working with Trautman and her ex."

"Why does Janet think it was Hart?" Jimmy asked, knowing Kwon didn't usually jump to conclusions without a good reason. "Why not just the ex?"

"Trautman implicated her. And Hart was there when Weaver died." Drake looked up at them. "She tried to save her, she didn't have anything to do with it."

"So why are you yelling at us and moping around like a teenager who's been grounded?" Jimmy threw back at him. Then comprehension dawned. "Christ, DJ, you didn't go and sleep with her, did you? Even you can't be that stupid!"

Drake whipped his head around. "Keep it down, will you?"

"He is that stupid," Andy put in. "Sleeping with a witness and now she's a suspect in a homicide? What were you thinking?"

Both of the older men glared at Drake like he was a kid caught playing hooky.

"Didn't you learn anything from last summer?" Jimmy muttered, his voice low.

"It's not like that. Hart is—"

"Going to ruin your career if Miller gets wind of it," Andy finished for him. "You'd better pray your girlfriend is innocent or there'll be hell to pay."

Andy treated them to lunch while Drake poured out a carefully edited account of his relationship with Hart. Afterward both of the older men shook their heads over his foolishness.

"You actually went over to her house this morning?" Andy asked.

Drake nodded. "To return her cell phone."

"And you found her there with her ex? This . . . King?"

"You sure they're not in it together, setting you up for a fall?"

"Or maybe King is setting up the missus?" Jimmy suggested, having the more devious mind. "It's an impossible case to prove any way you look at it. No witnesses worth anything. And no one would be fool enough to keep the evidence."

Andy shrugged. "So who cares about evidence? Go talk to this King guy, rattle his cage. Maybe he'll do something stupid."

Jimmy frowned at the retired cop's cavalier suggestion to stretch the rules. "Just don't you do something stupid," he warned Drake. "Like getting this guy so pissed he complains to Miller about you. After all, he saw you at Hart's house."

"Yeah, but he didn't know why I was there." Drake brightened at the idea of questioning King. "I think I'll head over to Three Rivers right now."

Andy watched through the window as Drake walked past the mouth of the alley, a spring in his step.

"He's in big trouble and he don't even know it," he told Jimmy. "How'd a smart guy like him get to be so dumb about women?"

Jimmy shrugged. "Dunno. You trained him."

"Yeah, well, you're his partner. You're supposed to keep him out of shit like this."

"Now you sound like Denise." Jimmy finished the last golden drop of Guinness. "And," he said, easing out of the booth and grabbing his hat, "since it's my day off and the kids are at school, I think I'll just go on home and give her a nice surprise."

"Nice for who?" Andy jeered as Jimmy slid into his coat.

·◦◦·

CASSIE PAUSED OUTSIDE of the pharmacy and checked her watch. Twelve-ten. Gary Krakov always, always took his lunch exactly at noon. She took a deep breath and pushed open the door.

The pharmacy workers barely glanced her way, too busy helping Neil Sinderson with a cartload of medications. She crossed through the front room, flinching as she passed Fran's empty workstation, and placed her hand on the door to Krakov's office.

What if it was locked? Then what would she do?

She turned the knob. It was open. Cassie slipped through the door and shut it behind her.

"Can I help you?"

She jumped. A young man sat at Krakov's computer and looked up at her with a smile.

"Who are you?" Cassie asked.

"Mike Romano. They sent me over from Information

Management to help Mr. Krakov finish his inventory."

She caught her breath and forced herself to smile. "Then you're just the person I want to see," she told him, daring to perch on Krakov's pristine desk. "I'm Dr. Hart from the ER—"

"You're the one who tried to save Fran." Mike's eyes darted toward the door and Fran's abandoned desk beyond. His voice dropped. "Is this something to help catch the killer?" He leaned forward, eager to be part of the investigation.

"Yes. So it has to be kept confidential, all right?" She felt a twinge of guilt, hoped she wasn't going to have this kid on her conscience, too.

"Sure. What do you need?" His fingers poised over the computer keyboard, ready for action.

"I need some way of comparing the most expensive drugs with patients who died. I thought maybe I could get a list of the drugs that cost the most from Mr. Krakov, take them to medical records, and compare them with recent patient deaths."

"You don't need to do that, I can do it all right here." He patted his computer.

Cassie looked over her shoulder. "When is Mr. Krakov coming back?" If she was right about Krakov, then he couldn't find out what Mike was doing for her.

"He isn't. One of the pharmacists upstairs in the ICU called in sick, so he's covering. He told me I could have his office to use since he won't be back today."

One less thing to worry about. "All right. Could you bring the information to my office when you're done?"

"Sure thing. I still have to finish the inventory for Mr. Krakov, so it'll probably be tomorrow."

His fingers started dancing over the keys, reminding her of the last time she saw Fran alive. She gnawed at her lip. She hoped she wasn't making a big mistake, but there was no other way to get the information.

If Fran's death had nothing to do with the missing FX but something else that she found, then Gary Krakov was the only logical suspect. The only man who knew Fran was working late, who could have known what Fran had uncovered, maybe even accessed her computer.

"Mike, don't tell anyone about this."

He didn't look up at that, merely nodded, already lost in the realms of cyberspace. "Whatever you say, doc."

CHAPTER 49

DRAKE CAUGHT UP with King as the surgeon was leaving his office.

"What can I do for you, Detective?" he asked Drake with a smirk on his face.

King had changed from his operating scrubs back into the well-draped silk suit Drake had seen him in this morning. It probably cost more than Drake took home in a month.

More priceless than the suit was the darkening swelling engulfing King's left eye. Hart's work. Drake couldn't help but smile.

King bristled under Drake's gaze. He locked his office door behind him. "I really must be going, Detective."

Drake leaned against the tiled corridor wall, hands jammed into the pockets of his jeans, taking his time. "Trautman worked with you."

"Not just with me. He was assigned to the orthopedic patients, not any one surgeon. Really, Detective." King smiled, his teeth unnaturally white, gleaming in the fluorescent lights. "My wife is waiting for me."

"Ex-wife," Drake corrected, standing straight,

stretching to his full height.

"Cassandra vowed to love, honor and cherish for the rest of her life. You don't know her like I do. When she makes a promise, it's for life. She's still mine."

"What's your hold on her, King?" Drake did not care for the other man's proprietary tone.

King flashed another smile. "I assure you, Detective, Cassandra makes her own choices, and has a will of her own. Of course, you've seen first hand how passionate she can be."

Drake twisted his fist in King's Italian silk and pushed the surgeon against the wall.

"Why you were there this morning?" he asked, his face inches away from King's.

King never flinched. "Really, Detective, I have no idea what you're talking about. There's no need to get so emotional about it. Of course," his grin widened, "there is the question of why you were at Ella's house this morning, isn't there?"

Drake slammed his palm into the tile wall a hairbreadth away from King's face. The sound echoed loud as a gunshot. A medical student entering a room further down the hallway looked over at them.

"Everything all right, Dr. King?" she called, cradling her clipboard close to her chest as if to shield her from the violence emanating from the two men.

Drake forced himself to open his fist and release King.

The surgeon smoothed out his shirt and smiled at the student. "Everything's fine, Maria." King lounged against the wall, watching Drake intently. "Cassandra's an intriguing woman, isn't she, Detective? So full of passion. She gets that from her Grandmother Rosa, you know. A gypsy witch from the old country.

"Ella's no different," King continued. "Believe me, I

know how she can turn a man's mind, twist his thoughts, make him do things he'd never consider otherwise." He paused and gave Drake a hard stare.

"You haven't come under her influence, have you, Detective Drake?" Then King laughed, a hollow sound that echoed off the tiled walls. "Of course not. You're a police officer, a man of reason. You'd never fall for Cassandra or her witchy ways." King strode down the hall. "Good bye, Detective. And good luck."

As Drake watched King go, he had the sudden urge to pound his fist into something. Like King's face. He swallowed the anger, unwilling to give the surgeon the satisfaction of seeing that his words had hit close to home.

✦

CASSIE STOOD AT the foot of Trautman's bed and watched the nurse change the bag of IV fluid. Dressed in scrubs and her white coat, the guard at the door hadn't questioned her entry. Trautman's eyes were both heavily bandaged. The silver gleam of handcuffs was visible above his right hand. She waited for the nurse to leave, rolled her shoulders, and took a deep breath before moving forward to wake the sleeping man.

"I've got to talk to you," she began.

Trautman stirred, a frown creasing between his thick eyebrows. His free arm waved toward her. "Who's there?"

She held her ground and said nothing. There was still time to back out. But this was the only plan she could think of, the only way to protect Drake. If Trautman knew who killed Fran, she could keep Richard out of it and Drake could make an arrest before Richard could do anything to discredit him.

Her hands clenched into tight fists. She spoke again. "I need to know, did you have her killed? Did you send someone to kill Fran?"

His head snapped in her direction. "Come closer, bitch and I'll tell you," he snarled. "Come see what you done to me!"

"Tell me the truth, and I'll drop my charges against you," she continued, hoping he couldn't hear the lie.

"Why should I tell you anything? I've got a lawyer, I don't need to talk to anyone."

"Your lawyer won't do you any good if I testify against you."

"King promised me he wouldn't let that happen. You testify against me, you're a dead woman. I may be blind, but I still got two good hands." He rattled the handcuff chain against the bed rail and lunged in her direction, grabbing her sleeve. "Maybe I'll do the job myself, and get me some satisfaction."

Instead of pulling away, she allowed him to believe he had the upper hand. "Just tell me about Fran," she pleaded, trying to sound weak instead of repulsed.

"I don't know any Fran, you stupid bitch." His speech was beginning to slur. His fingers slipped away from her arm.

"Now, go way, I don't feel so good." The last emerged in a drunken stutter. Trautman slumped back, all color drained from his face. His arm hung slackly over the bed rail.

"Trautman—" Cassie pinched his arm, trying to elicit some response. The man had fallen unconscious. She felt his pulse, it was weak and rapid. Then his arm flailed at her as he began to convulse.

She yanked the code alert from the wall. An alarm sounded in the hallway. She lowered the head of the bed and began to administer oxygen. The guard from outside Trautman's door ran inside.

"What happened?"

"He's seizing. Grab the code cart and get some help!"

"Ah, shit!" The guard ran back out into the hall. Soon the room was crowded with the crash cart, several nurses, and the guard who stood in the doorway, watching his prisoner as if he expected Trautman to leap to his feet and make a run for it.

"Does he have a history of seizures?" Cassie asked the nurse with Trautman's chart while she injected Valium into the IV. "What meds is he on?"

"No history of a seizure disorder, no known allergies. Only meds are Mefoxitin and Tylenol with Codeine."

Cassie reached for the medication bag attached to the IV. The label read Mefoxitin, a broad-spectrum antibiotic. She disconnected the IV and checked for any hives or other signs of an allergic reaction. Nothing.

They pushed another dose of Valium. Finally the seizure stopped, but so did his breathing.

"Damn it." She moved to the head of the bed and prepared to intubate. "Call for an ICU bed and page the attending on call for medicine." The nurse dialed the phone. Her comrade finished connecting monitor leads and ran a blood pressure.

"Heart rate dropping and I can't get a BP," she announced.

"I'm in." Cassie grabbed her stethoscope. "Keep bagging him." She looked at the monitor tracing. Heart rate was irregular and he was starting to throw PVC's. "Get me a tox screen, metabolic panel, and blood gas." Maybe one of Trautman's friends had somehow slipped him some drugs? What else could be going on here? "What's his blood sugar?"

"Hang on a sec, it's running." The nurse frowned over the small glucometer. "That can't be right. It says twenty— that's as low as it goes."

All right, finally something to treat. "Push an amp of

D50."

"No pulse! He's flatline!"

CHAPTER 50

"I KNOW WE got off on the wrong foot," Drake told Adeena Coleman, "but I need your help."

She gestured to the chair beside her desk and gave him a measured look. "Actually, I owe you an apology, Detective. I jumped the gun the other day. It's just so unlike Cassie to allow herself to lean on anyone for comfort, that I assumed—"

"I took advantage."

"Yes. I'm sorry. What can I help you with?"

"I need to understand why Hart is shielding her ex. Twice now I've come across them in circumstances that lead me to believe—hell, I know—that he's physically abusive. But she refuses to press charges or let me do anything. I confronted King, and he implied that she's protecting him because they're still involved. What kind of hold does he have on Hart?" The last came out in a rush, he leaned forward, waiting her response.

She shook her head. "I know what Rosa would say to that."

"I don't want more cryptic sayings. I've never met Rosa, but I'm already certain I don't like her."

"Don't be so quick to judge. You and Rosa would have butted heads—lord knew she and Cassie did, constantly—but I think she would like you. And you'd like her. It's because of Rosa that Cassie's who she is."

He sighed. Why couldn't she just give him a straight answer? Something he could take to Kwon and Dimeo, and use to nail King's ass.

"So Hart lets her dead grannie control her life from beyond the grave?" He raised an eyebrow. "I don't buy it."

"In my job it's not enough to only look at my client," she started. "I have to know the history, the family background, the supports available, the strengths and weaknesses of everyone involved so that I know what kind of services would be most helpful."

"Cut the social services crap, you know what I'm asking."

"It's not that simple. Do you know how Cassie's parents died?"

"Ed Castro told me he was there—"

"I know. When she was born, the first hands to touch her . . . Ed loves that story. Caitlyn, Cassie's mom, had cancer diagnosed during the pregnancy. She refused treatment for fear it would hurt the baby and died three days after Cassie was born."

Drake blinked. Christ, what a burden to lay on a kid.

"Her father, Patrick, died in a car accident when Cassie was twelve. Cassie was with him, and went to get help, but when she got back it was too late. So then it was just her and Rosa. Not that Patrick had ever been fully there for Cassie. He was a nice man, a wonderful father, but somehow it always seemed as if part of him was absent. It was as if when he held Cassie's hand in his, his other hand was always still reaching out for Caitlyn's."

"He couldn't give her up," Drake murmured, ghostly images flashing through his mind. "My dad died seven years ago. It devastated my mom, but she's been able to move on, get a life back." He'd never thought about the courage and strength that must have taken. He had been too busy with his own life. Drake promised himself that when this was all over he was going to take a vacation to visit his mother.

"Patrick and Caitlyn were soul mates in the true sense of the word," Adeena said. "But that doesn't make it any easier for a kid growing up, unable to command her father's attention when he's living with the ghosts of the past."

That explained Hart's home, a mausoleum for the family ghosts, not a house of the living.

"She thought she and King would have a love like that," he guessed. "When it didn't turn out that way—"

"Cassie did what she does best: she tried to fix everything. I blame myself partly, Richard had me fooled. I never twigged to the abuse until Cassie had already left him. She has a tendency to retreat, to go into a private mourning where she shuts out the outside world. Some would call it a situational depression. The first time I saw her do it we were nine, and her grandfather had died. Same thing happened after her father and Rosa passed. Took her weeks after she left Richard to leave her house to re-enter the world again."

"Why couldn't you or Castro get her help? Surely there's treatments, medications—"

"We tried. By being there for her when she's ready. It's what works for her. Rosa used to say 'small sorrows bring loud wails, great sorrows bring great silence.' She might've been a crazy old lady, but a lot of the time she was right. Why do you think Cassie's so passionate about her patients, her work? She's learned that the only way to live is to give it all or nothing."

He remembered the silent sobs he had feared would

choke Hart after Weaver died. "So, when Hart turned to me after Fran died—"

"It wasn't her usual pattern, which is why I suspected you of coercing her." Adeena smiled, laying her hand on his. "Now I see she was right to turn to you. You two seem to complement each other. Maybe you can help Cassie strike a balance. There are no gray areas in her life."

Drake frowned. Shades of gray. That was where he lived. Skirting shadows, fading into the background, following the rules to gather evidence, hunting all the details necessary to put a case together. He treated women the same way. He took what he wanted or needed at the time, and pulled back when they got too close. He had it down to a science.

His art was the only part of his life where he felt free to lose control. Until he met Hart. Now Drake was breaking all the rules that had grounded him for so very long.

He ran his fingers through his hair, and closed his eyes for a moment. God, he was tired. "King kept saying that it's her own choice, but I know something else is going on."

"She doesn't love him anymore, if that's what's worrying you. That died a long time ago. But, knowing Cassie, she still feels responsible for his actions."

"Why?"

"If he had the power to hurt someone, and she could stop him—then, King is right, she would do all she could to protect someone." Her eyes narrowed, and she looked at him. "Especially if it was someone she cared for."

Adeena's cell sounded. She glanced at the reading and frowned. "I'm late for a meeting."

"No problem. Thanks for your help. Other than King, Hart seems to have very good taste in her friends."

She smiled, gathering an armful of file folders. He opened the door for her. "Don't hold Richard against her.

No woman could have withstood his charms. Once Richard sets his mind to getting something, he won't take no for an answer."

"This time neither will I."

⋅⦿⋅

THERE WAS A flurry of activity as one nurse injected the glucose into Trautman's IV while another straddled him and began chest compressions. The hospital intercom began announcing the code and a breathless stream of residents, anxious to help, crowded into the room.

"Glucagon and epi are in," Cassie said. "Where are my lab results?" There weren't many drugs she could use to treat hypoglycemia and an absent pulse. Electricity wouldn't help, nor would any of the anti-arrhythmic agents. "Get me another glucose reading."

A respiratory tech took over bagging, and a medical student relieved the nurse doing CPR. An intern began a second IV while the charge nurse detailed the events to the senior resident.

"Still twenty," the nurse said.

"Damn it, it's not circulating. Push another amp of D50 and follow it with a fluid bolus," Cassie ordered. The medicine attending entered. She quickly filled him in, but he shook his head when asked if he had any other ideas.

"You're doing everything. How long's he been down?"

"Too long." Cassie tensed her shoulders in frustration. First, she had been powerless to save Fran and now the only link to her killer was dying before her eyes. Trautman hadn't killed Fran. But he might know who had.

Past tense, she thought with regret. "All right. Let's call it." The crowd around Trautman's body dispersed as Cassie stepped forward and lay her fingers over his carotid artery. Then she listened to his heart with her stethoscope.

The only sound she heard was the single monotonous note sounded by the monitor. "Nothing. He's gone."

A nurse turned the monitor off and for a single breath the room was silent.

"Leave everything," Cassie told the nurses as the room cleared of personnel. "The police will want an autopsy." She examined the IV bag once more, this time without touching it and adding more fingerprints. As much as she'd wanted Trautman to talk, someone else had wanted Trautman silent—permanently.

And she knew exactly who that someone might be.

CHAPTER 51

"DO YOU HAVE any idea how many prints there are in a hospital room?" Janet Kwon asked as she supervised the CSU techs from the doorway of Trautman's room. "They're second only to hotel rooms. Don't be expecting any miracles. Just getting all the elimination prints is going to take a few days." She nodded to the photographer and moved aside to allow the coroner's team approach the body.

"Yeah, right," Drake mumbled, his attention on the corpse before him and the debris scattered around the room. He'd arrived only to find that while he'd been trying to understand what was going on with Hart, she'd been hip deep in another suspicious death. "Where's Hart?"

"I sent her down to wait in her office," Kwon replied, her mouth twisted into a frown of disapproval. "Summers is canvassing the staff, seeing who had access to the medications. Which is pretty much anyone. Including Hart."

"What about her ex, King?"

She shrugged. "No one mentioned seeing him near Trautman, but he has other patients on the floor. They could be in it together, or it could be either one of them separately."

Drake kicked at the doorjamb. "Any ideas to cause?"

"Best guess? Someone added insulin to his IV. Fast acting, easy to get, undetectable at autopsy." Kwon gestured for him to follow her. She led him down the hall to the medication room beside the nurses' station. "Everything's locked up, except it turns out insulin is refrigerated." She swung the door of the small dorm-size refrigerator open, revealing rows of bottles and stacks of IV bags. "And there's no surveillance cameras. In fact, there's almost no surveillance anywhere except the parking deck, the psych ward, the nursery, and a few areas where they tape for teaching purposes."

"It's a big hospital, no way they would be able to monitor the cameras even if they were there. And patient confidentiality—"

"Just remind me to never be a patient here. My luck, I'd get that orderly creep I saw sneaking into rooms at night. Who knows what else goes on around here that no one knows about?"

Drake understood her frustration. "Who tipped you to the insulin deal?"

"Would you believe, Hart? I'm telling you, DJ, she's no good."

"Why, because she tried to save the guy?"

"Big question is: what was she doing here in the first place? The guy almost killed her last night, and she was alone in the room with him when he went downhill. I asked around. The docs say an OD of insulin acts fast, within five, ten minutes."

"She didn't do it." Couldn't have. But the evidence against her was mounting fast.

"How do we prove this insulin theory?" he asked, composing himself enough to stand and turn back to face

Kwon.

"Hart said to test the IV bag. It's labeled as an antibiotic, so there shouldn't be insulin in it. She also mentioned that her fingerprints will be on the bag." Kwon continued with a sneer. "She just happened to touch it during the code."

Drake clenched his teeth to smother his groan. He was certain Hart was only trying to be helpful. But why did she have to do it in a way that made her appear so goddamned guilty?

CHAPTER 52

——— ·✠═◈━━◗◉◖═━◈═╬ ✦——

AFTER DOCUMENTING HER part in Trautman's resuscitation, Cassie left a message for Richard to meet her at her office and retraced her steps back down to the ER. She stopped at the break room and grabbed her coffee mug from the shelf. The bright cobalt blue mug had the Three Rivers logo emblazoned on one side and her name printed in bold letters in permanent marker on the other. Administration had presented them to all of the ER staff in hopes of decreasing the expenditure on disposable cups. Cassie filled the mug and moved down the hall to her office.

She sat down at her desk and began to sort her mail, a mindless activity that kept her thoughts away from Trautman's death. Or the fact that Richard was probably behind it. After all, who had more to gain?

Could Richard also be behind Fran's death? Had he fallen that far? The man she knew, the man she'd once loved had been narcissistic, volatile—but not a stone-cold killer.

The big question was what could she do about it? Without forcing him to use the tape against Drake? She had no evidence, only a gut-twisting suspicion. Was that enough to convince Richard to trade her the tape for her silence?

Her name sounded on the overhead intercom, asking her to report to the nurses' station. Why hadn't Richard called her extension directly? The nurses' station was empty except for the bored looking clerk.

"Did you page me?" she asked.

"No, not me," he answered, turning the volume down on the Seether blaring from his iPod.

"Then who did?"

"No one here. It was the hospital operator. Why don't you ask her?"

Ed Castro was on duty and the ER was quiet, she saw no reason for Ed or anyone else to page her. Maybe Drake or one of his counterparts, looking for more information on Trautman's code? If so, they could come find her in person. She went back to her office.

Richard sat at her desk, feet propped up, drinking her coffee. "Hey, Ella." He swiveled around to greet her. "How can you drink this shit?"

The inferior grade of coffee didn't stop him from finishing the cup.

"I've got to talk to you." She forced herself not to smile at his black eye, her work. Despite the small room, their close proximity, or the fact that the man before her might be a killer, she felt no fear. She had none of the overwhelming sense of claustrophobia Richard usually elicited in her. Instead, she felt calm, confident. It was a pleasant change. "Do you know who killed Fran?"

"I told your friend Drake that you were coming back to me." He riffled through her mail. "He didn't seem too happy about it." He looked up with a wide grin.

"Drake has nothing to do with this. This is between you and me. I have no intention of coming back to you, not now, not ever. I notified the Medical Board that you're using again."

He tossed her mail back onto her desk and set her coffee cup down on her mouse pad. "I know. And the test came back clean. And they always will."

"How are you faking your drug tests?" He didn't answer. He merely smiled widely, his gaze smug. She tried another tack. "If you give me the video, I'll keep quiet about how you injected insulin into Trautman's antibiotic bag."

"Good try, Ella. But you can't fool me. You've got nothing." He reached a hand out to stroke her arm possessively. "Just remember. No one touches my wife and gets away with it. No one—not even a cop."

It took all her strength not to flinch or jerk away from his touch. It'd only make things worse—for Drake. She was silent, taking care not to provoke him further. He moved closer to her. He ground his teeth together, something he did only when very emotional.

"I told you, Ella. You're mine." His tongue darted out to lick his dry lips, and then he grabbed her by the elbows, drawing her near. She easily broke free of his grasp. His palms left sweaty stains on her sleeves.

He was sweating all over. She reached out and touched his flushed face. "You're burning up."

He lurched back against the desk. "Can't breathe," his words emerged in a gasp as he collapsed to the floor.

Cassie stared at him for a blank second. She should be kneeling at his side, opening his airway, checking his pulse, and getting him help. Instead, she was frozen in place, mesmerized by a bead of sweat slipping down his forehead, falling into his unseeing eye. He lay helpless at her feet. He could even be dying and for one brief moment the thought gave her a sense of elation, of freedom.

Her next breath brought her crashing back to earth with a heavy sense of guilt. She couldn't let him die. Conquering her primitive impulses, she ran out the door to the nurses' station.

"Call a code," she called to the charge nurse. "Get the cart down to my office. Now!" She raced back to Richard. His breathing stopped and convulsions began to wrack his body.

Ed Castro and a team of nurses arrived to help. They wrestled Richard's body onto a gurney and wheeled him down to the trauma room. Richard's jaws were locked together, making it next to impossible to force any air through to his lungs.

"I'm going to cric him," Cassie told the team, reaching for the equipment needed to insert an airway directly through his neck and into his trachea. She hoped it worked better on Richard than it had on the homeless boy last night.

"What's going on?" Ed asked as he started an IV.

"Temp's 105.6," a nurse announced. "Pulse ox dropping, heart rate 240, BP 210 over 150."

Cassie looked up from her position at Richard's head and met Ed's eyes. If they couldn't stabilize Richard soon they would lose him. She remembered her patient from the other night, Brian, her first Double Cross overdose. He had similar symptoms, but his had developed much more slowly. So had the boy's last night.

"Push Valium and pentobarbital," she told Ed.

"Won't do any good if you can't get that airway."

"I know." She was counting the seconds that Richard was deprived of oxygen. Brian had never been hypoxic, and his brain had still been fried by the potent drug combination.

She looked down at her ex-husband. She'd once loved the man. No matter how he had deteriorated, she didn't want to see him suffer. How could he have been so foolish, taking drugs here at work? What if this had happened when he was in the middle of surgery?

Splashing Betadine on his neck, she felt for the delicate membrane of tissue and inserted the scalpel blade until she had incised a tract into the trachea. She slid the tube in and began to force air through it, hoping she wasn't too late.

"I'm in."

"Pulse ox coming up," a nurse informed them. The other medications took effect, and the seizure stopped. Richard now lay in a coma, but one produced by the powerful barbiturates they had given to relax his body.

"Pentobarbital coma." Ed nodded in satisfaction as their patient's vitals began to drift back to normal. "Haven't used that since I was a resident back in the dark ages. Good thinking, Cassie."

"I used it the other night on a similar overdose." She didn't want to dwell on the ultimate outcome of that patient. Right now two parents were sitting at their son's bedside, waiting for the strength to turn off the machines keeping him alive.

"He wasn't down long. He'll be all right."

Cassie said nothing. The pessimism in Ed's voice said it all.

CHAPTER 53

THEY WERE WHEELING Richard out of the trauma room when Drake arrived. "What the hell happened?" he asked Cassie in a tone that made her stop short. "Do I have to lock you up to keep you out of trouble?"

"Not here." She led the way down to her office. Drake followed her inside.

"Richard came to see me," she started. "He collapsed from an overdose of the new FX/MDMA drug."

Drake frowned at that, his eyes narrowed. "King came to see you?"

"Yes. I asked him to." She hesitated. "We had some things to get straightened out."

"So you're not reconciling with him?"

"Of course not." She glanced up at him, and saw his face go from stony to relaxed. "You never really thought—"

"How did I know what to think? You weren't talking this morning."

"I'm sorry. I needed time to think."

"Why were you in Trautman's room when he died?" His gaze locked onto hers with an intensity that made her squirm and look away.

"I think Richard's been getting drugs from Trautman." It was the truth, just not all of it. "Something that isn't showing up in his urine tox screens. That's one of the things I wanted to talk to Richard about, but he collapsed before—" She stopped. Something was wrong. Things weren't adding up.

"Before what? He didn't hurt you, did he?"

Cassie shook her head, her gaze darting around the small room.

"Right before—Richard was drinking out of my coffee cup." She reached out a hand for the ceramic mug, and then drew back as if it was a viper.

Drake moved past her and examined the cup without touching it. "There's some kind of chalky residue in the bottom. A lot of it—" He looked at her appraisingly. "You're about half King's size. If you drank the same amount—"

"I'd probably be dead."

She sank back against the desk, her head reeling. Someone was trying to kill her. The same someone who had killed Fran?

Drake reached out to her, his fingers stroking the worry lines at the corner of her eye. "Let me get someone to secure this place, then I'll take you out of here."

"No."

"No what? You're not going to stay here. Don't you get it? This actor is after you. I'll take you down to the House, get your statement, and we'll figure this all out. I'm not going to let anything happen to you."

"I'm not going anywhere with you," she told him in a flat voice. Everyone who got near to her was in danger.

He stared at her, at first with concern, then with a frown. "You're trying to protect me, aren't you?" She said nothing. "I'm the cop, remember? I don't need your protection, if anything did happen, I can take care of myself."

"So can I."

"We are *not* having this conversation." He took her by the elbow, and steered her toward the door.

Cassie twisted free from his grasp. "Don't try to handle me, Drake."

He sighed, and ran his fingers through his hair. "I know you feel responsible for what happened to Richard—"

"It was my cup, damn it. Of course I'm responsible!"

"No, you're not!" His voice echoed off the cement block walls of the tiny office space. "You didn't put the fucking poison there! Just like you didn't shoot Weaver. And I'm damned certain you didn't kill Trautman."

"I'm the one who got Fran involved in all this. If I'd just minded my own business—"

"A lot of innocent kids might have been killed by FX overdoses."

Now who was playing God? "You don't know anything about it!"

"I know you take responsibility for everything that happens around you because you need to be in control!"

They were squared off, only inches separating them, forcing Cassie to tilt her head up to meet his glare.

"Guess what," he went on, in a low, relentless tone, " you're not in control—too fucking bad, welcome to the human race. What makes you think that you're better than the rest of us, anyway?"

"At least I don't get drunk and go whoring around!" Cassie clamped a hand over her mouth. Watched as he sucked in his breath, his entire body shrinking away from her as if she had slapped him.

The door opened and both of them jumped. Kwon stood there, a twisted smile curling her lips.

"Am I interrupting?"

CHAPTER 54

DRAKE FROZE. His face, his body, he swore even his heart stopped beating for a few moments until he recovered. He backed away from Hart, regaining breathing room and his composure, and joined Kwon in the hall.

"We need to secure the scene," he said to Kwon. "Richard King was poisoned by Double Cross placed in Hart's coffee cup."

Kwon clicked her tongue at that, her eyes narrowing as she stared at Hart. "Why am I not surprised to hear that?" She jerked her head at Hart. "Let's take this elsewhere, Doctor, shall we?"

Hart followed Kwon, her eyes on the floor, shoulders hunched as she walked past Drake. As if she was afraid he'd touch her, as if he'd hurt her as much as her words had wounded him. Maybe six months wasn't long enough, after all.

Kwon gave him a look of supreme disappointment as she opened the door to the break room and ushered Hart inside.

After Drake summoned one of the uniforms from upstairs to secure Hart's office, he joined them. Hart sat at the narrow table, palms flat against it, leaning forward, her face flushed in anger. Kwon lounged in her chair, sipping from a cup of coffee as if it was cream and she was a particularly satisfied cat.

She flicked her gaze over to Drake. He took a position in the corner of the room, out of direct eyeshot of either woman.

"Dr. Hart was just explaining how she came to be at," she ticked off her fingers as if counting, "five crime scenes in less than two days." She swiveled to face Hart once more. "No, excuse me. It's six crime scenes—if you count your original encounter with Jane Doe."

Kwon set her cup down and licked her upper lip. "Finding all that FX—knowing it could possibly lead back to you, that's what started it, isn't it, Hart? I understand. You were scared and felt trapped. You had to take action, to protect yourself."

Hart's face tightened into a scowl as the crimson that flushed her face crept down her neck. Her hands curled into fists. She pushed her chair back. Kwon remained seated, gazed placidly up at her.

"Sit down, Hart." Her voice cut through the silence like a gunshot.

Drake stepped forward, ready to intervene. But he didn't have to. Hart shook herself, gave Kwon a quick nod of acknowledgment as if she was keeping score and settled herself back into the chair.

"Let's start from the beginning," Kwon said, her voice smooth, unruffled. "Tell me about Weaver and the shooter. What did you see and hear?"

He watched grief crash down over Hart's features. She took a breath, and kept her eyes fixed on Kwon's. "It was raining very hard, and it was dark. I pulled a security guard outside with me. There was a shot. I saw a person running away. I think it was a man, wearing dark clothes, a hood or hat over his head. I didn't see his face."

"Could it have been Trautman?"

"No. He was much thinner, shorter. Trautman is what, six four or so?"

"*Was,*" Kwon reminded her. "The guard told us the man he saw was tall and stocky like Trautman."

Hart looked up in surprise. "He's wrong. The killer was lean, not stocky at all. And definitely under six feet."

"Conveniently rules out your husband as well." Kwon nodded as if she expected no less. "Want to tell me why you went out to the West End Bridge last night?"

"We had another overdose patient come in, and one of his friends recognized my Jane Doe. Said she'd seen her with some homeless kids near the West End Bridge."

"So you went down there to identify your patient?" Kwon's voice had a trace of skepticism. "Not because Trautman asked you to meet him there?"

Hart's expression was one of confusion. "Of course not."

"You and Trautman, you'd had dealings in the past?"

"He worked orthopedics, so he was in and out of the ER. You know, taking patients up to the OR, helping the ortho guys with fracture reductions and casts."

Kwon nodded her understanding. "That was your only interaction with Trautman prior to last night?"

"Yes."

Drake released the breath he hadn't realized he'd been holding. She was telling the truth—her face was open, eyes clear of deception. Trautman had lied about her involvement. But Hart's word alone wasn't good enough, especially not with Trautman dead. Not to mention the circumstances of his death.

"What about your husband? I believe he's an orthopedic surgeon."

"Ex-husband," Hart replied. "You'd have to ask him."

Her lips clamped shut as she remembered why that was impossible. Kwon merely raised an eyebrow at Hart's lapse.

"When he's better," she added, lamely.

"You mean out of his coma?" Kwon said with a bland inflection.

"Yes."

"I understand Dr. King recently returned from drug rehabilitation. Could Trautman have been dealing him drugs?"

"It's possible. I had my suspicions Richard was using again. His behavior has been erratic since his return. But he told me all his drug tests have been negative, and the hospital certainly wouldn't let him near patients if there were any suspicion that he might be impaired."

"You two must still be close for you to be defending him."

Hart bristled. "We're not close. I'm not defending him, I'm just telling you what little I know." She shifted in her chair, her gaze darting to the closed door, one hand pressed against her chest as if she needed air.

"Of course," Kwon agreed placidly. "Tell me about Trautman. He had a gun, didn't he? Why didn't he just shoot you?"

Drake was glad it had been six-four, two hundred-fifty pound Trautman out on that bridge with Hart instead of the slender Kwon. Kwon was entirely too rational, too logical about the most effective way to orchestrate Hart's demise.

"He put it in his pocket when he slapped me," Hart said, her fists clenching against the tabletop. "I kneed him in the groin and tried to run away, but he grabbed me and picked me up—" She broke off, looked down at her hands as she opened and closed them.

Drake remembered the terror that had gripped him

when he'd seen Trautman throw her over the railing and his gut roiled. He cleared his throat, a verbal nudge for Kwon to move on. She raised her index finger in acknowledgment.

"Why did you go see Trautman today? I'm sure after the events of last night you weren't a welcome visitor."

Hart hesitated. "I needed, I wanted to know if he knew who killed Fran."

That earned her a raised eyebrow. "You expected the man who you may have blinded for life, a man that you say tried to kill you and was a ruthless drug dealer, to confess to being an accessory to murder? Surely, you're not that naive?"

Hart was silent, her blush creeping up her neck once more. Kwon continued, "You called your husband, asked him to meet you. Why?"

"He wanted to reconcile, and I needed to make it clear to him that was impossible," Hart said, keeping her eyes firmly fixed on Kwon's, shoulders hunched once more as if trying to block Drake out. He caught a glimpse of her foot tapping below the table. Another lie. Was she protecting King? Or herself?

"Why? He's rich, handsome, a good doctor. Seems like a catch to me." Kwon leaned forward, just girls here, shooting the breeze.

Color suffused Hart's face now. She touched one finger to her lips before answering. "I told you, I had suspicions that Richard was using drugs again."

"Oh yeah, right." Kwon made a quick note. "It never occurred to you that your ex might be working with Trautman, might be involved with Weaver's death? Maybe Trautman's as well?"

Hart shifted, dragging the chair a few inches back across the floor, away from both Drake and Kwon. "Well, yes. That too."

"So there you are, in a small office, no one around but you and your drug-using-ex, who just might have helped kill your best friend, and you gave him coffee?" Kwon arched her eyebrow in disbelief.

"I didn't give him coffee," Hart snapped. "He took my cup and drank from it."

"So you were about to ask your husband if he helped to kill your best friend, but couldn't because someone else happened to slip poison into the cup he was drinking from? Is that how it happened?"

"No, of course not. I don't know how that Double Cross got into my cup. I was just trying to—" She stopped short.

Drake found himself leaning forward, anxious to catch every word.

"Trying to what?" Kwon asked. Hart remained silent. Kwon took a different tack. "How did you know it was Double Cross in the coffee? We're not even sure yet."

"His symptoms were the same as a patient I had the other night."

"How did that patient do?"

"He's brain dead."

"Guess your husband is lucky he's only in a coma, huh? Too bad Trautman and Weaver weren't as lucky after you tried to help them."

"You don't understand. You weren't there that night, watching Fran die, helpless to do anything, knowing that it was all because of you—" Drake watched her choke back her frustration and grief. After a deep breath she went on. "I had to try."

Kwon seemed skeptical, but let it pass. "Why do you think anyone would want to kill either you or your husband?"

"I don't know." The words emerged in a heavy tone as if Kwon had dragged them from Hart by force. They sank into a lengthening silence. Sweat gathered on Hart's upper lip. Her gaze kept darting to the door as if she were considering making a break for freedom.

She never once looked to Drake for help. Not that he could offer much if she did. He shoved his fists into his pockets, and kept his face impassive.

Kwon spoke again. "Awfully convenient, don't you think? That the one person other than Trautman who might be able to tell us anything is poisoned after drinking from your cup."

Hart started to open her mouth to protest, but the detective was already on a different track. "How did it feel watching your best friend die? I'm told you were holding her wound shut with your hands, trying to stop the bleeding."

Hart gagged and looked away. "There was nothing I could do. It was a mortal wound," she said, teeth clenched. Drake watched her dig her feet into the floor, ready to propel herself from the chair, from the room, and knew she was close to breaking.

He shuffled forward a half step, ready, wanting to stop this. But a jerk of Kwon's head stopped him and he held his ground. Reminded himself that finding the truth was the best way to help Hart. If only Hart would tell them the truth.

"Right." Kwon said, as if she'd forgotten this point. "I only ask because I understand you cut open your husband's neck. At about the same spot where Weaver was shot. Seems like a suitable revenge if he did kill your friend over drugs: first poison him, then slice him open." The detective flung these statements at her so nonchalantly that Hart blinked in surprise.

"I'm a doctor," she told Kwon in a voice choked with fury. "I save lives, I don't take them."

Kwon gave Hart a syrupy smile. "Surely you can do

better than that."

Drake winced. Did Hart have any idea how guilty she looked? She was acting just like any other perp.

Hart's glare had no effect on Kwon, other than to widen her smile. Moving in for the kill. "You see, you might have just made your first mistake by poisoning your husband. Trautman already gave us his statement—last night, in fact. Told us about how he caught you stealing FX and he blackmailed you into letting him in on the deal. If I were you, I'd start looking for a good lawyer. Oh, but I forgot," Kwon sat up straight, a look of sympathy pasted on her face, "your brother-in-law, the great and powerful Alan King, probably won't be in a mood to save the woman who just put his brother in a coma, will he?"

Hart's mouth opened then snapped shut again. After returning Kwon's stare for a long moment, she gathered her dignity like a moth-eaten shawl and scraped her chair back as she stood. "I've told you all I can, Detective. Please call me if you have more questions."

"I think you can count on that, Doctor." Kwon flashed a triumphant smile over her shoulder at Drake.

Hart caught their exchange and for the first time she made eye contact with Drake. Her wounded expression made him feel ashamed, forced him to take a half step back until he was against the wall.

She stalked across the room, toward the door he stood beside. Her face flushed with anger once more, giving her pale complexion a radiant glow. He remembered the colors that had enchanted him last night as they flowed over her skin, the light in her eyes after they made love. Those large, dark eyes looked up at him, just as they had last night, but now they were filled with pain and regret.

"I hope you found the show entertaining." She stood toe to toe with him, not giving an inch.

Drake was silent. He didn't trust his voice. Sweat

pooled at the small of his back, and he felt the ghost of her fingers dancing over that same sensitive area of flesh.

"I am free to go, aren't I, Detective?" she asked him. He nodded.

Her eyes blazed with indignation. He opened the door for her. She passed over the threshold, turning so that her back was to him, and marched down the corridor, back rigid, head high. And all he could do was watch her leave.

Kwon joined him at the door. "She's not a very good liar, is she?"

Drake grimaced and shook his head.

"Too bad it's all circumstantial. Not enough probable cause to bring her in. Yet," Kwon continued in a heartless tone. He knew she had purposely goaded Hart, trying to prove to him that Hart was guilty.

No matter what he believed about Hart being innocent of trying to kill her ex and Trautman, she'd definitely been lying about something. He was going to have to find out what. And who wanted to kill her—and why.

CHAPTER 55

CASSIE BARELY MADE it to the safety of the stairwell before she collapsed. Her chest was heaving, straining to pull enough oxygen into her body, her lips and hands were numb as waves of nausea crashed over her. Sitting on a concrete step, she hung her head between her knees, placed a palm against the cold cement block wall to steady her, and surrendered to the panic attack.

What had Drake said that first night? That together they could exorcize demons? Her vision blackened to a shadowy haze as her body shook, out of her control. If only it was that easy.

Slowly, by painful degrees, feeling returned to her. First a tantalizing tingling, then spasms of pain as her cramped muscles released their death grip. She raised her head. Black spots still danced in her vision, but she could see again. And breathe. And think.

But when she tried to focus, to come up with strategy, all she saw was Drake's face, watching her as he allowed Kwon to accuse her of murder. He thought she was lying.

Of course she was, but it was to protect him. Cassie ignored the tremors that still shook her as she hauled herself up onto her feet. She needed to get back to her life, to her world—where she was in control. Let the police take care of the rest.

And Drake?

The answer eluded her as she climbed the steps, one at a time in slow motion as if it was the summit of Everest that awaited her instead of the ICU three floors above. By the time she entered the unit, she felt reasonably in control of her body and mind. Enough to allow her to ignore the questioning looks from the nurses and staff she passed as she walked to the chart rack. Richard's chart was gone, probably with the group of neurologists gathered around his bedside.

She was reading Jane Doe's chart when a nurse rushed up to her. "Dr. Hart, I was just going to page you. Your patient's family wants to talk with you."

Cassie looked up at that, her pulse revving with excitement. "Jane Doe's family is here?"

The nurse frowned and shook her head. "Oh no, not her. The Winstons. Their plane was delayed in London, they just got in a few hours ago. They asked for you specifically." She glanced over her shoulder at the closed curtains around Brian's bed. "I think they didn't want to believe the neurologists. Someone told them you were the one who saved him in the ER, and," she shrugged apologetically, "I think they're hoping you'll give them better news."

"How is he doing?"

"They did a perfusion scan this morning and an apnea test." The nurse handed her Brian's chart. "Both showed no brain activity."

Cassie flipped through the chart to verify the test results. The neurologists had officially declared Brian Winston brain dead, and had documented their discussions with the family regarding withdrawing life support and possible organ donation.

She looked up at the nurse who gave her a look of condolence. It was the hardest part of her job, being helpless to offer anything, not even hope for a patient or their family. Thankfully, it wasn't a situation that arose very often down in the ER.

The price of getting involved, she told herself as she walked over to Brian's bed space and pulled back the privacy curtain. "Mr. and Mrs. Winston?"

Brian's parents stood at the head of the bed, but neither paid any attention to their son. They were engaged in a fierce argument conducted in hoarse whispers. The mother, a tall brunette with stylish short hair, large diamond and topaz earrings and a larger diamond pendant, had her fingers wrapped around the bedrail, shaking it as she accused her husband.

"It's all your fault," she was saying, her voice the sharp hiss of a viper. "You never spent any time with him, always too busy with your work, your clients—"

Mr. Winston stood several inches over his wife. He wore a form-fitting silk polo and sharply creased slacks. The Rolex on his wrist sparkled, reflecting the multi-colored tracings from Brian's monitors like Christmas lights. "You never complained before—not as long as my long hours gave you time for your Pilates and paid for your mindfulness coach and shopping sprees. Where were you? You're supposed to be his mother!"

Cassie coughed to catch their attention. "I'm Dr. Hart," she said as they both turned to her. "I took care of Brian," she directed her gaze on the comatose teen, hoping they would as well, "when he came into the ER."

"Doctor," Mrs. Winston said, "we heard how you saved our son. They want us to decide, to decide—"

"They say he's already gone," Mr. Winston put in bluntly. "I can't accept that. We wanted a second opinion.

From someone who doesn't just see him as a chance to bring in more cash through organ transplants."

Cassie forced herself not to react at his condemnation of her colleagues. She blamed it on their anger and guilt— all part of the grieving process. She wondered if they realized they'd already distanced themselves from Brian. Neither used his name or touched him. Instead they took a step back when she reached for Brian's arm to stroke it. His skin was warm, his pulse strong, although she knew the boy was already dead. Still, it helped to her to focus on what was really important here.

And for once, it wasn't her patient. Instead, she needed to help his family accept the worst thing that could happen to any parent: their child dying before them, as they watched, helpless.

⚜

ONCE HE WAS able to break free of Kwon's watchful eyes, Drake went AWOL, searching for Hart. Finally he found her at the first place he should have looked, back where everything had begun. With her patient, Jane Doe.

He stood inside the ICU doors, watching her sit with the teenager. Hart was combing the girl's freshly shampooed hair, murmuring to her in a quiet voice when he approached. He saw that her other patient, the Winston kid, was gone, his bed space empty.

"I thought someone should stay with her," she said, without looking up at him or pausing in her efforts. "Since I have nothing better to do." Now she turned her head to glare at him. "Unless you're here to arrest me?"

Drake shoved his hands into his coat pockets and shook his head. "No." He caught movement at the far end of the room and recognized Richard King lying in a bed. "How's King doing?"

"I heard a nurse saying he might have had a stroke, but I haven't been over to see for myself. Didn't want anyone to misinterpret my actions." Her voice was flinty.

Before Drake could respond, the doors slid open, and a tall, blond man rushed in.

"Where is he?" he demanded to the room at large as if everyone present should immediately attend to his needs. His gaze circled the room, lit on Hart, and blazed with fury.

Drake recognized Alan King from previous encounters in the courtroom. The older King looked a lot like his younger brother, except Alan's eyes were darker and, instead of Richard King's smooth poise, Alan's demeanor was one of constant urgency.

Alan King strode toward Hart, hands fisted in front of him. "You bitch. What the hell do you think you're doing here?"

Drake stepped between Hart and the agitated attorney, but she brushed past him to face King on her own.

"Not here," she said and left the ICU, King hurrying after her. Drake followed, watching from the doorway as she led King down the hall to a quiet corner beside the vending machines. Alan King's fury seemed to grow now that he had Hart alone, his voice was loud enough that Drake caught his part of the conversation effortlessly.

"How dare you come anywhere near him after what you've done!" King shouted. "I'll have you up on charges, get a restraining order. You'll never work in this city again when I'm done with you."

Drake debated joining them but Hart seemed to be doing fine on her own. He watched as she spoke quietly, saw the attorney's posture change. He didn't relax—he doubted Alan King ever relaxed—but he softened. He was impressed. Given Hart's quick temper, he expected her to lash back at Alan's unfounded accusations. Of course, she had long experience in dealing with the King family. Maybe that was why she seemed to have more patience with her ex than she did with Drake.

Then he saw Alan King's hand land on Hart's shoulder, and stay there despite her glare and movement to shake it off. The same possessive attitude Richard King had. Could Hart have been involved with both brothers? He watched her face darken with disgust and thought not. She glanced in his direction, and Drake took his cue, glad to be able to do something to help.

"Dr. Hart," he said in an official voice. "I need more information about your patient." He insinuated himself between them, giving Hart room to maneuver away from King.

King looked at Drake straight on for the first time. "Do I know you?"

"Detective Drake. We've met in court. The last time was when you got Lester Young off on a technicality after he emptied a TEC-9 at me and hit a van full of kids."

Alan King pursed his lips, and then smiled. "Right. Good old Lester. How's he doing, anyway?"

"He's dead." Drake didn't add that Lester died of the same drug that Richard King was now fighting. That seemed too cruel, even for a lawyer like King.

King shrugged as if the loss of a client was meaningless. As long as the bill was paid. Then his eyes cut back to Hart who stood at Drake's side. King reached out a hand, touched her cheek in a casual movement, and backed away again.

"We're not done here, Cassandra." He spun on his heel and returned to the ICU.

Drake watched him go—he could understand Kwon and Dimeo's fascination with implicating the King family in something dirty.

"Nice guy," he muttered.

"Alan? He's the worst of the bunch."

He looked down to see Hart wiping at the skin where King's fingers had touched her.

"Of course I didn't know that until after the wedding. Alan wouldn't think twice about casually walking into our bedroom, especially if he knew Richard wasn't there. Kept trying to corner me at family gatherings, too."

He raised an eyebrow, and she rolled her eyes at him. "Don't even go there. I might have been blind enough to fall for Richard's charm, but there's no way in hell I'd let that slime anywhere near me."

"Glad to hear it." Then he remembered why he had come. "Is there some place we can talk?"

"There are empty call rooms down here."

She led him down a narrow back hallway and into a small cave of a room furnished with a single bed, no headboard, a scarred bedside table with a ragged lamp and phone on it, and a single wooden chair. There were no windows, no mirrors, but there was an adjoining room with a toilet and a sink. Drake looked around. Most prison cells were larger. How many hundreds of nights had Hart spent in rooms just like this one?

He thought about her claustrophobia as she closed the door behind them. But she seemed totally at ease and in control here in a familiar environment, despite the confinement.

She sat on the bed, its plastic mattress cover rustling under her weight. The linens covering the bed had been starched and pressed so many times that they smelled charred.

"I'm sorry about what I said before, about Pamela," she started, pulling her knees up to her chest. "That was wrong."

"Lying to Kwon wasn't exactly a smart move either," he told her. "One thing about us cops, we hate being lied to." He spun the lone chair around and straddled it, facing her.

"That makes two of us. You told me I wasn't under suspicion. There's no way Kwon made up that crazy theory on the spur of the moment."

"I told you that you were clear in my book. The Task Force has been looking at you and King since the day you came to see Miller."

"The day I came to help you? Talk about no good deed going unpunished." She leaned back, and blew out her breath. "I almost wish I never—Fran would still be alive, Richard—none of this would have happened."

"We wouldn't have happened," he reminded her, reaching across the space between them to take her hand in his, softly stroking the scar at the base of her thumb. "Do you regret that?"

She tilted her head, and looked at him square on. "No. But you might. When I tell you the truth."

His fingers stopped their motion. "What is it? Who are you trying to protect? I know it can't be yourself, because you keep digging yourself in deeper with every lie."

"You. Damn it, I was trying to help you."

"Me? What the hell?"

"When we kissed the other day in the trauma room, the day after Fran died—"

"I remember." He wasn't going to soon forget. Her silent weeping in the dark had about broken his heart.

"We tape all our traumas, for teaching purposes. A video camera is activated when you turn the light on in those rooms."

Drake dropped her hand, breaking the connection between them. Shit. "Who has the tape?" As if he couldn't guess.

"Richard."

"King," he almost spat the name. "That's why he was

at your house this morning. He was blackmailing you."

"You didn't think that he was there to rekindle our romance, did you?" Her voice was tight with fatigue. "I'm sorry."

"What did you do to ensure his silence, Hart?"

CHAPTER 56

CASSIE SAT BOLT upright, planted her feet on the floor. "I didn't kill Trautman and I certainly didn't poison Richard, if that's what you're getting at!"

If Drake really believed she was capable of killing someone, then there was nothing more to discuss.

She needed to go. Escape. Return home to her life, her familiar ghosts. At least there she knew and understood what haunted her. Here with Drake she struggled through uncertain territory rife with danger—both seen and unseen. Best to run now while she still could.

Cassie pushed past him and opened the door. He took her by the wrist and raised one hand, his eyes blazing with emotion.

She couldn't help it, hated herself for it, but she cringed. The flinch lasted only a moment, but his hand flew off her, as if she had burned him.

Swallowing back bile, she rocked onto the balls of her feet, ready now to do physical harm to him if he tried to stop her, block her escape. He met her gaze, and she felt a surge of shame. She'd give anything for a chance to erase the look of pity from his eyes. Pity and disappointment—

his eyes reflected her own feelings back at her.

"I was just reaching for the door," Drake said in a soft voice, stepping back so that her escape route wasn't blocked.

Cassie heard a sound, a feral, inhuman whimper and realized it came from her. Her vision was blinded by tears. She slumped against the doorframe, shoulders bowed, energy sapped.

"Don't you think it's time you told me about King?" Drake wrapped her in his arms. He held her for a long moment. Finally she looked up at him and nodded. He led her to the narrow bed, cradled her on his lap.

"You can probably guess most of it," she whispered, her finger tracing up the inside of his arm. Touching him, feeling his strength, soothed the erratic pounding of her heart. She didn't want to do anything to jeopardize the comfort he offered her. "I'm sure it's a story you've heard often enough."

"I want to hear it from you." He gently but firmly moved her hand away, and held it within his. "King," he prompted.

She sighed and nodded again, her head resting against his chest. Then she pulled away from his embrace. She regretted leaving that warmth, fearing that after she told him her story, he would be gone from her life forever.

"We met when I was an intern and he was a senior orthopedic resident," Cassie began. "It was an opposites attract kind of thing. He was handsome, rich, from one of the oldest and proudest families in Pittsburgh, raised with servants, while I'd worked my way through school as a waitress and hotel housekeeper." She faltered, the memory of that first look Richard had given her expanding in her mind. No one had ever looked at her that way before.

"Our first date was something out of a movie. He took me sailing on a private yacht out on the river. We ate lobster, drank champagne, and watched the lights of the city. We danced until dawn." She sighed as she remembered.

"Ella—Cinderella," Drake put in.

"And he was my Prince Charming. A year later, after he'd finished his training and joined his father's practice, we were married. His parents gave us a house out in Fox Chapel as a wedding present.

"Of course I still had my residency to finish, and that meant night shifts, trauma and ICU rotations with every other night call, flying with the helicopter to accident scenes. There was work and there was Richard, nothing else. My grandmother died a few weeks before we were married. So Richard became my entire reason for being."

"He isolated you." Drake said, and she knew he recognized the classic pattern.

"I didn't see it at first. I was like a drowning victim caught in the riptide, not even knowing I was in trouble until I was too far out to swim back to shore or fight the current." Cassie winced, thinking of her naive, younger self. "That's when I found out about his temper—nothing physical, not at first, but when I did something that pleased him, it was like a honeymoon all over again." She gave a small derisive laugh. "Classic Pavlovian conditioning, but I fell for it.

"I told myself that I just had to make it through residency and everything would be all right. I'd find myself spending every waking moment thinking of ways to please him, to keep him happy so he wouldn't stop loving me. When the drinking began to escalate, I blamed myself that I wasn't there for him and so did he. Then one night . . ." Her voice trailed off.

Cassie closed her eyes as she remembered that night, dinner with his family and their friends at the Fox Club. It was past midnight and Richard was still regaling the table with stories, and reaching for another drink. She was sweating, trying hard to maintain a smile on her face and keep up her end of polite conversation about topics she could not care less about.

"Richard, don't you think you've had enough?" she'd asked quietly. "It's getting late."

All conversation had stopped at her words, and she found herself the uncomfortable center of attention. Richard set his tumbler down with a bang and shot her a glare. His brother, Alan, had chuckled and broken the tension.

"I'd say my brother's new wife has him wrapped around her pretty little finger," he said, lifting his own glass in a mock toast to Cassie.

Cassie bit her lip, uncertain how to respond. Then Richard laughed as well and took her hand as he stood up. He slid her chair out for her.

"What can I say?" he told the others as he lifted her hand to his lips. "We are still newlyweds, you know."

That earned them another laugh, and she felt her ears begin to burn with embarrassment. Richard pulled her into an intimate embrace, kissing her in front of everyone. Cassie froze, and he quickly broke it off. He draped his arm around her shoulder, casually laying his hand over her breast and turned back to the table.

"Thank you everyone. It has been, and it will continue to be," he winked at Cassie, "a wonderful evening."

Richard was silent as he drove them home. Cassie stewed, still flushed with embarrassment by his public display of affection. How could he have done that to her? He knew how out of place she felt with his family and their rich, country club friends. She'd seen the knowing smirks the other women had given her as they left. But she said nothing.

Once back at their house Richard followed her inside

to the living room, then surprised her by pulling her into another embrace.

She resisted at first, still angry with him, then forced herself to relax. Richard often told her that she was slower to respond to affection than other women, and that she needed to stop competing for control and trust him.

"I would never hurt you," he'd told her repeatedly when they were in bed together, and she believed him. She didn't understand why she couldn't respond the way he expected her to. "You'll learn," he assured her. "After all, marriage is a partnership. You just have to trust me."

So tonight, she forced herself to swallow her anger and return his ardor. "Did you see the way they all looked at us when you kissed me?" she asked. "I'll bet my face was bright red, I was so embarrassed."

He said nothing, but moved her back against the wall and began to slide his hands under her dress, his fingers catching the waistband of her panty hose. He knelt before her, tugging at the clingy material.

Cassie laughed, trying to maintain the romantic mood. "It's your own fault," she told him. "You're the one that insisted that no lady would ever dine at the Fox Club with her legs bare."

His fingers stopped for a second, then he wrenched the stubborn nylons down to her ankles. "That's right, Ella," he smiled up at her, lifting one foot onto his bent knee and slipping her shoe and the stocking off with a flourish. "I did. Guess I keep forgetting that you're no lady."

Cassie giggled again, shifting her weight to the other foot as he repeated his Prince Charming routine. His hands returned to stoke her inner thighs as he rose to his feet, and she felt her body begin to respond to his touch. He turned her to face the wall, his fingers teasing the zipper of her silk sheath dress down.

Sliding the dress over her head, he caught her wrists

in one hand and kept her arms extended in the air as his free hand glided down her side, tantalizing her with light, feathery touches. Cassie sighed in pleasure and leaned forward. This felt so much better, she thought, enjoying the time he was taking to excite her. She wished he would always go this slow.

She closed her eyes as he turned her to face him, arms still pinned over her head. His mouth closed on her breast. A shiver of passion swept over her. He moved his lips up her chest, and his free hand began to knead her breast. She could feel his erection through his clothes, and for once she was ready for him.

Then a sharp pain shot through her as he pinched her viciously. Cassie's eyes flew open. Richard stood over her, an unfamiliar grin crossing his face, his eyes cold and hard. Before she could say anything he slapped her hard, bouncing her head off the wall. She struggled, but he held her fast.

"You will never," he punctuated his words with a backhanded slap, "humiliate or contradict me in front of my friends and family again. I don't care how fucking drunk you think I am, you'll sit there and smile until I'm ready to leave." Without warning he released her, and she dropped to the floor.

"Do," he aimed a kick between her shoulder blades, "you," another against her buttocks, "understand?"

She'd scrambled away from his last kick, trying to regain her footing, desperately searching for a weapon, anything to defend herself with. He had chosen his battleground well. There was no place to hide, no loose objects she could reach.

Then he was on top of her, pummeling her, forcing himself on her.

CHAPTER 57

CASSIE OPENED HER eyes, pulled her legs up and hugged them against her chest, turning away from Drake. God, this was so humiliating, but it also felt good to tell the whole story, it was something she had never done before. And Drake was a good listener.

"I let him do what he wanted. But no matter how he tried, he couldn't perform. That made him furious." Her voice caught as she remembered how surprised she had been that night. "And that's when he hit me for the first time."

"For the first time?" Drake asked. "You mean there were more?"

She couldn't look at him, merely nodded her head, too embarrassed to say the words out loud.

"I know what you're thinking," she said. "I used to think the same thing myself about women I saw in the ER—that they asked for it, that it was partly their fault, that if they wanted to they could stop it. Until it happened to me.

"I moved out. I planned on leaving him for good. But he wore me down, he was so sweet and kind and gentle.

He sent me dinner when I was on call, and had presents waiting for me when I got back home.

"He blamed it on the alcohol, and he quit. He started AA—all for me, he said. He begged me to start over. By this time I only had a few weeks left in my residency and was taking some time off before starting my new job, so I let him talk me into it. I think I felt a little guilty. Maybe because of my long hours I hadn't seen the warning signs, hadn't taken the time to get him help sooner. And I still loved him.

"It was a honeymoon all over. Life was wonderful." She stopped and brushed her hair back from her face.

"He never acted drunk, not like he had before. But there were other things. Pill containers that weren't his. And he changed. He began to verbally abuse me, undermine my confidence, and trying to get me to have a drink so he'd have an excuse to join in.

"I tried counseling, Al-anon, asked a few of the psychiatrists and social workers I knew for advice. Everything I tried seemed to backfire on me. I felt as if I was drowning. Finally I confronted him, and told him I couldn't take anymore and that I was leaving.

"He was furious. He slammed the door, told me I would never leave him. I got mad and began to yell that I could do as I liked, and he said hell no, and before I knew it, I was reaching for the doorknob, and he hit me so hard I literally bounced off the floor.

"I lay there stunned. Part of me was scared to death of the look in his eyes, waiting for him to kill me, and the other part was waiting for him to apologize as he'd always done in the past." She stopped, unable to block the flood of memories she'd unleashed after burying them for so long.

"What happened?" Drake's voice came to her, and she realized he had moved close to her, wrapping her once more in the safe circle of his arms.

"I was lucky that time. He hit me a few more times and kicked me, but he passed out before he could do any real damage. I struggled to my feet and got my things together—"

"And that's when you left," Drake finished for her.

Cassie closed her eyes. It would be so easy to let it end there, to have him believe that. But she couldn't. Even if he would despise her when he heard the rest.

"No, that's when the phone rang," she continued, her voice a low monotone. "There was a patient who needed him."

"You told them that he was passed out drunk, you told them the truth, didn't you?" Drake asked, his arms falling away from her.

She shivered, wrapping her arms around her chest and keeping her eyes closed as if she could pretend it had happened to some other woman. "No," she whispered. "I told them Richard had a bad case of food poisoning. I didn't plan to say it, it just came out and once said I couldn't take it back—I just couldn't hurt him no matter how angry I was.

"I sat there staring at the phone, and I've never felt so low in my entire life. I left all of my things, and walked out into the street in the clothes I had on. Somehow I found myself back at my house, body aching and bruised from head to toe. It took me two days to build the courage to call Richard and tell him I was filing for divorce. Before I could hire an attorney, his lawyers served me with the papers, and it was over. I started my new job and a new life."

He moved off the bed, away from her, and her shivering grew in intensity. "And you never told anyone?" His voice sounded distant.

Cassie rested her head on her knees, hugging herself tighter. "Never."

Drake stood with his back to her, shoulders slumped.

"So it wasn't you that reported him to the medical board?"

"No," she admitted, her fingers digging into her calves. Someone else, Ed Castro, she suspected, had already done it before she could find the courage. But she wished she had. She wished she'd been the kind of person strong enough to do the right thing.

"Shit." The word came with an exhalation as if it were forced from him. His body grew rigid. Drake turned and looked down on her, his face expressionless, hands knotted into fists at his sides.

"I already told you I was sorry. What more do you want from me?" she demanded, angry that he seemed to resent her actions so much. Did he think she'd planned it this way? "I'll go talk to Miller in the morning." She got to her feet. "I'll explain everything, tell her it was all my fault."

She ached to have his arms back around her. She felt so desolate without his body near hers. Drake sank into the chair, his back to her, head cradled in his hands. Disappointed. In her. By her.

Cassie could understand why. She was disappointed in herself—had been ever since that night last year when she had protected Richard. Rosa and her father had not raised her that way. All she could claim was a temporary insanity. Bereft by Rosa's death, dazzled by Richard's attentions, she allowed herself to be lured into a world foreign to her own.

And had paid dearly for the trespass. But not enough. It seemed she was still paying.

·◦·

IF RICHARD KING wasn't already lying down the hall in a coma, Drake would have been happy to put him there. Damn the consequences. The sound of her voice cut through his fury, and he turned to Hart as she was reaching for the door.

"Don't go." He took several deep breaths, forced his anger aside. "Please."

She looked up, but kept her hand on the doorknob.

"Neither of us is in any shape to drive tonight," he went on. "Stay here. Stay with me." The words came in an uncontrollable rush. "There's nothing to be scared of. And," he took a step toward her, reached for her hand, "the only time I don't have nightmares seems to be when you're near."

"Me too," she said, her voice low, as if ashamed of her admission. She held her ground, considering his offer.

When she didn't come into his arms right away, he stepped forward into hers. He swept her up and carried her the three steps back to the bed. He tugged her shoes off, his high tops following right behind, and settled back on the noisy mattress with her on his lap.

"It's all right," he told her in a low voice. "I'm not going anywhere. Just sleep."

Hart said nothing as he turned the light off, but he felt her slowly relax in his arms. She turned onto her side, curled up into his chest as if burrowing into a warm, safe place, her head cradled against his neck. And, finally, she slept.

Drake wondered at the feelings that simple act of trust brought. Who would have ever believed that sleeping with a woman—his arms wrapped around her, offering her his strength, his comfort—would be as stirring as making love to her?

He eased one hand free to wedge the skimpy pillow between his head and the wall. Hart whimpered as if afraid he was leaving her. He tightened his arms around her, and leaned back. He allowed all of her weight to fall on him, and closed his eyes.

DRAKE WOKE TO a loud ringing. Hart leapt off him and before he could blink twice, she had the light on.

"It's mine," he told her when she looked around for her phone. He yanked the technologic intrusion from his belt. Kwon. He yawned and struggled to his feet, looking at the clock. Nine-forty. They had slept almost four hours.

He wrapped his arms around Hart, snuggling her close and kissed her on the forehead. Her body trembled with the adrenalin rush of her abrupt awakening and she was still too pale by far. But her eyes had regained their old light. "Any bad dreams?"

She smiled. "No. That was the best I've slept in days."

"Me too." His cell went off again. *Damn it, Kwon, take a Ritalin or something.*

Hart eased out of his arms, and headed into the tiny bathroom. He phoned Kwon.

"Something break? You need me to come in?" he asked.

"No." Kwon paused. "Actually, I was calling to talk to Hart. Thought I might find her with you."

"Why?" He looked up as Hart opened the door and emerged from the bathroom. "You don't want me to bring her in, do you?" He couldn't, he wouldn't put Hart through that. Not after everything she'd done to try to protect him. To hell with the job.

"Dimeo says we don't have enough to arrest Hart, not yet, anyway. But the search warrant came through. I was calling as a courtesy. Thought she might want to be there when we serve it."

Kwon's voice was cold, unemotional. Drake knew she was going above and beyond to warn him, trusting him not to make things worse. Trusting him not to screw up again.

His mind spun with the ramifications. Hart wasn't

guilty—that was the one thing he was certain of, even if he had no proof.

"DJ, can I talk to Hart?" Kwon's voice cut through his thoughts.

"Yeah." His voice was heavy with fatigue and regret. He handed the phone to Hart. "It's for you."

CASSIE TOOK THE phone, wondering what the bad news could be. "This is Detective Kwon," she heard. "We've a warrant to search your premises and are about to execute it. Customarily, if the homeowner isn't present we have the right to enter by any means necessary. But in these circumstances—" Her tone made it clear that Kwon in no way approved of the circumstances. "I'm willing to wait a few minutes until you get here to let us in."

She had to force the words past her lips. "I'll be right there."

"Hart?" Kwon's voice lowered as if she didn't want the people with her to hear what she said next. "Don't let DJ come with you. He's on shaky ground as it is, if he's seen with you—"

"I understand." So Kwon did have an ounce of compassion beneath that flint-like exterior, at least when it came to protecting her own. "Thank you, Detective." Cassie carefully hung up the phone. It was either that or hurl it across the room.

Drake stood there in his stocking feet, arms out at his sides, hands wide open. "I'm sorry."

She shook her head, batted away his apologies. She stepped into her boots, bent over to lace them. "I've got to go."

When she straightened, she saw that he was reaching for his shoes, fumbling with a knot in one of the laces.

"What do you think you're doing?"

"Going with you." He sat on the bed, tugging at the recalcitrant lace.

"No. You're not." His head snapped up, mouth open to protest. Cassie stepped between his legs and took his face in her hands, and kissed him. A deep, shuddering kiss, filled with the heat of her anger and frustration.

He dropped the high top to the floor with a thud and pulled her hard up against him.

"What was that for?" he asked.

"To thank you. For offering to come with me even though we both know it's about the stupidest thing you could do—for either of us," she added when he began to interject. She kissed him again, this one pure passion and warmth, a promise of things to come. "That one was so you don't forget me or Plan A."

"To hell with Plan A," he grumbled, drawing her tighter against his chest. His lips pressed hers with an urgency she shared. It took all of her strength to pull away.

"If I don't leave now, they'll break down the door," she said, ducking away from his lips. His arms held her in an unbreakable grip.

"Let 'em bust it into kindling." He planted his lips against hers once more.

"Drake, no. I couldn't let them do that—what would Rosa say?" Or the neighbors for that matter. She was certain there'd be a crowd watching the festivities. Police were not commonly seen on Gettysburg Street.

Drake sighed his surrender, and she stepped free of his embrace. He kept hold of one hand and gave it a tug.

"Hart, I'm tired of being bossed around by your dead grandmother."

She smiled, and leaned forward to plant one more quick kiss against his lips. And then she danced back out of his reach.

"Rosa would like you," she said and was gone.

⁘

THE DOOR SWUNG shut behind her, raising a whirling dervish of dust bunnies that sped through the room. Drake sank back on the bed, uncertain whether to be more afraid of her use of present tense when she spoke of a woman dead three years—or his own.

He shook his head, finished untying the knot in his shoe. He could head back home and get some more sleep. Or maybe crash at the House so he'd be there if something broke.

Drake jerked upright. Judas H! He was an idiot. He shoved his feet into his shoes. Hart had jumbled his mind so that he forgot about being a cop when he was around her, forgot everything.

Like the fact that someone in this hospital was trying to kill her. And he had let her waltz out the door. Alone.

He grabbed his coat and ran.

CHAPTER 58

DISTRACTED BY THOUGHTS of the police rampaging through her house, Cassie didn't notice the footsteps echoing behind her in the stairwell until she passed the third floor landing. She stopped. The steps above her stopped. She looked up into the dimly lit space but could see no one.

She wasn't the only one who found elevators distasteful. Of course, not everyone had their coffee spiked with poison today, either. She galloped down the stairs, anxious to get to the next floor. The clamor of her own footsteps camouflaged any other sounds. The second floor landing beckoned to her. Only a few steps to go.

A man's weight crashed into her, shoved her into the cinder block wall.

"I told you I wasn't finished, Cassandra," Alan King's voice came from behind her. He kept her pinned to the wall for a long moment, then lifted his weight off her. Cassie spun around to face him.

"Alan! What do you want?"

He leaned forward, one arm on either side of her. Cassie knew he thought he was being intimidating, violating her space, but his posture left several vulnerable targets open for her attack, if need be.

"You thought I wouldn't recognize your boyfriend, didn't you?" Alan continued. "But I did. He's the co-star of a certain video Richard left with me last night. And a medical student saw him assault Richard earlier today." He grinned at her. "I'm going to ruin his career. I'll take away everything he has."

She frowned. Alan clearly thought Drake was responsible for Richard's injuries. "Alan, Drake didn't give Richard that black eye. I did. He attacked me at my house this morning. Leave Drake alone."

Alan considered this, his gaze roaming down her body. "Give me a reason. What's in it for me?"

"For one thing, I won't have to arrest you for assault." Drake's voice came from above.

Cassie looked up in relief. Drake joined them on the landing. Alan ignored him for a long second, and then straightened, dropping his arms to his sides.

"Thought I'd escort you to your car, Dr. Hart," Drake said. "You never know what kind of predator might be roaming the hospital."

Alan chuckled. He pointed at Cassie. "You stay away from my brother. And you," he glared at Drake, "I wouldn't make any long term career plans, Detective Drake."

She watched him return up the steps to the ICU. "One of my favorite things about you," she said, intertwining her arm with Drake's, "is your impeccable sense of timing."

They continued together down the steps. Drake looked back over his shoulder in the direction Alan had taken. "Think he might be using the same stuff Richard was? That guy's a walking time bomb."

"No, that's just Alan. I used to think he was bipolar, but he's all mania, no depression."

They approached her car. He put his hands on her shoulders. "No matter what happens," he said, "don't forget that I believe in you. I'll be here for you."

He kissed her forehead, and then released her.

"And for God's sake, Hart, be careful."

DRAKE'S SIMPLE DECLARATION of faith helped to quiet her fears as she drove home. The streets were slick with snow. There were several inches on the ground already and no signs of letting up. She pulled her car into the alley behind her house after seeing that various law enforcement vehicles occupied the front spaces.

What a circus. She opened the door for Kwon and her team. They even had a drug-sniffing dog to help them. Kwon left her on the front porch with a patrolman. Cassie sat on the porch swing, trying not to grimace as she looked through the front windows and watched. They weren't destructive by any means, just very thorough. Apparently searching did not include replacing anything they moved, so within a few minutes the living room was strewn with displaced cushions, pillows and stacks and stacks of books.

And Rosa's floors! Bootprints, footprints, and dogprints marred the once shiny hardwood, melted snow puddles certain to leave stains. She sighed, pretended to read the thick wad of papers outlining the parameters of the search and tried to ignore the neighbors who wandered out from the comfort of their homes to see what was going on.

When they finished with the first floor, they allowed Cassie inside. She looked around the disruption surrounding her, and the weight of her exhaustion crashed down on her. Nothing was where it should be, where it had been for as long as she could remember. Her house was the one constant in her life. She'd never realized what an important touchstone it had become for her.

A dog's bark and a shout from above broke through her reverie. "Got something!" someone yelled from her bedroom.

No one stopped her, so Cassie climbed the steps to see what all the commotion was about. Had Richard brought drugs into her house this morning? Kwon, Spanos, and another officer with a dog crowded into her bedroom.

Kwon was holding her bloody T-shirt. "What happened here?" she asked Cassie.

"I had a bloody nose this morning." Cassie was glad she didn't have any swelling or black eyes like Richard did after their encounter. What would she say then—that she had run into a door?

Kwon didn't look convinced, and gestured to the broken glass, shattered remnants of the lamp and statue Richard had swept to the floor.

"I tripped," she answered the detective's unasked question.

"Right. When you got your bloody nose."

"That's right." Cassie kept her eyes level with the detective's, but knew Kwon didn't believe her.

"Want to tell us what's in the hamper?"

The dog was pawing at her dirty laundry, his handler holding his lead tight. "Nothing," she told them. "Just dirty clothes."

Kwon nodded to Spanos who began piece by piece exhuming Cassie's laundry. Spanos glanced over at Cassie with a leer that made her face flush. Out came dirty socks and underwear, clothes from work, a Kempo *gi*, sweaters, and jeans. The last set the dog to barking again.

"Nothing in the pockets," his handler said after searching them. The jeans were the only item the dog seemed to care about.

"Those are the ones I wore to the precinct house," Cassie remembered. "I had the FX in my pocket, it was wrapped in two plastic bags. Could he still smell it?"

The dog's handler nodded, praised his co-worker for his efforts. Kwon looked disgusted. "That's it?"

"Only thing in the whole house he alerted to. Rest of the place is clean."

Cassie wanted to pet the dog, tell it what a good boy it was, but refrained. Kwon and her men kept going, leafing through every book and piece of paper—which in the house of a history professor and his daughter, both voracious readers, was a herculean task in its own right—taking her computer, financial records, and poking their heads into every nook and cranny from basement to attic. The only thing remotely controversial was Rosa's ancient Luger, broken down and wrapped in oilcloth in a trunk in the attic. There were no bullets for it, and it wasn't the same caliber as the gun that killed Fran, but Kwon included it in her haul anyway.

Finally, at almost four in the morning, the disgruntled detective signed a receipt and explained to Cassie the procedure to retrieve her belongings if they weren't needed as evidence. Cassie watched as the policemen packed up their cars and left.

She closed the door and locked it, then leaned against the thick oak, surveying her home. Nothing looked familiar. It was as if she'd been dropped into some alternative dimension where chaos reigned. Sighing, she picked her way across the debris, found a cushion that fit the chair by the fire and shoved it into place, happy to have one thing appearing semi-normal. She turned the fire on. She hadn't eaten anything since lunch, but she was too upset to be hungry.

She stalked through the first floor of the house, her anger driving her, until she came up short in front of the buffet. A seldom touched bottle of Glen Morangie, her father's favorite, sat there, beckoning. It was usually kept below, behind the cabinet door, out of sight.

Why not?

She found the glasses stacked on the counter top beside a copy of Nietzsche. Cassie poured a few fingers of the single malt, watching the amber fluid slip down the side of the glass. The first swallow jolted through her—it had been a long time. Somehow, after Richard, turning to drink for comfort had not seemed appealing.

But this liquid fire that smoothed her ruffled temper felt so good. After another swallow, her toes began to tingle. She carried it back to her one habitable chair. Maybe she should dilute it? Cassie smiled. Paddy Hart would be rolling in his grave at the thought of his granddaughter spoiling whiskey that way—even if it was Scotch and not good Irish.

It was nice to think of Paddy with his Irish lilt and constant smell of moist soil and pipe tobacco. He'd grown up in Clifden, a seaside village northwest of Galway. Paddy despised the Brits but hated the Nazi's more after his sister, Brigid, died on the *Athenia*. He tried to join the Royal Navy, determined to avenge her, but had been assigned to the merchant fleet. Then, after he met Rosa, he left the sea behind to journey to a new land with new hopes and dreams.

She used to spend summers at their small farm in St. Augustine before Paddy died and Rosa moved in with Cassie and her father. She remembered nights spent under the stars, laying on Rosa's quilt, listening to Paddy spin his tales about the home country, and about the war. Her favorite had been the story of the first time Paddy and Rosa met.

"We was slinking along the coast of France, trying to avoid the Krauts and their bloody U-boats when it came. The siren sounded but 'fore you could do more than topple from your bunk, a Godawful shudder tore through the ship. Many's a boy who wet his pants, I can tell you that, gal."

"What happened?" Cassie asked, her fingers twisting a length of grass into a knot.

"That U-boat cap'n, he knew his business. Busted our lovely ship like your Gram guts a chicken. And their timing couldn't have been worse. It was a cold, blustery night, so cold that there was ice hanging from the rigging. A storm were raging, twenty foot seas, wind from the Northwest wailing like a banshee. We all tumbled into that godforsaken inferno of water certain we were breathing our last.

"Imagine eighteen men packed into a wee wooden boat being spun and tossed about like a whirligig," he continued, his hands weaving through the air, describing the raging ocean. "No lights or Jerry'd see us—as it was that bastard Kraut got two of our boats before he abandoned the rest of us to our fate. Men were howling, cursing, weeping and praying as that storm spat its fury at us." He took a puff on his pipe and shook his head. "God was pissed but good that night. I reckon he was already tired of this war and the pointless killing.

"We had no motor and lost most our oars when we launched. There was a bit of canvas, but no way to raise a sail—as it was, I thought the tiller would wrench my arm off.

"There was no choice but head for the coast and hope the Vichy treated their prisoners better than Jerry. Captain Cavendish sent an SOS, but we knew rescue weren't coming. Any other ship close enough would be a sitting duck for the U-boat and her cursed skipper. So we'd given up hope, thinking only that life in a prison was better than a certain death at sea. Although there were still some who argued the point, mind you. Myself, I was ready to take my chances with the sea, would have if the currents and wind had been fair. But God and nature seemed bound and determined to send us into the coast whether we liked it or not."

"But Gram, when did Gram come?" She bounced up and down with excitement.

"Patience child, patience. I swear you're just like Rosa, neither one of you can sit still worth a damn. Even if it means risking your fool life. And thank God for it, I say.

"Your gram had already escaped the Nazis once. They killed her entire family, so she made her way into France and joined the Resistance. She's a sneaky one, your gram, you wouldn't believe the hell her group raised. Chaos and calamity for the Vichy and their Kraut friends. Anyway, she heard our SOS. Knowing that them lazy Vichy coast watchers would be snug in their cottages drinking and playing cards, she rounded up every boat she and her mates could lay hands to and set out into the storm.

"Now, ya know Rosa can't swim—is terrified of water in fact. See, when your gram were a wee one, her own grandmother predicted she would die in the water. So's all her life she'd been cautioned from it. But that night, she rode out in one of the long boats, braving nature's fury without a thought to her own safety or comfort. She helped to find and haul in nine o' my mates 'fore they could drown or make it into enemy hands. The seas were churning all about them, threatening to swamp the boat. Waves higher than that barn there pounding them.

"But Rosa, she spotted one more poor soul floundering in the icy water. Her boat started to make its way toward him when he went under. Lost—the black ocean swallowed him whole!" Paddy's voice rose, and Cassie shuddered in anticipation. He paused and looked down on her.

"And do ya know what happened next?"

Cassie bobbed her head, hanging on every word.

"Well, I'll tell ya. There's that poor sailor boy, struggling for his last breath, fighting the sea with all's that in him and losing. And he knows it, too. Knows that he's good as done for. Then—" He took another puff of his pipe. "Then Rosa leapt out of her boat. Dove headfirst into the churning waters and swam to him. She moved through the water like a Selkie Queen returning home. And she found that sailor boy. Kept him afloat until they could haul 'em both aboard the rescue boat."

"And that was you, wasn't it?" She squeezed his hand. She knew the story by heart, but couldn't resist asking.

"Aye, that was me. More'n half dead I was. Icicles in me marrow, I was dreaming of heaven and what'd I be saying to St. Peter by way of greeting. Then I come to, me head cradled in Rosa's lap. I opened my eyes, saw her and told her she was an angel straight from heaven. I knew it must be true, 'cause who else could have pulled me back all the way from St. Peter's gates? So I asked her right then and there to marry me."

"And she said yes," she finished with a smirk. Paddy looked down at her with an indulgent smile and ruffled her hair with his calloused fingers.

"She did not. But that's another story." He looked up at the stars and gauged the time. "One that we've not the time for tonight. So off to bed with you now."

Cassie got to her feet and brushed the grass from Rosa's quilt. She started toward the house and turned back to where Paddy still sat, stoking his pipe.

"Am I really like her, Granda? Could I ever be brave and bold like Gram Rosa?" she asked in a soft whisper as if the words were too frightening to be said out loud.

"Aye child," he assured her. "You can and you will. Now to bed."

CASSIE RAISED THE glass of whiskey and sighed. To hell with ghosts. Just for one day, one short day, she wanted to live her own life, not the life they'd want her to live.

Another sip of the single malt and suddenly that actually seemed possible.

The cat, reassured by the restored quiet, came out from its hiding place under the sofa and jumped into her lap, settling in for a nap. Cassie grabbed Rosa's shawl from the floor and decided that sleep wasn't a bad idea at all.

CHAPTER 59

DRAKE WAS CRASHED on the couch in the third floor lounge when Kwon found him the next morning. She jostled his arm until he opened his eyes. As he sat up and stretched, she fed quarters into the vending machine and returned with coffee for each of them.

"King?" Drake asked, fearful the man had died, hammering another nail into the circumstantial case Kwon was building against Hart.

"No." Kwon sipped her coffee, looking down on him from across the room. Drake remembered it was only a few days ago that Hart had first stood there, a very similar look of appraisal on her face. "Miller wants to see you. She's pretty steamed. What did you do now, DJ?"

He shrugged. Miller could wait until he finished his coffee. "Find anything at Hart's?"

"You know damn well we didn't. She's too smart to keep anything incriminating."

"Or too innocent."

"Maybe," she allowed.

Drake swallowed the last dregs of coffee, crumpled the cup and aimed it at the trashcan. It missed, spinning to the floor beside the can. He scooped it up, deposited it on his way out the door. Time to face the music.

"Detective Drake, I believe you know Mr. King," Miller's voice was frosty as she made the introductions.

Drake ran his fingers through his hair. Alan King, sporting Armani, looking well pressed and well rested, and did not extend his hand. Instead he fastened the latch on an expensive snakeskin briefcase, stood, and nodded to Miller.

"You have our terms. We look forward to hearing from you, Commander Miller." The attorney shook Miller's hand briskly and glared at Drake before leaving.

Drake took the seat King had vacated and crossed his legs. "What was that all about?" He decided to pretend ignorance until he knew exactly what was going on.

Miller remained standing, stared at him with a caustic gaze. "I don't recall inviting you to sit down, Detective."

Drake got to his feet. Fast. Miller was known throughout the House as a disciplinarian, but usually not with her detectives. He stood at attention, silent, waiting for her invitation to speak.

"I assume you noticed the injuries to Dr. King?" she asked. He nodded. "Apparently they occurred prior to his overdose. His brother is claiming that they were inflicted by you. He's willing to forego any criminal charges if you tender your resignation by close of the working day."

Drake stared at her, stunned. "I didn't—"

Miller cut him off before he could finish. "According to King, a medical student witnessed part of the assault. I advise you to obtain counsel before you say anything, Detective. These are serious charges."

He caught his breath. Was this what Alan King and Hart had been talking about in the stairwell last night? "What exactly are the charges, Commander?"

"He says Dr. King found you with his wife, Dr. Hart, and he brought this as proof." Miller slid the security video across the desk. Drake didn't reach for it. "Apparently Dr. King went to," she checked her notes for a verbatim quote, "reconcile with his wife, found you there, you threatened him, and brandished your weapon at him."

Drake sank into the chair, and ignored Miller's withering look.

"Then, apparently you confronted him at his place of work. King described you to his brother as extremely agitated. He stated that you slammed him against a wall and physically assaulted him."

The rat bastard. King knew that it would be Drake's word against his. After all, who would believe the truth? Anyone seeing six-one King standing beside Hart would be hard pressed to believe that she could be capable of causing such damage. And that damned student wouldn't help any.

Clever rat bastard, Drake amended. He raked his fingers through his hair, trying to think of a way out of this.

To his surprise, Miller moved to close the door before resuming her seat.

"Want to tell me what really happened?" she asked, her voice actually approximating human.

"I did kiss Hart."

⚬

MILLER NODDED, SWALLOWING her flare of anger. Drake always had to push the limits of everything. Some days he was harder to deal with than her seventeen-year-old son. Why couldn't he be more like his old man?

In some ways the son was the better detective. He saw more, had a mind like a camera when it came to crime scenes and details, but he had a lot of growing up to do before he could begin to fill Drake Sr.'s shoes.

Drake sat slumped in the chair, eyes cast down, wringing his hands between his knees. God, he had it hard. Miller recognized love stricken despair when she saw it.

"And," she prompted.

"After Weaver's post mortem, I took Hart to my place." He looked up at her sound of disapproval. "It was her idea, but I have to admit, I didn't need much convincing." Miller could only imagine. She remembered the energy sparking between Hart and Drake on the West End Bridge two nights ago.

"Go on," she managed to keep her voice even.

"The next night we agreed to call it off, but—" his voice trailed off. "One thing led to another. She forgot her cell phone, so I went to her place to return it."

"That's why you were late to the task force meeting?" She raised an eyebrow. Sleeping with a witness was bad enough, but allowing it to interfere with the running of her task force was intolerable.

"I wouldn't have been, except I found her with King." He described the disturbance he witnessed, the broken glass, and King's injuries. "Yes, I went in with my gun drawn after hearing the commotion," he admitted, his face flushing as he disclosed his recklessness. "But, I never touched him, and never laid a hand on the man."

"And when you saw him at the hospital?"

Drake got to his feet and stood at attention. "He was threatening Hart. I admit it, I was too involved. I should have never gone there in the first place." He met her eyes with a level glance. "I grabbed his shirt front. I didn't shove him, but he was against the wall and I held him there for a few seconds. That was it. Other than that, I never touched him."

"Just long enough for a witness to see it," Miller concluded ruefully. "It still constitutes unlawful restraint and assault. He could win this. Any idea how Dr. King actually did receive his injuries?"

"Hart defended herself against him when he came to her house. I tried to convince her to press charges but—"

"You realize this only gives Hart more motive to have given King the Double Cross, don't you?"

"She wouldn't, she didn't. And I'm certain she had nothing to do with Trautman or the FX thefts."

He delivered the last with the earnestness of a schoolboy's recitation. Miller turned her smile into a cough. This was no laughing matter.

"Will Hart corroborate your story that she's the one responsible for King's injuries?"

Drake remained silent, his fists clenched at his sides, the muscles at his jaw twitching. Worse than a schoolboy in crush—he wanted to be Hart's knight in shining armor.

"We're talking about your career here, Detective. A once promising one, I may add. Do you really want ten years of hard work and service to this community to go down in flames?"

He remained silent. Damn the man. He was as proud as his father. Her mind flashed on the image of Drake Sr., his cheeks flushed, lips turning blue as he gasped for breath, hands clutched to his chest. His last words a faint whisper, begging her to watch over his son.

She had not been able to save the father. Could she possibly salvage the son's career? What an ungodly mess.

"Am I suspended?" Drake asked, his tone formal.

Miller considered. "Not until I say so. King gave us a little time. Let's use it wisely, Detective."

"Yes ma'am."

"And for God's sake, stay away from Hart."

CHAPTER 60

ANDY GREALLY LOOKED up from wiping the bar and scowled at Cassie.

"You've got nerve coming in here right now." He flung the stained bar rag onto the counter in front of her.

"Don't tell me, you think I'm a murderer too." She took a seat, ignoring the barkeep's surly mood. After what Kwon had said last night, she knew better than to call Drake at work. She'd hoped she'd find him here. "I told Kwon, I told Drake, and I'll tell you: I didn't try to kill my ex-husband, didn't kill T-man, and I didn't have anything to do with the FX thefts. I'm tired of being treated like a criminal. Where's Drake?"

"I don't care nothing 'bout the FX." Andy leaned his bulk against the bar and glared down at her. "DJ has enough problems without you playing the King family against him. I think he's well shut of you."

She looked up at that. "This is about the tape? I tried my best to get it back from Richard."

"Who cares about some stupid kiss caught on a tape? I'm talking about King's brother bringing charges against DJ for assault and battery. Is that what you like? To get men so hot and bothered that they'll fight over you? You're worse than that Pamela—" He faltered when he saw her smile. "What's so funny? It'll cost DJ his badge—"

"Andy." Cassie held up her hand in truce. "Drake didn't hit Richard."

"Like hell he didn't. Jimmy saw the pictures. King had a beaut of a shiner, and his nose was swelled out to—"

"I hit him," she interrupted. "Several times in fact. It's my fault, Alan warned me, but I didn't take him seriously. He's using Drake to get to me. He thinks I poisoned Richard."

Andy straightened, moving the bar rag a bare inch back from her. "You hit King?"

"Long story. Things got out of hand."

The ex-cop nodded, swiped at the counter in front of her and threw the rag under the bar. "Well, then, guess I owe you a drink," he conceded graciously. "Or at least some lunch. What'll it be?"

"Nothing, really. I just need to talk to Drake. You don't know where he is?"

Andy ignored her protests and ladled up a large bowl of beef stew for her. "Eat this," he ordered, crossing his arms and watching her in silence until she obeyed. "I don't know where DJ is and, after the lashing Miller gave him this morning, I'd stay clear of him for a while."

The stew was delicious. She hadn't realized how hungry she was until suddenly she was staring at the bottom of the bowl. "I'll go talk to Miller myself," she promised. "Although I'm not certain how much good it will do. Especially if she also thinks I poisoned Richard."

"Now, doc, you've got to admit you sure look good for that one. Trautman, too."

"Does Drake really think I could do that?" The question had been burning inside her. Cassie hated to voice it, and dreaded the answer.

Andy shook his head. "Of course not. Can't you see the kid's fallen, hard? I just don't want to see him messed up again."

"Like after Pamela?"

"He told you about her?"

She took a sip of the coffee he poured for her. "I can't figure him out," she confided to the barkeep.

"Maybe DJ's not as complicated as you'd like to think. Maybe he's just human like the rest of us, makes mistakes like the rest of us, even blames himself when something isn't his fault, and punishes himself for what he couldn't stop." Andy stared at her as if weighing Cassie's worth.

"The gun was his, he had been dating the woman, why didn't he see it coming?" There, the questions she wanted to ask were finally out in the open.

"I wouldn't say dating her, exactly. It was no long-term commitment. Pamela was a cop groupie, she'd gone out with a lot of the guys, always showed up at cop bars, softball games, parties, you name it. One night she'd had too much to drink. DJ took her home because Spanos and a guy from Zone Two were even more drunk and were going to take advantage of her. It caused a bit of a confrontation with Spanos, who ended up flat on his butt, I might add.

"Anyway, after that Pamela began to call DJ, stop by the House, and have the dispatcher page him. I think he enjoyed playing the knight in shining armor. Until he realized she didn't really want him, that she was obsessed only with the idea that he was a cop. So he broke it off. But then, a few weeks later—"

"She killed herself," Cassie finished softly.

Andy twisted the bar rag between his hands. "If she wanted to punish him, to humiliate him, she couldn't have planned it better. DJ doesn't think that's why she did it, he really believes that she did it out of desperation—some warped cry for help."

"You don't believe that."

"No, I don't. I saw her in here many a night, showing more flesh than any Liberty Avenue whore, hanging all over the guys, stroking their egos. I tried to warn DJ, but he wouldn't listen to me. I'll tell you, I think that dame belonged in Western Psych, and nobody's gonna convince me different."

She finished her coffee, feeling much better after hearing Andy's story and eating his stew. "Thanks, what do I owe you?"

"Nothing. Don't suppose you could get King to drop the charges against DJ?"

"I'll do my best," she promised, dreading having to face Alan again, but there was no other way. She offered her hand. He took it and shook it with a firm grip.

"You take care now, Cassie," he called out as she left.

⋅ᗉᔑ⋅

THINGS WERE GETTING out of control. Like a tornado building—with Hart in the middle. Ignoring Miller's orders, Drake headed out, determined to track her down. He'd stay by her side until they found the real killer. And she'd accept his protection even if Drake had to handcuff her to his bed.

That image made him grin.

He tried her home first, but she wasn't there, so he headed to Three Rivers. She wasn't at Jane Doe's bedside. He wandered down to the ER and was surprised to meet Janet Kwon coming in from the parking lot, dusting snow off her parka.

"Have you seen Hart?" he asked.

"I just hung up from talking to her. She's at home." She hesitated for a moment, and then looked up. "She actually called me, wanted to talk about the case."

"I must have missed her. Why did Hart call you?"

"She didn't want to get you into trouble—knew better than to contact you." Her tone made it clear she thought Hart was doing a better job of watching Drake's back than Drake himself was. "Hart told me she had suspicions about Krakov, the head of the pharmacy. Then the lab guys called. It wasn't Double Cross that poisoned Richard King, but a mix of pharmaceutical quality drugs that caused similar symptoms. I thought it'd be best to start from the beginning, re-think everything."

He matched her stride as they headed down to the Annex. A chance to close this once and for all, today? No way he could pass that up. They entered the pharmacy. Krakov's office door was ajar, and the sound of his voice was clearly audible.

"You don't work for Dr. Hart, you work for me! I don't care what it is you think you found, this is garbage. I swear, I'm going to dock your wages for the time you spent on this nonsense—"

"What nonsense would that be?" Drake asked, pushing his way into the office. Krakov was livid, standing over a scared looking kid in his middle twenties.

Krakov turned his ire on the detectives. "This," he dropped a thick computer printout onto his desk. "A mass of meaningless statistics that won't do anyone any good. And which wasted my personnel's time and energy."

"It wasn't a waste of time," the kid said. "Dr. Hart was right, there is something going on."

"What did Dr. Hart ask you to do?" Drake asked.

"She wanted a list of our most expensive drugs cross referenced with expired patients and what drugs they were on."

"She told him it'd help find the killer," Krakov put in. "Isn't that you people's job? Now, I suppose Hart will make a stink if I don't get it to her. Doctors, everything is an emergency to them. They think their time's more valuable than everyone else's." He turned to leave, but Drake restrained him.

"Mr. Krakov, I'm sure you want to assist us in anyway possible." He escorted the pharmacist to the desk chair. "After all, it was one of your people who was killed."

"You know, I have a doctorate in pharmacology. Do you think anyone bothers to call me Dr. Krakov?" the pharmacist sputtered, and then took a seat.

Drake cut his eyes to Kwon. She took her cue and slid into the chair beside Krakov's, effectively blocking his escape route.

"Dr. Krakov, couldn't you give us a few minutes of your time," she purred. Drake raised a hand to cover his smile. "You could explain these printouts to us so much faster—" She laid a hand on his forearm, and the pharmacist melted beneath her touch.

"Well," Krakov cleared his throat. "All right."

"So what are these?" Drake raised the top sheet of the printout and dangled the list of mysterious drug names in front of the pharmacist. He motioned to the kid to join them.

"Those are the top twenty drugs rated for expense. Most of them are chemo and immune therapy agents, and a few antimicrobials," the kid put in before Krakov could reply.

"So this top one, somaquin, how much does that cost?"

Krakov pursed his lips. "For a seventy kilo man, about twenty five hundred a dose. It's given four times a day."

Kwon and Drake exchanged glances. "That's more expensive than gold," she said.

The pharmacist nodded. "Yes, ounce for ounce, it is."

Drake thought about it. "If there was a way for

someone to steal these drugs, the profit would be much greater than dealing in FX. And the safety margin much larger."

"I don't know," Kwon argued. "There's no black market for drugs like this."

"And the people who died?" Drake called Krakov's attention to the rest of the printout. "How many were there?"

"Last month we had thirty-one deaths here in the hospital."

Not bad for a place with ninety thousand ER visits a year and over five hundred patients at any one time. "So that's about usual?"

"Actually not," the kid said, almost bouncing in his eagerness. "I think that's what Dr. Hart was looking for. I compared it to the same month last year and there were only twenty-two deaths. Then I compared the numbers for the past four years. For some reason we've had a marked increase in our mortality rates since March of last year."

"Why is that?" Kwon asked, her eyes racing down the statistics. "Sicker patients, higher acuity?"

The kid shrugged. Krakov adjusted his tie and answered, "Who's to know for sure? Certainly foul play wasn't involved. These patients were for the most part regarded as terminal prior to their admissions. None of these deaths would have been unexpected."

Drake leaned over Kwon's shoulder and perused the list. "But almost all of these patients were on the most expensive drugs."

"End of life care is the greatest health care expense. More money is spent in the last few months of a patient's life than at any other time."

"And what does this code, MM, indicate?" Drake pointed to the notation at the side of a patient's number.

"That means they were on the MedMark plan. Their

drugs were supplied by their HMO, not our hospital. It's a great cost savings. MedMark contracts with most of the major HMOs in the area. They buy in bulk and supply the drugs for patients all over the county."

Drake sat back while Kwon continued leafing through the data. "These drugs come prepackaged, ready to dispense?"

"Of course. Neil Sinderson owns the company. He personally delivers everything we need, twenty-four hours a day."

"So he had access to the pharmacy. Would anyone know if an IV bag marked somaquin actually contained the full concentration?"

Krakov sat up at that. "Neil Sinderson is a qualified pharmacist, he would never put a patient's life in jeopardy by diluting or substituting a medication."

Kwon looked up. "Did Sinderson know Fran Weaver? Know she was getting information for Dr. Hart?"

"Maybe, they were all together in the pharmacy the other morning. I don't know."

"He was here when Dr. Hart came in yesterday," the kid said. His eyes were wide with the possibility that he had been in the same room as a killer. "Do you think he might have killed Fran?"

"Sinderson buys one bag of somaquin," Drake mused, drumming his fingers against his thigh, liking how everything was finally fitting together. "Dilutes it, and sells it to patients at different hospitals. Some of them get better, some don't. They're all end stage, so no one's surprised either way. But the HMOs pay him for four doses when he's really only bought one."

"Why dilute the drug at all?" Kwon asked. "He could be giving these patients water, and no one would be the wiser."

He grabbed the phone and dialed Miller's direct line.

"It's Drake," he said. "We've got a lead. I need someone to pick up Neil Sinderson, he owns a company called MedMark."

"How'd you come up with this?" Miller asked.

"It was Hart's idea."

"Kwon said Hart thought there was more going on."

"Thanks to her, we may have just broke the case." Drake owed the good doctor. Big time. And wouldn't it be fun paying her back for her help? "I'm sending Kwon in with enough information to get us a warrant on Sinderson. Will you have Dimeo waiting? I'll be there in a little while, I just have a few things to wrap up first."

He hung up. Kwon was already on her feet, the stack of papers in her arms. Drake grabbed his coat.

"Thank you for your help, Dr. Krakov," he told the pharmacist. "And you," he held his hand out to the over-eager kid.

"Mike. You're welcome."

"Guess I owe Hart an apology," Kwon said as they walked through the lobby. "You know, I was kind of hoping she did do King—from everything I heard on the floor, he's a real piece of work. Would've been totally justifiable."

Drake looked down at her. Sometimes it was hard to know when Kwon was joking. He decided that she was now.

"I'll take care of the apology," he said with a smile. He spotted the hospital gift shop and stopped. "With any luck, they'll have Sinderson in custody when I get to the House."

"Don't be too long, or Miller will have everything wrapped up and the press conference done before you know it."

Drake couldn't care less about taking any credit for this collar. He just wanted to know Hart was safe and this nightmare was behind them. He entered the large, well-stocked gift store. What had his mother always told him? You could never go wrong with roses and chocolate.

Hopefully the two would work on Hart.

CHAPTER 61

CASSIE SURVEYED HER debris-strewn bedroom and began to reassemble her life. She was glad she'd told Kwon about Fran's theory that there was more going on at Three Rivers than the FX thefts. She still had a difficult time imagining Krakov stealing from the pharmacy, much less killing Fran.

Now that the police knew her theory, at least she didn't have to worry about Mike's safety. Or Drake's.

Surely they had arrested Krakov by now.

The snow was really coming down, she saw from her bedroom window. Almost a foot already lay on the ground. She looked around, the hamper was filled to capacity. Best get some wash started.

Cassie went back downstairs in her bare feet, carrying the hamper.

HE WAITED BEHIND the kitchen door, listening to her moving out in the living room. Hurry up, he urged her. He was on a schedule here. She was the last loose end to take care of.

Why did everything have to be so complicated? Life

had been so simple before Cassandra Hart had blundered her way into his perfect setup.

He reviewed his plan. The van was parked in the alley behind the house. With the snow covering his movements he should be able to get Hart out of here without being seen. He had his gun, duct tape, knife and, his ace in the hole, a syringe of ketamine, ready to go. The house in Uniontown was prepared. It was a perfect plan. The only drawback was that he couldn't shoot her, he had to remember that—only use the gun to threaten her.

All he needed now was Hart. He heard the padding of her bare feet on the hardwood floor. Come on, come get the treat I have waiting for you.

He smiled and tightened his grip on the gun as she began to move toward the kitchen.

⁙

CASSIE PUSHED THE door to the kitchen open, and a man's arm reached around her throat. Richard, was her first thought, as she flung the hamper at his face and aimed an elbow to his gut. Impossible. Richard was in a coma in the ICU.

She spun out of his grasp, pivoting into a fighting stance. Laundry was strewn everywhere, the hamper had bounced off him and landed in the dining room. It was Neil Sinderson, she saw with surprise. He was cradling his belly with one hand. The other pointed a gun at her.

A very large gun.

"On your knees," he ordered her, his face contorted in pain and fury. She hesitated for a brief moment. "Unless you'd rather see if you can outrun a bullet," he continued. "Fran couldn't."

The hand with the gun raised, aimed directly at her face.

Nowhere to run, and no way to disarm him without getting shot. She knelt on the cold tile of her kitchen floor.

She tensed herself to fight back when he approached her. Before she could do anything, he swung his gun high, bringing it down onto her head, and everything went black.

CHAPTER 62

THE MUSTANG SKIDDED part of the way down Gettysburg Street before finally coming to a stop in front of Hart's house. Drake struggled out of the car, arms laden with roses of every color and a large box of chocolates wrapped in gold foil. He climbed the steps to the porch, the snow spilling over the rims of his high tops. There, under shelter, he brushed snow from the bouquet and reached out to ring the doorbell.

He heard the bell echo through the house, but there were no answering footsteps. Damn it, he knew she was in there. He rang the bell again, toe tapping as he waited. He was nervous as a schoolboy on the way to the prom. And for some reason he couldn't stop grinning like an idiot.

Still no answer. He peered in through the large bay window. The fire was going in the living room. The place looked like a warzone. He wouldn't blame Hart for being furious with anyone carrying a badge after the wreck they'd made of her home. The lights were on, and her coat was there. He moved back in front of the solid oak door and shuffled his packages in order to pound on it.

"Come on, Hart," he shouted. "I know you're probably

mad at me for the mess the guys made, but I'm sorry. It's freezing out here. Willya let me in?"

The click of the lock sounded, and the door swung open. Drake rushed inside. "I've got good news—"

The muzzle of a gun touched the sensitive spot behind his ear. He saw Hart sprawled in the kitchen doorway, blood on her face. He felt his own face go cold as the blood rushed to his gut.

"Come right in, Detective," a man's voice prodded him forward. "Keep your arms where I can see them, please."

The door shut behind Drake. Idiot—hands full of junk while Hart lay there, maybe dying. Letting Sinderson get the drop on him. That's what he got for getting emotionally involved in a case. For forgetting all the rules.

"You might as well leave now, Sinderson." Drake's eyes never left Hart's still form. It was hard to believe his voice somehow escaped past the knot tightening his throat. "Get a head start."

"Ahh. So you did figure it out." Sinderson took Drake's Glock from its holster then emptied his pockets, taking his cell phone, car keys, and wallet. He stepped forward to face Drake, a Smith and Wesson Chief's Special raised in one hand and a strip of duct tape in the other. "Or maybe you're bluffing. Either way, I don't see how it should alter my plans. Hold your arms still."

Drake complied, his hands still filled with the gifts. What was he going to do, whack the guy with the roses, hope he'd have an allergic reaction? Sinderson quickly wrapped the duct tape around his wrists.

"What did you do to her?" He finally found the courage to ask.

"Don't worry. She's not dead." Sinderson added a second layer of the silver tape and moved back out of striking range. "She gave me a bit of a fight, so I had to knock her out. Then I gave her a shot of ketamine to keep her quiet. Now that you're here I may have to improvise. I think it would be better for you to drive."

"Drive where?" Drake asked, his mind exploring the possibilities. He'd heard of ketamine, Special K it was called on the street. An anesthetic similar to LSD, mainly used by veterinarians. He had no idea how long it would take for the effects to wear off, but if they were in a car, maybe there would be a chance to take control from Sinderson.

It was worth a chance. Better than being executed here and now.

"Out to the country for a little." Sinderson smiled. "Dinner theater. You and Hart are about to confront a very nasty drug dealer. Unfortunately, the methamphetamine lab in his basement will explode, and," he shook his head sadly, "I'm afraid neither of you will make it out alive."

CHAPTER 63

"WHY'D YOU DO it, Neil?" Drake navigated the Mustang through the slippery streets. "Why kill all those people?"

Sinderson had forced him to place Cassie's unconscious body on the floor of the front passenger seat, and then had climbed in, his legs straddling her, the gun never wavering from her head. Now they were on Route 51, heading south.

"I didn't mean to kill anyone," the pharmacist replied. "It's those damned HMOs."

"HMOs?"

"They wouldn't pay their bills. One of them owed me forty-one thousand dollars. How're you supposed to keep your business going if people don't pay their debts? But these HMOs—they're all about playing games with people's lives. They expect me to provide the drugs their patients need, dirt-cheap and no waiting, but will they pay me what they owe? No way. I even complained to the State Insurance Board and guess what? They make the HMO pay a fine, which comes out to less than one day's worth of interest the HMO earns off of my money that they're holding. But do I even get that? No. The fine goes to the

State, not me. So I'm screwed anyway you look at it.

"Then came the shortage of amphotericin. Suddenly, I'm everybody's best friend. Nobody can get the drug, its price quadrupled, but if I can get it for their patients, the HMOs will pay cash up front. So I figured, what the hell? I gave them their precious amphotericin. And some of the patients die and some get better, but I'm finally getting paid."

"But it wasn't really amphotericin that you gave them, was it Neil?"

"No, it was an electrolyte solution. Amphotericin is used for severe fungal infections; usually in AIDS or cancer patients who are going to die anyway. I figure these people are at a crossroads. Either God's going to save them or not, it's in His hands, not mine. So you see, I didn't kill anyone."

"What about Fran Weaver?"

Silence. Drake cut his eyes over at Sinderson and saw the pharmacist frowning.

"I never wanted to hurt Fran," Sinderson said after a moment. "I liked her. She was the only one halfway decent to me. But I heard her and Cassie talking about a problem with drugs and going to the police. Then the next day Fran calls, and asks me about some patients who died. So I told her I'd bring my records over, and we'd try to figure it out.

"I get there, and she's on the phone telling Cassie to come see her, there's more going on. I knew then I was going to have to do something. I took Fran's computer disks and tried to torch her hard drive, but the damned thing wouldn't burn.

"Cassie was coming, and Fran wouldn't tell me how much she already knew. So I took Fran out the back way, loaded her in my van and drove to where I could watch for Cassie's car. But I was too late. Cassie was already there. I panicked. I couldn't let Fran go, and I didn't know how much Cassie knew. So I called Cassie and made her come back to her car. I figured if I got them both in her car, then there wouldn't be any evidence in my van—just in case something happened."

Drake's hands clenched on the steering wheel as he thought about what that "something" was.

"Cassie had to go get that stupid guard," Sinderson continued, now sounding angry at his intended victim. "What could I do? I couldn't drag Fran back to my van with them watching, and she'd seen me, so I had to take care of her. I didn't have any choice."

Drake forced himself to remain silent. Keep him talking, be sympathetic, get on his wavelength. He tried to remember all the interrogation techniques he'd seen Jimmy Dolan use so successfully. Establish a bond so that it will be harder for him to kill you.

Of course, that hadn't saved Fran Weaver.

"You put the drugs in Cassie's coffee."

"Yes. Fran had told me how dangerous that new combo was. You know, if Cassie'd just minded her own business, we wouldn't be in this mess," he told Drake. "In fact, we were supposed to be going out tomorrow night. We had a date, me and Cassie."

Guess that's not gonna happen. Drake clamped his lips together before he could say something stupid. "So what's at this house?"

"I thought you guys, the police, I mean, will think Cassie and you tracked down the lab where the Double Cross was being made. You know how volatile those chemicals are, so I figure if there's an explosion, then the fire will take care of all the evidence. It'll give me time to get away."

Sinderson said this last with a note of pride as if he expected Drake to praise his ingenuity. Even though Drake was part of the "evidence" to be taken care of in the explosion.

"Yeah, they'd probably buy that," he said, "except for the fact that my team already knows all about you."

Sinderson smiled, his teeth white against the night. "Now you're trying to bluff me, Detective. Please, I'm not that stupid. Just pay attention to the road."

Drake did as he was told, furiously trying to think of a way past the man's wall of denial. Sinderson blamed his deeds on the HMOs, his victims, God's intervention— according to the man's logic, the only innocent party in all this was Sinderson himself. How to argue with that?

"Take Route 201 east," Sinderson ordered. Drake turned onto the narrow two-lane highway. The road was deserted, not even a snowplow or salt truck. The snow was coming down hard, a blanket of swirling white the Mustang's headlights couldn't penetrate. Drake geared down as they navigated several steep curves. He tried to divide his attention between the killer beside him and the treacherous driving conditions.

"You know, I could have been a doctor." Sinderson settled back in his seat, one hand absently stroking Hart's hair. "I was smart enough, and had great grades. But I couldn't stand the thought of actually touching people, all their disgusting private places and body fluids. So I got a doctorate in pharmacology instead. I thought, a doctor is a doctor. I'd still be helping people."

"Didn't quite work out that way, did it?" The Mustang fishtailed on a curve and Drake had to fight to control it.

"Careful, Detective. Cassie isn't wearing a seat belt. And neither are you." Sinderson laughed. "Now wouldn't that be ironic if we crashed, and I was the only one to survive?"

Drake remained silent but Sinderson needed no further prompting. "Do you have any idea how many medication errors are made?" the pharmacist asked. "And most of them are by doctors. I got tired of covering for them, of seeing them make all the money, driving health care costs sky high while all they cared about was their golf game."

"You know Cassie's not like that." Drake tried to force Sinderson to make a connection with her. "You saw how hard she worked to save Fran."

"I know," he admitted. "Turn here." He motioned to a small country lane that wasn't marked by a street sign. "It's out of my hands now."

That was when Drake knew there would be no reasoning with the man. Sinderson had disassociated himself so far from his actions that he saw everything as a drama pre-scripted, awaiting only the actors to play it out to its conclusion.

A drama that Sinderson had scripted to end in tragic death.

CHAPTER 64

CASSIE COULDN'T OPEN her eyes or her mouth. She tried to move her hands, but they were numb. It was as if her entire body belonged to someone else—someone very far away from her.

She was in a foreign place, a place where sounds transformed themselves into a cacophony of brilliant colors, where sight was meaningless and she couldn't touch anything. Did she even exist? Or was she dead?

A loud noise startled her, a bright starburst of scarlet flame. It came again, more intense. She struggled to understand. She began to feel parts of her body once more, to claim them as her own. She immediately regretted this as powerful waves of nausea racked her body, and acid burned her throat when she tried to vomit.

Then she felt cold steel pressed against her throat, and in that instant, her body and mind were rejoined.

"Stop it!" the voice commanded. She knew that voice, didn't she? "If you puke on me, I swear I'll kill you here and now!"

She fought to regain control of her mutinous body, to breathe, to force blood through her heart—it was hard work, these mundane processes of living. As she concentrated, her body stopped its jerking, and the wave of nausea receded.

"That's better." The voice was so close to her that it boomed and echoed through her mind like a thunderstorm, leaving in its wake the worse headache of her life.

"Don't move." Suddenly there were foreign fingers on her face, and a searing pain that forced a gasp out of her as something was torn from her mouth, taking a layer of skin with it. Then a second, more painful tearing of her flesh, but now her eyes could open.

She saw nothing but darkness and red flashes that kept time with the pounding of her headache. Where was she? The darkness was complete, she could not tell if she was sitting or standing.

The disorientation caused a vertigo so extreme she could no longer control her nausea. Rough fingers grabbed her hair, jerked her head to the side as she vomited. She emptied her stomach with fierce contractions that took her breath away.

She realized then that she was lying on the ground. Not outside though, it was too smooth. A cellar floor? She tried to concentrate on these tiny details. They seemed important, and they helped to distract her from the agonizing cramps that assaulted her body.

Then it was done. Her body went slack; she barely had enough energy to breathe. The foul smelling emesis slid across the floor, and soaked into her clothes and hair.

The hand pulled her upright, back against a smooth cold metal object that supported her. The knife returned to her throat.

"You need to do exactly as I tell you. Do you understand?" came the voice, softer now but more terrifying.

"Yes," she finally managed a hoarse whisper. Her

hands were jerked up in front of her, and the knife sliced through her restraints.

"Do you know what will happen if you don't do as I say?"

The blade forced her head backward until she could barely breathe. If she moved at all she knew what that knife could do.

"Please," she whispered the one syllable, not daring more, but still felt a sharp pain followed by a trickle of blood sliding down her neck.

Her eyes were starting to acclimate to the dark. The flashing was really a red light that was behind the man and a little higher than eye level. On a step, maybe? Then that was the way out.

The man's hand grasped more of her hair, this patch slick with vomit. He pulled away in disgust, shaking the foul fluid from his fingers, splattering her face with it.

"You're filthy."

She rubbed her fingers together, trying to get circulation restored. He left her on the floor and moved away. The fact that he didn't see her as a threat was frightening. Was he going to turn and shoot her like he had Fran? The thought made her choke with bile once more, and she doubled over with dry heaves, listening to his footsteps moving away.

She counted the thud of what sounded like five wooden steps until the red light began to move upward. Seven more steps, then everything was black again.

She tried to stand but immediately slipped on the wet plastic drop cloth covering the floor. She got to her knees, feeling with outstretched hands, and tried to crawl in the direction of the stairs. Her body was shivering so hard she had to clench her teeth shut to stop their chattering.

Think, Hart. It's a cellar, these stairs are the only way out.

Sinderson. The memory came to her as if from a distant century. Her heart began to race as she remembered his attack. He had grabbed her, and she fought back. She felt the swollen gash on her scalp, still wet with blood—had he shot her? No, he had hit her.

Where were they? And how was she going to get away?

CHAPTER 65

DRAKE WANTED TO howl in frustration. How could a simple piece of duct tape prevent him from getting to Hart, condemning them both? Kwon was right. The damned stuff should be outlawed, he cursed as he struggled to loosen his hands.

Once they stopped at the farmhouse, Sinderson had positioned him with his hands wrapped behind him, then secured him to the door handle, making it impossible for him to move around the interior of the Mustang.

He pulled against the handle. If he could just get loose from it, he could find something in here to free his hands. He jerked his body forward, bracing his legs and straining his shoulders until he thought he might dislocate them. The tape held.

He tried moving his arms back and forth, hoping the friction might loosen the adhesive. Finally after several minutes of furious effort, he felt the tape give a fraction. He pulled again, and it gave a little more.

Drake strained forward, his breath coming so fast it condensed on the windows and formed little clouds in front of him. Despite the dropping temperature of the interior of the car, sweat poured from his body, soaking though his clothes. He pulled forward again, but both the tape and door handle still held.

Goddamn it! He tried not to imagine what was happening to Hart. He couldn't let her die just because he was too stupid to figure a way out of this.

He resumed his struggle with the duct tape. Slowly, a fraction of an inch at a time, he felt the tape loosen from the door handle. He pulled forward, trying to keep tension on the tape, then again began to slide his wrists back and forth as fast as he could.

After several minutes of sustained effort, the tape parted. His wrists were still bound, but he was free of the door. He turned in the seat, moving across the gearshift to the passenger seat. It had been forever since he'd cleaned the glove compartment, his Swiss army knife should still be in there. He remembered a picnic last spring, trying to impress a grad student with his choice of wine and using the corkscrew on the knife.

Finally he ended up sitting backward on the front passenger seat, one leg over the gearshift, the other was wedged against the door. He flipped the glove compartment open, pulling the lid forward as far as he could, the edge digging into his back. His shoulders and elbows sent sharp messages of pain informing him that his body wasn't designed to move this way. Drake ignored them, forced his numbed fingers to search the compartment.

He shoved aside several maps and what felt like a service manual. His fingers groped toward the bottom of the deep compartment. If not the knife, then a pair of sunglasses he could pop the lenses out of—anything, he prayed. Finally his fingers brushed up against something metal.

Drake blew out the breath he had been holding.

Thank you, God. He stretched his fingers, and strained to open the knife blade. It took several attempts and some acrobatics, but finally he flipped the blade free of the handle, cutting his fingers in the process.

Now for the tricky part. He slid the knife through his fingers until it was aimed with the blade up and began to saw through the duct tape around his wrists. He almost dropped it once, and sliced himself several more times, but his hands were so numb he barely felt it. Then the tape split.

The blade that had just saved his life seemed a fragile weapon to go up against a madman. He made his way through the snow to the rear of the Mustang.

The snow had stopped, and the night was quiet. There were few clouds obscuring the stars and moon. Nothing moved inside the house. Drake opened the trunk and removed the carpet that covered the tire changing tools. He grabbed the jack handle, hefting its weight. It would do, he thought, pocketing the knife as well.

He crept toward the house, keeping his body low until he got to a window. Between the slit in the curtains he could see a living room, furniture covered with drop cloths, a dingy rag rug on the floor and yellowed squares of wallpaper where pictures used to hang. He drew back when he noted movement at one end of the room. A wooden door opened. Sinderson came through it and closed it again, locking it. That was where Hart had to be. He heard water running and crept to the front door, hoping the sound would cover his movements.

The front door was unlocked. Drake took a deep breath, opened it, slid through and shut it again before too much cold air could come through.

The water stopped running. He pressed himself against the wall that bordered the living room. He looked through the archway and saw Sinderson carrying a bucket that he set down beside a door. Sinderson took the Chief's Special from his waistband and opened the door.

·⟨◉⟩·

CASSIE BRACED HERSELF against the back of the steps. They had treads but no risers. She could reach through and grab Sinderson's legs when he descended. It wasn't much of a plan, but it was the best she could come up with in such a short time. The only weapon she had was her belt wrapped around her right hand, the buckle pointing outward.

If she got close enough, she could put his eyes out. If she got close enough, she could also be shot or stabbed.

A blinding light startled her, and she covered her eyes.

"Come out where I can see you," Sinderson called from the top of the stairs.

"What are you going to do?" She stalled while her eyes adjusted to the new light.

Stupid question, she already knew the answer. With the lights on she could see that the cellar had a concrete floor covered with sheets of plastic. There were vats of fluid set up on a long table. Several plastic drums labeled hydriodic acid and red phosphorous were arranged along the back wall.

"Come out now, or I'll get your friend and shoot him in front of you." Sinderson's voice seemed filled with regret. "Don't make me do it that way, Cassie. I want to make it as painless as possible for you both."

"What friend?" she asked, forcing her tone to stay neutral.

In response he tossed a wallet to her. She opened it. Drake, he had Drake.

Another wave of nausea almost dropped her to her knees. She sucked her breath in and slowly edged to the side of the stairway.

"Put your hands on your head and move to the front of the steps," Sinderson commanded.

She did as she was told, holding her left hand over her right, putting both hands behind her neck. She hoped that Sinderson would not notice her missing belt.

"Good, now kneel down."

Cassie obeyed, positioning herself near the stairs. She saw Sinderson reach behind him and lift a large bucket from the top step. He held the gun pointed at her chest as he slowly came down the stairs. She braced herself when he swung the bucket up, but still gasped as he threw the cold water on her.

Curling her toes under her, she dug in. She would only get one chance. He raised his leg to take the final step down.

CHAPTER 66

DRAKE WATCHED SINDERSON start down the stairs. Damn it, he left the door open behind him. Now Drake had to take the chance that Sinderson might hear him. He thought about rushing the pharmacist, pushing him down the stairs, but after hearing Sinderson's instructions to Hart, he knew it would be too risky. It might get her shot.

At least she was still alive. He wanted to run to her side, but he forced himself to remain calm. If he failed, and Sinderson killed him, Hart would be alone. No, he had to get help.

He saw a phone on a hall table. He crossed over to it and raised the receiver. It was dead. He looked around the living room but didn't see the car keys or his cell phone.

Now it was really up to him. If he couldn't take Sinderson out, Hart would die.

Drake wiped his sweaty palms and gripped the tire iron. He began to move toward the cellar door.

SINDERSON RAISED HIS leg, off balance for a precious

millisecond, and Cassie pounced. She pushed herself up, threw herself at him, tumbling him over. She grabbed his arm and tried to knock the gun free, but he gripped her throat with his free hand.

"You bitch," he snarled from his position under her, his fingers squeezing tighter until her vision began to darken. "I told you I didn't want to do it this way, but you wouldn't listen." She struck at his face with the belt buckle. He levered his body up, and shoved her off him.

"Why didn't you listen?" He wiped the blood from his face. He pivoted and kicked her in the gut, knocking the wind out of her. She grabbed his foot and pulled it into her, rolling her body weight against it. Sinderson slipped on the wet plastic and went down once more.

Before Cassie could move to take advantage of her position, footsteps pounded down the steps. Drake raced toward her, a tire iron in his hands. Sinderson raised his gun.

"No!" she cried. The sound of the shot ricocheted through the small stone room. Drake kept coming down the stairs, but she saw blood staining his shirt.

Sinderson fired again, this time hitting Drake in the thigh. Drake staggered, then tumbled down the rest of the steps, dragging the tire iron with him.

She grabbed Sinderson's gun arm from behind. She twisted it savagely, hoping to break it or at least dislocate his elbow. He pulled his knife and slashed her across her left forearm.

Cassie tried to hold on, but her hand was on fire with pain. Sinderson broke free and backslapped her with his gun, hitting her nose so hard that blood spurted.

She grappled with him. They both slid on the slippery plastic, but his greater weight gave him the advantage. She struggled to crawl away. Sinderson caught one of her legs, laughed as he pulled her toward him.

"No more running, Cassie."

Her hands flailed out in front of her, trying to gain a purchase. Then she felt the cold steel of the knife against her Achilles tendon.

"No," she whispered, "please, no."

He slid the blade up under her jeans, then down over her naked foot.

"Don't worry, it won't hurt for long. Not after the fire gets going, at least."

Cassie held her leg absolutely still. She raised her gaze and saw Drake was still conscious, staring at her. She thought for a second that she could hold on to the sight of those eyes forever. Then she followed Drake's glance down. Slowly, his breath coming in ragged gasps, he pushed the tire iron toward her, slid it inch by painful inch over the plastic.

She tried to ignore the ugly sucking noise that came with each breath Drake took and concentrated on stretching her fingers forward, reaching for the tire iron. *Please God*, she prayed, *not for me—don't let Drake die. Keep me alive long enough to save him. Please.*

Apparently God wasn't listening tonight. It was just too far for her to reach. She looked into Drake's eyes, but they had closed. Her heart stuttered for a moment—he was dead!

Then Cassie heard him take a deep, rattling breath and saw his body move. It was a heroic effort as he inched his body forward, pushing the tire iron with it.

Just as she felt the sting of Sinderson's blade slice into her flesh, Cassie connected with the steel rod and grabbed it.

With one fluid motion she arched her body into a sitting position and swung the tire iron into Sinderson's face. She felt the sickening crack of broken bones. He yelped, released her leg and dropped his knife.

He raised his gun, aiming blindly as blood filled his eyes, but she swung again, this time hitting the side of his head. She broke his skull with such force that the tire iron came out covered with blood and pieces of gray matter. Sinderson slumped to the ground, his hand still clutching the gun, his eyes unfocused.

He wasn't dead yet, but he was incapacitated. Cassie cautiously took the gun. She slid her hand under Sinderson's body and pulled Drake's gun from his waistband.

Then she took a deep breath. God, it hurt. She hurt everywhere. She turned to Drake, and carefully rolled him over. His breathing came in rapid gasps. He stared at her, his lips moved but no sound came from them.

"Sssh, it's okay." Her own blood mingled with his as her nose continued to bleed. She cut his shirt off with Sinderson's knife and ran her hands over his chest. Entry wound just below the diaphragm. Exit wound just behind the right axilla. Classic sucking chest wound.

Cassie cut a piece of the plastic drop cloth and placed it to cover the exit wound, then lay his hand on top of it.

"Don't hold it tight, let the air pass out." He nodded his understanding. "I'm going to try to get some help. Hold on, I'll be back."

She climbed to her feet. Her ankle was covered with blood, but she found she could still lift her foot enough to walk. That meant her Achilles tendon was at least partially intact. Enough to get the job done.

First she had to call for help. She found a phone in the first floor hallway, but the line was dead. Hell. Okay, Hart, focus. She looked out the front door and was surprised to see Drake's Mustang sitting in the drive.

Should she try to go for help? How could she—she didn't even know where they were.

Wanting to scream in frustration, Cassie grabbed one

of the canvas drop cloths and took it with her downstairs to where Drake lay, his breathing so loud that it echoed across the walls.

Sinderson had somehow crawled a few inches toward Drake, blood trailing behind him. He lay there staring at her, confusion in his eyes.

She ignored him. His head injury would be fatal without immediate surgical intervention, but there was nothing she could do about it.

Sinderson would soon be dead. She had killed a man. She was a killer.

Cassie squeezed her eyes shut, forced herself to think only of Drake. She might be able to save him.

Drake's breathing was labored and his color ashen. Using the cloth from upstairs, she dressed his leg wound. She gingerly felt his abdomen. He winced.

"Don't." The word rushed past his gritted teeth.

Cassie felt his pulse again. It was racing, and much too weak. The bullet had gone through his liver. He needed blood and surgery to stop the bleeding. Things she could give any patient at her trauma center but there was nothing she could do for him here. She looked up the stairs. If she tried to drag him out to the car she would kill him for sure, and she didn't think she was strong enough anyway.

His fingers tightened on her arm, pulling her close. "Cell phone," he whispered. She could tell that each breath was agonizing.

"Where is it?"

"Took it." She could barely hear him.

She looked over at Sinderson. His mouth was opening and closing like a fish out of water. He stared at her as she moved over to him, one hand reached out for her. She batted it away, and it flopped to the floor. She forced herself to feel his pockets, but there was no cell phone and no car keys either.

"Damn it, where are they?" she shouted at the soon-to-be-dead man.

He smiled at her, then his eyes rolled into the back of his head, and his body began convulsing. Cassie bit her lip as tears of frustration slid down her face. Sinderson would die soon—and so would Drake if she didn't find a way to get him help.

CHAPTER 67

———— ⠏⠕⠑⠕⠑ ————

"I'M GOING TO check upstairs," Cassie told Drake. She searched the dusty rooms of the first floor. Nothing there and nothing on the second floor either.

She sat on the bottom step in front of the living room and thought, tried to visualize herself coming in the door, car keys in her hand. There was no table to put them on, no coat rack, where was the closet? She stood up and looked around again. She found a tiny hall closet under the stairs. In it hung Sinderson's dark wool overcoat.

Please Lord. She pulled the coat from its hanger and began to search the pockets. There were two key rings in the right hand pocket, one of them Drake's. And, hallelujah, the phone was in the other pocket.

She dropped the coat and with trembling fingers, she flipped the phone open. She dialed the ER number, electronic tones sang at her, and she was rewarded with the desk clerk's voice.

"Three Rivers ER, how may I help you?"

"Jason, it's Cassie Hart. Listen closely. I need a helicopter transport and police here immediately. I have two patients: a severe head trauma and a gunshot wound to the chest and abdomen with internal bleeding."

"Where are you?" Jason asked.

She cursed in frustration. "I don't know where the hell I am, that's the problem. I'm calling from Detective Drake's cell phone. Call the police, tell them what's going on. See if they can trace this. I'll call you back in ten minutes."

"I'll try my best, doc." Cassie could hear the confusion in his voice.

"Just do it. I have two dying men out here." She hung up the phone. How much battery time did this thing have? How long would it take to trace it?

Her only hope was that Drake had some idea where they were. She went back downstairs, taking the coat with her. Drake was noticeably paler, for a second she wasn't even certain if he was alive. As she drew closer she could see his chest rise. She released the breath that had caught in her throat, lay the coat over him, and gently squeezed his hand.

"Hang in there," she urged him. "Help is on its way, but I need to know where we are."

His eyes didn't open, but his lips moved. She leaned down and was able to hear his rasping whisper. "South on fifty-one," she made out. "East two-oh-one."

"Okay, I've got it. Please, just hang on, it won't be long." She kissed his forehead then stood.

Cassie looked over to where Sinderson lay, his seizure over. He looked dead, but she didn't waste time finding out. She climbed the stairs again and went out to the front porch to look for a mailbox. She saw one down past the car.

She returned inside and grabbed another drop cloth to wrap around her. She looked for boots but could only find some old rubber shoe covers thrown into the corner of the closet. She put these on after wrapping her feet with strips of cloth.

Taking a deep breath, she stepped out into the cold, her feet burning as she crossed the snow-covered yard. She wrapped her arms around her, cursed her wet clothes that invited the wind to suck away all her body heat and energy. *At least the snow had stopped, they could fly.* She hurried down to the mailbox and squinted at the faded numbers, thankful for the moonlight.

Cassie made her way back to the house, tried to ignore her uncontrollable shivering, and called Jason again. This time he immediately turned the phone over to someone else.

"Dr. Hart, this is Sergeant Murphy," came a reassuring voice.

Murphy, she knew him, he was always stopping by the ER for coffee and gossip. "Murph, glad you're there. Drake says we're off Route 201, east of Route 51. The only address I could find was a rural delivery route number ten, house number ends in three-seven."

"Got it. We've state police standing by, we'll relay that information to them."

"Get a chopper in the air headed this way. Drake's really bad off, we need to get him into the OR."

"They're on the pad. I'll have Jason tell them to take off."

"Good. There's room to land on the front lawn. I'll turn all the lights on in the house and turn the car lights on."

"That's fine, Doctor. Just leave the cell phone on while you do that."

"Okay. First, send a message to the chopper crew to have six units of Oneg ready to go and a pleuravac and chest tube tray. A vent also," she said quickly, her thoughts racing. Most of that was gear the team would have anyway, but she wanted to be sure.

"We copy that," a second voice came over the phone. This one was overlapped by static.

"Zack, is that you?"

"Yes. We'll be taking off as soon as the blood gets here. Winds are pretty high, so weight's an issue. I've got a full crew and room for two, is that enough?"

Cassie knew that he was asking if she was functioning or if she was going to be another patient.

"That'll be fine, Zack."

"Glad to hear it. I'll talk to you soon to get LZ details. We're taking off now."

"Is the scene safe?" Murphy broke in.

She sighed. Except for the possibility of a good man dying, it was as safe as it could be. But that wasn't what Murphy meant. It was the first question any police officer, fireman, or paramedic was trained to ask: if they became a victim, they were only adding to the problem.

"Yes," she said. "The scene is safe."

He probably wanted to know about Sinderson, but she didn't want to tell him over an insecure phone line. Besides, she really didn't want to think about Sinderson at all. She wanted to focus all of her energy and effort on saving Drake.

Cassie sat the phone down, not waiting for their reply. She had no more energy for talking.

She quickly moved through the house, turning on any lights that she could find that still functioned. Then she moved Drake's car, pointing it so that the headlights aimed toward the power lines coming into the side of the house. She went back into the house and checked on Drake. He was unconscious, his belly now obviously distended, his pulse weak and rapid.

There was nothing she could do until the transport team arrived. Cassie cursed her helplessness. It couldn't end this way, it just couldn't. She wouldn't let Drake die, not after he had saved her life. If he hadn't been there, she'd be dead by now. The realization made her dizzy.

She took a deep breath, steadied herself, and went back up the stairs. She grabbed the phone and went out onto the porch, the drop cloth wrapped around her like a matador's cape flapping in the breeze.

"Zack, you there?"

"We just crossed I-70," came the chopper pilot's reply.

"Do you have my location yet?"

"The state police are supposed to be getting back to us any minute."

"Tell them to hurry, Drake can't wait. The LZ will be the front yard. There's electrical and phone lines coming in from the road to the side of the house. The yard slopes slightly, no trees, no ice that I can see—"

"Hang on a second, the Staties are on the other channel." She returned to the front room, glad to be out of the wind. Then Zack was back.

"I've got your twenty. Be there in five. Staties on the way also. Just hang on, doc."

CHAPTER 68

THEY WERE THE longest five minutes of Cassie's life as she scanned the skies for the lights of the helicopter. Then she saw blinking lights moving rapidly across the sky and soon after, she could hear the low throbbing of the Sikorksy's finely tuned engine. The chopper circled low around the yard and made a perfect landing.

She dropped her canvas cloth, couldn't risk it blowing into the rotor, and ran across to the front of the chopper. No one tried to talk as they rotated the gurney out of the helicopter and carried it through the snow to the porch.

"What've we got?" The flight doctor raised the visor from his helmet, and she was surprised to see that it was Ed Castro. Her boss never flew, he hated flying, even more than she did. She was thrilled to see him—Drake couldn't be in better hands.

"Thirty-four year old male, gunshot wound. One entry to abdomen, exit to right chest. Second through and through to right thigh. Airway intact, he's in shock, weak distal pulses, abdomen distended. Hemorrhage controlled from leg wound." She gave him the synopsis as the nurse and paramedic wrestled the gurney down the cellar stairs.

"You mentioned a head wound?"

"He's DOA."

"Holy shit," the paramedic muttered as he looked around.

"Get that oxygen on him." Cassie pointed at Drake. The medic turned to look at Cassie, and she realized that she must look bizarre with her wet clothes and blood covered body. "Ed, you'll have to start the IV, I don't trust my hands. How are his vitals?" she asked the nurse who crouched beside Drake.

"Holding steady." The nurse wrote the time and the vitals on a wide strip of tape stretched along the thigh of her flight suit.

"Hang the Oneg," Cassie ordered. "Let's C-collar him and get him on to the back board." Together they gently moved Drake onto the board then lifted him onto the gurney. Footsteps thudded overhead.

"We're down here!" she shouted. A burly state trooper appeared at the top of the steps, one hand on his holster. With his help, they were able to quickly move the gurney up the stairs.

"Hey, someone's got to stay and explain all this," the trooper shouted as they began to move out to the Sikorsky. "You've got some questions to answer." He grabbed Cassie's arm.

Ed Castro came to her rescue. "She'll not be answering any questions until she receives medical attention," he told the young trooper in a frosty tone—a tone Cassie was glad to not be on the receiving end of. The trooper shrugged and let her go. She quickly jumped into the chopper and strapped herself into the seat at Drake's head. She put on a headset and connected it into the box at her side.

"How're you doing, doc?" Zack asked as soon as he had them safely in the air and headed back to Three

Rivers.

"Just hurry," Cassie urged.

.⟨◉⟩.

FINALLY, SHE SAW the lights of Pittsburgh draw near. A few moments later she could make out the helipad outside the doors of her ER.

Zack brought them down gently, and they scrambled out of the helicopter while it was still running hot. Cassie kept up as best she could, but the waiting surgical resident and trauma nurse hustled the gurney through the doors, leaving her standing in the cold beside the helicopter. Ed Castro took her arm and helped her inside the ER where he sat her down into a wheelchair.

He began to push her down the corridor. Cassie saw the looks on the faces of her coworkers. From their expressions she must look half dead. No wonder, she was soaking wet and covered in hers, Drake's, and Sinderson's blood. Her nose was still dripping mucus and blood, she tried to wipe it, but was rewarded only with a wave of pain. It didn't matter, as long as Drake was going to be all right.

Then Ed turned the chair into one of the critical care rooms. "Take me up to the OR," she demanded.

"No." He closed the door behind him. "You need to be taken care of, I don't know how you stayed on your feet as long as you have. You're frozen, you've lost blood, your nose is broken. Lord only knows what other injuries you have. Was that really Neil Sinderson?"

She looked at him and realized it was futile to argue. Finally she nodded. "Yes, it was. I killed him."

Ed leaned against the sink. "Jesus, Cassie, what happened?"

"Sinderson killed Fran Weaver. And he poisoned

Richard. If it hadn't been for Drake, I would have been next."

"The press is going to have a field day with this." He shook his head. "We'll deal with them and the police later. First, you get out of those clothes." He opened the warmer and gave her two blankets. He turned his back and picked up the phone while she struggled with her sweater. "Rachel would you join me? Yes, it is Cassie Hart."

A few minutes later Cassie found herself on the gurney wearing a hospital gown and bundled in warm blankets. The nurse didn't ask anything, and Cassie was glad. This whole process of being a patient was so humiliating.

Ed examined her injuries, ordered an IV, lab tests, tetanus booster, X-rays and surgical consultation. Suddenly she wasn't a doctor or a person anymore, just the trauma in Room Two with multiple facial and extremity injuries. Her head CT was normal, urine dipped negative, nose was broken and would require surgical repair, as would her Achilles tendon.

Her forearm laceration was deep but did not require surgery so Ed sutured it himself while they were waiting for her room to be ready—there was a delay in processing the admission because Cassie didn't have her insurance information with her.

"Don't you have a wife to go home to?" she asked Ed after she finished arguing with the admissions clerk.

"Hold still." He placed a subcutaneous suture.

"How's Drake?" Every time she asked, no one would give her a straight answer—she learned you lose your clout when you became a patient.

Ed glanced at the clock. "You asked me that ten minutes ago. Believe me, when I hear something, you'll be the first to know."

She sighed. She'd asked Rachel to call his mother in

Florida and talk to his fellow police officers. Several of the detectives had tried to interview her, but Ed had chased them out each time. She closed her eyes, prayed for him to finish. God, this waiting was worse than anything. She sat up again.

"When are we going to hear anything? Will you call upstairs?"

"I said, hold still," he snapped. "I know why they say doctors make the worst patients."

"Goddamn it, Ed, I'll sign out AMA and go see for myself."

"Just a minute, only two more to go." He finished repairing the laceration, then stood up. "I'll go call—you," he said in a threatening voice, "stay put. Rachel, if she moves, put her in restraints."

Rachel applied antibiotic ointment to the laceration and dressed it. "We were so worried when you called," she chided Cassie. "Ed insisted on going in the helicopter, and you know how much he hates flying."

"I know," Cassie admitted.

Ed returned. "He'll be out of the OR and in ICU in twenty minutes. The surgery went fine, patched up his liver without problems, the bullet missed the vena cava."

"They ran the bowel?"

"Yes, no perforations."

Cassie lay back. Drake was going to be okay.

And that was all that mattered.

CHAPTER 69

DRAKE WOKE WITH a throbbing head, throat rubbed raw, and a hose running out of his nose. He'd been kicked in the chest by a mule, every breath was a surge of fire through his body. That was how he knew he was alive— being dead couldn't possibly hurt this bad.

He opened his eyes, but saw nothing except bright lights and white ceiling tiles. "Hart," his voice was barely a croak. He tried again. "Hart?" He tried to sit up, but his head spun and his vision went black. "Where's Cassandra Hart?"

"I already told you, she's fine. Now hold still while I give you some medicine," a woman's voice commanded.

"No." He batted her arm away. He struggled again to sit up, this time succeeding. He looked down at his body in surprise. Not only did he have a tube in his nose but there were also tubes coming from both his chest and abdomen. A small nest of three of them in his shoulder led to some bright yellow fluid hanging on a pole. One in his bladder too, he realized at the same time that he saw that he was naked under the flimsy hospital gown.

"Hold still, you'll tear your stitches," the nurse said, a

firm grip on his arm with one hand. With the other she pushed a button, and the head of his bed came up, just in time for him to slump back against it.

Damn, he felt as weak as a newborn. Where the hell was Hart? What had happened? He remembered her telling him that everything was going to be all right, but everything else was a fog.

"Where's Dr. Hart?" he asked again, his voice stronger this time.

The nurse looked at him and sighed. "I've told you a hundred times, she's fine. She had her surgery this morning. How about you go back to sleep? I'll give you some pain medicine."

"No, please. I need to know. What happened?" Drake could tell by the look on her face that he'd asked that before.

"It's the sedation, it disorients some people," came a friendly voice from the doorway.

Drake looked up and saw Hart smiling at him. Christ, she looked like hell. She looked wonderful.

Both her eyes were blackened and almost swollen shut, her nose and upper lip were also swollen with stitches in her lip bristling like black hairs. Her left arm was bandaged and she was wearing hospital scrubs, leaning on crutches, her leg in a cast.

But she was there, alive and relatively whole. Finally he felt able to breathe again.

"Dr. Hart, the patient really needs his rest," the nurse told her.

Hart took Drake's chart. "JP drainage minimal, chest tube to water seal, good I and 0's. You should be up and about in no time, Detective," she said. "When are they pulling the chest tube?" she asked the nurse.

"Dr. Alexander said tomorrow if his X-ray is okay."

"How about his gut?"

"Postop ileus. After he passes gas he can have clears." Both women looked at him expectantly. "Have you passed gas yet, Mr. Drake?" the nurse asked.

Drake closed his eyes. "I hate hospitals," he moaned.

He heard footsteps leaving the room and risked opening his eyes again. Hart smiled at him. Then he looked closer. There was a sadness in her eyes.

"Are you all right?" he asked. "You look like a truck ran over you."

Her smile faded. "I'm fine."

"What happened to Sinderson?" Parts of it were coming back. Drake remembered lying on a cold floor, watching Sinderson convulse, his head bloody and drool pouring from his mouth.

She took his hand as if preparing him for bad news. "He's dead. Thanks to you."

He frowned. "All I remember is coming down the stairs and the gun going off. I don't remember ever hitting him."

"You didn't, but you got the tire iron close enough to me so that I could grab it." She paused, a shadow crossing her face. "I killed him."

Drake was silent for a moment. Had he really done something so stupid as going down there armed only with a tire iron? How had she managed to kill Sinderson on her own?

Shame tackled him, grabbing his insides and giving them a hard kick. He should have been the one to take Sinderson down, not her.

"Are *you* all right?" he asked, squeezing her hand. But she let it lay limp in his, not returning the gesture.

"I'm fine."

He couldn't meet her gaze, what could he say to her? He was the one who lived with a gun at his side; she was the one who was supposed to save lives. How could she stand to be near him after he had let her down like that?

He looked into her eyes. The light there that had mesmerized him was faded, gone dull. Because of him, because he hadn't been able to protect her, to do his job—jeezit, it was almost as bad as Pamela. No, worse. Hart he cared for, he had thought—stupid, man, letting himself dream—maybe they had a future, a chance together.

He dropped her hand. "Well," he cleared his throat, suddenly his mouth was parched. "Just so long as you're okay."

He didn't risk looking at her face, he just watched as her hand lay there, next to his on the white sheet. Then, slowly, she pulled it away. He waited for her to say something but she was silent. Okay, so he was going to have to suck it up, do the hard work for both of them.

A memory of her bloody body lying on the floor at her house, when he hadn't known if she was dead or alive, flooded his vision. As much as he wanted to be with her, he couldn't ignore the fact that she'd almost died. And it was all his fault. He should have been a better protector, a better cop—a better man.

Pamela all over again. He blinked hard, hating the sting of tears. He sucked in a breath only to be sucker-punched by pain. The pain gave him the strength he needed—reminded him of what she'd gone through in that Uniontown cellar. He needed to make a clean break—she deserved that—before he could hurt her more.

"Look, Hart. A lot has happened—to both of us. It's going to take some getting used to."

There was another moment of silence. Then her breath whooshed out, circling above him. He still didn't risk looking up at her. Coward. But it hurt too much already. Cutting her out of his life was more painful than any cut the surgeons had made.

"Oh. I see." She gathered her crutches. "No problem. I

just wanted to make certain you were going to be okay," she told him, already backing toward the door. "Your mom and friends will be wanting to come and see you. Don't let them tire you out—doctor's orders." She paused at the doorway and he couldn't help himself, he glanced up. She gave him a heart-breaking half smile. "Take care of yourself, Mickey."

Then she was gone.

Drake looked at his hand, pressing it against his face. He could still feel her warmth. She had finally called him Mickey. He covered his eyes. Where was the nurse with her pain medicine when he really needed her?

⋅◈⋅

CASSIE SLUMPED AGAINST the wall outside Drake's room. Tears burned her eyelids, spilled over despite her best efforts to hold them at bay. She swiped at her face with her good hand, hating the stares two candy stripers gave her as they passed.

Drake almost died—because of her. Just as Fran and Trautman had died because she refused to mind her own business. And Richard still lay in a coma.

Not to mention Sinderson. Images of his lifeless eyes, blood splattered face, mouth opening and closing in silence cascaded through her brain. She clenched her hands around her crutches as she leaned on them, staring blindly at the linoleum at her feet. How could she ever forget Sinderson?

No wonder Drake wanted nothing to do with her. Who could blame him?

She hobbled down the hallway, paused at the door to the stairway, and looked at the elevator. Gritting her teeth, she punched the elevator call button. She'd been a fool to think that she'd ever been in control of anything—might as well start getting used to the idea.

The doors opened on the empty elevator and she pushed herself across the threshold. If she could kill a man with her own hands, she could bloody well face a ride in an elevator. Backing into the corner of the metal box, she hunched over, forcing herself to endure the short ride up two floors to the rehab unit.

The nurses there stared at her, then quickly looked away when she met their eyes. Even here, in the twilight quiet of the neuro-rehab ward where patients balanced between coma and wakefulness, they had heard that she was a killer. She glanced down at her hands, opened and closed them against the handles of her crutches.

Then she limped over to Jane Doe's bed. Sarah Yoder—that was her real name. The Holmes County Sheriff had called Adeena this morning with the news. A few hours ago the Yoders had arrived from their home in Millersburg, Ohio, driven by a Mennonite friend.

Cassie spotted the gray-haired couple at Jane-Sarah's bedside immediately. She raised her estimate of their ages, at least early fifties. They were both plainly dressed in homemade clothing and the wife covered her hair in a small white cap.

She took a moment to glance at Sarah's chart. Since being transferred out of the ICU yesterday, she'd begun to respond to stimuli. Although she hadn't fully awakened yet, it was definite progress.

"Mr. and Mrs. Yoder?" She approached them, leaning her crutches against Sarah's bed. They startled at her voice, their hands intertwined as they turned together to face her. "I'm Dr. Hart. I was the initial physician involved in Sarah's care."

She stretched out her hand, but they ignored it. The expression they shared resembled that of deer caught in headlights. "I'm so pleased that we were able to locate you," she continued, dropping her hand back to her side.

"The social worker said you went to considerable trouble for our daughter," the mother said, her voice hushed as if afraid they would disturb sleeping Sarah. "Thank you, Dr. Hart."

"You're quite welcome," Cassie said, feeling awkward at their gaze of appraisal. But they said nothing about her unorthodox appearance. Mr. Yoder turned back to Sarah's bed, gripping the bed rail in his rough-hewn hands. "Has she been gone a long time?"

Mrs. Yoder seemed to be the appointed speaker for the duo. "Almost two years now," she said in that same soft whisper. "Ran off with Bill Kleindietz. He was eighteen, much too old for Sarah, but she wouldn't listen."

"Where's Bill now?"

"Jail in Youngstown. Caught trying to rob a 7-11. When we heard about him, we thought we'd finally get Sarah back, but—" she shrugged. "It was too late. She'd gone off on her own." A single tear slipped down the older woman's cheek. "If you only knew what this meant to us—"

"She's not out of the woods yet," she told them, not wanting to give them false hope. "But every day she's showing signs of improvement."

"That's all we can ask for. The good Lord will take care of the rest. Thank you again. You'll always be in our prayers, Dr. Hart."

Cassie nodded, leaving them to become reacquainted with their lost daughter.

She went back to the hallway, thinking about the Yoders and their faith that things would work out for the best. God's plan. She was envious of such depth of faith. Wished she could share in it.

Was what happened to Sarah, to everyone since that night when Cassie had saved her, was that all part of a greater plan, somehow all for the best?

If she relinquished control of her life to a higher power, did that somehow absolve her of her role in the deaths of three people?

"I thought I'd find you here," Adeena's too-cheerful voice cut into Cassie's thoughts. The social worker was pushing a wheelchair down the hall. "You know you're not really supposed to be using those crutches yet."

She bundled Cassie into the chair, laid her crutches in her lap and wheeled her down to the elevator. "Once we get you home, you'll have to promise to stay off your feet and let me and Tessa take care of you. She's baking brownies and a London broil in honor—"

"I'm going home," Cassie interrupted her as the elevator arrived.

"Of course you are." Adeena pushed her inside the box where a man and two women already waited, the man holding the door open until Cassie was positioned inside.

The elevator began to move with a lurch that jolted through Cassie. Sweat began to pool, sliding between her breasts and down from her armpits. Her breath became ragged and her fingers grew numb. The crutches slid from her grasp with a clatter.

The women jumped back as if they were contaminated; while Adeena bent down to collect them. Cassie squeezed her eyes shut, swallowed against the nausea. Just as she was about to give voice to the scream that had clawed its way up her throat, the doors opened. They were the last out, the man standing against the doors to hold them open. Adeena thanked him, her voice a distant blur as Cassie hung her head, gulped in the fresh air of the lobby.

"I need to go home," Cassie told Adeena as they rolled outside into the frigid air and pulled up beside Adeena's waiting Civic.

"That's where we're going." Adeena handed her the

crutches so that she could transfer into the passenger seat, and then stopped, staring at Cassie with apprehension. "You don't mean your house? Cassie, you can't expect to take care of yourself, not after everything that happened."

Cassie felt her jaw clench tight at the thought of being looked after, scrutinized every second, unable to grieve in her own way. She'd never have her old life back—she knew that. But she still needed time to mourn its passing. She wasn't the person she thought she was, the person she hoped she was—the person Rosa and her parents had raised her to be.

So who was she? A doctor who killed with her own two hands? A woman who manipulated her friend into risking her job, her life? A wife that an ex-husband would kill to possess?

A lover who watched her love risk everything for her and almost die.

She sagged back down in the chair. She only had strength enough to raise her eyes and meet Adeena's. The social worker frowned, then finally sighed in surrender.

"At least come to lunch," she conceded. "Otherwise, I'll never be able to convince Tessa that you're all right." She crouched down beside the chair, her eyes level with Cassie's. "You are all right, aren't you?"

"I will be," Cassie assured her, feeling a tiny flicker of hope at her words. She might be a stranger even to herself, but she could take care of herself, and greet this new life of hers on her own terms. Maybe that was the most anyone could expect. She felt herself smile, the movement tugging at the tiny stitches, making her mouth feel lopsided. Adeena mirrored her smile, sun sparkling off Adeena's copper-colored beads. "I will be.

CHAPTER 70

DRAKE SIPPED AT his Guinness and paid no attention as Pitt came from behind to advance to the Sweet Sixteen. Andy Greally joined him.

"So when are you going to go see her?" he asked.

Drake didn't bother looking up. "What?"

"Earth to Drake. Did you even realize that the game is over?"

"Yeah, sure it is. Why are you bothering me? Don't you have other customers?"

"Just go see her, that way you can stop coming in here every day and making my life miserable." Andy shook his head. "You did tell her you were back, right?"

After he was discharged from the hospital three weeks ago, Drake had stayed with his mother, allowing her to pamper him and remind him constantly how his father had never gotten shot, not in thirty years of policing, so it better not happen again to her son.

He shook his head at Andy. "She doesn't want to see me."

"How do you know? She never said so, did she? You mean to tell me you find a gorgeous, gutsy woman who's willing to put her life on the line to save your sorry butt, and you're just gonna walk away?"

Andy looked up as Jimmy Dolan entered the Stone, a Pirates' ball cap covering his short-cropped hair. Jimmy took the stool next to Drake and nodded at them.

"Who won the game?"

Drake shrugged. Andy placed a Guinness in front of Jimmy.

"Pitt, came from behind."

Jimmy took a slug of the stout. "He still moping?" he asked Andy, gesturing at Drake.

"Yeah, won't you please take him back to work with you?"

"Can't do it. He still has to pass his psych eval and recert at the range."

"Why hasn't he seen the shrink yet? I thought he was supposed to go last week."

"Said he forgot, missed the appointment." They both looked at Drake.

"Would you two stop talking about me like I'm not here?"

Andy swiped at the bar with his rag. "He's your partner."

"Yeah, well, you trained him."

Andy walked down the bar. "Tell him to go see her already, why don't you?"

Jimmy picked up his Guinness and stood. "Grab your drink, we need to talk," he told Drake and headed toward an empty booth.

Drake sighed. Why couldn't everyone just leave him alone? But he followed Jimmy over to the booth.

Jimmy lifted his ball cap and scratched at his scalp. He stared at Drake. "You fucked up again, kid."

"I don't think so," Drake replied. "Actually, I've thought it through, and I think that I'm avoiding a lot of pain and trouble for both of us."

"So you made this decision for both of you?" Jimmy shook his head. "Your problem is that you've never been in love before. You don't know what to do."

"I've been in love many times," Drake protested.

"No, you've been in lust." Jimmy looked around the bar. "Look," he continued in a low voice. "This isn't something that I would tell anyone but my partner, but I'm not going to let you screw up again. See with Denise and me—we just looked at each other and we knew."

"Yeah, love at first sight, fairytale romance, I've got the picture."

"Would you for once in your life just listen? Like I was saying, for me and Denise it's different. She knows what the job is about, but we don't ever talk about it. We don't have to, it's just the way we are, been that way since the beginning. This is going to sound crazy to you, but Denise is the only woman I've ever made love to—and the only woman that I ever want to make love to."

Drake looked up in surprise. Was this his partner talking? He shook his head. "Sex is definitely not the problem." He took a deep drink of the stout. "The problem is that I acted like a fool out there. I almost got her killed, and then I almost got killed myself. I should have found some other way to handle the situation. Maybe taken the car and found a phone, gotten backup, waited until I had the drop on Sinderson instead of rushing down there, I don't know.

"All I know is that I couldn't think of anything but her being down there with him, and I couldn't stand it. I couldn't leave her there for one more second." He leaned back and rubbed his eyes. "God, what a fool I was. All my training, experience, thrown out the window because she was all I could think about. I don't like feeling that way. Out of control."

"And how do you feel now?" Jimmy asked.

"Like shit," he admitted. "I see a pretty model on a commercial, all I can think of is Hart. I walk by a store and see something nice and I want to go in and buy it for her. I read an interesting story in the paper, and I want to talk to her about it—God, Jimmy, I think I'm going crazy."

"Welcome to the real world. Why don't you just go talk to her?"

"No, everything is too complicated. Besides, I don't think she wants to see me. I remind her of too much pain."

"You selfish bastard. Is it her you're worried about, or yourself? If you let her go now, you'll always regret it."

"But we can never have what you and Denise have."

"Of course not, what works for us won't work for you. Hart won't be content to not ask the difficult questions, and she won't accept easy answers. Look at her, what she does—she needs to be involved. I know you. You always try to take the easy way out, and Hart's not gonna let you do that."

Drake thought about that. He thought about the way Hart pushed him past his limits, past the boundaries he'd drawn in his life. "I don't know if I can live like that."

"The question to ask is: do you want to live without her?" Jimmy finished his beer. "It's up to you to decide." He stood up. "I'll see you later. I've got to get home, see what Denise has planned for tonight."

"Hey, Jimmy," Drake called out. "Thanks a lot."

"Sure thing, partner."

A picture had been forming in Drake's mind ever since Adeena Coleman told him about Hart's parents. He left the Stone and walked home, colors and images swirling, almost blocking out the scenery around him.

A love so strong it didn't end with death. He remembered the photo of Hart's father, the way he looked only half in this world, yearning, longing for someone no longer there. Even as he held his daughter. Had Hart felt like she wasn't enough, never enough to command all of her father's love after her mother died? Was that part of what drove her?

Drake decided it would take a long time to completely understand Cassandra Hart. He took a deep breath and realized he was smiling. Somehow, he was certain the effort would be worth it.

He reached his apartment and for the first time since last summer, he felt ready to paint.

⚬

DRAKE PULLED THE Mustang up to the curb in front of Hart's house. He eased his way out of the low-slung car, his thigh muscles burning a bit, and reached for the brown-paper wrapped package from the rear. He was exhausted. He'd been up the past two nights sketching, painting watercolor drafts, working, re-working the visions that had insinuated themselves in his brain.

Most art theorists suggested that passionate affairs sapped an artist's creative drive, that the energy needed to sustain a relationship detracted from the art. But since meeting Hart, Drake had more ideas than ever before.

The framed watercolor was the best of the studies. He knew it might be weeks, months even, before he finished the full blown canvas. So he brought it as an offering.

He only hoped it was enough.

As he began up the steps to her porch he remembered sprinting up them the last time he was here, arms filled with roses and candy. Today it felt like climbing Mt. Everest. Halfway up his breath grew ragged, his head bowed by effort. By the time he made it to her front door, his heart was racing. He reached a trembling finger to the doorbell.

No answer. He returned to the Mustang, leaned against the side, catching his breath. He did fine on the four flights to his apartment, why was it so hard making it to her front door? Chalking it up to nerves, he looked around and spotted her car down the street. She was somewhere close by.

It was a brilliant spring day; no way was he going back up those steps to wait in the shadows of the porch. Her back yard had looked like an oasis even covered in snow, he'd wait for her there. He followed the narrow concrete walkway between houses to the back. A privacy fence ran along the property line, leading him to a gate in the rear alley. Drake unlatched it and entered Hart's garden.

And there she was. Sitting on a glider, sunlight streaming over her, eyes closed, head tilted back, basking in the warmth. Drake's blood surged through his veins as if his heart had only just now remembered how to pump it.

God, he'd been a fool thinking that walking away was the best thing for either of them.

The garden filled the entire yard. Drake could only imagine how it looked at the height of the growing season. Juniper, rhododendrons and azaleas grew along the shady side. In the center was a blazing circle of color provided by a rainbow of crocus and some petite yellow and purple irises.

"Hart." Adeena had said that Hart isolated herself the first few weeks after what happened, as much to guard her privacy from the reporters as to heal her soul.

She remained silent. He moved over to sit beside her on the glider. He lifted her cane out of the way. She'd lost weight, her flannel shirt and sweat pants threatened to swallow her whole. Her ankle was encased in Velcro and nylon.

He felt her tense; he'd been expecting that. After so long apart, after everything they'd been through, it was hard to bridge the gap back to where they had once been. That was his fault, he shouldn't have run away, he should have talked to her before now. But he hadn't known what to say to her. Still didn't.

"So, how are you?" When in doubt, go for the tried and true. Maybe he'd comment on the weather next.

It felt like a long time before she answered. "In a few days they'll let me start weight bearing, now I'm just doing range of motion and stretches."

Drake knew all about the torture methods of the physical therapists. He also knew that she knew he hadn't been asking about her leg.

"That's good," he said in a neutral voice. "Are you going back to work, then?"

She sighed, and shrugged her shoulders. Finally she opened her eyes and looked at him. Still, she was silent, watching, waiting for him to make the first move.

"You don't make it easy," he finally said. "It was you who ran away that first night—"

"I stayed the second," she reminded him. Was there a hint of warmth underlying her tone? Drake hoped so.

"And then kicked me out of your house the next morning."

She straightened, knocking the cane to the ground. "I already apologized for that."

"Sometimes you're too damned good at shutting me out. Why? Is it so terrifying to let me get close?"

"I'm not the one who ran away and never returned my calls."

He had that coming. "I know, I know. I just felt so—"

"Scared? Overwhelmed? Out of control? That's how I felt."

"Helpless," he finally admitted. "Ashamed. I let you

down out there. You saved my life. And I was helpless to do anything—"

"No, you don't understand." She took a deep breath. "I was ready to die. In my heart I knew I was going to, was absolutely certain of that fact. Oh, I was going to fight all the way, but Sinderson won—I had already given up.

"Then you came charging in like John Wayne, and I dared to hope again. For a brief second before Sinderson shot you, anyway." Her voice dropped even lower. "But you wouldn't give up. It was—" She searched for words. "Extraordinary."

She looked up into his eyes. "I don't know how you did it, but you somehow found the strength to push that tire iron over to me. You saved my life."

"I'm sorry it couldn't have happened differently," Drake told her. "I wish I'd been the one to use the tire iron."

She looked down, a shudder running through her body, and he felt her withdraw. "No," her voice was barely a whisper. "No, you don't."

He took her hand in his. She pulled away, held both hands out as if inspecting them for blood. "How can I ever go back after what I did? I killed a man. With these hands."

Drake felt his throat tighten as he blinked back tears. Jimmy was right, he was a selfish bastard. How could he have been worried about his pride when she was living through what had to be a physician's worst nightmare?

"You save lives," he told her, cradling her hands in his and lifting them to rest against his heart. "Don't you ever forget that, Hart. You saved my life—long before Sinderson shot me. I was lost, and you brought me back."

She raised her face, a frown of confusion creasing her features. Drake tried again. "I brought you a present. A family portrait."

"What do you know about my family?"

"More than you might imagine. Want to see if I got it

right?" He held up the thin package, and laid it in her lap. She slowly unwrapped it, her eyes constantly darting back up to meet his.

The painting depicted a family at the beach. A man with glasses, his gaze intent on his daughter as she danced in the surf, wind tousling her dark hair. At his side was a redheaded woman, equally engrossed in her daughter's antics. The adults' hands were joined together, forming a protective barrier between the girl and the storm-tossed sky behind them. Two adults united in their love of their child, solid and enduring against the inconstancy of the world beyond their circle.

A small choking noise came from Hart. She reached out her fingers, almost, but not quite, touching the figures of her parents.

"How did you—" Her voice was a hoarse whisper.

"It's only a study. I saw the photos on your mantle. I didn't think they really captured the spirit of your family, not the way it should have been in a perfect world. Not the way your parents would have wanted it to be."

"You found all that," she gestured to the painting, "in a few old snapshots?" Now her attention was focused solely on him, her eyes wide, filled with wonder. And the light that had so captivated him, the light he feared was lost, the light had returned.

"I found it in the woman who came from them."

A look of anguish crossed her face as she regarded the painting on her lap. Had he made a mistake, trusting his instincts after so long? But then she looked up and gave him a small, crooked smile.

"Thank you," she said.

Drake traced her smile with his fingertips. "All I want to do is take care of you."

"I can take care of myself."

"I know that. The point is, you don't need to—not

anymore." She gnawed on her lower lip, thought that over. "I'm not going to walk out again. I'm not going to abandon you in dark places. I'm not going away like your parents did. I will always be here for you."

"You can't be certain of that," she said.

Her eyes locked onto his, searching for answers he didn't have. Answers he hoped they could discover together. Drake wrapped an arm around her, and pulled her tight against him, a hint of lavender drifting from nearby. She responded by reaching out her hand, intertwining her fingers with his.

"Yes, I can. You're not alone any more."

Want More HART & DRAKE?

Their Adventures Continue In

SLEIGHT OF HAND

"There's an oath doctors take," Detective Mickey Drake said.

"Primum non nocere," the shrink supplied. *"First do no harm."*

⁘⟨◉⟩⁘

Two months ago Dr. Cassandra Hart was forced to kill a man. The man who murdered her best friend, almost killed Drake and seriously wounded her. Now she's back at work in her Pittsburgh ER, but nothing seems the same.

When she fears that a young boy is being abused by his "perfect" mother, her friends and colleagues worry that she's returned to work too soon, imagining dangers that don't exist. Others accuse her of trying to cover up her own alleged mistakes in the boy's treatment by making a false report of abuse.

Drake's facing problems of his own, trying to cope with the aftermath of the night two months ago when his passion for Cassie led to a confrontation with a killer. He's on desk duty, reviewing cold cases, and delves into the homicide case that killed his father seven years ago. But after so long, what good can he do, a cop without a gun?

The stakes escalate when Cassie is almost killed and Drake finds evidence that the killer his father was tracking might be planning to strike again–this time targeting a young boy. With the lives of two children at stake, how can they walk away?

SLEIGHT OF HAND

Available Now!
In Print, Audiobook, and e-book

Go to www.CJLyons.net
For more information

ABOUT THE AUTHOR

Pediatric ER doctor turned *New York Times* bestselling thriller writer CJ Lyons has been a storyteller all her life—something that landed her in many time-outs as a kid. She writes her Thrillers with Heart for the same reason that she became a doctor: because she believes we all have the power to change our world.

In the ER she witnessed many acts of courage by her patients and their families, learning that heroes truly are born every day. When not writing, she can be found walking the beaches near her Lowcountry home, listening to the voices in her head and plotting new and devious ways to create mayhem for her characters.

To learn more about CJ's Thrillers with Heart go to www.CJLyons.net

CPSIA information can be obtained at www.ICGtesting.com
Printed in the USA
BVOW08*0412130715

408458BV00012B/154/P